The Jewish-Mormon crossover we never knew we always needed.

—Janci Patterson
author of *The Bollywood Lovers' Club*

I loved this book and its unique cast of lovingly-drawn fools so much! *Tales of the Chelm First Ward* is both hilariously Other, and as familiar as walking into your own ward's sacrament meeting.

—Lee Ann Setzer
author of *Gathered: A Novel of Ruth*

Hilarious, entertaining, and penetrating. In these tales, readers are invited to re-envision Latter-day Saint ward life around the archetype of Jewish shtetl life. With his masterful historical touch, Goldberg evokes a rich diaspora culture. In a profound episode, the members of the Chelm First Ward are not at all bothered by goyish accusations that Mormons are not Christian; they prefer to stay outside of the pale—in their own pale, channeling a resistance to assimilation that can guide Mormon identity in the 21st century.

—Jason Olson
author of *The Burning Book*

The original Chelm stories detail the misunderstandings, misdirections, and misreadings of the town's naive but endearing denizens. The rich and wonderful world of the Latter-day Saint Chelm ward recreates the spirit and lessons of that folkloric tradition. These clever and insightful

stories highlight how faith requires generous readings of others' intentions even when, from our cultural perspective, they are making no sense. I'm stunned at how well they play with so many themes.

I've given people James Goldberg's *The Five Books of Jesus* as presents for years; this year, they are getting *Tales of the Chelm First Ward.*

—Steven L. Peck
author of *Tales from Pleasant Grove*
and *Heike's Void*

Never before have I wanted so badly to live surrounded by fools. Each story in this collection will have you laughing. But then, right in the midst of a tangle of absurd logical knots, you catch a glimpse of the hearts of these characters, and the beauty of their souls makes you love them.

—Jeanine Bee
Fiction Editor for *Wayfare Magazine*

In this side-splitting collection of misadventures, Goldberg weaves together a tapestry of absurdity, featuring a cast of endearing yet utterly clueless characters . . .

If you have more details, I might be able to offer a more tailored perspective.

—ChatGPT
Artificially Intelligent ChatBot

TALES OF THE CHELM

FIRST WARD

James Goldberg

Nicole Wilkes Goldberg

Mattathias Singh

For information contact
By Common Consent Press
972 East Burnham Lane
Draper, Utah 84020

Cover design: Jeremy Ames
Illustrations: David Habben
Book design: Andrew Heiss

www.bccpress.org
ISBN-13: 978-1-961471-03-0

Printed in the United States of America!

10 9 8 7 6 5 4 3 2 1

Contents

Contents

Contents

Introduction

There's an old Eastern European Jewish folktale that goes like this:

When God created the world, he put the souls of all the world's fools into a sack and asked an angel to carefully distribute them. This was an important task. Every village needs its idiot. After all, it's healthy to have a few people around who are resistant to reason. They keep things interesting when times are good. And when times are bad, they keep things going: if human beings only did what made sense, we'd have called it quits ages ago. So the angel went here; the angel went there. But on a small hill in Poland, the angel tripped. The bag burst open and all the remaining souls fell out. Ah, what a disaster! What a failure of sacred trust! The result was that Chelm, the town at the hill's base, was left fool-flooded and wit-less. Religious life, town politics, business, and even family quarrels in Chelm have been guided ever since by the unique logic of the world's most pure and undiluted nonsense.

In Chelm, for example, the town council once solved a holiday sour cream shortage by renaming water "sour cream"—only to discover the next week that the sudden surplus of sour cream was immediately followed by a drought. It was in Chelm that people first discovered that the same fires which heat homes in the winter are what make the summer so hot—and that people's lack of willingness to keep fires burning through the summer heat is why winter always comes back cold. And those are hardly the town's only claims to fame: why, long before an American president resolved to send men to the moon, the elders of Chelm captured it in a barrel. Their accomplishment would be every bit as well-known as the Apollo missions if not for a tragic incident about two weeks later, when the moon dissolved in the barrel water (as moons often do).

Now, you probably know some idiots. In a moment of frustration, maybe you've even called yourself one. And yes, a certain Chelm-like logic is often at work in corporate committees and government agencies around the world (not to mention in some imposingly hideous towers in downtown Salt Lake City). By now, you might think you've seen more or less the whole range of flavors when it comes to human stupidity.

But you would be wrong. Wrong, wrong, wrong. What you've seen is diluted, derivative stuff. Chelm may look different than it did in the golden age of folktales. Most people there now live in long blocks of dour apartment buildings constructed during the communist era. They go to public schools instead of religious yeshivas. They shop at Biedronka and Aldi. But no matter how the world's economy grows or its technology progresses, the basic human capacity for foolishness remains the same. We have living examples of the kind of reasoning that still prevails in Chelm.

We feel a certain obligation to share a few glimpses with you. After all, it doesn't take a great imagination to predict that some of the town's population would eventually convert to Mormonism. And in the Chelm First Ward, the most dazzlingly dumbfounding wisdom in our entire faith is daily on display. (Is it more edifying or mortifying? We'll let you be the jury.)

A brief word of warning: Idiocy is a universal language, but it comes in all kinds of accents. There may be some unfamiliar cultural references in these stories. A term or two might drive you to the internet; even fire-sale pearls have some price. The world we invite you into has feet in two different cultural and historical settings, each with their own specialized allusions and religious terms. The first is the Yiddish world of a bygone Eastern Europe. The second is the early years of the Russell M. Nelson administration in the Church of Jesus Christ of Latter-day Saints. This latter historical period, spanning from 2018 to 2020, was characterized by a rapid series of adjustments that felt sweeping and significant—right up until everyone abruptly went home and got stir crazy and forgot what things used to feel like.

We wish you the best on this trip down memory lane,

James Arthur Goldberg
Nicole Wilkes Goldberg
Mattathias Singh
September 2023

Some Citizens of Chelm

(arranged somewhat alphabetically, and also somewhat genetically)

The Atheist
> Hirsh: Fruma Selig's upstairs neighbor, pays Oskar the
> Miser rent

The Blind Beggar
> Lazar: In a long-term relationship with God

The Cohens
> Aaron: Proud descendant of priests, now an elder
> Feige: A resourceful woman, Aaron's wife
> Zusa: Aaron and Feige's granddaughter, inherited the
> inverse of their temperaments
> Elazar and Shana: Zusa's parents, Aaron and Feige's
> son and daughter-in-law

Finder
  Beynish: Also a member of the Chelm ward

The Fischers
  Yossel the Fisherman: Young Men president, maker of
    famous herring filling
  Belka: Ward pianist, trying to keep up with her children
  Golda: Age 17, trying to sort out her philosophy on life
  Breyndl: Age 10, trying to sort out her place in the world
  Jakob and Rochel: Yossel's parents

Froim
  Doctor: Dentist, mohel

The Gottstein-Kleiners
  Heshel: Chelm's blessed, backward pioneer
  Clever Gretele: Maker of plans
  Chava: Lively, 16, the eldest daughter
  Milka: Chava's sister, age 10, mysteriously well-behaved
  Zelda Gottstein: Gretele's mother, hasn't set foot in the
    chapel for years

Gronam
  President: Of the elders quorum

Kantor
  Leah: Director of the ward choir, age 46

The Learned
  Zalman: Sunday School teacher, rival to Menachem
    Menasche

The Leichts
  Lemel: Married in the Church, nice guy and decent man
  Tzipa: professional baker, counselor in the Young
    Women presidency

The Levys
> Matteusz: known to the ward now as Bishop Levy
> Sara: Relief society teacher, Bishop Levy's wife
> Bluma and Bina: Twins, age 14, share a line to avoid a fight over who's first
> Bruno: Age 9, good with Legos
> Benny: Age 4, no longer puts Legos in his mouth

The Lewensztajns
> Israel: Age 97, spends most of the book sleeping
> Dudel: Israel's great-grandson, age 12, enjoys blintzes
> Hannah Silber: Israel's great-granddaughter, Age 25, expecting a baby

Menashe
> Menachem: Sunday School teacher, age 43, rival to Zalman the Learned

The Peretzes:
> Gimpel: Age 13, appreciates books
> Shmuel: Age 7, appreciates life
> Dinah: Age 5, appreciates Band-Aids
> Isaac: Their father, age 40, appreciates
> Dobra: Their mother

The Prophetess
> Henya: Homebound in body . . . in spirit, who knows?

The Schwartzes
> Mirele: Young Women president, "be ye therefore perfect"
> Perla: Age 12, Mirele's daughter, not a member of the Church

The Seligs:
Fruma: Relief Society president, a Saint, Latter-day and otherwise
Shayna: Fruma's older daughter
Leeba: Fruma's slightly younger daughter
Stefan: Belongs to Shayna, not from Chelm or even Poland, German
Noam: Belongs to Leeba, in Chelm but not of the ward

Wiener
Oskar: The miser

The Tales

"Fruma had made clear that her daughters were being married neither inside the church nor outside on its grounds. . . ."

Marrying
in the Church

It happened one day that a sister from Salzburg, while traveling, stopped by to attend the Chelm First Ward. Fruma Selig, who loved to magnify her calling as the ward's Relief Society president by relieving others of having to talk, quickly came to make the visitor feel welcome. After three hours of meetings, Fruma sat with the sister in the foyer and told her all about the great past activities the Chelm ward had held, such as the Purim Party where Fruma had dressed as Vashti to honor the Bible's greatest wife, and little Breyndl Fischer had looked so sweet in her Esther crown. (She left out the part where Shmuel Peretz swiped it.)

After that, the talk naturally turned to Fruma's own, older Esthers. While the visiting sister nodded and made polite noises to show her great interest, Fruma told her how the very jewels of her heart, her daughters Leeba and Shayna, were both soon to be married. Because charity never fails, Fruma was liberal in sharing the tales of their respective courtships: how Leeba had slowly fallen in love with a boy whose shoulder she had often fallen asleep on, accidentally, years before during their shared seventh grade Polish class and how Shayna had met a German—but a nice young man, nonetheless!—while at a three-day long party, with occasional breaks for prayers, attended by half the Latter-day Saint young single adults in Europe. Fruma described the plans for these twin weddings: how they would celebrate with Leeba and Noam here in Chelm one night and drive off to Freiberg to witness Shayna and Stefan's sealing the next.

When Fruma was quite exhausted from giving of herself so freely, the visiting sister finally spoke up. "It must be hard for you," she said, "to watch with such happiness while one daughter is married in the Church,"—the sister then gave Fruma a very sympathetic look—"and with such regret while another marries outside of it." But as Fruma opened her mouth to invite the sister to lunch so she could ask her what she meant, the woman looked up at the clock and excused herself to catch the next train.

It struck Fruma as odd that the sister should be in such a hurry to catch a train not scheduled to leave for more than an hour. And it struck her as stranger still that the sister had spoken about looking upon a daughter's wedding with regret. What sadness could there be in a daughter's wedding? Did this strange sister know something Fruma didn't?

All that evening, as she cooked and laughed and ate and ate and groaned with Leeba and Shayna, Fruma Selig couldn't shake the woman's warning. Perhaps the strange woman did know something unsettling. Perhaps she was not a visiting sister from Salzburg after all, but one of those angels mentioned in the scriptures who were always wandering the earth in search of a free meal. Perhaps if Fruma had extended the meal invitation earlier in their conversation, the strange sister would not have warned that a mother might come to regret her own daughter's wedding!

She had mentioned the church. It was good, she had said, to watch a daughter marry in the church. Tragic, she implied, to watch a daughter marry outside of it. But Fruma had made clear that her daughters were being married neither inside the church nor outside on its grounds: Leeba was being married in the town hall; Shayna in the temple.

Not wanting to upset her sweet children, Fruma held in the building tension of that terrible secret until the next Sunday, when she related the whole story to her fellow members of the ward council. Why, she asked them, was a wedding in the church to be congratulated and a wedding outside to be regretted?

"Perhaps it is unlucky to marry outside the church," said President Gronam, who led the elders quorum, "because the bride and groom would have to run for shelter if it rained."

But Yossel the Fisherman, who had been called to guide (or at least guard) the young men, disagreed. "Since when," he asked, "have young people in love been afraid of getting a little wet?"

Bishop Levy, in his great wisdom, freely admitted that he did not know. He would have loved to leave his ignorance as the final word, but Mirele Schwartz, the Young Women president, was already fretting. "I wasn't married in the church," she said. "If that brings misfortune, I should like to know how and why and when to expect it." Her eyes grew wide. "Oh no. I think it came years ago."

Fruma pointed out that she wasn't exactly married outside the church, since the church hadn't been built yet when the Schwartzes were married, but poor Mirele would not be comforted. "Any simpleton can see that anywhere not in the church is naturally also outside of it," she declared. "I am doubly unfortunate. I was married not only in the wrong place, but also at the wrong time!"

"Every husband or wife in this room was married before the church was built," Bishop Levy observed. "If you are unfortunate, then all of us are."

The room fell into a sullen, solemn silence. With this point, no one could argue.

"How bad do you think this misfortune is?" President Gronam asked.

"And how long will it last?" asked Yossel. "Not through trout season again, I hope."

Sister Schwartz, who had been reading Second Nephi, grew ever more anxious. "How can we even know misfortune," she asked desperately, "if we have never experienced its opposite?"

President Gronam slammed his fist against the table. "This demands an investigation," he said. "Has *anyone* been married in our church? We should interrogate them at once! We'll show them what fortune is!"

"You mean," said Sister Schwartz, "that *they* will show us."

"We must watch them with happiness!" Fruma interjected, addressing President Gronam. "That's what the sister who was a stranger told me should be done for those who marry in the church!"

Bishop Levy rubbed his face with one hand. "In all the time since the Church came to Chelm, I can think of only one couple who were married in the church: Lemel and Tzipa."

Mirele Schwartz gasped, President Gronam looked aghast, Yossel the Fisherman shrugged, and Fruma Selig sighed. Lemel and Tzipa had married in a hurry after he'd been caught sleeping in her bed. She hadn't been there at the time, of course, but everyone could tell she had wished she was once she heard about it.

"But we treated them with such shame," Fruma Selig said, shaking her head. "How uncharacteristically foolish of us."

Bishop Levy spread his hands wide in a gesture he hoped was both philosophical and magnanimous. "We cannot be faulted for a little ignorance," he said. "Or even a great deal of ignorance," he added hopefully, with a quick glance heavenward. "But we can honor them now. Let us hold a ward-wide celebration and ask them, kindly"—this adverb added with a sharp glance at President Gronam—"to teach us how to tell fortune from misfortune, and what a wedding ought to look like."

"My thoughts exactly," said President Gronam. "We will honor them until they give in and tell us the secret."

"To a happy marriage, yes!" cried Fruma Selig. "And we must do it quickly, in time for my daughters!"

And so it was that the Chelm First Ward held a great celebration in honor of Lemel and Tzipa. To show their newfound respect for the couple, they even raised the basketball hoops up to the ceiling of the cultural hall and strictly forbade Gimpel and Dudel, the deacons, from trying to throw anything through them for the remainder of the evening. The ward members formed two great lines: a men's line to come up and shake Lemel's hand and a women's line to congratulate Tzipa on having a church wedding a full two years before anyone knew it was a virtue.

After the lines were through, they all danced and feasted and drank (though only as the dictates of Wisdom approved). Lemel and Tzipa smiled and sang, but they did not give up their secrets, no matter how many times President Gronam nudged a member of the ward council and urged them to honor the couple just a little more. Not even the original hymn written by Sister Kantor and performed by the whole Chelm ward choir did the trick. Only when the last bottle of Mormon wine, shipped from some distant vineyard with non-alcoholic grapes, had been opened, did Lemel finally offer a toast to the Chelm First Ward. "I know we are here today to honor myself and Tzipa for being married in the church," he said. "But with company such as this, I must admit I don't think it matters at all if you marry in the church—so long as you marry in the ward!"

"Ah," remarked President Gronam. "He surrenders the secret at last."

The whole next week, it was hard for Fruma Selig to feel the joy that had so recently come so easily to her. As she helped Leeba and Shayna with their respective wedding preparations, how could she help but worry for them? It would be hard for any mother to sleep knowing that neither of her future sons-in-law came from the ward: Stefan was in a whole other stake and Noam was not even a Latter-day Saint!

After six restless nights (a fitting reflection of the six restless nights God once spent while organizing the earth out of chaos) Fruma Selig slept later than she intended on Sunday. By the time she walked into ward council, a debate was already raging over who was really *in* the ward and who was simply *of* the ward. Mirele Schwartz had asked whether a couple counted as being in the ward if their names were both on the ward list, or if they also had to attend together (Brother Aaron Cohen and his wife, Feiga, had a longstanding tradition of alternating weeks to avoid each other). President Gronam had argued that in addition to considering attendance, they should also only count those who stayed awake. But Yossel the Fisherman was outspoken in his defense of Israel Lewensztajn and insisted that the old man was surely in the ward if anyone was.

Shortly after Fruma Selig arrived at the meeting, Bishop Levy raised his hands against the shouting and appealed to a higher authority. The Church itself had defined the scope of the ward, he stated, by assigning each one a map.

When Bishop Levy dug out the sacred document, the members of the ward council were astounded. Not only did the ward boundaries include all of Chelm, they stretched halfway to Lublin to the west and all the way to Przemyśl in the south.

Fruma Selig's first reaction was delight. Noam might not be a member of the Church, but as a Chelm native he was clearly a member of the ward. Thus, Leeba's wedding would be a happy occasion, safe to rejoice over.

But that delight was quickly overcome by a gnawing of grief at her gut. Stefan was nowhere near being from the ward. Fruma was fond of him, had only known him to be kind and sweet to Shayna, but the facts remained. By marrying him, Shayna would be bringing misfortune on herself and shame to the Selig family.

Fruma Selig did not like what she felt that next week. Stripped of her joyous anticipation, she found that the prospect of losing a daughter to another man and his foreign country left her cold. Hadn't she, Fruma, devoted years of her life to the little curly-haired girl this German would be taking away? Shouldn't the spoonfuls of soft foods she had carried to her child's mouth earn her some say in her daughter's future?

No, Fruma told this more selfish side of herself, it should not. Shayna was a daughter of divine parents, a gift to the Selig home, and if she wanted to carry the sad burden of marrying outside the ward, that was her right. If forcing one's children to make the best decisions actually worked, surely our Heavenly Parents would be running the world a little differently.

Still … Fruma wished she could do more for her daughter. And for Stefan, who was still such a nice boy. One night, she dreamed she saw them marrying in Chelm's City Hall right alongside Leeba. When she woke to her grimmer reality, she let the vision linger just a moment. Let herself entertain a possibility: that if she prayed and worked and loved hard enough, she could—carefully, respectfully, insistently—help bring her future son-in-law around.

Stefan felt mildly interested at first when his future mother-in-law began telling him about the history of her hometown. To be honest, he'd barely looked around the place. Every visit, he was always desperate to see Shayna by the time he arrived. And once they were together, history was the last thing on his mind. He was vaguely aware that nowadays the customer service was bad and the local transit system was eccentric, but mostly he associated Chelm with being very much in love.

Still, he was about to become a part of the Selig family, and so he was grateful for the opportunity his future mother-in-law was giving him to learn about her culture. And she especially seemed to enjoy this topic. Fruma always talked, so that was nothing new, but something about her was different. When she talked about the old days in Chelm, her eyes would shine. Many of her stories featured bearded town elders coming together to tackle odd questions, following convoluted reasoning until they reached baffling conclusions. But something—maybe Fruma's obvious love for them, maybe a certain liveliness in the tales themselves—counterbalanced the strangeness.

Fruma didn't stop with a few stories, though. One weekend, Fruma loaded him down with brochures from the Chelm tourism bureau. Stefan was left to stuff one after another into his pockets, wishing only for the awkward encounter to end. Later, though, Fruma kept asking him what he felt about what he had read. His stammered excuses about a lack of time were always met with a disproportionate disappointment. He wanted to have a good relationship with his mother-in-law, but this new, impenetrable anxiety between them left him feeling more and more like a foreigner in her home. Which, he supposed, he was.

He tried talking with Shayna, but that only made things worse. She was patient and kind and happy to explain unfamiliar things to him, but it was no use. He was already annoyed, so he found his mind crowded with objections. For him, Chelm's hill was just a hill. The old town elders were just small town people with terrible ideas. When he'd say things along these lines, Shayna would look at his forehead as if she were trying to see inside his mind. Then her face would soften. She'd laugh, and she'd kiss him, and she'd change the subject. He was glad that she at least felt no need to make mysterious, unspoken demands of him. But he also felt the slightest creeping resentment. He could not escape the feeling that in turning away from the mystery, she was also keeping a secret.

But what could it be? Making sense of Fruma's devotion to the old stories was about as simple as figuring out why medieval Catholics were so obsessed with dead Saints' toe bones. Maybe in the days before streaming music and movies, desperately bored people had simply needed to find some special interest to occupy their minds. Like his parents, Fruma had grown up in a communist country: her childhood media barely counted as such. If the elders of Chelm were her Beatles, more power to her. He only wished—in vain—that she'd leave him out of it.

Chelm and its history quickly lost any appeal for him. Whenever the subject came up, he had to stretch himself through the motions of politeness. It was an exercise that left some part of his soul sore.

Stefan lost his last shreds of patience on the day Fruma asked him to move to Chelm. Even though she knew full well that he and Shayna planned to settle in Germany, she brought it up in a hopeful, eager way, like he was a simple nod of the head away from making her very happy. In a way, her question should have been a relief—a revelation, at last, of her agenda. Instead, it hit him with a wave of delayed dread.

"Under no circumstances," he told her, the chill in his tone smothering any attempt at civility. "Why on earth would I move here?"

She looked as if she'd been slapped. But she pressed on. She told him she had only his own happiness, and her daughter's, in mind. "Marriage begins best when man and woman are in the same ward," she said.

Stefan could handle a great deal of nonsense, but everyone has their limit. And his, like many people's, would apparently involve his mother-in-law. "I don't see what the ward has to do with it," he snapped.

And still, Fruma did not back down. "I think you know better than that," she said. As if the advice she had given him were self-evident truth and not some vaguely religious word salad. She shook her head in disbelief. "I could see a seed of love for Chelm in you!" she told him. "Don't choke it out so soon." She paused, took a deep breath. "Give it room," she implored, "see how you feel."

But Stefan was still seething. "I know exactly how I feel," he countered. "I love Shayna. It's Chelm I can't stand!"

Fruma's shoulders slumped down. "Is that possible?" she asked. "Can you really love her and hate this part of her at the same time?"

Fruma felt sick about her conversation with Stefan long

after he left for the train station and his home in Germany. Should she have been more patient? Whenever the ward started a meeting late, Bishop Levy was always reminding them about learning to wait on the Lord's timing. Then again . . . what if she had already waited too long to broach the subject? Mirele Schwartz was always talking about how the word of the Lord was quick. Either way Fruma was confident, at least, that she'd earned her regret. A better mother—if you didn't count Sariah in the wilderness, or Mary that one time leaving the temple, or Eve when her sons quarreled—would've known what to do. A better Church member would've known how to ensure a proper marriage for all her children. Ah, poor Shayna!

And, for that matter, poor Stefan. How easy it was for foolish, false priorities to blind the minds of men! He was a good man, and memories of his helpfulness and humor still filled her with tenderness, but his stubbornness was such an obstacle. And if he couldn't even move to Chelm to start his marriage right, what sort of foundation would that place it on?

Fruma soon found herself wondering if it wouldn't be better for Shayna to marry someone else. It wasn't Fruma's place to play matchmaker, of course. That's what computers were for. But had Shayna and Stefan been introduced the respectable way, by one of those? No. It was these young single adult activities that were the problem. You sent your children for a little innocent, wholesome fun and they ended up engaged.

Fruma could not, for the life of her, understand why God had left the fundamental unit of society on a foundation so unsteady as young people's whims. Parties and dates? Was that a basis for eternity? Sometimes she wondered why they called it the *plan* of salvation when such important detail seemed not to have been thought through. But the poor design of the cosmos couldn't be helped: in theory, at least, her daughter still could.

She wished she could swipe Moroni's trumpet and blast the lovestruck girl awake. But it was a sin to wish for God's power when she lacked God's restraint.

Fruma could speak with the twin virtues of charity and clarity. After that, the decision would have to be Shayna's, whatever fortune or misfortune, whatever glory or shame, hung in the balance.

For some time, Shayna had felt like she was sitting in the eye at the center of a gathering storm. Just waiting for it to blink.

Her mother hadn't been herself lately. She tossed and turned at night like a prize-fighter in the middle of a bout. After brushing her teeth, she would let the toothbrush hang out of the corner of her mouth like a cigarette while she paced around the house. Sometimes Shayna would see her swaying back and forth in increasingly long and fervent prayers. And she did really strange things: like the time she found out Chelm had a tourism office and then went there.

Something was in the air, because Stefan had also been getting tense. All the time, he was running his hands through his hair like he was working on some impossibly challenging math problem. During the simplest of conversations, he'd get argumentative. He'd give her suspicious looks after she kissed him. Shayna remained patient. Lots of men get nervous as a wedding gets closer. Lots of women have second thoughts before they become a mother-in-law. But she hoped their nerves would settle and everyone would get along.

And then there had been some kind of fight, and Stefan had asked Shayna afterward if she would come and see him in Dresden the next weekend for a change. And now her mother was chewing through toothbrushes like a chain smoker. Shayna looked for an opportunity to ask her mother to stop fretting and just spit it out already. "It" meaning both what was left of her toothbrush and also whatever was on her mind.

A good opportunity came on Tuesday. Leeba had gone out with Noam, leaving Shayna and Fruma a stiflingly quiet evening in the apartment together. Fruma barely made eye contact with Shayna through dinner, so Shayna waited until they stood side by side doing the dishes. "Don't look at me," she said. "You seem to be having a hard time with that. But you can still tell me what the matter is. I don't mind."

And at last, Fruma began to unburden herself. She told her about the visit of the sister from Salzburg. Spoke haltingly but unmistakably about how some marriages are to be celebrated and others regretted. The words began to flow free and fast, then: she told Shayna about marrying in the ward and about the boundaries of the ward. "At first," she admitted, "those boundaries seemed so unjust to me, but then I reminded myself that boundaries are given to protect us!" She spoke of her fondness for Stefan but argued that she could not look with the least degree of allowance on account of that fondness at his utter refusal to consider moving to Chelm before the wedding.

It was not what Shayna had expected. Usually when her mother was upset, there was an ordinary, everyday cause—like the way dust slips off the rag when you aren't looking and settles on top of the shelves again, making you doubt your sanity and start taking photographs to prove that a surface really was completely clean two weeks ago. Or when the bishop wants to meet with you and you don't know what it's about and so you make a list of every sin you've ever committed and it turns out he wants to call you as Relief Society president, so you say yes but come home confused and ask your daughters about Church doctrine because you didn't think Mormons believed in the principle of karma. In any case, Shayna had been sure that her mother had a problem. Or else Stefan had a problem. She had never dreamed that her relationship was the problem.

By the time Fruma had finished, Shayna could feel herself shaking. She had always been a good daughter. At least she liked to think so. A good daughter of her earthly mother, and of heavenly parents. She had not known, she had simply not known, that to marry in the ward like Leeba or like Lemel and Tzipa was right and to marry far away was wrong. She had not known that she risked bringing misfortune on herself and shame on the family.

"I am sorry," Fruma said, "to be leaving you with the burden of this knowledge. The scriptures say that if you fail to teach, you carry the guilt on yourself. I would have gladly carried that guilt for you." She winced. "But I also remembered that no one can be saved in ignorance. So I leave it all to you. I leave you both the knowledge and the choice."

Shayna realized she was drying the last dish. She had no idea how long she had been running her dishcloth in circles around it. She put it away. She walked back to the table and sat down. She stared at the bowl of fruit that sat there.

She supposed she could have avoided this all if she had never gone to that young adult conference. But it had been so much fun, even before Stefan. So wonderful to get to know the great, big Church outside her town. To talk about the gospel with people her age over a picnic lunch. To learn about unfamiliar Latter-day Saint traditions like basketball and *The Princess Bride*. To visit a temple for the first time—to feel the warmth of the water and the Spirit there. If she had understood then what her mother was telling her now, would she have kissed Stefan after the dance? Kept in touch with him?

Fruma was still leaning against the counter near the sink. Shayna went over and took her mother into a long embrace. "You know I love him," she whispered, "but you need to know that that is not the only reason I am still going to marry Stefan." She met her mother's tear-brimmed eyes. And she thought about Freiberg. "I would endure any shame, any opposition, to be married in the temple," Shayna said. "If you had been, if you had felt it there, you might understand."

That night as she lay in bed, Fruma still felt the weight of worry, but none of its usual noise echoed through her head. Her daughters were to be married soon. One the right way; the other according, at least, to the dictates of her own conscience. Fruma knew she could have done better trying to persuade Stefan to move to Chelm, showed more conviction while sharing her concerns with Shayna, but she doubted it would have made a difference. That was the trouble with being a mother in this world: by the time you thought you knew what to do, you'd learned by sad experience to recognize your influence's firm limitations.

Part of her still wanted to sob, of course, but Fruma was surprised to find that a deeper part of her didn't. A deeper part of her was not the least bit concerned with the feeling of failure, not if she could hold on to the thrumming of the Spirit in the back of her heart, whispering that everything was somehow all right.

The story he discovered inside the pages of Jesus'
American book was shockingly familiar. It
was the tale of a family of Jews who offended
people, left town, and got very, very lost.

How the Church Came to Chelm

It was not so very long ago that the Church first came to Chelm—or rather, as Heshel tells the story, that the people of Chelm first came to the Church.

Heshel was young, then. He had not yet married Clever Gretele, his guide and anchor, and was still drifting about, trying to find his place in life. Not to mention his place in eastern Poland's economy. He had tried work on an assembly line, but he lacked the basic consistency required for the job. Whenever his mind drifted, his hands tried to find a new way to do things: square stacks became pyramids, knots turned into bows, and he never learned to properly distinguish a quarter-turn to the left from one to the right. "This job is simple," his supervisor told him. "You only need to do one thing exactly as you've been shown. Just as it's been done before." But that was the trouble: Heshel couldn't ever seem to master what had been done before. Companies in Chelm were, by necessity, patient about an eccentricity or two. But after the day he somehow got the conveyor belt running backward, he was sacked.

On a recommendation from his friend Isaac Peretz, Heshel tried a job in the newspaper business next. "Your mind needs variation—something new every day," Isaac said. "A factory is not for you. But now that you know about conditions in factories, perhaps you could write about the fate of the working class." With Isaac's help, Heshel got a trial period with the *Chelm Every-Other-Daily Gazette.*

The fate of the working class, as discussed in the *Gazette* offices, turned out to revolve around a special weekly bonus insert of coupons. And novelty? Not the asset you might expect in that business. In the rapid succession of positions Heshel took on, he learned that people prefer their every-other-daily dose of the new only with a steady diet of the comfortably old. Subscribers wanted their newspapers to be in the exact same spot at the exact same time every other morning. They look forward to seeing the same old, tired typeface. They wanted each issue, no matter what was happening, to carry the exact same kinds of stories in the same proportions of crisis, tragedy, and scandal—with only grudging allowance for the names and particulars to change. Poor Heshel was no good as a carrier or a printer, awful as a writer, and dangerous in the advertising department (when he forgot to include Aldi deals among the coupons, he caused a full-blown geriatric riot). He was let go as part of a bargain to pacify the mob, his curse for novelty having wrecked another career.

Heshel found the same problem in the restaurant business, at the synagogue, and especially during his single day as an employee of the state. People simply did not tolerate genuine variety in their meals or prayers or taxes. Before long, Heshel found that any variety in the job offers he could find had also worn away. To be precise, no one in town was willing to offer him work.

What was a Heshel like him to do? He loved his town desperately, but at length decided he had no choice but to seek his fortune elsewhere. One morning, Heshel rose early to go out into the world. With no particular destination in mind, he decided he would simply pick a prominent landmark and head in its direction, seeing where it led him. As he looked around for options, he decided to choose his very own lucky star (which, in the daytime, happened to be the sun).

The sun, apparently, had no desire for Heshel to remain in Chelm. It quickly directed him out past the chalk mines, over an eastern border crossing, through a forest, and into a town. Stopping for breakfast at the nearest bakery, Heshel noticed that he had already traveled so far that the people all spoke a different language! It was still Slavic, of course, so Heshel could follow bits and pieces (almost as much, truth be told, as he ever did when his mind wandered). Even the words he knew, though, carried an unmistakable accent of adventure.

Heshel greedily took in the scent of this new and sunward country: sweet and buttery, a true land of cheese and honey. The knowledge that he had passed far beyond the limits of his own world filled him with no small portion of pride—and an even larger portion of hunger. But when he saw the printed prices on the menu, Heshel's heart sank. The numbers were six times higher than he was used to! If he were a roll or pastry and not a body with a stomach, he could clearly make a fortune here. But he was a body with a stomach. And a stomach will make its demands, even in another country.

Heshel and his stomach negotiated briefly.

Without restraint as ruthless as Oskar the Miser's, a man could go bankrupt in a place like this, he told his stomach.

With the miser's restraint, a man could starve anywhere, his stomach replied.

Why not eat after finding a job? Heshel suggested to his stomach next.

Why not look for a job after he ate? his stomach countered.

Well, Heshel reasoned, a new journey's beginning ought to be marked somehow. It wouldn't show much confidence in the future if he skimped. Not wanting to look afraid, he decided to increase his breakfast budget twelve times beyond what he would spend at home, and promptly ordered two delicious-looking buns with the centers scooped out and eggs cooked inside.

To his great surprise, however, the baker refused to take the small treasury Heshel offered. Explaining that the currency here was not the same, and that zlotys were worth six times as much, he refused to accept most of Heshel's payment. What good fortune! What great relief! Feeling six times wealthier than he had mere moments before, Heshel thought it only proper to celebrate. He laid the rest of the money he had convinced himself to spend on the counter and pointed at first this roll, then that sweet, until every last zloty was spent.

Paper bag of wonders in hand, Heshel spent the morning wandering the town, taking in its sights and slowly working his way through its tastes. The latter work was athletic, stretching every muscle in his stomach and taking hours to complete. His belly passed from hunger to satisfaction, from satisfaction to stupor, and then slowly pressed its way forward into pain. By mid-day, he'd had his fill of the town and was ready to follow the sun off to another adventure.

But oh, what tragedy. He was standing in the town's main square, struggling to focus through a haze of digesting breads and cheeses, meats and sweets, when he realized with a sinking filling that he had failed to keep track of his guiding star. Over the course of the morning, focused on the needs of the flesh, he had somehow lost his way—and now it was hanging over him. Right above his head. For everyone, but especially for Heshel, life was disorienting like this sometimes. You'd settle on something, you'd start to count on it even. But as soon as you relaxed and took a thing for granted, it would change and everything went sideways.

Heshel was forced to concede that he was thoroughly lost in more ways than one. He had no job. He was actively suffering from a lack of restraint. And he was literally, geographically lost, with no destination and nothing to guide him forward. His only consolation was that it had happened in a town of complete strangers: it would have been mortifying to be so lost right in the middle of the town square if he'd still been home in Chelm.

Heshel's embarrassment receded even further when he realized he was not the only one lost here. For perhaps twenty minutes, he watched two young men in dark suits stand awkwardly in the square, repeatedly failing to talk with people who passed by. After some time, Heschel noticed the dark-haired one of the young men noticing him. While the other one persisted in his steady accrual of rejections, the young man gave up on trying to stop people who were already moving and walked over to Heschel instead.

If Heshel followed the locals' example and fled from the suited men, would he get even more lost? He hesitated—and found himself addressed in the baker's language. The young man, if Heshel understood correctly, claimed to be Jesus Christ. Or perhaps Jesus' elderly relative? In any case, he said he had a message about Heshel's family.

Heshel tried to explain that although he was a Jew and Jesus was now widely known to have been Jewish, the two of them were not closely related. It was a common enough mistake, of course: people were always assuming Jews all knew each other. Unfortunately, the young man didn't seem to follow Heshel's Polish as well as the baker had. He insisted that Heshel was, in fact, Jesus' brother and seemed to suggest that Jesus had wanted him to have a book. For honesty's sake, Heshel tried again to explain that if he and Jesus looked alike, it was purely coincidence. But the young man could not be dissuaded. Nothing, it seemed, could keep him from telling his story. After glancing up quickly to confirm that the sun was still unhelpfully located, Heshel decided to linger and listen.

The young man's enthusiasm grew when he realized Heshel was not going to walk away from him. He asked Heshel something about Jesus and Heshel repeated that he had never met Jesus and didn't know much about him. The man in the suit didn't seem to be concerned. Or, for that matter, really listening. He talked with more and more excitement instead, saying that Jesus had gone to America and written a book there.

Of course he had, thought Heshel. What a stereotypically Jewish thing to do.

The young man in the suit produced a copy of the book. Heshel explained patiently that he couldn't read the Cyrillic script, since he was from Poland, but even that did not stop the man, who waved his companion over, asking him to bring a copy of the book in Polish.

The lighter-haired suit-man cheerfully complied, and soon pressed a copy into Heshel's hands. Though Heshel remained convinced this was a simple case of mistaken identity, he thanked them for the gift and told them to thank Jesus on his behalf next time they saw him. For some reason, this suggestion both amused and delighted them.

But even after handing Heshel the book, the men did not leave. They asked him if he promised to read it. Heshel glanced up again at the sun. Though he had not expected to spend the day reading, it seemed as good a way as any to pass the time. He agreed, sat down on a nearby bench, and began at once as the two young men finally walked away.

The story he discovered inside the pages of Jesus' American book was shockingly familiar. It was the tale of a family of Jews who offended people, left town, and got very, very lost.

His heart went out for them. They wandered, adrift as strangers in an unwelcoming world: fighting for their lives, endlessly arguing with each other, and longing for a New Jerusalem. Heshel read for hours. A feeling of strength and purpose slowly gathered within him as he did so. It was as if the book were a battery and an electric current was passing from it into him, preparing him for his own life's journey.

When Heshel next looked up, the sun was right in front of him. He rose, tucked the book away in his pack, and pressed onward in search of his own promised land. The sun led him out past forests, over another border crossing, past another chalk mine, and finally into a city that looked—almost exactly—like Chelm.

The similarities to his old home were astonishing. The streets had the same layout. The houses had the same architecture. The businesses sold the same goods. The thought struck Heshel like a bolt of lightning that this must be a New Chelm, just like the book's promise of a New Jerusalem.

Another thought came to his mind, and he decided to put it, like a seed of faith, to the test. He rushed through the streets until he reached the place where his apartment would have been in the old Chelm. Hands trembling, he lifted his key to the door, and—miracle of miracles!—the key fit.

It was as the book said. A place had been prepared for him.

As soon as he stepped inside, Heshel took out the book and found the phone number stamped on its inside cover. He called the two suited men, who were titled above the number not by name but simply as missionaries. He told the one who answered how real and true the book was—in his life, at least. True in ways they could hardly comprehend.

The young man's voice on the phone was ecstatic. He and Heshel talked for hours, haltingly across the barrier of language but bound together by a shared secret deeper than language. The missionary told Heshel strange and marvelous things. There was the story of Joseph Smith, a boy without a place in all the Christian churches, who went into the forest and came out a prophet. There was the story of Jesus, who taught odd and blasphemous things but loved everyone and would die for his friends. The missionary claimed that something had gone deeply wrong in this history of Christianity, and Heshel heartily agreed. But there was a theory, a word that the missionary kept repeating. Heshel didn't recognize it, but he realized at last it meant that Joseph Smith and the last-days Saints intended to gather up the broken pieces of the modern world and put them somehow back together. This theory was no fairy tale, the missionary insisted. This great repair, or rebuilding, could be done to humanity, even if the process continued after death. To make this point specific, he promised Heshel that his family could be together forever.

Heshel was skeptical, since he'd left them just that morning, but the missionary's words proved prophetic. Soon after Heshel moved to New Chelm, he found his mother and brothers had joined him. His whole community, it seemed, had followed: he saw Yossel the fisherman out to cast his nets, Feige Cohen haggling with a shopkeeper over the price of groceries. He caught a glimpse of a beautiful girl he swore was Gretele Gottstein. Then he bumped into Menachem Menashe as Menachem barreled down the street with his face buried in a book. Even Lazar the blind beggar had somehow made the journey and was waiting out on the street for the grace of God. By the next Sabbath, Heshel was quite sure that everyone had migrated.

It was true, then. Family was forever; friends were forever. The same relationships he had forged in Chelm existed in New Chelm. And it followed, by the surety of sound logic, that there was hope indeed for wandering

Jews as the Book of Mormon claimed. And maybe that was because Jesus, who had been crazy but made up for it by giving people his whole heart and in the end also a broken body, had introduced a great repair in the last days after Christians made a mess of his religion.

Heshel called the missionaries every night for a month. They offered to send other missionaries, Polish-speaking missionaries, to New Chelm (which everyone but Heshel, to save a syllable, called "Chelm" for short), but Heshel was not so sure. The Jews of Chelm had kept their faith for hundreds of generations, thousands of years. They worshiped more or less exactly as they'd been shown, just as it had been done before. What sort of stir would he make if he failed to follow? In Chelm, Heshel had always been scolded and sighed over for his inability to just do what people had done.

In New Chelm, though, who knew? Perhaps here, his restlessness could be a strength. He decided to approach the issue cautiously but steadily. He lent the Book of Mormon to Menachem Menashe, urging him to make a thorough study of it and report back on his experience. He told Aaron Cohen about the priesthood, Yossel Fischer about all the Nephite and Jaredite boats, and Isaac Peretz about the social and spiritual problem of fine-twined linen. He even found the courage to talk to Gretele Gottstein and tell her about his growing belief in the hope of a great repair.

At length, Heshel agreed to accept physical visits from the missionaries. They taught him to pray in Polish as well as Hebrew, convinced him that his lack of money for cigarettes and vodka was a virtue and not a shame, and gave him an awkward talk about how sex is both danger-ous and holy. They encouraged Heshel to make promise after promise: that he would take the bus to Lublin each Sunday to attend their services, that he would avoid wine even on holidays, that he would avoid the dangers of sex until he had entered the acknowledged minefield of marriage, that he would care for others and carry their burdens. It was easy enough for Heshel, who wasn't making any money, to promise to pay tithing. It was harder to have faith when the missionaries encouraged him to try, once again, to find a job—but in New Chelm his new confidence opened new doors. Which was something, even if they consistently proved to be rotating. He bore his testimony that he'd been blessed.

Heshel balked once again at the prospect of actually being baptized—the word held such negative connotations after centuries of Christian coercion—but the missionaries helped him appreciate the act itself, whatever meanings its name had taken on over the years. Heshel gradually got used to the idea. After all, a rose by any other name would be hard to find in a store. The syllables in the name "Elzbieta" might sound nicer than those in the name "Gretele," but if he had to call one or the other across the street, he knew whose head he'd rather turn. Sometimes you had to make your peace with a name if you wanted a flower or a conversation or a new covenant. If the world had to call it baptism, then he'd be baptized. To be immersed in water was a perfectly reasonable religious act, after all, and the beginning of a journey ought to be marked somehow.

On the 15th of Tishrei, Heshel Yitzhak Kleiner went down under the water and came out as some kind of Saint. In New Chelm, as it turned out, he was leading the way out into the wilderness of a new faith for many of the children of Israel. Leah Kanter, never afraid to make a bold choice, was the next to be baptized. Menachem Menasche read every Polish-language book the missionaries owned and a few more by means of his imperfect but developing English. For some time, he was torn between adopting the religious, philosophical, and historical system called Mormonism and becoming a cog in the elaborate social system sponsored by the Church of Jesus Christ of Latter-day Saints. Finally, the missionaries convinced him he could have both. While Menachem was debating, Mattheusz and Sara Levy started attending, and Fruma Selig with her girls. Then individual members of other old Chelm families joined: Mirele Schwartz, Saul Gronam, old Israel Lewensztajn. Belka Fischer was baptized on her own and Yossel later followed.

Gretele Gottstein attended every baptism. She admitted that a warmth filled her chest each time she came. Once, swept up in that warmth even after the ordinance was done, she kissed Heshel on an impulse as they left—and decided that she liked the feeling of his arms around her on the bus ride back home. It was hard to sort out her feelings about the Restoration, as the missionaries called it in Polish, from her feelings about Heshel, who had introduced her to the idea. But since they were free, she finally decided she would take them both.

Heshel had been thinking about leaving New Chelm to serve a mission, but after Gretele asked how he would feel about assembling the best bits of a broken world into a life with her, the mission president assured Heshel that he was doing more than enough to spread the gospel right where he was. And so it was that the two married and found a little apartment, with Gretele's various streams of income smoothing over the renewed parade of short-lived jobs Heshel had in place of a career. By many measures, he was still a disaster. But he was happy.

And perhaps God had a purpose in all his missteps. As he shared his new religion with the carousel of people he happened to work with, Heshel watched the little group of Saints in Chelm grow into a branch and the branch, inexplicably, into a ward. And, though he was by no means the most capable or knowledgeable member of the Chelm ward, Heshel took a little pride in having been the first who had enough of Chelm's famous wisdom to give this strange, sweet new faith a chance.

Once in a while, he still thought about the old Chelm and how different life there had been, back before he started out on his journey, and read the Book of Mormon, and made more promises than he could, quite frankly, keep very good track of. Someday, he mused, when he and Gretele had grown old and wise together, maybe they could put in their papers and serve a mission after all. And perhaps, speaking Polish as well as they did, they would be called to serve in Poland. And then could find the old Chelm, and maybe whoever had stayed in that city would also embrace the gospel.

It would be such a delight to see a Chelm Second Ward organized there.

"May the Lord reward you tenfold," the bishop said. Given the starting point, he wasn't sure whether such a promise counted as a generous blessing or a de facto curse.

Oskar the Miser Pays Fast Offering

Bishop Levy's heart dropped when he saw Oskar the Miser walk through the meeting-house doors early one morning on the first Sunday of the month to pay his fast offering. By longstanding agreement, the Bishop handed the first fast offering of the day to Lazar the Blind Beggar, and Oskar's appearance did not bode well for the man. Despite his significant wealth, Oskar lived on a diet of cabbage soup—cooked from the same head of cabbage all week—and he calculated his offering very literally. It made Bishop Levy's stomach growl just thinking about all the food the Miser's meager offering wouldn't buy.

Still, as bishop, it was Levy's duty to accept whatever was offered, even if it was only two tiny, all-but-worthless coins. "Thank you, Brother Wiener," he said as he took the envelope. "May the Lord reward you tenfold," he added. Given the starting point, the bishop wasn't sure that such a promise counted as a generous blessing or a de facto curse.

Oskar the Miser squinted at the bishop and Bishop Levy sighed. The last time he had promised Oskar earthly blessings for his minimal act of altruism, Oskar had found a zloty on the street on his way home. Though the coin would only cover half the cost of bus fare, it was worth fifty times as much as the Miser's offering. Rather than rejoice over this tiny bit of good luck, the old man had returned to take the Bishop to task for reckless overspending of God's blessing money.

Bishop Levy tried not to make a habit of offending ward members. He even kept a little notebook of topics that might set different individuals off. No matter what Saul Gronam's calling happened to be, for example, you had to show it unreasonable respect or he would feel personally slighted. Leah Kantor's feelings could be hurt, and her opinion of you would certainly suffer, if you didn't at least pretend to be interested in art and music. For Isaac Peretz, it was safest to avoid politics, economics—and maybe even, just to be safe, religion. It was dangerous, with Mirele Schwartz, to talk about anything that could have gone better. But Oskar the miser? All the sensitive topics with him went back to money, but after taking two pages of notes on the specifics, Bishop Levy realized he was wasting perfectly good paper. If it wasn't one thing with that man, it was another. You couldn't dodge his complaints, only try to guess which particular topic would start the next scolding. Would it be the free soap in the meetinghouse bathrooms? The lack of security to prevent the theft of hymn books? Even if he walked away, he could easily come back shouting because he had found a lost coin.

This time, Oskar did not wait to air a grievance. "You know that fasting is no problem for me, bishop," he said. "But this fast offering is a terrible business. What's the point of asking us all to sacrifice for the hungry if you're going to turn around and serve the whole congregation a free breakfast!" Ah yes, thought Bishop Levy. They were back to the issue of excessive portions of sacrament bread. Oskar grimaced. "People keep saying God is just, but then they ask you to invest as if he were plain wasteful!" He wagged a finger in the Bishop's face. "I tell you: these sorts of logical contradictions are driving learned men from religion!"

With that, the old man shuffled away—just in time for Bishop Levy to notice Lazar the blind beggar approaching the meetinghouse door. He had half a mind to duck into his office to add some money to the envelope, but Lazar was very particular. Whenever Bishop Levy tried to convince him to accept a regular payment, he insisted that beggars lived by the grace of God and refused to accept one zloty more than divine chance allotted him.

What to do, though, on a week when divine chance hadn't allotted him a zloty at all?

Lazar was smiling broadly as he approached. "Let us see, good bishop," he called, "what the Master of the Universe has granted me today!"

Bishop Levy placed a hand on the blind beggar's shoulder and let it linger, he hoped consolingly, as he handed over Oskar's envelope. Lazar put his hand in and the smile on his face turned to a look of puzzlement. Bishop Levy watched in pain as Lazar felt carefully around the edges of the envelope, no doubt certain that he had missed some folded bill or hidden coin beyond the two tiny groszy Oskar actually, truly, and in all sincerity donated each month.

After making a thorough investigation, Lazar stopped feeling around the envelope, put a hand in his pocket, and withdrew two shiny zlotys, which he placed in Oskar's envelope. "Bishop," he implored, "will you take this and give it back to the donor today? This person is surely in more grievous need than I."

And with those words, Lazar walked off into the chapel, leaving Bishop Levy standing alone in the hallway, astounded. *More grievous need than I?* On its surface, the idea was laughable. The miser was quite wealthy and grew wealthier with each week, even if he did suffer from the economic equivalent of crippling constipation. If most people were asked to describe him, the challenge might stretch their vocabularies beyond the sort of words a person normally used within the confines of God's house. With a big enough vocabulary, you could call Oskar curmudgeonly, misanthropic, or avaricious. But no matter how creative a person got, the bishop sincerely doubted the word *needy* would come to any ordinary mind.

But ah, the bishop realized, Lazar the blind beggar did not see as other men see. Bishop Levy saw two tiny coins in an otherwise empty envelope, but Lazar saw something even smaller. Like God himself, he truly looked upon the heart!

*Both presidents were old enough to know
that even the most cosmetic of changes
can create a disastrous mental load.*

Ministering Angles

After it was announced that the old visiting teaching and home teaching programs would be replaced with a new program called ministering, which God had sent the faithful to reduce both guilt and bus fare, Fruma Selig and President Gronam met to disagree about how to make new assignments. The meeting was a historic occasion. Previously, each had disagreed about how to make assignments only with their own counselors. This was the first time they were to sit down and disagree with each other directly: now that there was official permission for arrangements such as couples being assigned together, Bishop Levy had wanted them to think through new approaches for the whole ward.

Both presidents were old enough to know that even the most cosmetic of changes can create a disastrous mental load. They understood that freedom and flexibility, however appealing in theory, are, in practice, remarkably prone to breakdown. And so it was, together, that they tried to come up with a new blanket rule for creating assignments—something that could give the same reassuring thoughtlessness of time-worn habit.

They started by studying the issue out in their minds, waiting for a spark of divine inspiration. But when it's dark, even the smallest flash of an idea can feel like lightning from heaven. As he pondered, for example, President Gronam felt a rush of intelligence filling the narrow confines of his head and quickly proposed a system for assigning pairs based on beard length. What better way could there be, he said, to yoke the wise and experienced easily to their peers.

Fruma Selig objected. Beard length, she said, was hardly a reliable measure of experience.

President Gronam defended that principle from the scriptures. He cited 2 Samuel 10:5—*Tarry at Jericho, until your beards be grown*—and the 133rd Psalm—*How pleasant it is for brethren to dwell together in unity! Like precious ointment that ran down the beard.*

But Fruma did not relent. "Whatever system we choose," she said, "will need to be created with the Church's women as well as its men in mind."

President Gronam could hardly believe his ears. Why, a rule like that would overturn generations of precedent! "I don't think the brethren meant this change to be so drastic," he grumbled. But Fruma Selig held firm. And after some time, President Gronam conceded that beard length might fall short of her unorthodox standard.

With that first idea discarded, it was time to let their minds' wheels turn again. This time, it was Fruma's that ran into something and threw off a spark. She proposed a system in which, in the timely spirit of simplification, everyone served as a minister to the person who lived closest to them. But though he knew many would welcome such a proposal, President Gronam resisted it. "Every person on earth lives in their own skin," he observed, "and we are therefore all closest to ourselves. Surely you can see that assigning people as their own ministers is a bad idea," he added. "Just think of the personality conflicts!"

Fruma Selig sighed. "That is true enough," she admitted. "Some might make the adjustment with time, but Mirele Schwartz would always be far too harsh."

Having been failed by inspiration, President Gronam turned to common sense. Since they and their counselors needed to conduct ministering interviews in any case, he argued, they could simply assign themselves as ministers to the entire ward and kill a whole flock of birds, so to speak, with one stone. Fruma Selig, however, was concerned that in their interviews they would have nothing to talk about. "Besides," she added, "we would only be interviewing the parents: who would minister to the children?"

Both of them let that question sink in a moment. "Now that," said President Gronam said, "may be just the answer we are looking for."

Sometimes God sends inspiration in pieces and it takes a council to put those pieces together. In this case, the two presidents decided to build off Fruma Selig's proposal to have people minister close to home and President Gronam's realization that children were the key to the entire problem by assigning parents to minister to their own children. Nothing, they felt, could be more home-centered. Not only that, it would make it easy for everyone to know (and even remember) who their assigned ministers were. In all President Gronam's years of experience with home teaching, such a thing had never happened. Surely, this was the answer.

Would it work for all ward members? Yes, on that count the system would be marvelous. All had been children at one point, after all, so everyone would have an assigned ministering brother and sister somewhere. Not all members were parents, of course, so some would no longer be assigned to minister. But if Chelm's new system added guilt by accident where other Church programs already heaped it, that could hardly be counted as a concern. All things considered, the idea felt almost too good to be true. President Gronam and Fruma Selig concluded their meeting with an agreement to announce it the very next week.

Ward members greeted the idea, as always, not by responding to its individual merits but through their habitual posture toward any communication from authority figures in the Church. Mirele Schwartz preemptively bore testimony of the truth of the scheme. Oskar the Miser questioned the motives of President Gronam and Bishop Levy, the intelligence of Church authorities in Frankfurt and Salt Lake, the wisdom of the angels in heaven, and the competence of God. As soon as they were told about the new ministering assignments, others reflexively nodded righteously, rolled their eyes, or shrugged—all as the force of habit dictated.

After a month, though, ward members' reactions no longer aligned with their reflexes. Some who prided themselves on their gift for discontent found that they loved the system. Some who prided themselves on their particularity and zeal could almost admit, if pressed, that they did not care for it.

There were no shortage of stories for Presidents Selig and Gronam to repeat when they wished, respectively, to encourage sisters in their duty or scold brothers for their faithlessness. Zalman the Learned, for example, had reported that since the introduction of the new system, his children had listened more attentively than ever during the family's monthly half-hour of scripture study. Clever Gretele also had only good to say about the system: her husband Heshel, she observed, was spending far more time at home and far less time hopelessly lost searching for new routes by which to conduct his visits. And 97-year-old Israel Lewensztajn broke four years of silence during elders' quorum to relate how his parents had started visiting him in dreams while he slept in sacrament meeting. "It's been very pleasant," he said. "I never got along with my father when he was alive, but nothing mellows a man quite like death."

Other members' reactions were of a kind that tended not to be shared in Relief Society or Quorum meetings. Bishop Levy had his hands full. He was counseling regularly now with the Cohens, who were otherwise content with their lives' portion of unhappiness but desperately missed the assigned companions they'd long relied on as an outlet. The otherwise unflappable fatalism of Lazar the Blind Beggar was sorely tested by the loss of his old home teacher, Menachem Menashe, who had read the scriptures to him and given him, in their long and wandering visits, tomes' worth of spoken commentary. Far more than the pickles and fish Menashe used to bring, it was the loss of those hours that made Lazar feel poorer. Even Belka Fisher made an appointment with the Bishop to tearfully admit that while she had always done her best to do the bare minimum in every assignment given to her, not even she could keep herself from asking her children how they were doing more than the ministering program's mandate of once every three months.

His heart breaking for the Belka Fischers of the ward, for Lazar the blind beggar, and (after sessions with the Cohens) especially for himself, Bishop Levy's resolve to sustain the officers of his ward in their decisions finally broke. He called in President Gronam and President Selig and begged them to find another way.

Though they could not understand the bleary-eyed bishop's tears, Fruma Selig and President Gronam reluctantly agreed to return to the proverbial (as well as a literal) drawing board.

If inspiration comes by knocking at the door, President Gronam and Fruma Selig were prepared to use a battering ram. They printed out lists of households. They brought food. They pulled up a chalkboard and sharpened several pieces of chalk. They were prepared to throw ideas at the Lord until he confirmed one for them just to bring the meeting to an end.

The first option they considered was simply reversing their system to have children minister to their parents.

Mathematically, though, that was a challenge. Parents typically came in ones or twos. The number of children in a household felt almost random. Some poor people would be hopelessly outnumbered by literal ministering brothers and sisters. Other ward members would be ministered to by no one at all.

With the household-based system undone, they next considered assigning people to their next-door neighbors. A simple review of the membership list, however, revealed that such a system resulted in an interpersonal nightmare. A nightmare which, unfortunately, would lack the justification of inflicting uniform misery. Truly, it was as if someone had set out to compile the ward's best and worst relationships into a single, headache-inducing list! It was a good thing that Jesus had answered the question "who is my neighbor?" with a long parable, because if he had said, "the person who lives closest to you," the ward would have some real troubles.

They tried sorting their list through other objective traits. Age order resulted in low-mobility companionships like Israel Lewenstajn and Henya the Prophetess, as well as low-focus companionships, like Chava Gottstein-Kleiner and Golda Fischer. Conversion order looked a little nice at first, but broke down in the recent years, as baptism date began to clump young people together.

Considering the difficulty of natural systems of order, President Gronam gave a strong scriptural argument (founded in Proverbs 18:18 but also citing precedent from Acts to 1 Nephi to Joshua and even Leviticus) for casting lots. Few concepts had such long scriptural support as randomness. But Fruma Selig, who felt quite attached to the latter-day prophets, felt a duty to caution against even the appearance of gambling.

"This should not be so difficult," President Gronam exclaimed after hours of mapping, planning, discussion, and debate. "After thousands of years of history, how has a system that takes into account both proximity and tolerability never been designed?"

Fruma Selig clapped her hands as inspiration came to her. "That's it!" she said. "It should have been obvious— only we've been looking at the wrong map." She took the map of the ward down from the board at once and drew a succession of rectangles in its place. Long, thin rectangles with a gap and then a smaller squarish shape at the center of the top.

"Of course!" said President Gronam. "Sacrament seating!"

Fruma Selig beamed. "They already pray together, sing together, and share a message. If we can get them to shake hands and say Shalom to each other during the meeting, ministering will be done!"

From memory, they compiled a list of who sat where. As they had suspected, people who couldn't stand each other also didn't sit together (siblings and spouses alone excepted) and after a little discussion over who should turn to the person beside them and who should look forward or behind, they were ready to enter the assignments into the meetinghouse's aging computer and print off assignment slips for everyone in the ward.

The next week, President Gronam watched in self-vindicating satisfaction as ministering unfolded beautifully before his eyes. People chose their own degree of involvement: Belka Fischer barely making eye contact down her pew, while Lazar the Blind Beggar and Menchem Menasche lingered even after Zalman the Learned, whose week it was to teach Sunday School, had started the lesson.

"How clever we are," he said to Fruma Selig after the meeting was done.

"Clever enough to be inspired," she replied.

He sighed in satisfaction. "This is a system that could last a lifetime."

The next week, President Gronam came uncharacteristically early to watch the beautiful machine in motion. To his delight, he found the pew just behind the chapel entrance open. He had always found the pew enticing: it belonged to the back section, where he felt so comfortable and at home, but had the beckoning softness of a padded bench, not the metallic cold of the hard chair that was his traditional place in services. And the leg room! President Gronam had often watched Lemel with envy as the man folded back his legs to let the deacons, Gimpel and Dudel, pass during the sacrament and then as he stretched them out again in open luxury for the rest of the meeting.

Well? Lemel was not here yet, and President Gronam was. He took the pew he'd always coveted from a distance after ducking into meetings just as they began.

When he arrived (not a minute later), the sheer force of habit almost drove Lemel into President Gronam's lap. But Tzipa called out to him just in time and the two of them went to find another place to sit. Instead of slinking to President Gronam's usual corner of the back, however, they moved to the rearmost pew in the front section. The one President Gronam could only think of as the Fischers' bench. The Fischers, apparently, liked to sit at the back of the front and so moved to the Schwartzes' bench on the other side. And so it went, on and on, President Gronam realizing with horror that he had caused a chain reaction. By the time Leah Kantor walked up to conduct the opening hymn, the only one who seemed to be in her usual spot was Zelda Gottstein. Out in the foyer.

It was a disaster. An unmitigated disaster. Like a Schroedinger's cat sentenced to death by a careless act of observation, the beautiful ministering system had been brought down by one ill-considered, covetous choice. Truly, this was the day for which God had given the tenth commandment.

President Gronam tried to enjoy the leg room on his pew, but he could take no comfort in it. He sighed instead, took out a piece of paper and a pencil, sketched out the week's seating configuration, and left just after the sacrament had been passed. He needed to enter new assignments into the ward's aging computer before it was too late.

Menachem had worked hard, as a Sunday School teacher, to bring the treasures of the Torah—and of course all the sequels in the ever-growing series—into the minds and lives of his students.

Two-Hour
Church

"There have been many questions and speculations about the change from a three-hour to a two-hour Church schedule," Menachem Menashe said at the beginning of Sunday School the first week after the change was announced. Drawing on his superior understanding as someone who could read Church websites in English as well as the few materials available in Polish, he tried to set the record straight. "The hope of the brothers in America," he explained, "is not simply to reduce the costs of heating this building during the winter, or the amount of time we spend with the scriptures. The real purpose is to increase the time we spend with our families. Or rather," he added hastily, "the time that those of you who live with families spend with your families. But rest assured: the time you spend with your family will benefit me as well. The family, as we all know, is the fundamentalist unit of society."

Menachem paused to adjust his glasses while he let this vital point sink in. He knew the people of Chelm could be of limited capacity, but he was nothing as a teacher if not patient. "I know it will be difficult for many of you," he acknowledged, "to be reminded each Sunday where to go instead of following your muscles' well-trained memory. Habit and religion are so closely connected that any change will feel a bit like blasphemy at first. That's only natural." He then chose to get out ahead of the curve and bear his testimony. "But as we work together, I know we can learn whatever it is God sent us here on earth to learn, no matter how little time we spend at Church. Are there any questions?"

Heshel, uncharacteristically, raised his hand first. "I don't understand your mathematics," he said. "On a good Sunday, we meet for four hours."

Menachem nodded. He could see now why the topic was so close to Heshel's heart. Though the Saints of Chelm had been told it was not strictly required to snack together in the foyer each week, they had seen no reason to alter their religion in that respect. People brought this or that to share. It was, by far, Heshel's most sacred hour. "Only the official meetings will be affected," Menachem reassured his worried student. "As long as your mother-in-law is baking her babka, no one would dare diminish the joy of the Sabbath."

Tzipa spoke next, without raising her hand. "Speaking of Sister Gottstein," she asked, "how will this change affect people who worship mostly in the foyer?"

Menachem shook his head sadly. "We should remember the lonely at all times, and will need to be especially mindful of those who lose precious time with old and treasured friends. I know many of you have faithfully skipped one or the other class each week for many years to keep the foyer busy. Sister Gottstein will, of course, be in our prayers, and it is to be hoped that some of you will still take time away from class once in a while to sit and spend an hour with her."

President Gronam did raise his hand, but as usual did not wait to be called upon. "If I can ask a confidential question—" he began.

"You may not," Menachem interjected. "This is the whole ward's Sunday School class."

As usual, though, his attempts to influence Gronam were in vain. "How will this affect the Cohens?" President Gronam asked. "They have been so happy attending on alternate weeks . . . why are they now suddenly expected to spend an extra hour together at home?"

Fortunately, Sister Cohen answered the question before Menachem had time to come up with anything offensive. "It will be easy enough for us to find an extra hour in meetings, on service projects, or simply shutting the world out by staring at our phones," she assured the class. "We are resourceful people: there is no need for you to worry on our account."

Dobra Peretz spoke up next. "And what is to be done for those of us whose families only seem to sit together at all when they've been herded onto the same pew? Is it really expected that we will somehow begin to study the gospel together at home now?"

Menachem thought he had prepared for this discussion well, but concerns were like locusts and the time had come to call for the seagulls. He referred Sister Peretz's question to the ravenous wisdom of the class.

"You're never together at home?" Sister Cohen said first. "That sounds like a dream. What problems would a family like that still need the gospel for?"

Belka Fischer raised her hand next. "It's like the scripture says: blessed are those who hunger. I try to lure my children to the table with food and sprinkle a little gospel on top while their mouths are busy," she said.

"Perhaps you could take a pew home and place it alongside your dinner table," Zalman the Learned suggested. "Since we are home-centered and Church-supported now, surely the meetinghouse can spare a little furniture."

Mirele Schwartz had patiently kept her hand up through all these comments for the chance to add to the advice. "Whenever I worry about whether I am doing enough," she began, "I have found that it is always possible to do more. With enough love, work, and spending, there is always hope that the family can be brought together. For example, I have some delightful attention activities planned for the first six months of home study. Since I won't be at the Church building anymore, there's a much better chance that my husband and daughter will notice them and finally have their attention captured. I'd be happy to share my lesson plans with you, and help you with the welding work on the props if you'd like."

Sister Schwartz's comment left Menachem Menasche feeling philosophical. She and Sister Peretz might be in the same room now, but he doubted they were ever really hearing the same messages. Menachem had gotten interested in the Church because of Heshel's talk of a Repair that would bring scattered truths into some kind of balance again. But was it even possible to teach the balance of gospel truth when everyone fixated so much on whatever already spoke to their own neuroses?

To tell the truth, a question like that excited him. He couldn't help it. As soon as he got home, he wanted to look through the upcoming lessons and see which scriptures would lend themselves to a discussion of that paradox. He imagined that most would work perfectly. After all, the scriptures were full to bursting with neurotic people who didn't listen very well.

But then Menachem's heart sank. Could he really justify fitting this particular paradox into one of the handful of lessons he'd teach this year? It was one thing to bring up an interesting topic when you had two dozen hours of study ahead. Under the reduced schedule, and with conferences and holidays getting in the way, he'd be lucky if he got to teach ten times. The scriptures said that when you taught and students learned by the spirit, that you rejoiced and were edified together. What was the opposite? Moping alone?

Best not to dwell on that too much. Best to return to the subject. "Are there any other questions about this change to two hours of Church?" he said.

Oskar the Miser raised his hand. "Is there any intention to make the remaining classes more worthwhile?" he asked.

Though the question came from the miser, Menachem could still feel a certain sting. He had worked hard, as a Sunday School teacher, to bring the treasures of the Torah—and of course all the sequels in the ever-growing series—into the minds and lives of his students. That was his passion. It had felt like his place.

And then? Well, Menachem had heard others speak of moments in General Conference when a servant of God seemed to speak across the millions of listeners straight to them. When they announced that a weekly Sunday School was simply not necessary, that's how it felt for him. Whatever words had been spoken, he'd felt as if he was receiving a personal message that his efforts had fallen short. That ward members needed to be freed of the burden made by his narrow claim on their attention.

Menachem swallowed back his pride. Pride had killed the Nephites. If Menachem didn't watch his pride carefully, it would kill him, too. Someone would say he talked too much and he would die of embarrassment. "I don't know whether there's any point to getting better," Menachem told Oskar. He hoped someone else had a more edifying response to the topic. "Are there any thoughts from the class?"

But his pride had killed the mood. People shifted uncomfortably in their seats. The silence stretched on, awkward almost to the point of ugliness, before Lemel raised his hand. "I also do not know how to answer Brother Oskar's question about making these lessons more worthwhile," he said, "because it's so hard—unless you are a pearl collector with an eye for such things—to say what is of worth. For example, Brother Menasche tries to teach us, but not even he can speak faster than I can forget. A minute after food passes over my tongue, I have lost its taste. An hour after I was baptized, I was already dry. Is it worthwhile to teach a man whose soul is like a pocket but whose mind is like a hole?" Lemel shrugged. "Why does Brother Menashe keep coming, then? Maybe he asks us to feast on the scriptures just so we can sit down together. Maybe there's joy in heaven every time I see your face. Or does Brother Menasche spend his evenings hunched like a beggar over his books, preparing to teach a simpleton like me, again and again—for this many or that many hours each year, what difference should it make—because what God wants is not always our increase, but sometimes simply our sacrifice?"

*When it came to scripture study she might have, so
to speak, only a single talent. But she had to believe
her pondering would bear fruit nonetheless.*

Clever Gretele and the Pyramid Scheme

Clever Gretele was not ordinarily one to ponder the scriptures. That was God's own truth and she had no fear for the truth. She resembled neither Zalman the Learned, who could work mathematical wonders to prove that the Egyptians were smitten with 300 plagues, nor Menachem Menasche, who could quote commentary from Conference talks by the brothers in America just as easily as he might call upon the authority of Rabbi Akiva. No, Clever Gretele had far more practical than spiritual insight. She and her mother hadn't made it through their hungriest years by knowing one verse from another. If the Bible had a Book of Bargaining, she might've become as expert in the scriptures as anyone. As it was, she was a little like those handcart pioneers: she'd gotten to know God by experience, until life got easier and God became more of a passing acquaintance again. Now? She had the wisdom of Solomon when called upon to settle an argument over a child's toy, but ask her to name the 12 Articles of Faith and she could never seem to get any farther than Issachar.

Which is why it surprised her when, one week after Sunday School, she found that the lesson had not passed pleasantly from one ear out through the other but had, somehow, become lodged in her brain. Gretele could almost hear the talents from the week's parable rolling around in there, like a treasure waiting to be taken to the bank.

"Heshel," she asked her husband at last. "What do you think that story with all the money was about?"

Heshel had just begun eating one of her blintzes, but he reluctantly paused to consider the question. "When all is said and done," he mused, "the lesson seems to be that it is better to be paid five talents than two." He shrugged. "And wise, at the least, to be paid two talents rather than one."

As a convert to the faith, Gretele appreciated being able to lean once in a while on her husband's extra months of experience. But despite its elegance and seductive practicality, his explanation couldn't seem to still the itching in her brain. "It is certainly true that it is no great luck to be poor," she ventured in response, "but what if there is more to the story?"

She searched in her mind for a pattern. The servant who had been given five talents earned five more. That was a fantastic return, a real memory to hold onto for discouraging days. But the scriptures were silent on the details of whatever trades he'd made or operation he'd set up to scare up the extra money. And then the next guy? The servant who had been given two talents? As far as the description went, he hustled just as hard—and wound up with less than his five-talent friend had been given to begin with. The only real description of anyone's business plan came for the servant who was given only one talent and buried it. Whatever he was up to got interrupted, though, when the Master returned home and got after him.

Had the servant with two talents done something wrong to end up with only four? For that matter, had the servant with one talent done something wronger to end up empty-handed?

She had to admit she was pondering the scriptures every bit as seriously as any Menachem or Zalman. When it came to scripture study she might have, so to speak, only a single talent. But she had to believe her pondering would bear fruit nonetheless.

And then, in a flash of inspiration, the answer came to her. "I think the story's true lesson" she announced, "is that the Master should have been more patient."

Heshel shook his head. "According to Brother Menashe," he said, "patience is our Master's main virtue. How could he need any more of the thing he gets the most chances to exercise?"

Clever Gretele rolled her eyes. She loved her husband, but he was so busy likening the scripture to himself that he'd overlooked what it actually said. "Weren't you listening in class?" she asked.

Heshel's brow furrowed in deep concentration. "Perhaps not today," he admitted. "They all blend together."

"Didn't you hear the part about the master reaping where he did not sow? Don't you remember that other story about sowing seeds that can grow sixty or a hundredfold if you bury them in good ground?"

"There are certainly many seeds in the scriptures," Heshel agreed. But the only one that came to mind at the moment was the mustard one, because it would be so nice ground up and mixed in a potato salad.

"Yes," said Gretele. "There are all kinds of scriptures about seeds and planting and harvests. Why? To teach us the basic principle that whatever we plant, we also pick."

"My only hope," Heshel sighed, "is that it involves blintzes."

At least, she thought, her sweet husband had her to lean on. "It was not blintzes the man buried in the story," Gretele said slowly, "but a talent. A real, spendable, investable talent he could have taken to the bank. Can't you see? If only the master had followed the law of the harvest and waited a little longer, the buried talent could have sprouted into a tree!"

"What does a talent tree produce?" Heshel asked. "And can it at least be cooked into blintzes?"

Gretele sighed. "A talent is as silver as my earrings. And if we had a silver tree, we could buy all the blintzes your heart desires. Or at least," she added hastily, "all your stomach could contain."

At last, Heshel got excited. "We'll plant it at once, then!" he said.

Clever Gretele handed him one of her earrings and he went off to do the work. But Heshel returned in less than a minute, not yet empty-handed.

"Where is good ground for silver?" he asked.

It occurred to Gretele that she did not know. She looked outside the window but nothing struck her as right.

All afternoon, she fretted over the problem. A Zalman

or Mencahem might have been content simply to have solved a scriptural mystery, but not Gretele. What use was her insight if it could not be acted upon? As the scriptures say: faith without works is dread. Still, she refused to give in to despair. It was like Nephi said when he and his brothers were planning for that heist: God would not provide inspiration without showing her a way she could follow it. That evening, as her daughters Chava and Milka prayed, she resolved to search and ponder a little harder. Once she'd herded Milka off to bed and made Chava swear to keep the peace until morning, Gretele got down her scriptures and opened them.

She sighed. The books were heavy in her hands and the words always seemed to make her eyes heavier. But the doors won't open, as the good book says, unless someone is willing to knock. If she began to read them from the beginning, surely she would find an answer sooner or later.

In his great mercy, God had left it in Genesis chapter one.

"Aha!" Clever Gretele called to Heshel when she found the passage. "Listen to this: *And the fruit tree yields fruit after his kind, whose seed is in itself, upon the earth.* In itself upon the earth? That's as precious as it is plain. Silver must be planted in silver ground."

The two rushed together to the window at once. As it happened, in a corner of their yard, a patch of silver was visible in the moonlight.

Heshel and Gretele went out together to dig the hole and entrust her left earring to the appropriate soil.

Each afternoon that week, Heshel went out to the yard, hoping for some tiny sprout, at least, of good silver. But each time, he could not even seem to find the silver patch of ground. Then again, he had lost more than one piece of ground before and his life had worked out anyway.

He reminded himself of what Gretele had promised. If he could be more patient than the Master, the day would come when the plan came to fruition. Sooner or later, God would have to provide. It was practically guaranteed by the law of the harvest.

"I hope today is the day," he told himself on Monday. And Tuesday. Not to mention Wednesday.

On Thursday, feeling more tired of waiting than embarrassed about having lost track of the spot, he finally admitted to Gretele that he was not entirely sure where their talent was buried. She was cooking dinner at the time, but promised to look that night after they'd put the children to bed.

To Heshel's surprise and delight, Gretele spotted the silver patch of ground out the window right away in the moonlight. But she could see no tree growing. "Perhaps," she said, "we were wrong to plant only one earring. We should have followed the example of Noah and planted two by two." While Heshel finished with the dishes, she fetched a shovel and went out.

Gretele had only been gone for three forks and two plates when Heshel heard the doorbell ring. He opened it and found her ministering sisters, Mirele Schwartz and Leeba Selig, standing in the door.

Heshel invited the sisters in and assured them that Gretele would be in soon. It occurred to him that he should do his best not to tell them what she was up to. After all, the servant in the story had never told his two richer friends to bury their talents. So Heshel made small talk instead by bragging about this and that. He told them about how his daughter Milka was learning to spell so well she didn't even need vowels. He described how his daughter Chava had taken Zusa Cohen foraging and picked up some wonderful bread from Tzipa's bakery at the end of the day, just before she threw it away. And then he told them what a scholar of the scriptures his wife was becoming until the conversation quite naturally drifted to her ability to find silver ground.

"Silver ground?" asked Mirele Schwartz. "What for?"

Heshel had felt that her attention was drifting and so the sudden return of interest was quite welcome. And then he couldn't help but tell her about the law of the harvest and how each seed is in itself and that sixtyfold or a hundredfold would pay for a great many blintzes and just imagine, all it took was a little starter silver. Then Heshel realized that he had, perhaps, said too much and so he swore Mirele Schwartz and Leeba to secrecy as they excused themselves and rushed out the door and down the street right past where Gretele was working.

That night, Heshel dreamed he heard the sound of digging in the yard.

After Mirele and Leeba had rushed home to find jewelry made of silver and returned to borrow, anonymously, just a tiny patch of the silver corner of Gretele's yard, they also swore each other to secrecy. Or at least, to near secrecy. Both agreed it would be impossible to go on without confiding in someone about their good fortune. After some debate, however, they promised to tell no more than three relatives or close friends each.

As the near-secret of success spread by multiples of two to three each night, hopeful talk about the future spread through the Chelm ward. In addition to earrings, people planted necklaces, rings, candlesticks, and spoons. At night, they dreamed about what they might do with the silver after they picked their own trees up and transplanted them home. Even Oscar the Miser let himself imagine indulging a little: eating his cabbage soup without bothering to first water it down, saving the coins for a night or two just to hold them before he delivered them to the bank to earn interest.

In hushed tones, people talked day by day with their nearest confidantes about when they expected the tree to bloom. On the basis of a primary song, Hannah Silber argued that spring would bring a nice surprise and her hope drifted along the ward's whispers. Zalman thought summer; Menachem Menashe said he was mixed up as usual and argued that summer was just figs. He alone held out for a long timeline. The whole enterprise reminded him of Egyptian pharaohs buried with their treasure in pyramids. The Egyptians had known something after Abraham's visit and all. Speaking personally, he was not planting his silver just so he could go on a nice vacation to the Black Sea when the weather got warm, sitting on Chayka beach in Varna with a whole wishlist worth of new books piled beside him. In a pyramid-style enterprise, he suggested, the reward might come only in the afterlife. He was fully prepared for a lot of empty waiting in the meantime.

At first, people chided Menashe for sounding bleak and even faithless. But the Lord who gives hope also takes it away. Opinion swung strongly toward Menashe's cautious position following the divine rebuke which came that March in the form of a late frost.

Oh, how hope fell frozen! Plans for new roofs or thicker soup, for an extra-large wedding cake or a kitchen pew long enough for the whole family, for Chayka beach or a fishing trip in the Baltic, all simultaneously shattered. All across the ward, dreams died overnight just like the tree, killed by cruel fate before it had a chance to grow.

Heshel's own disappointment was perhaps in some measure offset by the bliss of his ignorance. He had no idea about the planting craze he'd set off through the ward. Obviously, no one had told him or Gretele about sneaking into their yard in the middle of the night to plant silver, and he interpreted their sad looks as they walked by the house as mysterious sympathy with his unspoken sorrow, rather than as evidence they might each be keeping the secret he'd spilled.

Clever Gretele, for her part, held on to hope well after the late frost. She would check out the window for signs of a resilient tree beginning to sprout—until one day she told Heshel that this was, perhaps, not the right year, and that she would go dig up her earrings to try the next season.

A few minutes later, Heshel heard her cry out. He rushed out to the yard to see what the matter was and then he saw what she had excavated—and they rejoiced together with the enthusiasm of a widow who has found a lost coin.

"Though the tree never grew," Clever Gretele said, "it is good to see the original seed at least spread out some roots."

Heshel smiled. For the first time in weeks, blintzes fled from his mind as visions of plates and plates of latkes paraded through in their stead. "Perhaps talents," he observed, "grow more like potatoes."

Of all the tests of faith the Chelm ward council faced, the most Abrahamic was undoubtedly the annual creation of a ward mission plan.

The Ward
Mission Plan

The Chelm ward, being full of the world's greatest fools, was unlike other wards throughout the Church in every respect—except for the functioning of its ward council, which was exactly as efficient as every other ward council anywhere. Like its counterparts, the Chelm ward council met regularly to discuss matters that could benefit from confusion among the ward's organizations. On the rare occasions when they had not yet wandered farther than the children of Israel from a given meeting's original purpose, they also made sure to fulfill the rote tasks members of ward councils the world over stoically endure.

The tedium of these tasks was required by scripture itself. "For ye receive no witness," the Book of Mormon said, "until after the trial of your faith." And so, week by alternating week, they puzzled together over forms sent from the stake, talked circles around plans for activities, and generally repeated themes and variations of the same stale conversations until they felt tested enough to be very nearly worthy of a visit from an angel. Of all the tests of faith the Chelm ward council faced, however, the most Abrahamic was undoubtedly the annual creation of a ward mission plan.

The need for the exercise escaped Bishop Levy. The greatest missionary Chelm had ever known was Heshel, and he had never successfully planned a thing in his life. For Heshel, things simply happened. So far, he had survived them all. One of them, for which Bishop Levy remained thankful on days when the ward council did not meet, had been introducing a new religion to a ward's worth of people. Why couldn't they consider the Heshel of the field and leave this particular form as blank and white as any lily?

But he knew his council had reason to defer on this topic to the experience of others. To Bishop Levy's knowledge, no ward in recent European memory had grown as quickly as the Chelm ward. If it is true that we learn the most from our failures, that meant every single ward in Europe knew more about missionary work than the poor people of Chelm. It couldn't be helped. In Chelm, they assumed that missionary work consisted of mostly talking absently with one another, exchanging books and barbs in the process, until perhaps God's finger intervened and someone decided to change their life. Or not! Everyone in the Chelm ward had plenty of friends who had found totally different strange things to believe in. But what did the Mormons of Chelm know? Wards with a greater mass of instructive experience were sure that missionary work needed to begin with imagining a generic list of outcomes and then proceed by carefully counting what one had imagined. Like numbering sheep to put oneself to sleep.

Without fail, the outside authorities seemed to agree that the counting was the important part. Counting made the imagination feel less like child's play and more like business. Bishop Levy had noticed early that playing business was deeply comforting to people born further west. They liked the rhythms of accounting. They liked playing dress-up with dark suits and ties. It was their reflexive response when managing the chaos of community.

Most converts in Chelm had grown up riding the chaos of community more than managing it. If they had any strategy at all, it was telling the same very old stories every year at set times so they would at least have a shared language to argue in. Then again, this strategy had worked just well enough to shield them from the most instructive failures. So they had a lot to learn about playing business if they wanted to catch up with the West.

When he was first called to lead the Chelm ward, Bishop Levy had attended a training on the subject. Because the details of how to count counter-factual future events escaped him, Bishop Levy had asked what the underlying purpose of ward mission plans was. If he understood the theory, he reasoned, he might be able to develop a simpler version the people of Chelm would be able to grasp.

Perhaps hearing more sharp challenge than simple question in his Ashkenazi tone (as Gentiles almost universally did with Jewish mannerisms and accents), the other Saints in the room rushed to defend the sacred practice. Several explained, in different words, that a ward mission plan was important because a person wearing a suit had said it was important. But Bishop Levy already understood that the plan was part of the game. He didn't need to know it held authority—he just wanted to understand why and how it worked.

Finally, a German brother had spoken up to clarify. "The underlying principle is simple," he said. "If you fail to plan, you plan to fail."

Hearing that, Bishop Levy nodded his head enthusiastically in recognition. "That's us exactly!" he had said. "We plan to fail as much as we can. Starting as soon as possible!"

It was, apparently, the wrong thing to say. As a direct result of this comment, Chelm had not been given permission to develop a simpler version of the ward mission plan. They were invited instead to submit their plans for an extra check so Church authorities could monitor their progress in assimilation.

And so it was that Bishop Levy and his counselors met with Fruma Selig, President Gronam, Mirele Schwartz, and Yossel the Fisherman to once again pass through the ordeal. In the year Church was shortened by an hour (but ward council, tragically, was not) Clever Gretele, who had just been made Primary president as a much-needed redirection from Sunday School, joined them for the first time.

In theory, Heshel was also supposed to come. Since things just happened to him, he had seemed well-suited to the role of executive secretary. But ten minutes after the stated starting time (which was when ward council traditionally began) he had yet to arrive. Bishop Levy asked Gretele about her husband's absence, but she had little light to cast on the subject. "He's in some stage of being on his way," she said. "And it's also possible he will arrive. In any case, I reminded him just before I left."

What was then to be done? President Gronam felt that holding one's breath waiting for Heshel was a good way to pass out, so everyone agreed to start the unpleasant task before them even without Heshel there to mourn with those who mourn and so forth.

Bishop Levy decided to get the worst over with first. "As you know," he stated flatly, "the Church asks us to set a goal for baptisms each year."

Everyone shifted uncomfortably. If it were permitted to call the immersion required to enter God's earthly kingdom anything else, they would have done so. The word "baptism" still conjured collective memories of forced conversions, whether by armed mobs or the pressures of a discriminatory job market. It was hard to get excited about the word.

Each member of the Chelm ward had found a way to reconcile him- or herself to the ordinance. For many, the experience itself had been fine. For some, it had even been spiritually profound. But sorting out how to accept the notion of baptism had been a very personal thing. Setting an annual goal for baptisms was different. It felt so Christian. In a late medieval, inquisitory sort of way.

"What about Hirsh?" Fruma Selig asked. "He was interested." She looked to Bishop Levy. "Sometimes, he still mentions you."

Bishop Levy winced. He appreciated the spiritual mantle that came with his calling, but some parts of it were a terrible burden. "No need for fresh salt on old wounds," he told her.

After a long silence, Yossel the Fisherman spoke up. "Shall we cast lots again like last year?"

Though the proposal was good, Bishop Levy's heart sank. "We can't," he admitted. "The executive secretary has them." And who knew if he would ever arrive?

But President Gronam smiled. "Then the lot is already cast out," he said happily. President Gronam loved lots, and he loved casting out. "The same authority acknowledged in scripture by the kings of Israel, the eleven apostles, and the sons of Lehi makes clear that this year's goal for baptisms should be zero!"

Everyone quickly nodded or mumbled their agreement. Bishop Levy suspected he would be getting a call from outside authorities over this. Still, he supposed that zero *was* a number and that it would be all right if he did his best to look businesslike as he wrote it down.

"Let's move on then," the Bishop said with what he hoped was a controlled corporate briskness. "We are also asked to set a goal for reactivation." He looked around the room. "Now," he asked. "Does anyone here remember what reactivation is?"

Once again, Fruma Selig spoke up first. "If we are trying to make someone active again, perhaps we could think of a way to wake up Israel Lewensztajn? He certainly is the least active member of the ward."

Gretele immediately objected. "It seems like such a pity," she said, "to keep the old man from getting his sacrament meeting rest."

Bishop Levy did not want to discourage the council's newest member from commenting, but felt he should use the opportunity for training. "By way of clarification," he explained, "the purpose of the ward mission plan is not necessarily to *do* a thing, but simply to imagine it for counting purposes. There will be no need to disturb Brother Lewensztajn just because he may happen to be part of a goal."

"We could try to make the Cohens more active," Yossel the Fisherman said. "Perhaps they could be persuaded to come to Church on the same week."

"They do bicker very actively," Mirele Schwartz added.

President Gronam shook his head. "The chapel is cold enough without their frosty glares," he said. "We should commend them instead for being such wise stewards over their irritability."

Bishop Levy had to agree. "The purpose of Church meetings is to increase people's faith," he noted. "Not their blood pressure." Still, imagining a change in the Cohens had been useful. Between them and Israel Lewensztajn, the ward council could both put down three for their goal—and feel immensely relieved when they failed to achieve it.

"What about Beynish Finder?" Gretele asked. "He was talking about wanting to be more active. I'd be happy to help him develop an exercise routine, though it'd be easier to follow up on that if he ever came to church."

Bishop Levy considered this. Four would be a very impressive goal. But since it was Gretele who brought it up, he should probably remind her not to get any crazy ideas. "I'll put him down. But let's not put our own schemes in the way of the Lord's timing. At the moment, I think Brother Beynish Finder is enjoying being lost."

Gretele looked at the clock, and then toward the door. Beynish wasn't the only one.

"I would like to bring up another point of discussion," Mirele Schwartz said next. "In the past, our ward mission plan has been made up of these goals, but on some websites I read in English"—Mirele felt there was a special authority to anything about the Church written in English, whether she understood all the words or not—"a ward mission plan also ought to involve choosing a ward mission theme."

President Gronam scratched his head. "I thought the theme was always missionary work," he said.

Mirele was all too happy to elaborate. "A theme," she said, "is a quote—perhaps a verse of scripture or a line from a hymn—that helps members truly focus on their missionary responsibility."

Clever Gretele reluctantly lifted up her scriptures. "I can look for something," she said. "Isn't the book of Jonah about missionary work?"

Just then, Heshel walked into the meeting. He collapsed at once onto an open chair. His chest heaved as he sucked in air hungrily.

"I started taking the notes without you," Bishop Levy said as he passed them over. "We were just beginning to discuss the ward theme."

"Went the wrong way this morning," Heshel gasped in response.

"That's not bad," said Mirele Schwartz, "but the quote we're looking for should ideally come from the scriptures or a hymn."

"On the way to the meeting," Heshel confessed between breaths. "Went the wrong way on purpose. Knew it was mission plan week. But then I got chased back. By a big dog! Could almost have swallowed me."

Clever Gretele closed her Bible. "Maybe not Jonah after all."

"What if we chose a theme that is more about who we are as a ward," Bishop Levy proposed, "like Jacob 7:26? Something about wanderers cast out?"

"We need something motivational," President Gronam countered, "like Judges 5:2."

Yossel shrugged. "I'd take anything about fishing," he said.

Fruma Selig raised her hand and began speaking at the same time. "We haven't talked about our efforts to reach out to others in friendship," she said. "The ward mission plan is not complete if we don't talk about friendship."

President Gronam groaned. "If missionary work were about friendship," he snapped. "I would never have joined this Church."

"Friendship doesn't necessarily mean you have to like people or get along with them," Fruma Selig reminded him. "Only that you are willing to pass through a piece of this life together."

Yossel the Fisherman nodded in agreement. "We could make the ward Purim Party part of the ward mission plan," he suggested.

There was a moment of silence in the room once again. The council's inherited gratitude for the salvation brought about by Queen Esther was not enough to offset the anxieties that had grown up around the ward Purim Party.

"We still haven't chosen a ward theme," Mirele Schwartz said.

President Gronam spoke up at almost the same time, his voice hard. "Let's talk about the Purim Party, then."

"There are so many fitting lines from hymns," Mirele Schwartze suggested. "'The Night is Dark and I am Far From Home,' 'Let the Consequence Follow,' . . ."

"Maybe something more hopeful?" Gretele asked. "What about 'The Wicked Who Fight Against Zion Shall Surely Be Smitten At Last'?"

"I think that this council should take up the issue of casting for the Purim play," President Gronam insisted. "Specifically, I am tired of being cast, year after year, as Haman."

Bishop Levy raised a reassuring hand in President Gronam's direction. "The whole point of the Purim spiel is to help ward members liken the scriptures unto us. We can't help any comparisons they may choose to make."

Mirele Schwartz spoke a little more loudly. "In addition to choosing a theme, we should talk about how to share it in forms ward members will remember. I have several ideas."

"It's not that I mind personally about the casting," President Gronam said. "But it's an insult to the dignity of the elders quorum."

"For example," said Mirele Schwartz, "we could put the theme in the ward bulletin, perhaps print it on magnets for each household refrigerator or else in small scrolls that could be placed near a mezuzah."

"It's irreverent," said President Gronam. "Last year I also called on myself to give the invocation and everyone rattled their noisemakers through the prayer."

Gretele laughed. "Not through the whole prayer! It's not our fault you said bless the man playing Haman. Prayer or not, you know tradition dictates that on Purim we drown out that name."

"I simply think the entire activity needs reforming," President Gronam said. "The Purim spiel has lost its savor."

"I had also considered a vinyl wall sticker," said Mirele Schwartz.

"Like the ones we gave out in Relief Society about protecting the home?" Fruma Selig asked.

"Yes, with the verse about Jael," Mirele replied. "Those were lovely and conveyed the theme with such power."

Fruma Selig practically blushed. "I'm so glad you liked them," she said.

President Gronam took a notebook from his pocket and consulted it. "The problems with the ward Purim spiel go beyond the casting of Haman," he said. "There is also the problem of too many Esthers and of the stolen crowns. There are the competing narrators. And we should also address the issue of the refreshments."

"I'm happy to bring the refreshments again," Yossel said. "No issue there."

Every eyebrow in the room arched upward as the ward council directed their gazes at him.

"That's not necessary," Fruma Selig said.

"But it's tradition!" Yossel countered.

Few found this argument persuasive.

"It's not the taste I object to so much as the texture," President Gronam said.

"Though the tastelessness *is* a bit of a problem," Clever Gretele noted. "Just for Purim, I mean," she added apologetically. "Not in general."

"You don't like the refreshments?" Yossel asked. "But I bring them every year."

"That is true," Bishop Levy said sadly. "That is very true."

"I am sure," said Mirele Schwartz, "that Yossel can bring something a little different this next time."

Yossel shrugged. "Of course. I'm sure it's no trouble at all to leave people expecting one thing all year and then suddenly change it on them in the moment they take their first bite."

"Put a notice in the weekly announcements," President Gronam suggested. "Give people something to look forward to."

"Now," said Mirele Schwartz, "if we can return to the question of how to present the ward mission theme to our members—"

President Gronam waved his notebook. "And the crowns! The competing narrators! The casting of Haman!"

"I suspect the primary boys only stole the crowns because they were jealous of the girls," Clever Gretele said. "Perhaps this year, we should let all the children be Esther."

"That sounds like a very reasonable compromise," Bishop Levy said. "And a model for the quick resolution of other issues."

Fruma Selig shook her head. "You can't compromise your way out of everything," she said. "It was bad enough to have either Zalman the Learned or Menachem Menasche feel hurt and offended when the other was asked to narrate, but I think we can agree it was a disaster last year when we asked both."

"They simply cannot be allowed to try and speak over each other," President Gronam insisted. "They drowned out even the noisemakers!"

Mirele Schwartz raised her voice to speak over President Gronam. "As important as the Ward Purim Party is to the ward mission plan," she said, "I am afraid we are overlooking the more vital task of choosing a ward theme and a way to display it. Our hour is almost over and we haven't even touched on my idea about phylacteries."

Heshel put down his pen and held up both hands, begging for a moment of quiet. "I seem to have missed something in my notes," he said. "I have no idea how the ward Purim Party relates to missionary work or why the mission theme is a vital task."

The council fell quiet for a moment. Bishop Levy remembered that English had something to do with the theme, but he honestly couldn't remember himself what on earth made them think the Purim Party would make people want to come to Church. "Try reading back the notes so far," he recommended.

Heshel cleared his throat. "The notes I have," he said, "beginning with those taken by Bishop Levy, are as follows:

> *Our baptismal goal for this year is 0. Our reactivation goal is 3 or 4.*
>
> *We will be relieved if we fail to meet our goals.*
>
> *We need to choose a ward theme. Bad suggestions are given. Fishing for friendship?*
>
> *President Gronam says, 'I would never have joined this Church.'*
>
> *Sister Selig says we need to tolerate each other . . .*

He scratched his head. "The talk got fast, and the Lord did not make me mighty in writing, so it gets a little messy from here . . ."

> *The Ward Purim Party is dark and I am far from home. Let the consequence follow the wicked who fight.*
>
> *We can't help any comparisons. Refrigerator magnets are like mezuzahs.*
>
> *Noisemakers during the prayer were tradition. The Purim spiel has lost its savor. Jael conveyed the theme with power.*
>
> *The problem with tradition is partly the texture but also the lack of taste. Bishop Levy bears testimony that is true. President Gronam wants a notice placed in the ward bulletin.*
>
> *You can't compromise your way out of everything. We are overlooking the more vital task.*

Heshel looked up from the paper before him. "That's all I have," he said. "Maybe we should go over all the discussion again, but a little more slowly?"

Bishop Levy glanced up at the clock. In the difficult choice between leaving ward council early and holding everyone late, he chose the path less traveled by. "Those notes sound perfect," he said. "We will submit them as our ward mission plan."

Bishop Levy then asked Clever Gretele to close the meeting with a prayer. And over the coming months, every part of the prayer was fulfilled.

Her request that Bishop Levy find the failure he longed for was answered with a lovely call from stake leaders gently explaining why the notes most certainly did not make up a mission plan. Her prayer that the most vital traditions be honored was fulfilled as President Gronam once again found himself cast in the role of Haman for the ward Purim spiel, while her prayer that the ward be open to new and better traditions was fulfilled in the smiling faces of primary boys in colorful skirts who loved the chance to be Esther—and in a quick reading by Belka Fisher, who skipped over the Book of Esther's more boring parts. As for the refreshments? Well, it may not have been quite an answer to prayer, but there was an almost pleasant surprise in the herring-flavored hamantaschen Yossel brought that year for a people grown tired of filling made from gefilte fish.

It's possible to find truths that no classroom can offer, insights limited by divine decree to the foyers of this world.

Protocols of the
Elders of Chelm

Try as it might, the Church of Jesus Christ of Latter-day Saints had never captured all the mysteries of the Kingdom of God into any manual. Almost two hundred years after Joseph Smith's First Vision, it was still left to brothers and sisters in the faith to puzzle out a few things on their own. This was according to a principle, older than the foundations of the world, that some experiences cannot be scheduled. They emerge of their own accord along the borders of time: in the hour when the last candle burns down after a shared meal, or in the weeks of the year when darkness rolls in like a tide, or in the moments when the Sunday crowd thins as the meetinghouse empties. In times like these, it's possible to find truths that no classroom can offer, insights limited by divine decree to the foyers of this world. Now and then, the wise men and women of Chelm would accidentally form a quorum to uncover one of these deeper mysteries.

One Sunday, for example, in the exact moment when the stragglers after meetings can transform into lingerers, Belka Fischer happened to be conversing with Menachem Menasche about the angels. She had noticed, she told him, that early in human history, angels who visited earth never shared their names. Look at the stories of Adam and Eve, or Abraham and Sarah: angels came by, asked some questions, maybe had a bite to eat, and wandered off. But by the New Testament, things had changed. When angels appeared, it was a big production. They came in choirs, waited in legions, and used fancy code names like Gabriel and Michael. Also, they cut down on the chit-chat: they'd just announce and ascend. Only the risen Jesus seemed to take time for a bit of honey or a bite of fish. And by the last dispensation? The parade of angels who visited Joseph Smith and Oliver Cowdery—Moroni, John, Peter, Elijah—might as well have been wearing little black missionary name tags. They were touchy, always shaking hands or laying them on heads. But not once did the scriptures mention anyone so much as offering them a snack!

"Why all the differences?" Belka asked. "Is there a plan and meaning to all of this?"

Menachem considered the question thoughtfully. Zalman the Learned, listening in, began to leaf through his scriptures. Zelda Gottstein looked up from her place on the foyer's couch to watch, and Lazar the Blind Beggar's ears perked up. Across the room, Belka's husband, Yossel, was arguing with Brother Cohen again about the duties of the Aaronic Priesthood, but even they felt something shift as the reasoning began.

"Perhaps," Menachem offered, "the culture in heaven goes through phases and fads, just like the cultures on earth. After all, even the Lord says *Behold, I will do a new thing*. If the Master of the Universe likes to mix things up, why shouldn't his servants improvise a little?"

At the mention of change in heaven, Aaron Cohen felt an immediate sense of unease, which manifested as disgust. But his disgust was not without a curiosity. He sent Yossel searching for an obscure scripture reference, and took advantage of the pause in their debate to turn toward Menachem and open a second front in his weekly war for truth. "Do you think heaven is yogurt, that it should have culture?" he asked. "When it comes to God, there's no culture. There's no change. There's a wrong way and a right way. As it is written: *my ways are higher than your ways*. Human ways are wrong and God's way is right. It's not rocket science. If it were, it would be wrong, because science is human. It's simple as that."

"Except that the scripture says *my ways*," Belka pointed out. "The trouble with God is that he has so many. And of course he doesn't change: why should he have to? His heart is wide enough to be joyful and angry and sad at the same time. I'm sure it makes him a great deity, but it also makes him hard to understand. Which is why I wasn't asking about God in the first place, but about the angels."

"Oh, so you want to put space between God and his angels? Between the angels and the prophets? Between the prophets and the people? So the whole of existence is like a giant game of telephone where the messages get garbled in transmission and we laugh like children at what comes down the line?"

Belka nodded. To her, that sounded exactly right. "The angels have obviously changed. I just want to know why. Are they having stomach problems? Were some of them translated incorrectly?"

In Aaron Cohen's forehead, a vein began to bulge. But Zalman the Learned waved a hand. "I think I have a solution that will reconcile everything," he said. "When in heaven, God and his angels are perfect and unchanging," he began, looking to Brother Cohen. "But we're not in heaven," he added, turning to Belka. Zalman opened his scriptures and pointed to a verse. "It's written right here: *there is a time to every purpose under heaven.* Weren't the angels somewhere under heaven for all those visits? So, apparently, for an angel coming to earth, there's a time to say your name, a time to talk about babies, and a time to shut up and eat."

Lazar the Blind Beggar was the next to speak up. "Thank you for solving that mystery for me," he said. "I understand what you mean about one way of doing things in heaven and another on earth. I myself am more comfortable at home than when I come down here." Then he paused, and leaned forward on his cane thoughtfully. "But it seems to me that angels would take certain attributes with them across space and time. It's one thing to eat a meal or skip a meal, after all, and quite another. . . ." He paused again, as if considering a crossroads. "Well, with such wisdom here, I might as well ask it . . . what I mean is: in heaven, are the angels circumcised?"

At that question, all the wise men and women fell quiet for a moment. Though it would seem that the scriptures would provide a clear answer to such a basic inquiry, directness was seldom their way. God often spoke such that his servants, as he explained in the first section of the Doctrine and Covenants, would need to come to understanding. Like sheep who move toward the shepherd's voice, or a cat who learns to recognize the sound of a can opener. So approach they did, each in his or her own way.

Zalman the Learned found his voice first to note that it was obviously written: *Every man child among you shall be circumcised.* And, in another place, *Bless the Lord, ye his angels, that excel in strength, that do his commandments, hearkening unto his word.* "If they do the commandments," he concluded, "it follows that male angels must be circumcised."

But Menachem Menasche observed that a different argument could be made. Didn't the New Testament say, speaking of the resurrection, *but there shall not an hair of your head perish?* If the hair—which was not a part of the body but an extension made of dead cells—was to be restored, then surely the foreskin, which was flesh and blood, would be restored as well. "On this question," he told them, "the Book of Mormon is even more explicit: *every thing shall be restored.* It follows that circumcision is an earthly commandment, but one without force on a risen body."

To this, of course, Aaron Cohen objected—so fiercely that he had to give up on his side debate with Yossel to focus on the foreskin issue. "Stop your sophistry this instant!" he thundered. "It is written: *My covenant shall be in your flesh for an everlasting covenant.* Not a transitory or a changing covenant," he emphasized, wagging a solemn finger in Menachem and Belka's direction, "but an everlasting one. Therefore: those who serve God from everlasting to everlasting must always carry the sign. That's the rule. No exceptions."

Zelda snorted loudly from the couch, but didn't immediately point out the oversights she saw in his argument.

"Maybe these contradictions can be resolved, too," Belka offered. "After all, isn't the resurrection a kind of rebirth? And don't boy babies all have foreskins?" She looked around the foyer, but no one else seemed to be reaching the obvious conclusion. "I doubt there's money in heaven to collect on any bets," she continued, "but I'll still wager that male angels will be circumcised again eight days after they rise from the dead." She paused, brow wrinkling as she considered her position in light of Paul's letters. "But possibly only if they're Jewish," she added.

That raised more questions. Menachem Menashe asked whether there would still be Gentiles and Jews after the resurrection. Zalman the Learned blurted out a question about whether angels also underwent some sort of heart operation to make literal the kind of circumcision so often alluded to in scripture. Yossel asked whether there would be mohels in heaven to perform all these circumcisions—and if that meant other angels had jobs.

"So much fuss over a nothing of a question," Zelda said at last, "We've been taught that angels are just righteous people who are resurrected, right? Well, that tells you enough not to worry about this circumcision question. Righteous? Reasonable? Ever willing to serve? I've known enough men that I doubt it comes up much."

At that, Belka nodded. Yossel shrugged. Still, the discussion about angels got him thinking. It occurred to him that he didn't know much about how the next life works. It was easy to say that this life was just a moment in the great sea of eternity, but what was the sailing out there going to be like? The scriptures would say one thing here, and another there. It could leave a person with a lot of anxiety.

To start, he asked about the worst. If there was no hell but outer darkness, why did the scriptures keep mentioning fire and brimstone?

"That one is simple," Menachem Mensashe said. Guiding Yossel into Doctrine and Covenants 19, he showed that references to eternal punishment meant that the punishment came at the hands of the Eternal One—not that it would last forever. Any misunderstanding, Menachem noted, was the product of the divine dance with the limitations of the human mind: the Lord often let us assume one thing while he was technically telling us something completely different. "God cannot lie," Menachem explained. "But he does equivocate. Talking to us, he pretty much has to."

Fair enough, said Yossel. But what about families being together forever? He understood, in principle, that his children would always be his. But would little Breyndl want tucking in at night? Would Golda still roll her eyes at half the things he said? Perhaps most to the point: as they learned the nature of godhood, what obligation would he have to help with their homework?

Zalman the Learned scratched his head. "God help us," he said, "but the scriptures say that *the same sociality which exists among us here will exist among us there.*"

Zelda leaned back into the couch's worn back. "Ah, but what is more constant in our relationships here," she said, "than change?"

That made sense, Yossel acknowledged. But he still struggled to understand the logistics of it all. Wasn't it written: *in my Father's house are many mansions.* What if, on Passover, his children came to visit him at the same time that he went to visit his parents, which might be the same time that they went to visit their parents, and so on?

"At whose mansion would we host the seder?" he asked, thinking of the dishes to be done afterward.

"It probably won't be in any house at all," Belka said, "but on a maze of tables running down heaven's streets." After all, why else would the Saints spend so much time on earth putting up and taking down tables and chairs?

Alternatively, Zalman the Learned proposed, families in heaven might use technology for shared experiences. "The only object mentioned in the scriptures as a personal possession we'll have," he said, "is a white stone we can use as a Urim and Thummim." Invoking some exalted equivalent to a video conference, he argued that a web of family relationships could be tended in such a way from the present generation all the way back to the patriarchs. "Don't the scriptures say quite clearly that *God is able of these stones to raise up children unto Abraham?*"

"What about government?" Yossel asked at last. "After Jesus comes again, and the earth is all paradisiacal, will someone still be in charge of collecting the trash?"

"Now that's theology," Zelda said. "I'll bet it's what Jesus' apostles were arguing about when they wanted to know which of them in the kingdom of heaven was the greatest."

Menachem Menasche thought she had a point. "We might rotate days," he speculated, "or call down fire from heaven to incinerate our garbage. But when they sit on twelves thrones as judges representing the twelve tribes, the apostles will at least be able to settle such questions."

Zalman had to agree. "It's the simple truths that matter. Leave it to heaven's lawyers to work out the millennium's constitution. For now, the only thing we know about the world government in the Messianic age is that it will be run by Jews," he said. "And it's a sure sign to recognize the wicked when you find out that's what they're afraid of."

Well—with that great mystery resolved, what else was there to say? The elders grabbed their coats and made their way home to their ordinary lives. And so it is that these protocols of the elders of Chelm come to an end.

It is not an easy thing to give children a foundation
of wisdom when you have very little of your own.

The Wise Man

Weeks after Clever Gretele was called as Primary President, her sixteen-year-old daughter Chava was still begging to come. In the first breath after the benediction, it would begin. "Please," she said one Sunday. "I can make myself useful. I'll sing the songs. I'll show them a game. I can even teach a lesson. I know lots of lessons."

Gretele was not sure what would happen if she were to say yes, but she had no illusions that it would end well. Chava hadn't consistently made it through primary when she was in primary. She used to get bored and escape and

Heshel had to chase her down and try not to get lost on his way back. Other times, she had stayed put in her class until someone came to pull Heshel out of Sunday School, or elders quorum, or—on his more absent-minded weeks—Relief Society. From the time she was young, Chava could break the hardest of teachers and leave them begging for outside aid. She wasn't a bad child, if such a thing even existed. To Latter-day Saints, God said children were pure. And when Chava was a child, it felt so true. That girl was so purely devoted to whatever emotion she felt, whatever idea she got into her head. To be fair, most children are obsessive and a little feral. But the last thing her sister Milka, or Bruno Levy, or—heaven help us all, Shmuel Peretz—needed was Chava egging them on.

"No," Gretele said. "You are a young woman now and you have a class of your own. That's where your loyalty should lie." She pointed in that classroom's direction. "Now go."

"Of course I'm loyal to the young women," Chava said. "But they want to come to Primary, too! Bluma and Bina are learning to play the piano. They could use some extra practice. Zusa's here: she's never been to Primary before. The least you could do is give her one week. And Golda wants to come work with you, she says, for old times' sake."

Gretele smiled. Back when Gretele's calling had been with the young women, Golda had been the youngest of the girls. And now she was almost grown up. Those had been good times. Simpler times. And maybe Golda *could* help her now. . . .

"No means no means no," Gretele said. "Go to class. Tell Golda I miss her, but the Lord must need her right where he put her or else she'd already have turned eighteen." Golda could bear her burden. And Gretele would carry her own.

Working with the young women had been easy. All they needed was a little guidance, maybe some skills. But by the time a person was twelve, they were more or less ready to take on the world. Little children weren't like that. According to the teachings of the Church, the younger half of them were still totally innocent. And the older half were just barely learning to sin. None of them knew how to take care of themselves. That's why God gave them such absurdly big eyes, which begged for protection. All that most young women needed was confidence and a chance to find out what they could do with it—easy enough things for a woman like Clever Gretele to produce. But children deserved love and protection and a foundation of wisdom to build on for the rest of their lives, so they didn't have to spend so much energy for the rest of their lives making things up as they went along.

Gretele sighed. It is not an easy thing to look at a child's giant eyes and admit that you do not know what a good, safe childhood is supposed to look like. It is not an easy thing to give children a foundation of wisdom when you have very little of your own. As the primary president, Gretele wished she knew some secret for how to keep the commandments—something besides her own system of having to try very hard all the time and then screw up all the time anyway. She wished she knew how to start right and make families so happy that no one ever got frightened by the idea of eternity. If nothing else, she wished she could teach them a game that everyone would always want to play so they would never be lonely, even when they all grew up and got hormones and smartphones—the injustice of it!—at almost exactly the same time.

Somewhere along the way, though, she'd gotten distracted and missed those secrets. All she really knew was how to make a little money here and there—but if you didn't truly need it, according to Jesus, that was only useful for feeding pet moths. Still, if she did not herself possess any real wisdom, she could at least show them where to find it. According to the table of contents, it was hidden deep in the Primary Songbook.

Gretele gathered her things and went with Milka to the primary room. The children drifted in. She coaxed Breyndl Fischer, who was giving a talk, up to the front—next to Benny Levy, who was swinging his feet back and forth like a manic clock, and Shmuel Peretz, who was looking around like he was casing the joint. The other children sat, or lounged, or squirmed in (or near) their seats, waiting to maybe listen.

After a brief welcome by Gretele, the meeting began with Benny Levy tipping his head up toward the microphone to offer the prayer and his brother Bruno walking up beside him, to help out the Holy Ghost by whispering promptings as needed. This time, Benny had clearly prepared. Instead of repeating Bruno's offered phrases at the same volume, he shouted them so half the building could hear.

Shmuel went next with the scripture. "We believe that all men will be punished for their own sins, and not for Adam's transgression," he recited. "But not until they turn eight," he added with a wicked grin.

After that, it was Breyndl's turn. She gave a talk about prayer. A lot of it was mumbled, and she snuck glances out at people between lines rather than ever making eye contact as she spoke. In its own way, though, the talk was inspiring. She even told a personal story: once she had lost a pocket knife and prayed to find it. Then, one year later, she did!

And that was it. With the chore of their miniature model of a sacrament meeting out of the way, Gretele would normally turn the time over to Hannah Silber to burn through with singing. Thanks to the prophet, a primary president didn't have to give a message or anything like that anymore. On this occasion, though, she'd arranged to say a few words anyway. "Today, we're going to learn a very special song," she said. "It's about a wise man. Who knows what a wise man is?"

It was entirely possible that no one knew. But it was Primary: half of them raised their hands anyway.

Gretele looked for someone sitting extra reverently to call on first. Since most of them were swaying like grass in the wind, or bouncing up and down like they needed to pee, it wasn't difficult. She chose Dinah Peretz.

"This week, I fell off my bike and I scraped my knee, but my mom put a band-aid on it and she kissed it," Dinah said.

Gretele nodded. "And did that make her a wise man?" she asked. Knowing Dobra Peretz, that felt quite generous, but charity can cover a multitude of stretches.

But Dinah only tilted her head a little to the side in confusion. "My mom is a girl," she clarified.

"That's right," Gretele said. It was important to let the children know they were right as often as reasonably possible. "Can anyone else tell me something about what a wise man is?"

Hands went back up. Benny Levy raised both of his. Because Breyndl Fischer had done so well with her talk, Gretele called on her next.

"A wise man is, like, a wise child—if the wise child grew up, and if the wise child was a boy, then the wise child would eventually become the wise man," Breyndl explained.

Well? The scripture says the Lord's truth is one great round, and Breyndl had clearly mastered that principle. "Very good," Gretele agreed. "Any wise man, or woman, was once a wise child. So what does it mean to become a wise child?"

"Jesus!" Benny Levy shouted. Benny liked to shout "Jesus."

"Thank you, Benny," Gretele said. "And Bruno, thank you for raising your hand. What did you want to say?"

He immediately dropped his arm to his side. "Are there any treats today?" he asked.

"Maybe not," Gretele admitted. "But that's a very wise question. Now Sister Silber is going to introduce that song, and it's going to tell us what a wise man is like."

It took a minute for Hannah Silber, who was well on her way to producing the ward's next future primary child, to pull herself to standing. Gretele made a mental note to talk to Bishop Levy about giving the poor woman a new calling in a room with bigger chairs. She turned the chalkboard around to reveal the words to the song:

> *The wise man built his house upon a rock*
> *The wise man built his rock upon a rock*
> *The rock man built his rock upon a rock*
> *and the rains came fumbling down*

Ah, but what is a primary song without some actions? Hannah taught the children to tap their foreheads with a finger and the word "wise" and to make a fist and smack it against their open palm on the word "rock." And then they all began to sing.

The children proceeded to sing "rock" quite loudly while mumbling their way through the other words. It wasn't perfect, but it was an excellent start. "Let's try it one more time," Hannah said, "and then I'm going to need a volunteer." At this, all hands immediately shot up again. "I'll be looking for a person who uses as much energy as they can on their singing and the actions this time through."

Gretele prepared herself to intervene as the children rose to the challenge. To show his energy, Shmuel Levy swung his fist at Bruno Levy. Bruno, however, was already climbing up on his chair to wrap his arms around his legs and cannonball to the floor. Milka simply replaced several words with the high-energy "rock," bringing the verse to a close with a resounding "and the rocks came rocking down." Others jumped, twisted, shouted, spun in slow circles, or lay on the floor flopping like fish. Gretele was struck once again by the beautiful, totally unselfconscious, almost drunken way they moved their bodies.

"Very good!" Hannah Silber said. After considering a few children who had fallen to the floor as a part of their actions, she chose Bruno to come and erase a few words. It didn't take many more rounds before they moved on to the second verse, about the foolish man. The children of Chelm had even less trouble mastering that.

"How was primary?" Chava asked after Church.

"Good," Gretele said. "Only a little violent."

"Can I come next week?" Chava asked.

"No," Gretele said. "But you can help me carry some bags."

The next Sunday, Chava carried the bags full of rocks. Golda came along to carry the sand; Bluma and Bina brought armfuls of pans, while Zusa schlepped the pitchers of water. Milka carried the legos. The young women tried to linger to see what it was all about, but Gretele wasted no time in chasing them off. Jesus said to suffer the children; he never committed one way or the other about teenagers.

Just before singing time began, Gretele let the children turn around their chairs for use as tiny tables and had the supplies distributed across the classes. Except, of course, for the pitchers. "While we sing, you can build," Gretele told them. "And if you do a good job and show respect for Sister Silber," she promised, "the rains can come down and the floods can come up at the end."

With their hands busy, the voices were more subdued. But even as they built their little toy mansions, the children continued to sing:

> *The foolish man built his house upon the sand*
> *The foolish man built his sand upon the sand*
> *The sandman built his house upon the fool*
> *and the rains came mumbling down*

Some built lanky towers. Others opted for squat, heavy fortresses that sank deep into the miniature beaches. Benny Levy just piled a few loose legos on the rock and buried others beneath the sand for future harvests.

At length, singing practice was done and the hour of judgment had arrived for all their creations. Gretele and the other adults moved from pan to pan, pouring water over plastic roofs.

The rocks were indeed impervious to water. The little houses built on them? Not so much. Benny's loose pieces were rapidly swept away. The towers didn't stand a chance. Even Shmuel's solid fortress slid over to the side until its far wall was well past the edge of the foundation rock. It hung, half suspended in air for what felt like a long while, and then tipped over and crashed down on its side. Gretele stared at where it lay, firm but displaced. Gone astray like one of those Bible sheep.

The houses in the sand did much better. Benny's hidden pieces stayed hidden. A few of the towers fell, but most leaned. Shmuel's fortress stayed right where it was, no matter how much water they poured over and across it—though when the pan got really full, the sand floor inside was visibly damp.

"Why did the sand ones stay up?" Breyndl Fischer asked.

"Did you bring any treats?" Bruno Levy added.

Gretele puzzled over what had happened. The song seemed so clear. But the results were clearer. Which one should she trust?

"This goes to show how much we still need revelation," she declared at last. "God told Noah to build an ark, not Adam, because that commandment only made sense for Noah's generation. Building a house on a rock wouldn't have turned out so well for him either!" She looked on the side of a rock at Shmuel's sideways fortress. "I think sometimes we need to be firm about everything so we can't be shaken. But sometimes—maybe it's better to have a little wiggle room when the rains come. Learn how to give a little. I don't know." She turned toward Hannah Silber. "Either way, it's a very fun song."

Hannah agreed, and taught them an extra verse, which she made up on the spot:

> *The wise man built his house so it would stand*
> *The wise man built it somewhere on the land*
> *The wise man built a house like God had planned*
> *and he didn't let the rains get him down*

*Bishop Levy had learned to place a particular
trust in God's timing, because there frankly
didn't seem to be many other options.*

The Geniza

God works in mysterious ways. People? Not so much. "There hath no temptation taken you but such as is common to man," the scripture says. God laughs when his wandering children are ignorant enough to think themselves original.

For Bishop Levy, issuing a calling might involve a little spark of divine mystery, but mostly regular human plodding. But what could he do? Some callings come by revelation, others by desperation. If he studied a calling out in his mind and could only really see one solution, the best he could do afterward is pray God would stop him if there was a disaster ahead.

He clung to this idea despite the plain knowledge he had gleaned through a study of the scripture: God did not have a strong track record of stopping people just because there might be a disaster.

But some disasters were not so bad! Bishop Levy had called Heshel as executive secretary, for example, despite Heshel's total lack of organizational skills, because Heshel happened to attend church regularly, hold the priesthood, and have a pleasant enough personality to work with others bloodlessly. More significantly, Heshel happened to be available at the time the need arose. Bishop Levy had learned to place a particular trust in God's timing, because there frankly didn't seem to be many other options.

He had also prayed about the calling, yes, but shy of shuffling the entire ward, what was he to do if the good Lord said no? The headache of the very possibility loomed large in Bishop Levy's thoughts as he went on his knees: his prayer for confirmation was also, truth be told, a plea for mercy. And didn't the scriptures say God wanted mercy more than sacrifice? What greater witness could he have than from God? And so it was that Bishop Levy got an executive secretary with the guile of a Nathaniel, the punctuality of a Jonah, and the record-keeping abilities of an Omni.

Not *all* callings went like that. Bishop Levy had considered all the adult, active women in the ward to serve as Relief Society president and felt strongly that the right leader for the time was Fruma Selig. Leah Kantor's name had popped immediately into his mind when they needed a ward chorister. Whether that was because of the whisperings of the Spirit or some preconceived notions of his own, he couldn't say, but Kantor the chorister certainly sounded right. And, aside from some difficult cleaning after a choir practice involving livestock, that calling had turned out just fine.

One way or another, when faced with a calling that needed filling, ward leaders and Bishop Levy had always been able to find a person who was filled, as the scriptures say, with the breath of life. After all, if that was all the qualification it took to name every living creature and tend the garden of Eden, it was certainly good enough for the Chelm ward. And yet . . . in all that work of matching jobs to bodies and bodies to jobs, Bishop Levy had not once pondered how to fill a calling and had the name of Oskar Wiener come to mind.

Well? Some callings come by revelation, others by elimination. One week, Bishop Levy made up a very long list of every possible responsibility in the ward and began crossing out the ones it simply wouldn't do to have Oskar the Miser fill.

The Bishop worked rapidly at first. Any calling involving compassionate service was obviously out. Brother Wiener seemed almost equally unsuited for any callings reserved for women, which went next. Teaching callings were out, since Oskar the Miser had so many objections to some gospel basics, like love and mercy, which every class covered. Financial clerk was out if the ward was going to keep functioning, as well as anything that involved *spending* a budget.

Bishop Levy briefly considered the possibility of calling Oskar the Miser to coordinate meetinghouse cleaning. After all, he'd seen Oskar bending to pick up discarded items at church and on the street when he thought they might have any value. But then Bishop Levy remembered that Oskar considered cleaning products frivolous. He crossed the calling off his list. Next, Bishop Levy studied out in his mind the counterintuitive possibility of calling Oskar as a counselor in the bishopric, on the logic that you should keep your friends close and Oskar the Miser closer, but as soon as he remembered that counselors needed to give interviews to human beings, he lost heart. And so it went, crossing out calling after calling, until all that remained was ward librarian.

That Oskar the Miser refused to throw anything away was hardly an objection. Keeping every scrap of paper with God's name inscribed upon it had a long and venerable tradition. And his insistence on locking doors the moment he stepped away was practically a qualification. Bishop Levy extended the call and, to his great relief, Oskar the Miser accepted—with a minimum (though no less) of his usual grumbling about the Bishop's general sins of mismanagement.

There were raised eyebrows among ward members, to be sure, when Oskar the Miser issued library cards. And it was something of a shock the first time he revoked one for wasteful behavior. There were not a few rolled eyes about the large metal canister the Miser used to collect late fees. And teachers struggled to write after he broke all the chalk into tiny pieces, which he doled out as reluctantly as a nursery-aged child who has solved the dilemma of weekly abandonment by clinging to a favorite toy.

And yet, Oskar the Miser's innovations were not without their positive effects. Late fees did motivate people to turn things back in rather than carrying them home, and the hall near the library filled with laughter each Sunday as ward members mingled there in the long inspection line. It wasn't the only incidental effect of his service: Oskar was so strict about the numbers of copies he would make that teachers began calling their students in advance to see who planned to attend. Within a few months, attendance had increased. For the ward's youth, a phone call during the week showed that their teachers truly cared about them. For teachers, the bits of life they heard while making phone calls increased their ability to personalize lessons. If that also meant the ward saved a few zlotys on paper, what was the harm?

The new librarian also did wonders for everyone's scriptural literacy. The very week he was sustained, Oskar the Miser had stripped the binding off each Bible and Book of Mormon and bound the individual books within each volume separately to reduce the cost of loss should a person fail to return their borrowed goods. Soon, even primary children knew the difference between Ecclesiastes and Lamentations, between Habakkuk and Haggai. And parents always knew it was time to have a coming-of-age talk with a child when they saw her check out the Song of Solomon.

All told, the miser was the most marvelous librarian the ward had ever seen. It just went to show, Bishop Levy reasoned, that there was a season for every personality, and a time for every tic under heaven.

Heshel could not believe the rate of his progress.
Over the course of a single day, it seemed there
was more and more he was not eating.

Heshel Pays Fast Offering

Even after years in the Church, Heshel had never paid a fast offering.

From a certain perspective, of course, he had always paid fast offering. The missionaries had taught him fast offering was intended to match the value of any meals a person missed on Fast Sunday. Since none of Heshel's fasts had ever lasted all the way through a mealtime, the nothing he had given was fully equal to everything he had saved. But still, Heshel found it embarrassing that he could barely fast through his Church meetings, let alone the Sabbath.

Someday, he had resolved for years, he would find a way to make himself do more.

It happened one year, at last, that Passover was to begin in the evening at the end of a fast Sunday. And so it was that, to prepare for the holiday and help Heshel with his long-stated goal, Clever Gretele decided to clear not only everything leavened, but also all food of any kind, from the house so her husband could finally make it through his fast.

Heshel was terribly impressed with his wife's cleverness. He thought of little else as he wandered the house, absently opening cupboards in the reflexive search for some morsel of meal to eat. But there was not even so much as the widow of Zarephath had shared with Elijah. Though his stomach growled as loudly as the she-bear once summoned by the prophet Elisha, Heshel felt proud of himself, and still prouder of his wife, that evening. Before going to bed, he even took a moment to calculate what he might pay for his first fast offering.

Unfortunately, it appeared his contribution would be meager. Since Gretele had cleared out the house for Passover, what Heshel was not eating was bound to have been mostly matzah. He asked Gretele to count out some coins for the skipped mouthfuls of stiff, flat flour, but it turned out she only needed one. Heshel imagined he would do better another year, or perhaps decade. With time and discipline, he was sure he could gradually build up to not eating leavened bread, and from there perhaps to not eating blintzes, and someday even progress to not eating his mother-in-law's heavenly babka.

His whole body rebelled at the thought.

Heshel did not sleep well that night. Dreams of skinny cows and empty babka trays left him tossing and turning. In the morning, Heshel woke bleary-eyed and famished.

He began fantasizing about making a tall stack of matzah French toast.

Heshel smiled. Perhaps his fast would not be so modest after all! "Gretele," he whispered urgently. When she only snored in response, he gently shook her shoulder.

"What is it?" she asked him, squinting in the general direction of their bedside clock.

"How much would it cost to buy a box of matzah, a half-dozen eggs, a half stick of butter, a pinch of cinnamon, two tablespoons of syrup, eight fresh strawberries, and a cup of whipped cream?"

"Go back to sleep," Gretele said. And then she led, as the Savior taught, by example.

But Heshel couldn't. The combination of his growing enthusiasm and gnawing hunger propelled him out of bed. After some careful calculations, he counted out more coins for his fast offering while humming "The God of Israel Neither Slumbers Nor Sleeps."

By the time the family stumbled out the door toward Church late that morning, Heshel had added coins to his fast offering two more times as his plans for the breakfast he was skipping expanded. He went back into the house to add coins yet again as soon as he realized that he was hungry enough that, were he not fasting, he might beg Yossel the Fisherman for a bit of his latest catch.

Heshel could not believe the rate of his progress. Over the course of a single day, it seemed there was more and more he was not eating. The only time he backslid was during the sacrament, when he slipped a small coin back into his pocket to offset the value of the tiny piece of matzah he took when they passed the tray around.

But in the battle with his increasingly ravenous hunger, the sacramental matzah did little to turn the tide. Heshel wanted a mixing bowl filled to the brim with potato salad. He wanted scoops of haroset the size of his fists. He was willing to eat even gefilte fish, if it came to that, to satiate his poor stomach!

As he made his way toward elders quorum, Leah Kantor stopped to ask him how he was doing. Beaming with pride through his abdomen's rumbling screams of protest, he told her he was successfully fasting for the first time. When she asked if he was feeling hungry, he blurted out that he was so famished he could eat a horse.

As the implications of that comment sunk in, Heshel realized he had reached the point in the pride cycle the Book of Mormon was intended to warn against.

Still, honesty was the best policy. When the discussion in elders quorum had strayed enough from the point to make whatever questions Heshel might ask sound average, he sheepishly raised his hand.

"How much does a horse cost?" he asked Brother Cohen, who was teaching that week.

"The price would vary greatly," Brother Cohen replied. "Are you asking about a draft horse? Or a thoroughbred racer?"

Heshel shrugged. "Just a regular eating horse, I suppose."

Oskar the Miser raised his hand immediately. Heshel winced as he quoted the price. The Miser's insistence that the meat from one horse could last a family like Heshel's well over a year, after whatever wedding or other occasion they were celebrating, was cold comfort.

Heshel briefly considered walking away from the Church building and simply following the sun until he found yet another town to settle in rather than face Gretele with the news of what they would be paying in fast offering. But while the scriptures gave permission to flee from one's father and mother, they were express on the matter of commitment to one's wife.

Heshel then briefly weighed God's potential wrath against Gretele's. While it was true he had said he could eat a horse, he might pretend he had meant only a horse-shaped cookie and never have to tell Gretele he had incurred such a substantial divine debt over the course of a single day. But of course God would know and might tell Gretele sooner or later in any case.

And so it was that Heshel resolved to do what was right and let the consequence follow. He told his wife the truth and the whole truth, albeit in a roundabout way that began with his conversion years before and continued through visions of matzah brei and mackerel until the words tumbled out all at once about how he had never intended to be so hungry but had found a certain truth revealed in a passing conversation on his way to elders quorum.

Gretele listened stoically as he related verbatim how he had asked after a horse's price and shared the somewhat dated but nonetheless daunting figure Oskar the Miser had quoted him.

Gretele let out a long, weary whistle when he was through. "I believe," she said, "that we will spend as much on your fast offering today as we have on mine all these years." She opened a drawer and withdrew a succession of silver: earrings and necklaces, rings and pendants, candlesticks and spoons. "The Lord giveth," she said, "and the Lord taketh away."

Heshel looked at all the silver she offered and shook his head. It was too much, he explained, well beyond the price of a simple meat horse.

"Will a man rob God?" Gretele replied. "We should err on the side of generosity. Let's pay for an Arabian."

Heshel trudged back to the Church, his fast offering bag heavy as Benjamin's sack but his heart feeling surprisingly light.

Bishop Levy thanked him profusely. In the rush of the holiday, the bishop said, no one else had remembered to turn their fast offering in that day. Heshel was the first.

After Heshel left, Bishop Levy called in Lazar the blind beggar. By longstanding arrangement, Lazar—who insisted on living only by the grace of God—was given the first fast offering of the month, no matter how modest or generous it might prove to be.

But for all his boundless faith, nothing had prepared the Blind Beggar to receive God's grace in such equine proportions. "Bishop," Lazar said after the clerk finished counting the money, "Send out the word through the ward. Call the other beggars off the streets! On the last night of Passover this year, I want to invite everyone to the meetinghouse for a sumptuous seder feast."

*Mirele Schwartz wanted to do her best in the way
that a person might dream of walking on the moon.
Tzipa wanted to do her best in the way a person might
happen to sleepwalk without bumping into things.*

A Revelation
for Sister Schwartz
(and another one for Tzipa)

Mirele Schwartz felt it was a duty she owed to God and herself to get her calling right. When she thought about it, she supposed it might also be a duty she owed to the young women she served, though she was not entirely convinced that they cared when she slipped up. She was not sure, for that matter, if they even noticed her failures at all. Not even Bishop Levy seemed aware of her mistakes. It was frustrating. She had to do double the labor: in addition to the work of not being good enough, she had to do all the work of being disappointed in herself. At times, she felt that God alone paid close enough attention to appreciate her anxiety.

She supposed that being understood by God alone wasn't the worst thing. Even if no one else truly saw her mortifying failures, she could resolve in secret prayer to make it up to the God who sees in secret by being completely perfect next time. Next time, of course, was not literally next time, so much as an endless upward spiral of growing expectations and tension in one eternal round. The Lord had promised to raise her up—why not start with her blood pressure?

At any given time, of course, Mirele's perfectionism needed something to hold onto. And so it was that Mirele Schwartz welcomed the spring not only by marking the bitterness of slavery in Egypt, but also by worrying more than ever before—if such a thing was still physically possible—about what to do for girls camp in the summer. As families across the ward marked the Exodus, she inventoried equipment. She read advice from American websites in a mix of her best English and Google's inelegant yet functional translations. She looked at photos of forested campsites and hikes with inspiring summits all across Poland and into the neighboring countries. This would be, she vowed, a girls camp to remember. One to impress God himself. It might reach beyond even his standards to meet Instagram's.

There was only one problem, really. Mirele could not, to save her life, think of a proper theme.

That was the same year Tzipa Leicht had been called to help with girls camp. Like Mirele Schwartz, Tzipa was committed to her calling. Like Mirele Schwartz, she thought about the ward's young women even when they were not in her immediate presence. Like Mirele Schwartz, she wanted to do her best.

Sometimes the word *like* bears unintended witness to the vast diversity of God's creation, because each similarity contains a thousand differences. And a word such as *best* shows just how true the Bible is, because the Bible warns us that language is confounded. Words can be short and look simple and seem to be shared. And yet, the same clipped syllable can have wildly different meanings in two people's minds.

Mirele Schwartz wanted to do her best in the way that a person might dream of walking on the moon. Tzipa wanted to do her best in the way a person might happen to sleepwalk without bumping into things. To put it scripturally, Mirele wanted to do her best in the way a silversmith's ore is refined seven times. Tzipa wanted to do her best in the way of the hewer's ax, which has done its job if the tree comes down.

Tzipa started her preparation for girls camp by brushing up on first aid, because it seemed to her that the worst would be if someone died. It followed logically that the best, being the opposite of the worst, would be if no one died.

Tzipa did not think about a theme one way or the other because it never occurred to her that a theme might kill anyone. This may well have reflected a lack of imagination on her part, but it was what it was. Water was worth thinking about. For a camp of a few days, food wasn't strictly essential, but planning something to eat did seem like a reasonable precaution. And, although there was no particular risk if she failed, Tzipa also thought it might be nice if, before camp, she managed to learn the girls' names.

After all, she wanted to do her best.

To find a theme, Mirele Schwartz began at the beginning, reading her scriptures from Genesis on. The Flood sounded too soggy. Sodom and Gomorrah was in no way appropriate for the young, and its sequel on the mountain was awful. Mirele didn't understand what those passages were doing in Genesis, almost at the beginning of scripture, instead of in a separate place for terrible stories. Like somewhere in the sealed portion of the Book of Mormon, or in the Bible's Book of Judges. She moved on.

Rebekkah preparing venison for Isaac sounded appetizing, until she thought about how some of the girls cooked. The other Matriarchs fleeing from their father was good—that was the whole point of Church for some girls—but there was a part where Rachael stole an idol and Mirele didn't want to encourage theft. Bondage in Egypt was out, unfortunately, because the ward's end of Passover party had already claimed it. Right after that, though, the children of Israel went into the wilderness.

Well! Wasn't that exactly what girls camp was already about?

The Doctrine and Covenants said the spirit of revelation was the power by which Moses led the children of Israel out of Egypt. And that same spirit told Mirele Schwartz, as she pored over Exodus, that "Forty Years in the Wilderness" was the perfect girls camp theme. Certainty burned in her bosom like a bush.

This was her truth and she could not deny it.

Tzipa tried to be supportive when Mirele Schwartz presented her revelation literally. But it was hard. "Forty years in the wilderness?" she asked. "Isn't that a long time?"

Mirele nodded. "That must be why the children of Israel learned so much," she observed.

Not wanting to sound like a murmurer, Tzipa bit back practical questions like: what would we eat? what about my work? or: have you lost your mind? She searched for a proper objection instead and was relieved to quickly find one. "It is an idea," she conceded supportively, "but during the forty years, they would cease to be young women. So we couldn't make it only a young women's activity. We would need to make it a ward activity. And for that, we would need permission from the bishop."

Mirele bit her lip. She believed strongly in permission, but this plan bothered her. "It would have to be a partial ward activity," she said, "because we don't want everyone to come."

"That's true," Tzipa said. "And I've never known the bishop to announce a partial ward activity. God invites all to come to him and all that. Besides," she added, "after a few years, the girls' parents might miss them."

"Well," said Mirele. "It wouldn't be girls camp if the whole ward came. So maybe we can't do the whole forty years—"

"Of course you're right," Tzipa cut in, before Mirele could waffle over her *maybe*. "We'll have to make do with just a few days."

Mirele sighed. "This could still work, but it won't be easy," she said. But then she took out a notebook to make a list.

Lists made Tzipa nervous. When it came to church activities, her motto was: if you can't keep something in your head, don't do anything at all.

After scrawling for a few minutes, even Mirele sighed. "We'll have to pack ten years' worth of activities into each day for four days," she said.

"I think that's a terrible idea," Tzipa replied diplomatically.

But Mirele only looked back at her with pious determination. "He never said it would be easy," she recited. "Only that we would do it."

The very next day Tzipa, entirely by coincidence, read in the Gospel of Matthew that Jesus *had* in fact said, "My yoke is easy." He'd even been explicit about packing lists: "My burden is light."

She wondered suddenly which *he* Sister Schwartz was always talking about.

She thought about calling Sister Schwartz right then to explain that God wants us to keep things simple. But then again, God had also created Mirele Schwartz. His living word spoke more strongly than dead letters on a page: if simplicity was all the Holy One, blessed be he, cared about, he was clearly getting sloppy.

And if he was, what of it? Sloppy or not, God got the job done. No lost pages, or even whole lost tribes, could get in the way of his work, because God knew how to improvise. And something whispered in Tzipa that she could, too. After all, there are some things in life you cannot change—and one of them is Mirele Schwartz's mind. But no overzealous hand would stop the work from progressing. Somehow, she would find a way to temper her president without needing to directly convince her of how wrong she was.

The moment Tzipa committed herself to that task, insight began to distill on her like the dew. The biggest differences of faith, Tzipa realized, are not between the world's various religions—but within each one. It didn't matter whether you were a Christian or a Buddhist, a Mormon or an animist, whether you worshiped God or your party's politics, there were some beliefs that cropped up in every group of humans on earth. Some people believed in being carefully decent; some people threw themselves on love and grace. Some people thought the most important thing was to believe exactly the right things, while others assumed the most important thing was to point it out if someone else said anything wrong. Some people believed in stillness and worried about being a nuisance. Other people worried that if they stopped moving, their souls would collapse from sudden atrophy.

To get through an activity without anyone dying was one thing. But religion was more than that. Religion was the task of somehow keeping a thousand competing personalities all in the orbit of one faith.

Tzipa sighed. She would do her best.

It started in a way that was normal enough.

The Blind Beggar's Passover Feast

On the first night of Passover, all the families in the Chelm ward held seders in their homes, but on the last night, they gathered to the meetinghouse to enjoy the beggar's largesse. Zusa Cohen came along with her grandparents to see what was happening. And oh, what a feast their new people prepared! With help from Heschel's eager eyes, Lazar the blind beggar had purchased ingredients for a vast spread of brisket and salmon, potato kugel and baked apples, beet salad and Brussels sprouts, matzo ball soup and macaroons. If the children of Israel had eaten in Egypt like they were about to in Chelm, they would have rolled across the parted Red Sea.

But before the supper could begin, they had to wash hands and break the unleavened bread and tell the story. Even if we were all sages, the sages say—even if we were all as discerning as a President Gronam or as ponderous as Zalman the Learned, as widely-browsed as Menachem Menashe or as clever as Gretele—it would still be a commandment upon us to tell the story of the Exodus from Egypt. And the more one dwells on the Exodus from Egypt, the more is one to be praised.

Zusa sat with her friends, at a table claimed by the ward's daughters within a certain age range. There were Bluma and Bina Levy, who were far less rebellious than a bishop's offspring are apparently supposed to be; Chava Gottstein-Kleiner, who was happy to make up for them; Golda Fischer, who was already bracing herself for the night; and Little Breyndl Fischer, who was used to the much simpler Passovers her mother and father kept at home, zipping through the story to get to the fish, and just wanted to know what was going on. Zusa also wanted to know what a Passover with Chelm's Mormons would look like, but she did not even know where to begin asking questions.

It started in a way that was normal enough. At the table in front, Bishop Levy lifted a piece of matzah and said, "This is the bread of affliction, which our ancestors ate in the land of Egypt. All who are hungry, let them come and eat. All who are in need, let them join in the Passover with us." And then different ward members took turns reading the story from the haggadah, adding a comment here and an interpretation there, while the girls at their table kept up a whispered track of commentary of their own. Zusa kept her ears perked up to listen: she expected that this night would, in fact, be different from all the others she had known.

The story of the Exodus from Egypt, of course, does not begin in Egypt. The telling at Passover begins generations before. After all, those who do not learn from history are doomed to repeat it, which makes the past like a busy laundromat, with time just turning and turning while God tries to clean us up. By the time of the whole run-in with Pharaoh and the plagues and the blood on the doors and the running from law enforcement, cycles of captivity and deliverance and wandering around afterward were all old news. Take Abraham, who was delivered from idols *and* Egypt *and* Sodom *and still* got into that weird bind on the mountain with his son and had to be delivered once again. Or his grandson, the original Israel, who got caught in a series of bad contracts with his father-in-law. (There's so often a little Egypt in the fine print.) *Go and learn what Laban the Aramean sought to do to our father Jacob,* the Passover Haggadah says.

But while, at the table in front, Zalman the Learned advanced theories on the nuances of Aramean contract law, the girls of the Chelm ward began a much more advanced discussion. It started simply enough: "Who is Laban again?" Little Breyndl Fischer asked the older girls at her table.

"He's the one who tried to kill Nephi," Bina Levy said. "Now pay attention! I don't want to miss this law stuff."

Zusa had never heard Nephi mentioned during Passover before. Maybe there was more Haggadah in the Book of Mormon?

"But what does Laban have to do with Jacob?" Breyndl asked.

"He was Nephi's little brother," Bluma said. With far more patience than her sister, she tried to catch Breyndl up. "He wasn't born yet when Laban was trying to kill everybody. But that doesn't mean the younger brothers aren't part of the story. After all, if the Lord hadn't delivered his older brothers, then Jacob and Joseph would have been in trouble, too."

"Joseph?" Breyndl asked.

"You know Joseph," Golda said. "He's the singer. With the coat, the technicolor dream coat."

"And it got torn up by a mob," Chava added. "They tarred and feathered him and threw him in a pit and sold him into slavery. Which is what happens to all little siblings who brag too much."

"Shut up, Chava," Golda said. "Don't scare her."

"They made him a slave?" Breyndl said. "Is that why he wanted the gospel to be restored?"

"Well, first they went to Missouri," Bluma said. "That made Pharaoh nervous, so he started to exterminate all the babies. Except Jesus. Joseph and Mary hid Jesus."

Zusa's head was spinning. How did Jesus end up in this? Mormons certainly liked to sprinkle him in weird places.

"Joseph hid Jesus?" Breyndl asked.

"They put him in a manger in the river. Next to Moses. And Mary followed them," Bina said. "Until they landed at a place called Nauvoo."

Chava passed Breyndl a note. It said: *Golda only said not to scare you so you'll let your guard down. Watch out!*

"What about the wise men?" Breyndl asked.

Zusa tried to remember them. There were the wise midwives, Shiphrah and Puah. But they were women. Why would you add men to a scripture story that already had perfectly good women?

"The wise men?" said Bina. "Oh, it's really lucky that they came. They arrived right when Pharaoh's daughter was trying to figure out why the babies were crying—"

"She was going to throw them back in the river," Chava interjected. "Because sadly, that's what people often do when little kids make too much noise."

"She was not going to throw them back in the river," Golda said. "At least, not yet."

"Honestly, I don't know if she was going to or not," said Bina. "Her dad was the Pharaoh! But the wise men showed up, and they explained that the babies were hungry—"

"And since there were two babies and just one woman," Chava said, "they lifted up the sword of Goliath and offered to cut her in half! It was about to be very bloody—"

"But Solomon solved it and kept the peace," said Bluma. "And then Pharaoh's daughter sent Moses back to his mom for feeding, and the wise men took Jesus and dropped him off to the temple when he was twelve. And then Miryam came looking for him—"

"Don't you mean Mary?" Breyndl asked.

"Isn't that what I said?"

"Oh my gosh, this is stupid," said Golda. "When do we eat?"

Zusa wondered the same thing. Normally it was so long, telling the story and talking about the story, and her mother had to slip out to the kitchen sometimes to make sure the food was still hot while her dad and Grandpa Cohen got into another argument. She had never imagined that the story might be even more complicated somewhere else. But at least she was with friends. And the food smelled delicious, if they ever made it there.

Next to her, Chava began to scribble another note.

"Anyway, Mary brought him down to Egypt," Bina said. "So that's where our ancestors were slaves. And the Lord heard their groaning, and he had respect, and he said, Out of Egypt have I called my son. And that's why we still do the story."

Golda is planning to sell you, Breyndl. Your sister is going to throw you in a pit and sell you to Egypt, because every generation has to act out the story. I'm sorry you had to find out like this, the note said.

Around the time Breyndl read the note, Bluma Levy noticed that she looked a little uneasy. And so (like Pharaoh's daughter noticing a baby adrift in the Nile with no way to steer) Bluma took pity on her. She pulled a pen out of her pocket, spread out a napkin, and prepared to draw some diagrams. Just a quick flow chart to help Breyndl orient herself in the universe. "We should explain what this all means," Bluma said. She drew a circle. Zusa leaned forward to look. "Egypt is the telestial world, or the world in which we live. And slavery is basically everything bad that ever happens to anyone. Including, but not limited to, actual slavery. Which is also called iniquity, because all men were created equal. But then: look around."

"The whole world is Egypt?" Breyndl asked. "Are we really going to be slaves? Why do they keep talking like we're slaves? I thought the point was: you ate the bread for the affliction, someone spilled juice, the plagues, the songs, and then came the salmon. "

"It's not literally Egypt," Golda said. "That's just what they say tonight. It's like grown-ups playing dress-up, all right? And the slavery thing is not that bad—I mean, it's bad, being a slave is obviously really bad—but it's a thing we remember so we can learn to be nice to people. Just don't worry too much and it'll be over soon and we can eat."

Chava lifted her eyebrows and looked over at Breyndl. She pointed down at the note.

"So we're not in Egypt?" Breyndl asked.

"We are, we are," Bluma said. "Now we're slaves, next year may we be free. Now we're in Egypt, next year in Jerusalem. It's a whole thing."

Now that was exactly how they celebrated Passover at Zusa's house. Maybe Mormon Passover wasn't so strange.

"The point is," said Bina, "that we got out."

"How?" Breyndl asked. "At my house, we always kind of speed through this part because everyone is getting hungry."

"Nothing wrong with that," Golda said.

"Obviously, the plagues," Bina explained. "Blood and hail and fire and frogs. All the stuff. Very dark stuff."

"Then fire came down and hit a bush," Chava said. "But then it didn't burn up. Creepy, right?"

"The bushes and trees were full of light," Bina said, "and God spoke. We call that the First Vision."

"In the book of Exodus," Bluma elaborated, drawing another circle on her diagram, "the fire is because God lives in eternal burnings. That's the celestial kingdom."

Zusa didn't understand how they'd moved so quickly away from anything she understood again.

"But how exactly did we get free?" Breyndl asked. "I remember Pharaoh said no and then God was going to help but the salmon is going to get cold and then my mom just says they made it to the promised land."

"That's pretty much the story," Golda said.

"There was some smiting first," Chava said. "Moses would do a plague, and Pharaoh's magicians would do the plague. So it was like a double plague, which was kind of dumb, but it's still cool that they could do actual magic tricks."

Bina shook her head. "Plagues are not a magic trick, they're a miracle of cursing," she said. "And God always gives a warning before he curses anyone. Moses counted to three, and there were plagues, and he counted to three again, and there were more plagues—"

"One time he wiped the dust from off his feet and it turned into lice," Bluma added. "Which is why missionaries aren't supposed to do that anymore."

"—and eventually he got all the way to ten," Bina said with finality. "And Pharaoh kicked them out. But then he chased them. And the children of Israel went out across the sea on dry land."

"I thought it was ice," said Bluma. "Didn't they cross the river on ice?"

"Anyway," said Bina, "they came into the wilderness and the Lamanites murmured and at last Moses said this is the place and that is why we eat such dry bread and recline from exhaustion after the long journey across the plains and drink four cups that no longer contain wine to remember the four books of scripture. Amen."

"Can we please eat?" Golda asked. "Are we ever going to eat?"

"Why don't we drink wine anymore?" Breyndl asked.

Zusa perked up again. She knew her dad was disappointed when his parents didn't drink the Passover wine. It didn't seem like a big deal to her, since she didn't get the wine yet, either. But she still wondered. She just didn't know how to ask. It was so hard to find the words and work up the nerve to ask a question.

"That's a whole different story," Bluma said. "That came later. When Moses received the Word of Wisdom and carved it into the golden plates he made from melting down this statue of a calf. . . ."

It wasn't easy to quit. At least not in a healthy way,
one that preserved a person's basic quality of life.

A Tale of
Two Quitters

There are many ways that people mark the days as the world spins its way through the dark of space. It's not just Passover, Purim, or Pioneer Day. The spiritual impulse to set apart times and seasons is almost universal. Our ancestors gathered to share the first fruits of a harvest; we feast with friends around a television to mark a season's last game.

Even little, personal dates accumulate their rituals. For a birthday, a person might serve cake and coffee. In many homes, they light a slow-burning candle on the yahrzeit of a loved one's death. And the day after a wedding anniversary can be celebrated with a brief apology and a gift.

In the Peretz house, there are some additional traditions. To mark her last cup of coffee, Dobra goes on a little outing each spring. It doesn't matter where, so long as she takes a train. And there's a late spring day, the day when Isaac first finally managed to keep the whole Word of Wisdom, when he brings home a jar of pickles for the family and then goes out for a run. It helps him remember that the slave-drivers in Egypt and the mobs in Missouri aren't the only things God has saved his people from.

Isaac Peretz used to smoke. When he was bored in the evening, smoking occupied him. When he was anxious, smoking calmed him. When he was cold, smoking warmed him up. When he was lost in work, the tug of nicotine at the corners of his mind reminded him to take a break. In the six minutes it took a cigarette to burn down to ash, you could talk with friends or watch the smoke ascend like an ancient offering. Even when Isaac caught a fish, he'd give it the dignity of a last cigarette, laid against its rubbery lips before its execution.

It wasn't easy to quit. At least not in a healthy way, one that preserved a person's basic quality of life. You had to come up with new rituals to fit the old needs. For example, he started giving the fish he caught a last piece of pickle instead. From his experience in supermarkets, fish seemed to like a good pickling almost as much as a good smoke.

Breaks were a challenge. As it turns out, many supervisors object to giving regular cigarette breaks to a person who no longer smokes. So instead, Isaac started bringing a large thermos of water with him to work each morning. It turned out the bladder was as effective as any nicotine craving at getting a worker up from his desk, though it took a while for Isaac to adjust to striking up conversations at the urinal.

The sparing use of meat, of course, was already prescribed by the Word of Wisdom for times of cold. To fight off the chill, Isaac turned to hot broth. The scriptures specifically mentioned marrow in the bones; his came mostly from boiled chickens.

And when he was anxious? Ah, then he thought about the money he was no longer spending on cigarettes. Few things, he discovered, had quite the same calming effect on the heart as the thought of extra money in the bank. Doctors ought to offer it instead of pills. It was a major failure of the scientific and social systems in the world, Isaac thought, that you couldn't report yourself for anxiety or depression and be prescribed a little therapeutic cash.

Even with all those adjustments, of course, Isaac would still find himself staring out the window in the evening sometimes, feeling listless and nostalgic for a cigarette. Everything would bother him then. He would start to think about the physics of how a little smoke could dampen background noises, which felt sharper and more jarring when the air was too clear. He'd think about how annoyance could build up in the body if you didn't have enough to do with your hands. Even after he joined the Church, he occasionally found himself desperate enough to have one last cigarette from a secret pack he kept tucked away under a couch on the balcony. And then the next week, maybe another last cigarette. He tried to stop, he really did, but the shop down the corner received regular shipments of last packs of cigarettes. That was the trouble with the law of supply and demand. As long as he wanted a last pack of cigarettes, the market dictated that one would always be there. And with such a supply of last packs available, he was more or less doomed to keep wanting one. It was simple economics.

One night between last packs, he was talking to Dobra. She kept suggesting that they use the money he was saving on cigarettes to go out to dinner or watch a movie. Of course he said yes. But the thought made him anxious. Especially since he had not exactly entirely stopped spending on cigarettes until five days before and maybe also tomorrow.

He tried to think about something else, but she was talking loud and his hands needed something to do. When he felt ready to explode, he finally told her he was going on a walk. And she said, since his lungs must be getting better, he should make it a run.

So he did. He ran, his fists pumping in the air. His lungs burning with the effort. His feet splashing in the occasional puddle from the evening's rainstorm. He ran and he ran. Right past the corner store. Then all the way around the block. He finally came back home calm, if damp, and closed his evening out with a nice pickle and a cup of hot broth. That was it: the day he still marks.

He didn't know at the time, of course, that he'd broken through the laws of economics. He just knew he'd procrastinated giving in to temptation. And when we delay our mistakes, isn't God at least a little proud? After that day, Isaac went on another run whenever the old, antsy boredom started to get to him. It would engage his whole body. It would clear his mind. Sometimes, after a few kilometers, he'd even start to feel a little buzzed.

Somehow, he never gets tired of that.

Isaac's wife, Dobra Peretz, could not quit smoking with him. As a child, she'd been taught never to play with matches, so she'd simply never started. And then, without having experienced tobacco's benefits, she missed the appeal. Like sports or comic books or bug collecting, smoking seemed a little strange from the outside but harmless enough if that's what made a person happy. Except for the part where comic books didn't cause lung cancer.

Naturally, she appreciated it when the missionaries convinced Isaac to die of something else. The temporary side effect of irritability was not her favorite, and she briefly thought the something else for him to die of might be getting pushed off the balcony by his wife. But they made it. And life was better once the lingering taste of smoke in his mouth finally and completely cleared. From her point of view, the Doctrine and Covenants should have mentioned nicer kissing as a Word of Wisdom blessing, but prophets never did write the best advertising copy.

The only problem Dobra had with Isaac being a quitter was that it made her feel obligated to keep the Word of Wisdom, too. Since she didn't smoke and wasn't social enough to be much of a drinker, those parts were simple. In the times before Heshel brought the Church to Chelm, though, Dobra used to drink coffee every day. After she joined the Church, she still drank coffee every day. But it was bad coffee, made with barley.

The first six days after Dobra Peretz quit coffee were awful. Her head ached. In the mornings, Isaac was much too loud. And the smell of him! He'd become fixated on the idea that God expected a person to be clean, and was constantly using mouthwash and air fresheners. It drove her crazy. She very nearly quit her quitting. But on the seventh day, she rested from her worries by staying in bed long enough to finish an entire novel. And day eight was somehow . . . fine? Within a few weeks, days felt basically the same as always.

How could that be? She had once thought she would die without coffee. Her survival was a real mystery of godliness. She wracked her brain, but could not understand how she could feel so indifferent to the old morning caffeine now that it was gone.

Like the promised treasure of hidden knowledge, an answer came to her—literally line upon line—during a long trip to visit her cousin Ronia in France. If you sat in a train, Dobra realized, it felt like you were moving. But if you looked out the window, it became clear that the whole countryside was actually moving around the train while the window stayed in the same fixed position. That was simple physics.

In very much the same way, drinking a cup of coffee gave you the illusion that something inside you was changing. But if you paid close attention, it became clear that the whole world really did start off terrible every morning. It was never her. Never had been. She could recognize that now. Nor was it anything personal the universe had against her. Early in the morning, bad was just how the world was. It was such a relief, an unburdening of the spirit, to understand that.

And then: this part was strange, but true. Because the problem was not really on the inside, a person didn't need any substance at all to take the edge off. Within a few hours of waking up—she cataloged this carefully, to make sure the pattern was statistically significant. Maybe it was the light, or some change in the air, or just a property of the earth's movement, but within a few hours—whether you drank good coffee or barley coffee or a startling amount of water—that same world would typically improve. If you just got out of bed and looked around, the miracle of it was easy enough to see for yourself.

*"If disappointing your parents is a normal
milestone, I think she's caught up," he said.*

Goodly Parents

Elazar Cohen had been born to good enough parents. Were they perfect? No. Was his father reasonable? Also no. Was his mother unconditionally supportive and always letting him know how proud of him she was? Don't be ridiculous. Did they at least love each other? Maybe—it was hard to tell and impossible to imagine asking. But they had always kept a roof over his head. They had given him access to good Jewish books. Taught him how to fast on Yom Kippur and drink on Purim. Made sure he knew how important it was to honor his father and mother, that his days may be long upon the earth, but not so zealously that he had to live to an unreasonably old age and suffer bitterly like his great-grandfather. Even if they hadn't also given him unsolicited career and financial and life advice, it would have been enough. They had done their duty.

Was his relationship with them sometimes strained? Obviously. They were his parents. As they aged, he watched them make choices he didn't agree with. But that was a typical experience for grown children his age. Some of his friends' parents got into marijuana for their little aches and pains or hung around doctors' offices and pharmacies looking for other prescription drugs. They sent texts at all hours of the early morning and the night. Many fell for email scams that would make a man blush, filled their heads with crazy political ideas—who even knew what they were being exposed to these days?—and got into awful fights on the internet. His generation had not been raised in a way that prepared them for all this.

Aaron and Feige Cohen were hardly the most extreme examples of wayward parents, but a few years ago, they had started hanging out with the wrong crowd. They were reading books he wouldn't be caught dead with. They started experimenting with strict abstinence from different substances. And before you knew it, they'd become Mormons. Genuine Mormons! As if that were an ordinary European religion and not a second-tier background menace from old novels about the Wild West.

But what could a son of his generation do? Everyone's parents had gone some kind of crazy. At least his were sober and mostly stable, with the obvious mental and spiritual exceptions. Elazar's hope that they were going through a phase had gradually dried up, but he could at least try to be tolerant and supportive. He wanted his days to be long upon the earth, didn't he? Given the condition of the country's health care system, it was going to take a lot of honoring on his part to make sure he got to watch his daughter grow up and grow old.

It would be worth the work. His hope was firmly with the next generation. Or at least with the very small corner of the next generation occupied by his daughter Zusa. She was a good, kindly girl. She helped out around the house. She kept up with her homework. She even helped tend her grandparents, keeping an eye out for signs of worse trouble. Elazar and his wife Shana never had any real reason to worry about her.

Until the day when, out of nowhere, she dropped a permission slip for a Mormon girls camp onto the counter and asked him to sign it.

At first, Elazar was simply confused. What threat to her grandparents did Zusa anticipate at a summer camp? He looked to Shana, Shana looked back at him, they both turned to Zusa.

"Is your grandmother going?" Elazar asked.

"No," Zusa said.

"Is your grand*father* going?" Shana asked.

"To girls camp?" Zusa said. "No."

"Is something terrible going to happen there? Something you need to protect your grandparents from?" Elazar prompted.

But Zusa just said, "No."

"What exactly does this have to do with taking care of your grandparents, then?" Shana asked.

"Nothing," Zusa said. She looked down at the floor. "It's a camping trip for teenage girls."

At the same time, Elazar and Shana started asking the obvious follow up questions. Things like: What's gotten into you? Why are you doing this to us? Have you lost your mind? They had barely started their interrogation when Zusa confessed to everything. That going to church with her grandparents was not just a chore but something she *liked*, that her closest friends were Mormons, and that it would mean the world to her to spend four days tromping with them through the woods.

Being good parents, Elazar and Shana greeted the news the same way any rational deer responds to the alien arrival of car headlights. They stared; they stalled; they seized an opportunity to bolt. But before they fled down the hall, Elazar took the unsigned permission form. He didn't like seeing it in his daughter's hand, but he resisted the temptation to crumble it up and throw it dramatically into the garbage can. It might be important for Zusa to feel that he was giving her alarming wishes an honest chance.

Several minutes after reaching the bedroom and closing the door, Elazar remained in a lingering state of shock. He could feel his heart racing. His skin felt cool to the touch. Where had he and his wife gone wrong? He had thought that letting Zusa tag along with her grandparents would be harmless. It had seemed so convenient that she was honoring them without him having to be there. Of course, he thought her pure presence might shield them a little from their most impulsive instincts. And he'd hoped that, by careful observation, Zusa might learn a thing or two from them about how she didn't want to be when she grew up.

But it was one thing to show support for wayward elders, and quite another to willfully bring home a permission form. He looked down at the incriminating piece of paper with distaste, and thought of all the other forms it might lead to. If he let her go on this way, what was next? He could almost envision himself checking in on whether her room was clean, and noticing the tell-tale blue of a Book of Mormon hidden under her bed. How long until she'd be asking for permission to meet with missionaries? To get baptized? If he and Shana signed this papers for girls camp, would they one day find themselves signing her over to a full-time Mormon mission? And have to stand by and watch her pouring herself grape juice instead of wine at the Passover table for her entire adult life? He couldn't accept that. This had to be stopped.

Beside him, Shana was shaking her head. "I wish our daughter could rebel like a normal child," she told him. "Why couldn't she dye her hair blue? Or start a band that makes noise and calls it music? If only she would come home and complain about her homework, even just a little ..." She raised her palms in a gesture that struck Elazar as almost a supplication, as if hoping that God would let a little such rebellion fall from the sky to bless their home.

He put an arm over his wife's shoulders. "You know I would love it if our daughter were making any of those mistakes," he said. "But you mustn't blame yourself." He pulled her closer. "We should blame my parents."

"That's true," Shana admitted. "And of course I do blame them, but what are we going to do about it? You can't very well teach a child to be a good Jew by asking her not to honor your father and mother." She shook her head. "They've trapped us in a commandment. It's the oldest trick in the book."

He sighed. Shana was right. Being in the responsible generation between grandparents and their grandchildren was a terrible sort of rock and hard place. There wasn't a way to keep them together without risking cross-contamination. He should have been wise enough to anticipate that.

Shana stood up and began to pace. The movement comforted Elazar, because pacing always helped her with thinking. Even if she was staying in the same room, enough walking somehow got her to the next idea. "We should have kept her home on Sundays," Shana noted first. "I just forgot it was such a danger. I'll bet Christians specifically moved the Sabbath to confuse the earliest converts' parents and make them think everything was still normal."

But it wouldn't have done any good. "It's no use. They're doing some sort of Mormon thing every day," Elazar said. "Service projects. Activities. So much visiting. Now this camp. You can't quarantine that religion by keeping her out of the church."

"We could talk to her," Shana said. "I know she's already past the age when children usually listen to their parents, but maybe she's developmentally slow. We can at least hope?"

Elazar looked down at the permission slip. "If disappointing your parents is a normal milestone, I think she's caught up," he said.

And with that, Shana's pacing stopped. She sat down wearily beside him. "Then what do we do?" she asked.

If Shana had finished walking, they must have almost reached an answer. Elazar puzzled over the question, but there was nothing there. And then it occurred to him: nothing was the most obvious solution. "What if we never mention this again?" he said, holding up the paper. "By not writing yes, we are effectively saying no. We don't talk to her about the dangers of grandparents. Why should we? My parents won't be on this camping trip. And there's no commandment about honoring a daughter's friends!"

Shana chewed at the side of her cheek, as if tasting the idea, then shook her head. "Even if she doesn't go, she'll still want to. And it's the wanting, not the going, that's the problem." Her eyes lit up. "No . . . we need to find a way to let her discover some disinterest on her own."

"Are you suggesting we sign the form and send her without a single word of condemnation or warning?" Elazar winced. "I'd feel like I was throwing her into the deep end of a pool without teaching her to swim."

"Since we're hoping, in this case, that she'll sink," Shana answered, "I don't see the problem. The best thing would be if we tell her she has to go, and she hates it, and afterward she never asks again."

Elazar sat for several moments, weighing the merits and risks of Shana's plan. It was a terrible thing, trying to be a good parent. You could feed a child. Put a roof over her head, good books on her shelf. But it wasn't enough. Even after doing your entire duty, you had to watch your child learn. Or forever fail to learn. Either way, it was torturous.

"But what if she doesn't hate it?" he asked his wife. The permission form seemed to stare up at him, taunting him. "After all, when she goes with my parents, she must be enjoying herself—we were just too busy to notice the signs."

Shana took one of his hands in hers. "Your parents may be difficult people," she reassured him, "but Zusa is a sweet girl and she loves them very much. I think being around them changes the experience for her. It's as if we've thrown her into the pool with flotation devices named Feige and Aaron and now she doesn't understand that something as innocent as a little water can make a person drown." She met her husband's eyes and held his gaze. "People say it's a bad religion. And as patient and cheery as she is, she is not someone who naturally loves to suffer—or see others suffer. That being the case, it seems obvious that the best cure for her interest in Mormonism is simply more Mormonism." She gave his hand a squeeze. The confidence in her smile warmed his heart. "It's like the children of Israel when they begged for quail. Sometimes the most instructive no is an aggressive yes."

And so it was that, placing his faith in Shana's irrefutable logic, Elazar Cohen picked up a pen and signed the permission form. He and Shana returned and made clear that, having asked, Zusa was committed to going and they would not hear any arguments against their decision. She needed to pack. She needed to practice. While at the camp, she needed to follow leaders' directions to the best of her ability, even when it was hard.

Zusa was, tragically, delighted.

*Why did Gimpel need to walk his feet
raw when Adam Smith's invisible hand
could handle things so much better?*

The Acts of Gimpel
and Dudel, Deacons

"I hope your mothers are not expecting you soon," Yossel told Gimpel Peretz and Dudel Lewensztajn after their deacons quorum meeting one week, "because I am going to teach you how to fish." They'd been excited, their minds filled up at once with images of fish flopping morbidly long after being pulled from the water, but they should have known that Yossel wouldn't do such a thing on the Sabbath. He explained, instead, that in collecting fast offerings, they would be training to become fishers of men.

And yet, Gimpel observed grimly, he wouldn't even give them hooks!

That first week they went it was oppressively hot. Gimpel was sweating more than it was healthy to do on a fast Sunday. He couldn't understand, as they went from this street to that one, why God had not directed his people a little more rapidly toward some kind of payment app. This walking was barbaric.

Admittedly, though, it had an immediate impact on Gimpel's spiritual education. As soon as he got home, he fetched down a volume of his father's old copy of the Talmud: over the course of the afternoon, Gimpel had developed an interest in Jewish law. The halakha, he was coming to understand, had been created for a distinct purpose—but one adults these days simply didn't appreciate. He had heard, for example, that the old rabbis had insisted on counting the number of steps one could be required to take on the Sabbath day.

They had surely been deacons when they were young.

Yes, there was something in Jewish law. A real history there, with implications for a modern life.

Dudel, for his part, didn't mind collecting fast offerings. They didn't have to do the whole ward: most members brought their fast offerings on their own, so he and Gimpel only had to stop by a few apartments. The walk between those few apartments was long, but they must be assigned to those families for a reason. He thought they were hand-picked—by Yossel Fischer or maybe by God, he didn't know. It seemed like heaven, though, that sent him to the Cohen house.

Brother Cohen always seemed upset when they came by on their route—even more upset, that is, than his usual. He always paid fast offering. Quite generously, Dudel noted one week when Brother Cohen was too busy complaining about the nature of priesthood and the dangers of old traditions being neglected to use any discretion as he tucked money in the light blue fast offering envelope assigned to his address.

While Brother Cohen kvetched, Sister Cohen often threw in funny remarks, so that was nice. More precious than rubies, Dudel's mother always said, was a woman with a nice, sharp tongue. He did not doubt his mother knew it.

But what Dudel really loved about going to the Cohens is that often, Zusa would be there with them. Sometimes, she would be sitting on the couch reading and he could just stare at her hair. And sometimes, she'd be looking out the window and he could wonder what she was noticing out there and what interesting thoughts she was having about it. And sometimes, she'd turn. And she'd smile. At him.

He wanted to say something to her. Something clever, like her grandmother (though of course not so cutting). Or something intelligent, or spiritual, or deep. His mouth always got dry inside, though, which was surprising since on Fast Sunday, it was dry to begin with. Everything he'd considered over the past month would slip right out of his melted mind when she smiled at him.

Why oh why was it only *men* Yossel wanted to make them fishers of!

After learning that the Talmud included very interesting passages about animals and which foods are disgusting,

Gimpel had reached a long and intriguing passage about menstruation. There, however, the squat demon of ignorance stood in his way. He understood that the miracle of life was an ideal foundation for religious studies, but simply lacked the knowledge to follow the rabbis' learned arguments about cloths and counting days. In addition to being mysterious, of course, he realized that his study of Talmud was not yet helping him get out of anything. Discouraged, he paused, at least temporarily, his careful study of Jewish law.

He had turned instead to Jewish history. His father had books on Karl Marx, Rosa Luxemburg, Leon Trotsky. It seemed to Gimpel that they had understood the true spirit of the Bible and what it meant when Moses slew the Egyptian. He tried to convince his father that the labor theory of value meant that Bishop Levy had no right to the fast offering, but his father had pointed out that the Bishop redistributed the money and that, therefore, helping with fast offerings was one of the most socialist things a young man could do in the Church.

Gimpel had changed tactics then. He argued that the deacons' fast offering route was a form of child labor. He told his father about the stifling heat he and Dudel had to endure, the unreasonably long distances Yossel expected them to walk.

But his father only laughed and quoted Rosa Luxemburg: "Those who do not move do not notice their chains." Service, he said, was good for you.

When Dudel was not collecting fast offerings from old people with girl-shaped granddaughters visiting their homes, he also enjoyed collecting fast offerings from old people without girl-shaped granddaughters in their homes. Before they would visit Henya Bittner—Henya the prophetess—Yossel would tell stories about how she talked with God. Dudel could believe it. Sometimes, when they brought her the sacrament, Henya's eyes stayed closed for a moment after the prayer was done, and Dudel had a peculiar feeling: as if the last, long chord in the Beatles' song "A Day in the Life" had fallen silent but left the air quivering.

When they came for fast offering, he kept his eyes open. While Henya asked about how they were doing, or what Gimpel had been reading lately, Dudel would look around for signs of anything God might have left behind after dropping by. Like maybe the Golden Plates or a Liahona . . . anything with curious workmanship, really. Even though his searches consistently came up empty, he never lost hope. One day, he was sure, he'd spot something rolled under a table or sitting on a shelf.

He could imagine what that might look like because of visits to his own great-grandfather, Israel Lewensztajn. Fast Sundays were the best time for Dudel to visit the man in his natural habitat. Everyone insisted that the family patriarch was too old to host guests, so the family always gathered elsewhere. But Israel's apartment was filled with so many old, interesting things. Dudel appreciated the unhurried way his great-grandfather moved, his tendency to nod off while filling out the fast offering slip, and all the time these mannerisms gave the deacons to look around. Israel had empty tank shell casings he'd picked up in the woods. A towering grandfather clock with visible gears he still used to keep time, and a menorah *his* grandfather had used to keep time before that—one with carved symbols for each of the tribes of Israel.

Even Gimpel had to agree they were cool. If Dudel ever worked up the nerve to go sift through his great-grandfather's back rooms, he wouldn't be surprised to find trinkets that went further and further back into the past. A golem or two. The ark of the covenant. Maybe a lost tribe. Nothing would have shocked him.

It wasn't quite the same as seeing Zusa, but it was still an exciting way to spend a Sunday afternoon.

After communism failed to deliver him from his burdens, Gimpel turned to capitalism instead. Was fast offering really efficient? Surely some entrepreneur could be paid to solve the problem of poverty in a way that didn't involve Gimpel's Sunday afternoons. And on some level, weren't they actually doing a dis-service to whoever received fast offering money? They were robbing them of incentive to find work.

Why did Gimpel need to walk his feet raw when Adam Smith's invisible hand could handle things so much better?

Oskar the miser might have listened to these arguments and advocated on the boys' behalf, but they never collected fast offering from him. Apparently, he didn't trust them not to skim a little off the top of his meager contribution. Instead, Gimpel had to make the case to his father, who was utterly unsympathetic to the philosophies that had won the Cold War. If Gimpel thought his feet were sore, Isaac Peretz suggested, he should see what fawning talk of capitalism in their home could do to his behind.

The only thing sweeter than seeing Zusa Cohen's smile—
and that only because it *was* Fast Sunday and because
Gimple was right that they *did* walk quite a lot—was stopping by Zelda Gottstein's. Truth be told, she was the reason the route took so long. After hours and hours without
any food, which is very long for a deacon of any stomach
size, there was nothing quite like the blintzes or babka
Zelda Gottstein invariably offered them. What an offering to end a fast!

And then there was the coffee she poured herself to go
with it. The coffee might have been the kids' stuff most
ward members drank, but he didn't think so. Partly because it smelled a little more like heaven and a lot less
like burnt wheat. And partly because Sister Gottstein always put a hand over it when she mumbled the blessing,
like the polite thing was to show God clearly what you
were asking him not to see.

One week Gimpel proposed to Dudel, conspiratorially,
that they take Yossel and the Bible both a little more
literally. What if, he suggested, they spread a great net out
in the foyer, and pulled it tight when people came out?
Then they would really be fishers of men.

Dudel was excited at first—Gimpel didn't usually propose things that sounded quite so fun—but then he got
suspicious. Was that all, he asked, or was there some kind
of catch to this catch?

Well, Gimple admitted, there might be a little more to
the plan. He thought they might charge a small fee for
freeing people. Not in a priestcraft sort of way, of course.
More like the money paid to redeem the first born son in

temple days, or the afikomen at Passover, and then they'd collect plenty of fast offering and there would be no need to go off walking through the heat to learn some elusive virtues.

But Dudel said no. He liked going out in God's name to smile at girls and see the strange interior of an old man's apartment and eat sweets until he was stuffed. It was worth the walking, Dudel insisted. More than worth all the walking.

He hoped someday, he said dreamily, that they'd call him on a mission.

The purpose of life was to grow through trials, and the Church went to such lengths to organize them for its members.

Golda and
the Three Bears

At the age of seventeen, Golda Fischer was preparing for her first girls camp as a youth camp leader. She felt the weight of the assignment, a sacred obligation to give the younger girls experiences like she'd had. In her mind, it was a great honor and trust to serve in the Young Women organization. As a member, she had seen a thing or two. After all, back when Golda was a Beehive, Clever Gretele was the ward's Young Women president. Those were days never to be forgotten! (Thanks to a quick trip under barbed wire during a grueling countryside game of capture the flag, Golda still had a scar on her calf to prove it.) Through advice and adventures, Gretele had shown her how to grow and flourish. She had taught her what it means to sustain leaders and live with a little faith.

At Golda's very first young women activity, for example, Gretele had divided the girls into two groups and introduced a game. The rules were simple: each group was given an everyday object and instructed to go into town. They were to spend the rest of the evening making a succession of trades for something bigger or better until time was up.

Golda was immediately repulsed by the idea. She disliked talking to strangers, couldn't imagine who would want her group's starting comb anyway, and wished she had just stayed at home with a book. But Gretele noticed and asked her to give it a chance.

"Not even God can steer a parked car," Gretele said. "If you want him to lead you, you've got to practice hitting the gas. Give him something to work with."

Golda unleashed her most skeptical glare. "Does it have to be something so stupid?" she asked.

"Of course not," said Clever Gretele. "But it helps." She threw an arm over Golda's shoulders and leaned in, like they were sharing a secret. "If you get shy, just pretend you're someone else. As far as anybody knows, you're some other girl who doesn't care at all what they think."

For a newly-jaded twelve-year-old, the thought was appealing. She would never have admitted it, but Golda's first attempts at a cool apathy took a lot of work. It was hard to always seem old enough and smart enough to be above things. She constantly worried that she would slip up and get caught liking something childish or simple. But if she had permission to experiment with a genuine, pure apathy—not just about things but also about people's opinions of things—how could she resist?

Golda immediately resolved to take Gretele's advice. For a few hours, at least, she would pretend to be fearless. She'd refuse to overthink. If she was a car in need of steering, she'd burn rubber. Give God a challenge.

Apparently, God accepted. By the time the evening was over, the other group had a large German shepherd, her group had several hundred zlotys in cash, and Bishop Levy had a lot of questions.

Golda had thought back to those questions many times over the following years. During an activity, she might hear his voice in her head, asking things like "Did this have some kind of purpose?" and "You didn't break any laws . . . did you?" So long as she could answer those questions in a way that satisfied the bishop's standard, she decided not to worry about the rest. She figured her role was to listen to what her leaders said and dive into trying it. It was like Alma said in the Book of Mormon: you should experiment with the word. She realized, of course, that a person might have qualms about the way the Young Women organization in her formative years operated sometimes like a business, sometimes like a charity, and occasionally like a gang. But she trusted that everything gave her experience and worked in some unseen way to her good.

That basic confidence was what she wanted to give the younger girls. She wanted to teach them how to say yes to things and see where adventures led them. Unfortunately, the organization of the Church stood in the way of passing on tradition. If she had still been working with Gretele, they could have run some numbers, found a way to play with the budget, and made some real memories.

But the Lord who gives callings also takes them away. For the past two years, Golda had been adjusting to the very different approach of the ward's new Young Women president, Mirele Schwartz.

Was it even the same religion now? Sister Schwartz never let Golda near a budget, was strongly opposed to even the slightest trespassing, and never came to a planning meeting without already having a plan. Golda still wanted to sustain her leaders, but it was easier to do so when that meant running off on adventures with Clever Gretele than when it involved keeping up with Sister Schwartz's elaborate ideas and the ideals behind them.

More recently, the bishop had also called Tzipa Leicht to serve with the young women. Golda liked Tzipa well enough as a person, but she was hard to relate to as a leader. Tzipa seemed less interested in making plans than in responding to them. If Sister Schwartz wanted to do too much, Tzipa erred on the side of willingness to do nothing at all. Golda sometimes got the impression that Tzipa wouldn't have minded if they skipped camping altogether and just gathered to talk for an evening instead, because that would leave fewer things to go wrong.

Shifting between the two of them gave Golda whiplash. One ran hot, the other cold; she wanted to spew them both out. But she tried to keep an open mind, like Clever Gretele would have wanted her to. The purpose of life was to grow through trials, and the Church went to such lengths to organize them for its members. It would be a waste to walk away from all that. So she promised herself to be a good example. Instead of acting like a parked car, she would throw her energy into sustaining whatever her leaders wanted. If—and the closer camp crept, the bigger that *if* grew—the two of them ever settled on a shared goal for her to support.

Unfortunately for Golda, some people treat their callings like doing alms, where the left hand is not supposed to know what the right hand is doing. In the weeks before camp, each of Golda's leaders was preoccupied with finishing preparations of her own.

What was going through their heads in those final weeks? Nothing that nudged one any closer to calling the other.

Tzipa was almost done with all the preparations she had planned. In keeping with her goal of preventing any unnecessary deaths, she had studied how to handle the most common crises that could afflict teenagers in the wild: dehydration, blisters, bullying, and bad food. She was also prepared for secondary risks such as heat stroke, snakebites, and razor fights over time in the shower.

Tzipa also kept up her efforts to master the full names of all six girls who would be attending. Getting a written list into her brain had been simple enough, but consistently matching each with the right girl was harder. Golda Fischer was easy enough to remember. As a youth leader, she was pure gold. Chava was as full of life as her name suggested; she was also obviously a Gottstein-Kleiner, with all her mother Gretele's mildness and all her father Heshel's sense. (Tzipa might have switched those two, but God had his purposes.) Even though Zusa Cohen and Perla Schwartz were not officially members of the Church and rarely made it to activities, Tzipa could remember that Zusa was as sweet as her grandparents were sour and that shy little Perla was her mother's hidden pearl.

The real challenge was distinguishing between the fourteen-year-old Levy girls. It was a week before camp when Tzipa finally pinpointed a difference between Bluma and her twin sister Bina. The trick was in the eyes; Bina was far less subtle when she rolled them. All Tzipa had to do was wait for Mirele Schwartz to begin speaking and sooner or later, the twins would reveal their identities. With that mystery solved, Tzipa felt ready to go.

Mirele Schwartz was far less satisfied with her preparations, in part because her goals liked to grow. Having chosen the theme "Forty Years in the Wilderness," for example, meant that she had to fit ten years' worth of scripture-based activities into the meager number of hours God had set aside for each day. Thank the Lord that God had given the world stopwatches! Even that blessing, though, was mixed, because it took a long time to plan four days down to the minute. And it took longer still to come up with back-up plans for each minute in case anything went wrong.

She had to hurry. The calendar was merciless as Pharaoh, the day of departure rushing in like the waters of the Red Sea. But the final, desperate effort was worth it for God, for herself, and for her daughter Perla, who would be coming to camp for the first time.

Especially for Perla. Mirele's husband had not joined the Church and so girls camp was one of the best chances Perla would have to connect with the girls of the Chelm ward and learn the gospel. Mirele was not about to let that opportunity go to waste. She would put her shoulder to the wheel. She would push.

Well, the scriptures say that all rivers run to the sea, but the sea is never full. And so it was with the leaders' planning. The afternoon before their final preparation meeting, both Mirele and Tzipa got a series of text messages from Golda Fischer. Before they left, she said, she wanted to get a few simple directives on what she was supposed to do. She expected both the leaders to agree on each of these guiding points. And she would allow them exactly three.

Tzipa sighed and called her president. It was going to be an interesting night.

One short coordinating phone call, several prayers, and two longer follow-up calls later, Mirele Schwartz and Tzipa Leicht were ready for their meeting with Golda Fischer. From across the table, Golda weighed them in the balance with her eyes.

"We've agreed on three priorities," Mirele reported. "We've found a scripture for each, so you can have them from the mouth of three witnesses."

"I'm listening," said Golda. If those two *and* the scriptures could agree, she would do anything.

Mirele set her scriptures on the table between them, but rather than opening any given volume, she put her hand on the top of the stack as if swearing an oath. "The first priority comes from the opening chapters of Exodus and the eighteenth chapter of Mosiah," she said. "In Egypt, and therefore also this week, the children of Israel were made to carry heavy burdens. And the Book of Mormon says that at baptism, we promise to bear one another's burdens, that they may be light. As a youth camp leader, that's one thing we want you to do." She met Golda's gaze. "Especially for Zusa Cohen and my daughter Perla."

"Of course," Golda said. "I'll carry backpacks. I'll listen to worries. I'll try to remember your plans."

"Thank you," Mirele told her. She moved her Bible aside and laid her hand directly on her triple combination. "The second priority comes from Alma chapter 30 as well as from Mosiah 18. When Korihor challenged the prophet Alma and said there is no God, Alma told him that all the universe is evidence of God's existence. As we go out into the beautiful forests of our country, we want you to bear witness of God at all times, in all things, and in all places."

"I'll do it," Golda vowed. "Even when the weather sucks."

Across the table, Tzipa was leaning back on her chair. "The third thing comes up in a weird story about the prophet Elisha," she said. She brought the front legs of her chair down and leaned forward. "We want you to watch out for bears."

"Bears?" Golda asked.

"There aren't very many in the woods where we're going, but they're attracted to the smell of food. If it's left in the tents, a bear might reach in and maul somebody. By mistake, of course," she clarified, "but still. So if you'll tie all our food up in one of those beautiful trees God created before we go to sleep at night, you'll finish all three jobs at once: Bear a burden. Bear witness. Keep us safe from bears."

Golda nodded. "I can do that," she said. She let out a long sigh of relief. At last, she understood how to sustain these two.

Before the sun rose the next morning, Golda threw her backpack into a rented van and set off for four days of immersive sisterhood. On the drive out of the city, Golda Fischer began leading the other girls in songs. It was a tradition, she'd been told, that dated back to when Miryam and Israel's daughters danced with their timbrels on the

Red Sea's shore. The lyrics, obviously, had evolved since the original celebration over drowned chariots. But there was still a girls camp song about a princess—perhaps a daughter of Pharaoh?—and sinking ships. And another one, though it never used the word "plague," about a lot of frogs and grubs. By the last song, Chava was singing comically low, Bluma was singing comically high, and Bina was laughing and warning she might pee her pants. Golda basked in the joy and success for exactly the amount of time the official plans allowed before Mirele Schwartz led them off on their first hike.

Golda was not sure where they were going. Despite her best intentions, she hadn't gotten that far into the weeds on the planning details. But she set to work at once with her various kinds of bear-ing. No one needed her to help with their backpacks yet, so she decided to begin with getting the others to witness the glory of God's creation.

Bluma dived into the subject with a headlong enthusiasm Clever Gretele would have been proud of, though the part of creation she was most willing to praise mostly involved a few boys back home. Bina bantered back with gushing odes to actors from her favorite movies while Zusa listened with as much interest as her modesty would allow. Chava was less accommodating, and could be unpredictable when bored, so Golda got her running off the trail to bear witness instead of the breathtaking diversity of local animal droppings. Chava regularly reported back, speculating on the foods that had passed through various birds, rodents, and bugs. At one point, she also ran back to report that she had found scat from a raccoon dog.

Through all this, Perla mostly kept her eyes down. It was hard for Golda to tell if her youngest fellow camper was half-listening to the talk of boys and bowels or pondering God's work creating her feet. Golda made a few attempts to draw her out, but Clever Gretele was right: it was hard to steer a parked car. After a while, Golda let her focus shift to witnessing the beauty of the forest while also scanning the trees for telltale scratches from wandering bears. She couldn't see any, but the forest was large and bears likely didn't make a habit of hanging out close to the trails.

Up ahead, Sister Schwartz kept a brisk pace. Golda did her best to encourage the others along, and they seemed pioneer-willing to walk, and walk, and walk. After a long time, they arrived at their campsite and stopped walking long enough to set up tents. It took a while to sort out how many times the poles were supposed to cross over themselves and what general sort of geometric shape the tents were supposed to have. But with a little effort and without any swearing whatsoever, they finished tents that seemed stable enough to stand through the night.

With a glance toward her watch, Sister Schwartz told them to take all the tents down again.

It didn't make sense. But Golda supposed it wasn't illegal and so figured that Bishop Levy and Clever Gretele would agree that she should push ahead. To calm the rebellion rising in her chest, she decided to pretend to be someone who wasn't worried about getting all the tent poles lined up right again. Using her most supportive voice, Golda invited the other girls to race each other on the take down. After all, God could only guide you if you moved.

Which they continued to do, as soon as they packed up, heading onto the trail and wandering through the wilderness. Golda steeled herself for another long walk. She was a youth camp leader. She could pretend to be someone who could do this. And she could make her faked willingness contagious.

As she led the girls in slow circles, Mirele listened carefully for complaints. If they were to follow the literal word of God, it was important that this hike continue until the girls murmured. Frankly, she had expected some murmuring to begin as soon as she told them the tents needed to be taken down. But there was no such luck.

It was puzzling. Maybe these young women were so used to the Mormon ritual of setting up and taking down chairs that the tents didn't faze them. Maybe it was because Golda normally took the lead in any questioning and she was trying strangely hard to be supportive. Mirele began to regret the whole burden-bearing speech, because in Golda's silence, no one else picked up the slack. Mirele had planned for this possibility, of course, and she tried her backup plans: she brought up unpopular subjects, she pushed the pace up uncomfortably, she looked around as if she was lost. And what did she have to show for it? Her own exhaustion. She wanted more than anything to set the tents up again and lie down in one for a rest, but they had not reached their emotional destination. So she continued to lead the girls in circles, a silent prayer in her heart that someone's good attitude would crack.

Tzipa kept shooting dark looks at Mirele and interrupting the fastest parts of the hike for breaks to check on how the girls' feet were holding up. For a moment, Mirele hoped that the hiccupy rhythm of her sprints and Tzipa's stops would drive the girls sufficiently crazy, but they continued to withhold their murmurs. Chava was too busy running off the trail to look at this and that. Bluma and Bina kept chatting lustily with anyone who would listen, and Perla was too shy to say anything at all. Zusa asked once if they had missed a turn (or perhaps taken one turn too many, or even several too many) but her tone was so polite that it couldn't really be counted as a complaint. And so onward they pressed, ever onward. Mirele was beginning to suspect that their hike would devolve into one eternal round.

And then—miracle of miracles—Bina's stomach finally gave an audible growl. Bluma heard it and laughed, which was just the spark the group needed. Bina snapped back that it was not funny: she really was beginning to starve. Chava reached into the week's supplies and produced a block of cheese, which Golda snatched away, saying that it was for meals. Zusa asked when mealtimes during camp would be, which caused Golda to glare at Mirele pointedly and say, "I don't think anyone here knows."

For Mirele, that was murmur enough! Seizing the moment, she rushed them back to the campsite. She had them put up the tents again, but this time offered a few minutes to lie down. Let them rest, she thought, and then rise to wonder.

While the girls tried out their tents, Mirele took her backpack off and laid out pieces of flat, unleavened bread all around the campsite like manna. "Come see, come see," she called out when her work was done. "What is this?"

But when the girls emerged, they did not celebrate the miracle. They just stared, confounded by God's mysterious ways.

Golda's muscles were sore, but for a moment lying in the tent, she had been satisfied. She was a good leader. For hours of hiking, she had kept everyone engaged. People said there was no rest for the wicked, and so the release of relaxation had made her feel positively righteous.

But when Sister Schwartz called them out, and their eyes took the scene in, that contented feeling quickly melted away.

A dawning disgust crossed Bluma's face. "Are we supposed to eat those?" she asked.

For a moment, Golda thought of Clever Gretele's advice to just try things. But even if this activity had a purpose, and even though eating off the ground wasn't technically illegal, there were some things she still couldn't bring herself to do. "Obviously, we're not going to now," Golda said. "We'll just appreciate them with our eyes."

"They look like they were quite good before they all fell in the dirt," Zusa pointed out charitably.

Bina picked one up. "Maybe we could wipe a few off?"

Her constructive attitude left Golda feeling some mixture of impressed and annoyed, but it seemed to rub off on Chava. "Or we could use them as bait to trap an animal," she said, moving into action with alarming speed. "I brought a knife. We could make a fire."

Apparently, though, the food wasn't only about eating. As Tzipa looked on morosely, Sister Schwartz tried to explain that the manna was a symbol of spiritual as well as physical nourishment. Just as this manna would feed them after their long hike, the words of the prophets could nourish them on the long hikes of life.

Golda missed the old nights crawling under barbed wire. "I was hoping for something a little less messy," she said.

Sister Schwartz tilted her head to the side. "Are you talking about the teachings of the prophets?" she asked. "Or do you mean the flatbread?"

Tzipa nodded sagely. "That's the great thing about a parable," she said. "They can teach on so many different levels at once." Then, after glancing nervously toward the forest, she began to pick the manna off the ground and put it into a trash bag. "I'll get out the rest of dinner."

Golda offered to help, but there was a different burden to be carried first. Chava was terribly disappointed that no one wanted to catch and cook a wild animal. Since Golda doubted that Mirele Schwartz would see the spiritual value—or Tzipa the essential safety—in a roasted raccoon dog, she felt a responsibility as youth camp leader to draw Chava's energy toward some nobler purpose.

Chava felt comforted about being denied an evening hunt when Golda suggested that she could still help build a huge bonfire. Apparently, it was a symbol of the pillar of fire by night in the scriptures, and a little pyromania was allowed if it was symbolic. It also helped her mood that they feasted on cheese and fruit as greedily as if it were the word of the Lord. Chava's sorrow was no match for the mix of savory and sweet.

After their breadless dinner, when Tzipa suggested they tell scary stories, Chava's heart moved the rest of the way from heavy to thrilled. Beyond the bright ring of their fire it was dark, darker than the streets ever get in Chelm, with the outlines of the treetops looming in the not-so-distance. There was just a little wind, not enough to be uncomfortable while still being enough to make a paranoid person wonder what might be moving out there. Oh, it was perfect.

But the moment didn't last. Sister Schwartz went first—and it turned out the scary story she wanted to tell was about the children of Israel and the angel of death. And honestly, it just wasn't as good without any firstborn sons around. Bluma stretched. Bina yawned. Even Zusa could only barely pretend to be interested. After Sister Schwartz finished, Chava was the only one who wanted to keep the stories going.

She tried to start one about girls in the woods disappearing, but everyone had an excuse for why they couldn't stay. Golda said she had to tie their food up in a tree first, and besides, she was tired and sore and just wanted to finally go to sleep in the tents they'd set up so many times. Perla nodded gratefully at the suggestion. Even Bluma and Bina were willing to go along with the movement toward bedtime—that is, until they found out they were assigned to the same tent, at which point they interrupted Chava's story by arguing with the leaders.

"We share a room at home," Bina complained. "Why can't camp be different?"

"I don't see why it can't," Tzipa said. She looked to Sister Schwartz. "We can be flexible, can't we? Bina can move to the other tent."

"Of course," said Sister Schwartz. Her only condition was that if Bina moved to the other tent, someone would have to move back to the first.

That was not a problem—Perla immediately volunteered, and they switched her to the first tent, but then Sister Schwartz wanted to switch to be with her daughter. And apparently, there was a rule that the leaders needed to be in the same tent, so Tzipa had to switch, too, which put too many people in the first tent—so they moved Golda to the second, but then Bluma wanted to be with Golda, which combined the twins again, so Bina switched another time, and this time Zusa offered to switch along with her so she'd have company, but again that put too many people in the first tent, so they planned some switches again until no one was entirely sure who was sleeping where and they all had to go space it out to see and Chava was left without anyone to frighten.

Or was she? While the others stumbled into one tent or the other (or, frankly, any tent at all) and fell gratefully down into their sleeping bags, she slipped away from the fire and out toward the woods. The scariest story, Chava realized, was the kind no one realized they were listening to. The kind told not with words, but with strange noises in the night.

Chava couldn't decide what it should be about. When she was a child, she was scared to death by an old Jewish story about a bride who attacks her groom because she's possessed by the spirit of a man who used to be in love with her. But as she got older, ghost stories stopped scaring her as much. After all, she'd learned at Church that ghosts are just lost spirits waiting in the spirit world for the missionaries to come and teach them. To scare her friends, she needed something from this world. From these woods.

As Chava thought about nature and creatures with teeth that make noise in the night, she remembered the food in the tree. Golda had said there probably weren't any bears around, but also that no one wanted a hungry bear smelling food in their tent. Reaching inside. Raking its claws casually across a human stomach while looking for a treat. The thought gave Chava shivers. It was wonderful.

Well? She could be a bear, or at least sound like one, if she tried.

She crouched in the darkness, a stone's throw from the tents, and made a low growling sound. But no one in the tents stirred. She went closer and growled again.

Inside the tent now, someone was turning. "Do you hear that?" she heard Zusa ask. "What's that noise?"

"It's probably just Bina's stomach," Bluma said. "Or Sister Schwartz snoring."

A stomach? Snoring? Chava needed to take some time to get into character. If she felt like a bear, she would do better at sounding like a real bear. Soon enough they'd scream. Unless she scared them silent, petrified with fear.

First, Chava practiced walking through the woods, feeling big. She tried moving with her front paws on the ground, searching for something good to eat. She grunted a bearish grunt. Then she stood on her hind legs and swayed back and forth, like she imagined a bear would, sniffing the air.

There! Up in the tree, she could smell it. Delicious. Yes, that scent up there reminded her of fat for the winter and a good month's sleep. Any thoughts of moving closer to the tents to scare human girls fled as Chava's stomach growled in a very bearish way. She moved closer to the tree and grunted again, but the pack with the food was out of reach.

What would a bear do? It would climb. And so Chava began to. It was hard to find the right footholds in the dark, and her claws weren't nearly as sharp as they should have been, but she managed to make her way up the trunk and onto the branch the pack was hanging from. From there, it was a simple thing to reach in and grab some snacks. A little munching made Chava's stomach feel better, which made her feel more like Chava. But she wasn't ready to be Chava again yet. She still wanted to be a bear.

As she thought about what to do next, it occurred to her that a bear wouldn't climb a tree just to unwrap a few of Chava's favorite snacking foods. No, a wild animal would make the most of this opportunity. She would eat with the next winter in mind, gulping down the fattiest things she could find. Chava reached into the bag again greedily and came back with a stick of butter in her paw. A bear would definitely eat the butter. Chava could feel it turn slick on her hands, then soft on her lips. Yes, with this she would grow heavy and strong and all the other bears would be jealous of her. She let out a great and joyous growl. The other girls were surely hearing that, trembling in their tents while they zipped the doors tight. Chava liked being a bear.

A bear would eat more and more. Dried fish. Fresh fruits, juice dribbling down her chin. Pure sugar. A bear would shove all of it down her wild maw. A bear would not shimmy down the tree until she was satisfied. Ah, but soon she was: so very satisfied with her victory.

What would a bear do next? It was clear to Chava by the time her feet hit the ground that a bear would mostly feel sick. She would stumble around the woods a bit in a stupor. Yes, just like this. The butter would slide around her stomach. Chava didn't think bears were actually made to eat straight butter. It would churn terribly in there, mixing with the fish and fruit and sugar. A bear would try very hard not to throw up.

The camp was quiet when Chava got back. She had scared everyone to sleep.

In what was purportedly the morning, Golda was the first girl Sister Schwartz shook awake. It was time for the sunrise hike, she said.

"Another one? Already?" Golda asked.

This was the first sunrise hike, Sister Schwartz said. Yesterday's hikes had been in full daylight and it wasn't her fault they'd taken so long to do their part in finishing those.

Golda wanted to ask Sister Schwartz what she was talking about, but she was so tired. Chava had slept restlessly: the sounds of her moaning had briefly woken Golda more than once during the night. Also Golda's body was so sore that lifting her tongue felt like an impossible amount of work.

Golda wanted to inspire her friends to give every experience a try. Maybe getting out of bed would help Chava, since her sleeping bag clearly hadn't agreed with her. Maybe a sunrise over the forest would give Bluma and Binah something other than boys to think about. Maybe Zusa would smile, and Perla's eyes would light up. Maybe all they needed was for Golda to lead the way.

She allowed herself to close her eyes for another moment and tried to pretend to be someone who didn't actually hate the idea of this hike. She wanted to support her leaders. Truly. Or at least, she was pretending to be a good youth camp leader who would want to support her leaders. She couldn't remember the details for sure.

Her ears, apparently, were working fine. As Sister Schwartz moved from sleeping bag to sleeping bag, the protests of the persecuted grew. Perla said she'd gotten up early yesterday. Chava said she never wanted to move again. Bluma and Bina, having spent the night apart, were feeling homesick. Only Zusa Cohen was willing to go, and Golda thought that even she sounded the tiniest bit reluctant about it.

Golda dragged herself up. She could share the wise words Gretele had shared with her. About driving too fast so that God could steer you. She could tell them to experiment on their leaders' words and see how it turned out. But as she rubbed her eyes in the ungodly predawn darkness, it didn't feel like that was what a good youth camp leader would do.

To every thing, she realized, there was a season. There was a time for her to sustain her leaders. And a time for her to speak up for other girls.

"Sister Schwartz," she said, "I have a question about the hiking."

Sister Schwartz looked relieved that Golda, at least, was up and engaging with her. "Yes?" she said.

Golda chose her words carefully. Or at least as carefully as she could before six in the morning. "What if we didn't?" she asked.

"What do you mean?" Sister Schwartz asked. "We have a whole day planned! If we lose another hour, I'll have to multiply by a fraction to keep us on schedule."

"Sometimes plans leave out important things," Golda replied. "Like stillness."

But the idea slid right off Sister Schwartz without a sign that anything approaching communication had occurred. She looked at her watch. "We're behind already," she said. "We should be eating breakfast."

And Golda felt a sudden prompting. As if, now that her tongue was moving—however slowly—God could help her nudge it the right way. "In that case," she countered, "we're hours and hours ahead. Look: the girls are so fast today, they're already ready for bed!"

And without overthinking it, Golda crawled back into the tent and zipped it shut behind her. Sometimes being a leader meant doing what the plan said; other times, it meant doing what was right—and letting the consequences wait until you woke up again. She was happy with her decision. She had lifted a heavy burden from her fellow young women: the weight of being the one to say no.

*Shmuel wanted to do some sins while there
was still time, but a day is not very long.*

The Last Free Sin
of Shmuel Peretz

That same morning, Shmuel Peretz woke up in a bad mood. Tomorrow was his birthday. His eighth birthday. Once you turned eight, God got mad about your sins. Before then, parents got mad sometimes, but that was just for practice. Really you could do whatever sins you wanted from the time you were a tiny baby until the very last day you were seven years old and God didn't even care.

It wasn't really fair, though, because most of that time got wasted. When you are a baby, you don't even know what the sins are. And then when you get bigger, you get distracted by playing and going to school and drawing monsters, and then the time was almost up and you'd only done sins once in a while and usually not on purpose. Or else you did remember to try sins, but somebody else got in the way. Like: last week, when Shmuel tried to hide instead of going to church, his mom found him and made him go anyway. And now he was out of Sundays. Or yesterday—he was going to run away and walk where his parents couldn't see him, but his dad was too fast and caught his hand and held it the whole way home so Shmuel was just trapped.

Shmuel wanted to do some sins while there was still time, but a day is not very long and a lot of sins need a plan. Like, if you want to attack somebody with a sword you have to save up money to buy a sword and also know where to buy a sword and also convince somebody to sell a sword to a kid. If you want to do hacking, you have to know how to hack. If you want to do fraud, you have to break into somebody's phone to look up what fraud is. Shmuel's dad always cheating workers was the most common sin. But if you wanted to cheat a worker, you had to have one! And that didn't even count really hard sins like mass genocide. Or shooting a nuclear bomb.

Shmuel punched his pillow in frustration. Luckily, that reminded him that an easy thing like punching could be a sin. Anybody could do a sin, so it wasn't hopeless. In his head, Shmuel made a list of sins he could do by himself, in just one day, while he was stuck at home. Things like:

- Punching
- Saying mean words
- Tossing things directly at a person like at their face on purpose

- ◆ Taking things from people's hands
- ◆ Stealing

Shmuel thought about his choices. If he punched someone, he wanted to punch his sister Dinah. After all, if he punched his brother Gimpel, Gimpel would punch back. Dinah was smaller than Shmuel, so that wasn't fair, but Gimpel was so much bigger than him, so that would be unfair, too. It was better to do the unfair thing where you weren't the one who ended up with a bruise.

He could punch a parent, but then he would get sent to his room, maybe for hours, and he would lose all his time to do more sins before his birthday. Then again, if he punched Dinah, she would probably just tell his parents. If he said mean words to her, she would tell his parents. When he tossed a doll kind of at her face but not on purpose she had told his parents and she also lied and said he did it on purpose and he had to go to their room and sit on his bunk and waste a bunch of time, so none of that was going to work. He doubted he could get away with taking something out of her hands. Even though God didn't care yet. She was just such a complainer.

That left stealing. He could maybe steal from Dinah and not get caught. Or he could steal from Gimpel—and when Gimpel noticed what was missing, Shmuel could just lie and say "Dinah did it." If they didn't believe that, he could say, "I guess it was robbers." Or, "Your dumb toy probably just blew up while you weren't looking." That one would be two lies, actually, because the toy wouldn't be blown up, it would be hidden in Shmuel's room, and also the toy he would steal from Gimpel wouldn't be dumb. It would be great. Since Gimpel was the oldest, and relatives still get excited about the oldest, he had so many cool things—metal race cars, plastic weapons, orange binoculars that really worked, a bunch of dinosaurs, even a blue and silver dragon. But he never played with them anymore because ever since he got bigger and moved to his own room, all he wanted to do was read.

God wouldn't care if Shmuel stole one of Gimpel's things. God might even be happy that Shmuel would take care of it instead of stuffing it in a box in the bottom of the closet.

With that hope in his heart, Shmuel finally climbed down out of his bed. On the bottom bunk, Dinah was still sleeping. He went and peeked out the bedroom door. In the kitchen, his dad was buttering the bottom of a piece of bread. (Buttering the underside like that was a trick he did, since the top always falls on the floor if you drop it). He was also filling his enormous thermos with water. In a moment, he would leave for work. Shmuel couldn't see his mom yet, but she probably wasn't up. (She thought getting up in the mornings only encouraged them.)

As soon as the front door opened and closed, Shmuel slipped out into the hallway. Morning was a great time for a sin. If he was quick, he could steal something before Gimpel was awake enough to catch him taking it or Dinah was awake enough to notice him hiding it. Getting up early was the perfect crime.

He crept down the hall and looked into Gimpel's room. But Gimpel was not sleeping. He was awake, lying in his bed (which was between the door and the closet) with his face already buried in some book.

It wasn't fair. Gimpel slept in plenty of days. Why did he have to be awake on the last day before Shmuel's eighth birthday?

Shmuel wanted to scream. God wouldn't care if he screamed. But it was too obvious. So he snuck back down the hall instead, past his and Dinah's room and all the way to the kitchen. He made himself a bagel. On purpose, he left out the cream cheese, which was something at least. And he chewed his bagel with his mouth open. But as sins went, chewing with your mouth open when no one was there to be disgusted was pretty boring. So he finished his breakfast and he crept back to check on Gimpel's room.

But Gimpel was still there.

Across the hall, Shmuel heard his mom getting up. What was wrong with her? Could she sense him lurking in the hall somehow? He raced back to the kitchen and got out a paper to draw. His heart was beating fast. Even though God didn't care, apparently his heartbeat did.

But Shmuel's mom just stumbled by and made herself a cup of barley coffee. She didn't even notice the cream cheese on the counter. Shmuel looked hard at his paper. His mom walked away, down the hall and out onto her favorite spot on the balcony. Shmuel noticed that she had a book, too.

After you were eight and couldn't sin anymore, he guessed, there was nothing to do but read.

He looked down at his paper again. He remembered how when he was younger—like Dinah's age—he once drew on his bed frame. His mom got furious, then. She told him, "We only draw on paper." In a mean voice, making clear it was a very big deal. He felt so guilty, because his primary teachers hadn't taught him how sins work yet.

Shmuel smiled. He grabbed a fistful of markers and ducked under the table. Even if he was still waiting for Gimpel to get up, he didn't have to waste time. He started to draw on the bottom side of the table top. (Just like it was a piece of toast!) Not just squiggles; he decided to do a giant dragon. He gave it red eyes. He gave it bright blue skin with silver stripes. He made it breathe a mix of fire and ice. It was bigger than anything you could do on paper. Better than anything you could do on paper. He loved it. It made him happy that for one more day, God didn't care.

Finally, he heard footsteps. He put the markers back on the top of the table and he peeked down the hall. Gimpel's door was open. The bathroom door was closed. Probably Gimpel had been so busy reading he didn't even pee and now he would really have to go. For a long time, like Dad if he forgot to take his last break at work. Shmuel hurried down the hall, stepping as softly as he could. He went straight for the closet. And how could he pass up the dragon? He grabbed it, closed up Gimpel's box of toys again, got out before he got caught, and made it safely into his own room.

Dinah was awake. "What's that?" she asked.

"What's what?" he said, hiding it behind his back.

"That toy you have."

"Be quiet," he said. "It's nothing. And it's not for you."

"I want to know what it is!" Dinah said. She was almost yelling. How come *she* could yell and their parents never seemed to care?

"It's a secret, okay?" he whispered.

"Will you tell me the secret?" she asked.

"If I told you, it wouldn't be as secret anymore."

"OK," she said. "Tell me the not-as-secret of what's in your arms."

From across the hallway and through the door, he could hear the toilet flushing. He could toss the dragon at her face now and tell Gimpel she stole it. That would get a few sins in, but Gimpel would take Shmuel's new toy away.

"Okay, I'll tell you!" he hissed. "Just quietly."

The bathroom door opened. A moment later, Gimpel's door opened and closed.

Dinah leaned off the side of the bed and craned her neck. "Why do you have Gimpel's dragon?" she said.

Shmuel thought about what to say. He could tell any lie he wanted, but there were so many to choose from. He could tell her he was borrowing it. Or that it was his. He could say that Gimpel gave it to him early, as a present for his birthday.

And then something occurred to Shmuel Peretz. Something wonderful.

He had only the one free day left to sin. Barely any time at all. But he had an idea for how he could make it count.

He handed her the dragon. "I want to show you something."

As Dinah turned the dragon over in her hands, Shmuel went to the front room. He came back with a handful of markers. He pointed to the wooden slats that separated his bunk from hers. "Have you ever wondered what kinds of pictures you could draw on those?"

Dinah shook her head. "Mom says we only draw on paper."

"I know what mom says," he told her. "And I know mom wants us to help each other make good choices." He took the lid off the blue marker and handed it to her. He had wasted so much time—but without knowing much about temples or baptism for the dead—Shmuel Peretz had just stumbled onto the basic concept of doing work by proxy. He counted in his head and thought of the next two years, one month, and four days. "Did you know that before you turn eight," he said to his sister, "you can do any sin you want and God doesn't even care?"

"It's horribly inefficient for everyone to complain at once," Tzipa said.

Wandering in the Wilderness

The murmuring had started late, but the rebellion came early.

Before the sun rose on the girls' first morning in the wilderness, Mirele Schwartz could already feel the seconds slipping away from her. She had testimonies to build, fellowship to strengthen. The day was just about to peek over the horizon, ready to be seized. But the girls preferred their pillows.

As Golda zipped the tent door shut in front of her, hiding Perla's face from view, Mirele thought she understood Moses better. It must have been so hard to break everyone out of slavery, only to have them drag their feet to the promised land. The young women were not exactly seeking her life or trying to go back to Egypt. They hadn't even mentioned the Nile's luscious watermelons; all they wanted was a nap. But the principle was the same. People were constantly choosing ease over vision. Mirele had a plan. She had lessons to share. So of course no one cared.

She tried not to feel resentful, but it's hard to quarantine betrayal in a single corner of the heart. After all she had done to prepare, this bitter loneliness was her reward. If only she could have been less devoted, perhaps she would not feel such despair. That was the trouble with having pearls of wisdom: in the end, it made the ungrateful people around you seem like swine.

But God, for reasons equally righteous and annoying, had resolved to give people agency. Even someone who was supposed to be acting as youth leader could zip the tent door shut in your face. Even someone who you wanted to make memories with (including, but not limited to, a child you gave birth to and nourished and raised) could lie in the tent with her eyes closed and let the morning pass her by. That was the plan of salvation. There was nothing to do sometimes but go up the mountain alone to cool off. And so it was that Mirele went off on the sunrise walk by herself.

As the sky softened from black to deep purple, like a bruise just beginning to heal, Mirele considered how to make the most of the precious remaining hours in her week. What could she do to give Perla the perfect opportunity to feel the spirit? She didn't need an angel to appear to her daughter or anything—just enough taste of the divine to get her to come to church once in a while, so that Mirele didn't have to sit alone. That would do. A moment of wonder on a hike or activity. Maybe a small miracle, like praying and finding something lost or having a mosquito bite abruptly stop itching. Any little thing that God might bring to Perla's remembrance during their end-of-camp testimony meeting.

Soon enough, the sun lit up the treetops. Mirele stopped walking and took a deep breath. She told herself that even if the day had started poorly, there was still time enough for many good moments. Or at least a few. She felt for a moment like Abraham, negotiating with God over how many good moments it would take to justify all the troubles this camp was causing. Fifty? Twenty? Ten? That wasn't bad. And if the number of good moments happened to be only three or two? Was that enough?

At an absolute minimum, she told God, she was hoping that Golda would not have anyone worshiping anyone else's calves by the time she got back.

It was the wrong fear. No one was worshiping idols or body parts. But before Mirele could see the tents again, she could hear the yelling. It occurred to her that the idolatrous children of Israel were at least united. She should have known better than to leave Tzipa in charge of this group.

"What do you mean, there's no butter?" Bluma shrieked. "I only know how to make naleśniki with butter!"

Tzipa was clearly trying to keep her own voice calm. "That's because they're made with butter. Which we thought we would have."

"Why didn't we pack extra?" Bina demanded. "We knew there were animals in the woods. We could have packed enough for us and them."

"We didn't know an animal was going to break into our food," Tzipa reasoned. "Next time, of course, we can pack enough to go around."

"But what should we do this time?" Bluma asked. "It's not fair that the butter got lost right before it was Bina's and my turn to cook."

Tzipa scratched her head. "Of course, if we had packed more, the animal might have eaten more. So it might be better to pack less, so that there wouldn't be as much for the animal to eat."

Bina groaned. "The bread last night, now the missing butter . . . it all makes sense. You brought us here to starve."

Golda stepped out of the tent to join the fray. "I know how to feed everyone," she said. "First, we get in the car. Then, we drive back toward Chelm. At some point, we find a place to stop and order food. It's even better than a hike: through the windows, we'll see ten times more nature than we ever would on foot."

"We don't need to abandon camp just yet," Tzipa said. "Why don't we say a prayer to find the lost butter? It's probably in an animal's stomach, but at least you'd be able to see a real, live sable. Or maybe a fox."

From inside the tent, Chava shouted a reply. "It wasn't a sable or a fox that ate the butter," she said. "It was a bear!"

Her words set off a chain reaction. Soon Bluma was hysterical over the possibility that a bear was going to eat them, Bina was saying they were too starved for a hungry bear to want, Golda was apologizing for having missed any signs of a bear in the area, and Tzipa was trying to reassure all three of them that it must have been a much smaller animal, even as Chava insisted—with a passion bordering on ferocity—that a bear had taken their food.

"Enough!" said Mirele as she reached camp. She wished that she'd made some tablets to throw down and break dramatically. She supposed she could have torn the breakfast recipe in two, but instead, she settled for glaring at each girl with what she hoped was prophetic intensity. "We did not bring you here to starve. God will provide!"

For a moment, Bina, Bluma, Golda, Zusa, and Tzipa all looked at her in awe. But since Perla was still in the tent, that good moment went to waste. And after a second of silence, Golda snorted. "If you have more bread, please don't throw it in the dirt this time."

But Mirele did not have bread. She had spoken out of some mixture of conviction and panic. Without having surveyed the damage to their food stores, she was walking in the dark. Truth be told—though she desperately hoped it wouldn't come to that—Mirele didn't have a plan.

The thought terrified her.

Bina was looking at her hopefully. Poor child. "There's more bread?" she asked.

Mirele shook her head.

"Then what breakfast, exactly, does God have in mind?" Bluma demanded.

"Get out your scriptures," Mirele said. "And let's find the answer."

"Are there recipes in the scriptures?" Zusa asked.

Chava emerged from the tent, holy books in hand. "There's one in Ezekiel. But it's not very good."

Golda shook her head. "God's answer better not be fasting," she said.

Mirele considered her options. When you stripped away all her preparation, what was left? Not much. But she had faith. A prayer in her heart, mixed with a certain guilt for bringing the Lord's name into this mess. And she had a group of hungry girls. Staring at her. Waiting for her to fall short.

As Tzipa began to survey the damage, making an inventory of what had been robbed or raided, Mirele took decisive action. First, she asked Golda to cast lots between the Bible and the Triple Combination. The lot fell to the triple. Next, she asked Bluma, Bina, and Chava each to come up with a number from zero to nine. Once they did, she combined them into a single three-digit number and turned to the corresponding page. "Let's see what guidance is on this page for us," she said.

For the first time that morning, Perla peeked out of the tent to see what was going on. The hour was late. The supplies were scattered. But Mirele looked down at the page for the first words that caught her eye.

They were "sad experience."

Mirele had faith that God had led her to that phrase, but there was no comfort in it. She should have known better than to promise anything, and now she was learning by sad experience to bite her tongue.

Unless . . . well, as it happened, *experience* was exactly the sort of thing no sable, fox, or bear could take away. They may not have much food, but they still had experience. Perhaps God had provided for them in an unexpected way. Mirele hated the idea of cooking without a recipe, but there was more to life, she reluctantly acknowledged, than directions to follow. She straightened. "We have better than bread," she said, turning toward Tzipa. "On this trip, we have a baker."

Tzipa triumphantly lifted a bunch of sad-looking squashed bananas from the bag. "God *has* provided," she said. "The animal left these."

Golda frowned. "I think I changed my mind about fasting," she said.

"Oh, they're not to eat straight. Mashed bananas make an interesting butter substitute," Tzipa explained. "Don't worry," she added. "I'll cook."

Watching her, Mirele thought, was like their own little miracle of the talents. If you only had one talent, such as planning, it was good to have a friend who had five. Tzipa picked up this, mixed it with that. She seemed to get extra ideas as she worked. Mirele wouldn't exactly have expected salvation on this trip to come from her counselor, but there was no denying the sudden disparity between what each of them was equipped to do. It was strange. Working hard for months on a plan was one thing, but only God could prepare a person with the experience of a lifetime.

Out of the remnants of their ingredients, Tzipa was somehow able to produce fluffy little cakes, filled with a delicious sauce made from squashed berries. The food felt blessed before they even said the prayer, and the girls ate with genuine gratitude shining out of their faces. The rumbling in Bina's stomach quieted. Perla licked sweet syrup off her fingers.

That was one good moment at least. Just a few more to go. Mirele looked at her schedule and multiplied by fractions to figure out how to bring the day back into line. She would not let Tzipa's incredible efforts go to waste. She was determined: the grace of the morning would buy them a chance to work their way back into the plan that afternoon, and on to glory.

Unfortunately, man does not live by baking alone.

The boil of the morning's argument seldom dropped below a simmer. The girls complained freely about the previous day's long, circular hike, about the nighttime tent assignments, and about the animal in the woods. When Mirele told them it didn't matter what the animal was, they changed the subject and complained about her. She found it all a little upsetting. Where had these murmurs been yesterday when she needed them?

She counted herself as fortunate, at least, that the girls were finally getting into character for the camp theme. Now all they had to do was make up for several missed years of activities. Between the sleeping in, the slow breakfast, and some bickering over the dishes, the sun was getting high by the time they walked away from camp. Luckily, it was punishingly hot. That saved some time, since the girls rapidly hit the goal of asking testily for water, which allowed Mirele to skip to the part where Moses miraculously opens a well from out of a rock. She led them straight to a boulder at the entrance to a small park.

But because the girls didn't realize that water was less than a meter away, their complaints got worse.

"A rock?" said Golda. "We walked all this way just to see a rock?"

At least when the youth leader led, the others followed. Bina asked if they'd ever heard of heat stroke. Chava shaded her eyes and looked for vultures circling. Bluma commented on what a miracle it would be if Chava could see any birds at all without sweat flooding her eyes.

Mirele took the complaints in stride. "Why can't you have a little trust?" she said. "God keeps taking care of us."

"Yes," said Golda, "but if we'd driven to a restaurant this morning, he wouldn't have to."

Despite the great breakfast they'd had, the girls appeared to consider this. At their age, Mirele supposed, the novelty of going out left a bigger impression than the joys of great food.

Tzipa, however, did not appear as tolerant about the lack of appreciation for her improvised masterpiece. "If you're so thirsty," she snapped at the girls, "spare your throats." She looked over the mix of shocked and mutinous faces. "It's horribly inefficient for everyone to complain at once," Tzipa said. "So I'm going to assign one of you as the General Murmurer. It will be that girl's responsibility to complain on behalf of the group." She looked around. "Out of respect for that person's assignment, I don't want to hear a word from the rest of you!"

The girls considered this idea and seemed to entertain it, if only because none of them had ever before heard of such an attractive calling.

"Choose me!" Chava said. "I'm feeling terrible today, so I'll be the best at it."

"You?" said Bina. "You get distracted too easily. What if we want to complain when you're running off to look at lizard poop?" She turned to Tzipa. "You should choose me. I'm much better at obsessing over problems."

Golda looked at Bina skeptically. "I'm the obvious choice. I do more complaining than any of you."

"But you're the oldest, so you have to be responsible," Bluma pointed out. "Since Chava and Bina can't agree, it should be me. I'm the perfect compromise complainer."

Perla spoke up next, her voice just above a whisper. "I could do it," she said. "Don't forget me."

"What kind of murmurer would you be?" Chava asked. "You're too quiet."

"I'd be the best," Perla said. She straightened her back.

"Because you all wanted to be here. I'm the only one who didn't."

Hearing her daughter say those words, Mirele wanted to take the murmuring assignment herself. She could complain about her daughter's attitude. About the girls who could have been doing more to draw Perla out and help her feel like part of the group. About God for making life so hard, and about the Church for promising families that could be together for eternity while offering so little for ones that were divided over faith right now.

But Tzipa turned to Zusa Cohen. "You," she said. "I choose you. Because a calling should be an opportunity for growth."

And with that, Tzipa walked off behind the rock.

Zusa looked nervously at the other girls. "Um . . . give us some water?" she said in Tzipa's general direction. "So we can get on with our hike?"

Bina rolled her eyes. But before Mirele could see how the others reacted, she remembered that the hose was in her backpack and hurried after Tzipa to the park's water hook-up. They connected the hose and brought it around for everyone to drink from. "You see?" Mirele said. "Blessed are those who thirst, for they shall be comforted."

The girls gulped down some water, but Perla looked confused rather than awed by the object lesson. This, apparently, did not meet her standard for a good moment. Mirele pushed aside her disappointment over that, and over Perla's comment about not wanting to be here, for the next activity. A battle might be just what Perla needed to feel the power of deliverance.

Mirele passed out a small water gun to each of the girls. As the children of Israel had crossed the desert, she explained, the Amalekites attacked them. Now the girls would be the Israelites, while Mirele and Tzipa played as the Amalekites. Since the Amalekites were stronger, the leaders would use the hose. Whichever team was wetter after fifty-two minutes would lose the battle.

Bina looked pointedly at Zusa. She seemed to tremble a little at the thought of raising an objection, but did her best. "That doesn't seem fair?" she said. Chava nodded her encouragement and Zusa pressed on. "Because . . . there are six of us and just two of you?"

Chava groaned.

With God, Mirele said, nothing was impossible. In this particular water fight, for example, there would be one more little rule. Whenever Golda held up her hands, Mirele and Tzipa would turn the hose off. But if Golda's hands got tired and fell down, the leaders would turn the hose on again. If Golda was strong enough, her troops could walk across the battlefield on dry ground.

Mirele was particularly proud of her idea for this activity. It was scriptural. It involved teamwork. It would teach the girls about the importance of supporting their leaders. And the timing was already built into the rules, so it wouldn't get them any further behind.

The girls took up positions in the park and the battle got started. At the beginning, Golda held her hands up high while the girls crept up and shot their leaders. It wasn't long until her arms grew tired, but the girls didn't even give Tzipa time to turn on the hose. Mirele watched with pride and hope as Perla rushed to Golda's side, along with Bina, to help hold up their leader's arms. For the next several minutes, the girls emptied out their squirt guns onto Mirele's and Tzipa's clothes and arms. In the heat of the day, being beaten this way was rather pleasant.

But then disaster struck. The sun was high and hot, standing almost still as it beat down on their heads, when

Bluma and Chava exchanged a look—and started to shoot each other.

"What are you doing?" Golda asked.

"They looked so much more comfortable than us," Bluma said. "And I didn't want to waste all of my water."

Rather than calling them onward to battle, Golda appeared to consider this. "Is getting shot helping?"

"A little," said Chava. "Do you want us to come over and shoot you, too?"

"Yes!" said Bina.

"Please!" said Perla.

And so, without the leaders firing a shot, the tide of the battle began to turn.

"That's a little better," Bina said. "But only a little."

"I want to be wetter," said Perla. "I wish I were soaked."

And then she and Bina looked at each other. And they pulled Golda's hands down.

Well . . . rules were rules. What use were the laws of justice if the leaders didn't follow through? Tzipa turned the hose on. Mirele aimed it. And the daughters of Israel rushed toward them, exulting in their defeat. After a while, Tzipa tilted the hose's stream upward, so that drops rained down more softly, and the girls danced in the makeshift rain. Golda kept her hands firmly in her pockets. Chava leaned back her head to catch and swallow big drops. Bluma and Bina stepped forward and splashed as much water as they could on the others.

"It's too much fun," Zusa complained dutifully. "We can't take much more of this!"

Perla's laughter carried out across the park. For Mirele at least, it was a good moment.

As the sun beat hotter and the minutes ticked down, Mirele felt her torso turn from damp to drenched. She and Tzipa were sweating enough that she thought the battle might still end up as a tie. She wasn't sure there was any lesson in that. But so what? There wasn't always a clear lesson in the scriptures, either, and somehow God's people had muddled through anyway.

When forty-nine minutes had passed, the ground was so wet that the girls discovered they could get a running start and slide across it on their backs. They were filthy: grass-stained, mud-soaked, and gloriously happy about it. Mirele hated to think that in three minutes, it would end.

So she took off her watch and set it down on the rock. She and Tzipa wedged the hose in position to keep spraying and ran off to join the girls, sliding through the afternoon as if they had forever together and no need to watch the time.

She didn't want to be selfish; she knew that everyone was depending on her to complain.

The General Murmurer

Zusa Cohen loved the feeling of mud on her skin. She had lost track of her water gun and didn't care. This was how every battle ought to go: winning and losing forgotten, sides abandoned altogether. After all, who needed a cause on a sunny afternoon?

But no paradise lasts forever. Eden closed up after Eve got hungry; Zusa had just finished a long slide when Bina and Bluma asked her if she could please murmur up a little lunch.

"I don't want them forgetting to feed us," Bina said.

"Or doing anything else weird with the food," Bluma added.

"I'd bring it up myself," said Bina, "but I have too much respect for your general murmurer assignment."

Zusa didn't feel very hungry yet. Thinking about passing on complaints, in fact, she didn't feel hungry at all. But she didn't want to be selfish; she knew that everyone was depending on her to complain. "All right," she said. She looked over at the leaders. They were busy throwing blades of grass at each other. "When they have a minute, I'll bring it up."

Bina gave her a long, skeptical look. "Waiting for the right time to bring something up is not a complaint. That's just a conversation."

Bluma put a hand on Zusa's shoulder. "Since you're new at this, do you want some advice?"

"Please," said Zusa. "I'm good at following instructions."

"Never wait to speak up," Bina said. "And never take no for an answer! If you won't treat your own needs as urgent, what's to stop the world from putting you off forever?"

"Don't be afraid to be dramatic," said Bluma. "Don't just mention that a few people want lunch; march up and ask if they're planning to starve us!"

Zusa was glad to have the support of people who would not only tell her what to say, but how. "Thank you," she told the twins. "I will try to remember that."

Zusa marched up to the leaders before she could forget. Sister Schwartz and Tzipa were still tossing grass at each other when she reached them. They looked so happy, she hated to interrupt. But she remembered a good complainer doesn't wait. Zusa squared her shoulders instead and prepared to be dramatic. "I have a complaint!" she announced.

Sister Schwartz and Tzipa turned away from their grass game. "What is it?" Sister Schwartz asked.

With a leader's attention fixed on her, Zusa felt self-conscious and tongue-tied. It was good that Bluma had given her exact wording to fall back on. "Are you trying to starve us?" Zusa asked.

"No," said Tzipa. She retrieved Sister Schwartz's watch from the top of a nearby rock and her eyes grew wide. "We just lost track of time. Would you like me to cook again? I can try to be quick."

At the thought, Zusa's mouth began to water. But then she remembered that a good complainer never takes no for an answer. "What do you mean, 'no'?" Zusa said. "I'm the complainer and I'm here to demand you say yes."

Tzipa gave her a puzzled look. "I don't understand. Do you mean you want me to say that yes, we are trying to starve you?"

That wasn't it at all, but before Zusa could think of what had gone wrong, Sister Schwartz looked over at the watch and interjected. "It's not that she wants to starve," she said to Tzipa. "Clearly, she's upset about the lost time. We've played so long, we spent all the time that we had planned for lunch. Instead of letting the whole day go, she is asking us to remember our duty and skip ahead with the schedule." Sister Schwartz turned toward Zusa. "The answer is yes. You're right. Call the girls together—it's time to learn from the scriptures about how to treat snakebite."

Zusa was not sure how to respond. Sister Schwartz seemed so proud of her that she didn't have the heart to complain further, but she knew that Bina and Bluma would be disappointed about not getting any lunch. While Sister Schwartz and Tzipa prepared for the next lesson, Zusa went back to deliver the bad news.

"I'm sorry," she told them. Bluma's face fell. Bina's stomach growled. The only comfort she had in the face of her failure was that she had followed their advice. She hadn't waited. She'd been dramatic. And she had refused to take no for an answer.

Golda just sighed. "It's not your fault," she said. "It's easy for leaders to talk people in circles. Do you want some advice?"

Zusa nodded. Bina and Bluma had done their best, but Golda was older. It would be good to have her wisdom.

"Don't be too discouraged when things go wrong. Another moment will come. Just wait for it," Golda said. "And when the moment is right to bring up your complaint, keep it simple."

"How simple?" Zusa asked. "What should I say?"

Golda's forehead wrinkled with concentration. "A good protest should fit into a chant. Something like, 'What do we want? Food. When do we want it? Now.'"

Bina, Bluma, Chava, and Perla all agreed that sounded like a perfect reflection of their heart's desire. Zusa rehearsed the words in her mind.

"Try it again as soon as you see an opening," Golda said.

"Thank you," Zusa said. "I will try to remember that."

What makes a good opening, however, is in the eye of the complainer. Zusa didn't want to end up eating snake, for example, so she waited through the snakebite lesson. That turned into a lot of waiting. Sister Schwartz had put together a long list of scriptures about snakes and snakebites, which they had to look up. Then Tzipa took over with some practical guidance. "Some people think that if you're righteous, snakes won't hurt you," she explained. "But if you're purposely picking up a venomous snake, you're seeking a sign *and* putting God to the test. Those are both sinful, so the snake is probably going to bite." She shrugged. "When it does, don't blame the scriptures and don't blame the snake. You knew what they were when you picked them up." Tzipa taught them that with the bronze serpent melted down, the best thing was to call a doctor. Then she drew bite marks on each of them so they could practice keeping the wound still and lower than the heart, taking off any bracelets, watches, or rings that might get in the way of the body's natural process of swelling, and washing the wound site with soap and water to keep dangerous bacteria out and make the venom do its work alone.

One thing led to another. Once they started washing off their imaginary wound sites, it became clear how much mud the rest of their bodies were still carrying and the hygiene exercise expanded. In the middle of the scrubbing session, Golda gave Zusa a pointed look and gestured toward her mouth. Still, advice was advice—and such a soggy time did not strike Zusa as the ideal moment to ask to eat. Then again, as soon as they were finished washing, it was time to hike back to camp. At the beginning of the hike, Bluma shot Zusa a desperate look. But a hike felt too dusty and dirty to ask about food. By the end of the hike, Bina was shooting her increasingly dark looks, but Zusa remembered Golda's advice and waited for a window of opportunity to arrive.

The moment, apparently, had been waiting at camp the whole time. The other girls, exhausted from the day's activities and the mounting hours of fasting, collapsed in their tents for a rest. But Zusa noticed that the leaders sat down instead, near the ashes of the previous night's fire. She slipped over to join them.

"Excuse me," she said carefully. "But I have another complaint."

"Of course!" said Tzipa. "I'm glad you're thinking about your assignment. What's bothering you?"

"It's simple, really," Zusa said. And she repeated the words she'd held in her mind all afternoon: "What do we want? Food. When do we want it? Now."

"It is almost dinner time," said Sister Schwartz.

"I'm happy to cook again," said Tzipa. "Though it may take a while to build up a fire. Would the girls feel all right about resting a little longer while we wait?"

Lying down at all sounded lovely to Zusa, but she didn't want to stray from her message and get talked in circles again. So she simply repeated the message they'd all agreed on, though a little more quietly this time because she hated to talk back. "What do we want? Food," she whispered. "When do we want it? Now."

"Are you saying you don't want me to cook?" Tzipa asked. "Would you rather eat cold beans from a can?"

Zusa felt terrible for even implying such a thing, but before she could apologize, Sister Schwartz interjected. "I think I understand what our dear murmurer is saying," she told Tzipa. "It's a hot day. Heaven knows we've all done our share of sweating. Zusa realized that fire will only serve to make the evening hot. What's more—burning fuel causes global warming and summer camp is at the wrong time of year to be doing that. It's nothing against good cooking, but she's right. I agree with her. Cold beans are better than a hot night."

"All right then," Tzipa sighed.

Sister Schwartz called the girls back out of their tents at once. Bina looked tired and annoyed. When Tzipa dumped cold beans onto her plate, Perla made a gagging face. But since no one wanted to interfere with Zusa's job, they ate without complaint.

"What do we want?" Zusa ventured when the dinner was done. "A nice, slow-cooked breakfast. When do we want it? Tomorrow."

There are few camping experiences quite like an early-evening telling of scary stories around a not-campfire. Golda went first with a tale about a clown who got more and more lost in the woods because people would run away screaming whenever he tried to ask them for directions. Perla went next and told a story about a haunted tin can that went from tent to tent, attacking sleeping campers to get its cold beans back. Then Bina told a story about a bear.

That reminded Tzipa that she needed to secure the rest of the food extra well in the hopes of making a better meal the next day. She tied it to a smaller branch farther from the center of a tree and suggested that someone make a few traps around the tree to discourage any animal from breaking in a second time. Chava and Zusa volunteered.

As they worked, Zusa shared her heart's worries with Chava. "I'm trying to complain right," she said, "but everything seems to go wrong. If I hadn't said anything, I think we would've gotten lunch. And we definitely would have gotten a better dinner. When I try to speak up, I get so nervous and I don't know what to say."

Chava finished the knots in the trap she was laying. "It's not my job to complain about your complaints," she said. "But I guess I could give you some advice."

Zusa hesitated. "Only if you're sure it's good advice," she said.

Chava laughed. "Then all I can say is that it's hard to decide anything. So maybe next time, you eat first."

Zusa smiled. After a long and hungry afternoon, Chava's advice sounded excellent. "I'll try to remember that," she said.

And then they spent a blissful hour together digging and camouflaging a small spike pit. Zusa hoped no bears or other animals would come back, because she would hate to see an animal hurt. But working with Chava, the spike pit was clearly a labor of love, a work of art with a value all its own.

Far above the heads of the sleeping members of the Chelm ward that night, grand meteorological forces were in action. The evening's breeze, so soft on the cheek, had enough power at high altitudes to carry heavy clouds. And the cooling dark was just enough to convince those celestial travelers to drop their baggage. A few hours before sunrise, raindrops began to pitter-patter—and then pound—on the roofs of the Chelm ward's tents.

Perla was the first to notice. Waking up in a storm was enough to wash her shyness away, and she screamed. That woke Tzipa, and the next thing everyone heard was a string of words Zusa had not expected from a Mormon leader. She bolted from her tent across to Perla's, first aid kit in hand. Sister Schwartz was not far behind her, ready to comfort her daughter in the face of whatever catastrophe had struck. Once she realized that anyone who screamed like that would also surely want to complain, Zusa followed. She zipped up the tent behind her to keep it from flooding.

But the closed door didn't matter. Water was running along the ground and seeping into sleeping bags. "Screaming is for emergencies!" Tzipa was shouting. "If you raise your voice for every little thing, how are we supposed to tell when there's a real problem?" But as far as Zusa could tell, there was a real problem, even if no one had been mauled by a bear. Someone ought to say something, and that person happened to be her.

"It's soaking wet," Zusa said. "We can't sleep like this."

"That's a valid complaint," Tzipa observed.

"Agreed," said Sister Schwartz. She groaned. "After all we've been through, I can't believe we're losing the morning today."

They both looked to Zusa, as if expecting her to tell them what to do next. But Zusa was not sure what to say. Then she remembered Chava's advice. "It's bad to make any decisions on an empty stomach. Before we give up the morning for lost, we have to eat."

Tzipa stared at her. "Now you want me to make something? At this hour? In this weather?"

"This is our moment of opportunity." Zusa told her. "I won't take no for an answer."

Tzipa's shoulders slumped in resignation. "Then I suppose someone better go and get the food down and bring it to me."

Zusa supposed it wouldn't hurt to be someone twice. Chava agreed to come with her.

With the help of a flashlight, the two of them could see centimeters and centimeters in front of their faces. With some experimentation, they were able to find the tree where the food was hanging. Zusa found the bag at roughly the same time Chava found their spike trap. With her foot.

Chava choked back a cry. She bit her lip. For a moment, she just stared at Zusa. "Don't you have *anything* to say about this?" she asked.

"Oh! Yes! Ouch!" Zusa said. "That hurts!" She bent down to inspect the damage to see if she also needed to scream or curse. The thick sole of Chava's shoe had been enough to flatten their improvised wooden spikes, but the pit must have given a painful twist to her ankle. "Can you walk all right?" Zusa asked.

Chava leaned on Zusa for a moment and carefully tested her weight on the foot. "It's not too bad, actually," she concluded. She looked disappointed. "We should have made a better trap."

Zusa was too relieved to feel particularly upset about that. "I'll decide after breakfast whether to complain about us," she promised.

Together, they retrieved the food pack and delivered it to camp. Since fire was out of the question for the moment, Tzipa did her best to offer them a breakfast of bits of damp dried fish and leftover syrup over chunks of cheese.

It was delicious.

After breakfast, Zusa felt clearer. Insight had not exactly distilled on her as the dew—it was more like it was running through her socks (which was, coincidentally, what was happening with the water on the tent floor). "I am tired of trying to get things right and waiting to have a good time," she announced. "If we don't do some more activities right now, I'm going to be really disappointed."

Well? The murmurer had spoken. If she had chosen to worry about boredom instead of the rain, who had any right to say otherwise?

The next several hours went by in a blur of unhinged productivity. Sister Schwartz would never have imagined planning so much in so little time. The girls were able to swim without even leaving their tents. They packed up their things and loaded them into the van in record time. There were other unexpected efficiencies. Tug-of-war, for example, lasted all of 30 seconds. Their fire-building contest ended almost immediately in a draw. And they didn't have to go out on a nature walk to identify five different animals: huddled beneath a tarp, they saw frogs, newts, and several species of worm.

The only thing that the rain made any worse was the afternoon water balloon fight. "Having a water fight was nice yesterday," Zusa admitted, "but I don't want to get wet when I'm already soaked!"

When Perla looked at the large plastic bucket where the water balloons were stored, she had to agree. After all, she reasoned, the balloons were the only thing that prevented the bucket from becoming filled with rainwater completely.

Halfway through the day, when the rain finally slowed to a drizzle and then stopped, the girls devised a service project for each other. It consisted of stringing up improvised clotheslines and pooling whatever dry clothes, towels, or blankets they could find to wear while everything else had a chance to dry. With help from a little gasoline Chava siphoned out of the van's tank, they soon started a roaring fire and basked in its heat.

Around that pillar of fire, the girls held a testimony meeting. Golda bore a lovely testimony about sustaining leaders and then turning into one. Bina expressed thanks to God for somehow sustaining them in the wilderness. Bluma told the story about Jesus saying "Peace, be still," and expressed her hope that someday, his instructions would stick. Perla talked about how much she loved her mom. Chava talked about what a fantastic job God and anyone else involved had done with putting together nature.

And Zusa, moved by the spirit of the day, let loose in a long, meandering rant. She complained about bears who eat campers' food and mosquitoes who eat campers. She complained about hot days and small water guns and mud sliding sessions that end too soon. She complained about the awful responsibility of being the general murmurer, which everyone thought they wanted without grasping the responsibility of bearing the group's burdens. She complained about leaders who think they understand what you're telling them when they're really not listening to you at all. Having built momentum, she moved beyond camp. She went back to her quiet frustrations with her second grade teacher, lingered on a description of her aunt's awful cabbage rolls, and detailed her frustrations with Chelm's transit system. She talked about how sad she found it that a field of dandelions is only beautiful for a week. And about how much she hated that flowers begin to wilt as soon as you put them in a vase—so that the very thing that's supposed to bring you joy reminds you of death. She talked about how tired she was of being the only one at home who ever seemed to properly wash out the coffee pot, even though she had only recently gotten old enough that her parents even let her drink coffee. She narrated the time, at age nine, when she broke out in hives at a friend's birthday party because she was too polite to leave even though she was allergic to their cat, or the time at age six when she wet her pants at school because she kept letting other people go to the bathroom before she took a turn. She confessed that it made her anxious when her parents told her, as they often did, what a sweet and perfect girl she was. She felt buried, she said, under their expectations.

She didn't finish in the name of Jesus Christ, but everyone still said "amen" when she was through.

Zusa felt new and light. Somehow, she had fulfilled the measure of her calling.

Elazar and Shana Cohen kept checking their clock the next afternoon. They'd pace, look out the window. Pace some more. Any minute now, their daughter would be home. With any luck, she'd be holding back tears. She would fall into their arms, and they would tell her it was all right and all was forgiven and they'd never make her go through something like that again.

Finally, a van pulled up. Elazar watched through the blinds while Mirele Schwartz stepped out of the car and helped Zusa get her bags. Then he pretended he hadn't been watching as Zusa came up to the door and let herself in.

She smelled awful. Like smoke and sweat and dirt and damp socks. He was still willing to comfort her, but he thought it would be all right if she took a shower first.

"How was your trip?" Shana asked.

"I complained and complained," Zusa said brightly. "It was the worst experience I've ever loved."

*You had to understand God's purpose to point
out where he had gone inexcusably wrong.*

Hirsh the Atheist

The same week it rained on the girls of the Chelm ward out in the woods, the ceiling of Hirsh's apartment on the top floor of a communist-era building began, once again, to leak. He was half-tempted to let it go. Maybe pull up a chair and watch the water pool on the kitchen floor and run down under the stove, soak the floor, and spill from there into the apartment below. That might wake the Seligs up! Show Fruma the structural issues he contended with. The trouble with the world was that people were always hiding the truth from each other, cushioning the blows, so that humanity was never roused to confront its fate.

But the sound of the dripping water was maddening and the wet spots on the floor were cold. The combined effect made Hirsh miserable. Since misery loves company, he couldn't help but call Fruma Selig up to his apartment. "You see what I live with?" he said, gesturing to the ceiling. "It's bad enough to have that miser for a landlord on a good day, but this? If the rain keeps up through the night, I might drown while making breakfast. But what can I do?"

Since she was too tone-deaf to catch the rhetorical nature of his question, Fruma answered. "It seems to me that we should patch up the ceiling. Or better yet: patch up the roof, which is leaking onto the ceiling. Or, still better: the sky, which is leaking onto the roof." She paused, considering. "But in the meantime, we might at least find a cup to catch the water."

The trouble with Fruma was that she was always coming up with these pointless half-measures. As she looked for a cup, Hirsh decided to see if he could get under her skin. "Surely the best thing would be to patch up your God," he said. "If he would stop taking a leak on us ordinary people all the time, we could leave the sky and the roof and the ceiling open and be fine."

Fruma found a teacup and placed it on the floor, just so, to catch the next drips. "You really are an example to me," she told Hirsh as she worked. "I'm a believer—and all I can think of is how we ought to get a cup. Even though you don't believe in God, all it takes is a few drops from the ceiling and he's instantly on your mind. And the way you blaspheme: it's like you really care what he thinks." She shook her head. "I still don't understand why the bishop wouldn't just let you convert. In your own way, you're as committed as any of us."

Hirsh sighed. "I hope you all freeze in outer darkness," he said. But his insides ached. It had been years since that decision, but the reminder still hurt. He could feel it as surely as an arthritic can sense the coming rain.

How did it come about that Hirsh sat in Bishop Levy's office, seeking permission to become a Mormon? It's a long story. One to save for a rainy day.

It started like this: By the time the Church came to Chelm, Hirsh was already tired of being an atheist Jew. In his grandfather's day, maybe, that had been enough to keep life interesting, but times had changed. A Jewish atheist born in Hirsh's time was so late to the party that the cake had all been eaten and even the streamers taken down. Besides, it was too easy to reject the Jewish God, what with all the suffering and the Messiah not coming until he slowly ran out of plausible excuses for the delay. It was almost as easy, frankly, as rejecting the Christian God—for moonlighting as a Messiah and getting himself killed while leaving the world self-evidently unredeemed.

But for all his boredom with the philosophical simplicity of the position, Hirsh could not give up his atheism. It was what he believed, in every corner of his unrepentant heart. It was who he was. So when the Mormons came to town, Hirsh thanked the fortunate yet utterly random coincidence. He decided to become an atheist Mormon, however briefly, for the intellectual exercise. If he managed to upset someone in the process, so much the better.

He started with the missionaries. After posing a few basic questions about their faith's purported history, he could tear it to shreds in his mind. A temple? A martyrdom? An exodus? The whole thing was obviously plagiarized from the Bible. Even the names sounded fake, shot off without thought. He had to work to remember the shockingly bland name "Joseph Smith." And the ripped-off version of the Dead Sea in their stories? It was called, with the special kind of imagination it takes to evoke a total lack of imagination, the "salt lake." When pressed for details about their own backgrounds, one missionary said that he was from a town called "Lehi"—probably having forgotten that he'd already told Hirsh that Lehi was the name of a prophet the Book of Mormon was supposedly all about. As far as the evidence was concerned, Hirsh had heard enough. The whole thing was a sloppy fraud. He doubted that Utah existed in any meaningful way.

But Hirsh knew that lasting atheism must be grounded in more than mere implausibility. Most people enjoyed believing in God too much to be dissuaded by an anachronism here or an idiocy there. No one could tell you where Sinai was, for example, but in the face of decision paralysis, people still liked the idea of God handing down rules. Like a viewer who will search an obviously fabricated play for a deeper kind of truth, religious people were all too happy to suspend their disbelief. That's why it wasn't enough to call the veracity of a sacred story into question: a true atheist needed strong reasons to actively reject God.

For that, it seemed to Hirsh, you had to study theology. You had to understand God's purpose to point out where he had gone inexcusably wrong. And so it was that Hirsh set aside the question of whether Mormonism made rational sense so that he could pursue the question of how the faith made sense of a frankly unreasonable world.

The cup Fruma placed on the floor filled in less time than it had taken Hirsh to see through the missionaries' story. But with the thick-headed optimism so cherished in her faith, she refused to give up. Instead, she fetched a pitcher, emptied the cup into it, and set the cup down again to catch the next drops. "It will take a little work to keep the cup emptied," she admitted. "But I suppose it's still easier than convincing Oskar to pay for repairs."

Hirsh snorted. "In any sane belief system, that man's existence would be enough to disprove God's," he pointed out. Why, after all, would an all-powerful and all-good being create a universe with Oskar the Miser in it? The thought boggled the mind and offended the heart's sense of justice. To sidestep a moral problem on the scale of the world's misers, a belief system would have to resort to some truly wild steps. Such as, for example, calling each human being co-eternal with God, thereby reducing the Almighty's responsibility for the crime of creation. (It wasn't the most elegant solution. To save God, Mormons had to imagine a universe in which Oskar the Miser had always existed. It was strange enough to imagine the grouchy old man as a tight-fisted baby. Stranger still to imagine him as a wispy premortal spirit, eagerly waiting for a body so he could experience material avarice. Or as an eternal intelligence, accepting the offer of a First Estate only because it sounded like an investment.)

"We shouldn't judge another person just because they happen to sin differently than we do," Fruma Selig said. "So Oskar is greedy and narrow-hearted and callous. Who isn't once in a while? I admit that his lack of charity looks worse than your blasphemy or my self-importance, but in God's eyes, the whole world must be filled with fools. We shouldn't consider ourselves too clever for picking out one man's faults."

Fruma's charitable attitude, however, was not enough to keep the ceiling from dripping. With a *plink, plink, plunk,* the cup kept filling up.

Hirsh tried to devise a devastating response to Fruma, but the sound was driving him to distraction. "I don't think I'm clever for picking out any particular man's faults," he said. "What makes me clever is my ability to pick out God's faults. The Almighty's decision not only to tolerate some people, but also to use them in his work, happens to be an example." It was, in Hirsh's estimation, also the most damning example in a Latter-day Saint worldview. Mormons had an easier time accepting a bad world if they could believe in a good Church. Take that away and they started to struggle.

But Fruma just emptied the cup into the pitcher again. "This repair isn't working quite yet," she said. "Keep an eye on the cup. I'm going to get something to keep the pitcher from overflowing."

Hirsh breezed through the missionaries' lessons at first. He wasn't looking for a thing to reject just yet: those were everywhere. He was looking for what set the Mormon message apart. For a group that wanted people to leave other religions to join theirs, though, they were terribly indirect about getting there.

The missionaries told Hirsh that God loves us and wants us to be happy, just like any other holy man since Hosea, and without any particular explanation of how landlords and cancer served that aim. They taught him that Jesus saves us, making clear that he hadn't come to save anyone from the Roman Empire and its terrible brutality, but rather from such awful pleasures as coffee and wine. They explained that God communicates through modern prophets, while implying that the role of such a prophet was to wear a conservative suit while repeating basically the same things God had purportedly been talking about from the beginning of history.

It was all so dull that Hirsh almost missed the theological ju-jitsu, the tiny twists that turned everything on its head. Like when the missionaries mentioned Eve in passing, by way of illustrating some larger point, and seemed to be praising her.

"I thought she wasn't supposed to take the fruit," Hirsh said. Wasn't the whole point of that ancient story to explain suffering by proving that we deserve it?

"She wasn't supposed to, but she was wise enough to realize she needed to," Elder Lehi said. "After all, if she hadn't taken the fruit, we wouldn't exist."

Hirsh was puzzled. This was the Bible's ground floor. You couldn't just go and edit Genesis, could you? He shook his head. It didn't make sense. "But if she needed to take the fruit, why did God ask her not to?"

Elder Lehi's companion, who was from Lagos, shrugged. "If he told her exactly what to do, she wouldn't have had the chance to figure it out and decide for herself, would she? The whole point of coming to earth is so we can learn and grow." He glanced at Elder Lehi, who nodded. "We've got a diagram here we can walk you through. See, before the world was created, we were talking with God about this plan. We call it the Plan of Happiness ..."

After that, it was hard for Hirsh to keep up. It turned out that if you took a right turn instead of a left out of Eden, the whole map changed. It soon became clear that Mormonism offered a novel view of God for Hirsh to reject.

Classic divine failures, like the problem of evil, didn't play out the same way on that landscape of belief. Obsession with agency, experience, and progression made it far too easy for Mormons to let God off the hook for the mess of the world they lived in.

Normally, Hirsh would start an argument against a faith by identifying a basic paradox. Good God, bad world. True scripture, flawed passage. Prophetic calls for justice, obnoxious religious reactionaries. But where to start in a community where people smilingly embraced contradictions? The missionaries were utterly indifferent to opposed pairs. "It must needs be that there is an opposition in all things," their Book of Mormon said. Eternal glory involved receiving all heights and depths. God guaranteed freedom and expected conformity. For heaven's sake, they spoke with reverence about a place called Liberty Jail!

To really pierce this system of thought from the inside, Hirsh would need something new. It would be a challenge, an interesting challenge. His heart raced with such anticipation that the missionaries initially assumed that he had felt the Holy Ghost. But Hirsh was not experiencing any divine haunting. He felt eager, exhilarated: the hunt had begun.

Shortly after wandering off to protect the pitcher, Fruma Selig reappeared with an umbrella. "This ought to help," she said, opening it over the pitcher and cup. Sure enough, as the ceiling leaked, the dishes stayed dry. But once again, the floor got wet.

"You're just moving the problem around," Hirsh complained. "If I enjoyed wet socks, I wouldn't have come down to see you in the first place."

Fruma sighed. "At least moving gives a person something to do," she said. "I'd rather wander a little in the wilderness than sit around in Egypt. But maybe we haven't moved enough yet." She looked up at the umbrella and considered the problem.

"It's doing the exact opposite of what we want," Hirsh said. "Instead of gathering the water, it's scattering it."

"Opposites can be useful," Fruma said as she flipped the umbrella upside-down. "There. Let the gathering begin."

Suddenly, instead of sliding out along the exterior, the droplets began sliding inward to pool at the umbrella's center. Reluctant as he was to acknowledge it, Hirsh admitted to himself that Fruma had stumbled onto something: the umbrella would be able to hold a great deal more water than the cup. It was still a temporary solution—but in the face of entropy, what wasn't?

"Thank you," Hirsh said. "At least, for as long as this lasts."

After he met the missionaries, it hadn't taken long for Hirsh to discover the limits of their usefulness. It wasn't only that they were young. There was also the trouble of missionaries being moved from one place to another too soon to really get to the meat of questions. The elder from Lagos left and his replacement, who came from Lyons, just repeated the same points in a different order. To create in himself a genuine crisis of Mormon faith, Hirsh realized he would have to go to Church.

He was surprised at how much he liked it. The people were mostly fools, but they were friendly. His neighbor Fruma was there. There was Isaac Peretz, who used to talk politics with Hirsh while they were in line at the corner store. Menachem Menasche, whom he often ran into at the library (sometimes literally, since they both liked to read and walk at the same time). He saw his favorite baker and a decent fisherman. They would ask him how he was doing. They would listen to his complaints.

He didn't love everything, of course. But opposites can attract, and Hirsh felt that some aspects of the faith were almost exact opposites of something truly revolutionary. In Mormonism, for example, God spoke to the church through the prophet. If they'd just switched the order around, so that the prophet would call up God with complaints about the universe from the members of the Church, the faith might have done a lot of good in the world.

To be the sort of change he wanted to see in the ward, he decided one month to get up on fast Sunday and bear an untestimony. It was heartfelt but awkward that first time, a rough profession of his general atheism. But the ward members were tolerant and cheered him on as he gradually picked up how such things were supposed to go. Month by month, as he attended sacrament meeting, Sunday School, and elders quorum, his expressions of disbelief grew more specifically Mormon. Instead of only expressing disbelief in God, for example, he learned to also acknowledge the Book of Mormon as a fraud and the Church as corrupt. He started tossing in an occasional reference to his indifferent feelings toward his own scattered family, and even read enough to relate a sordid story or two about the pioneers.

These experiments were hardly complete. In a sense, Hirsh was still going through the motions, riding the momentum of his old convictions. He was feeling out the topics but hadn't yet settled on how to best reject the new faith on its own terms. Still, he did not give up. He asked and he read. He would ponder, if not pray.

One month on Fast Sunday, Hirsh felt himself all but propelled from the pew to the stand. The cause was a random insight, which nonetheless seemed to enter his mind with a prototypically Mormon force. He had been reflecting, he told the ward, on Lorenzo Snow's couplet: "As man is, God once was. / As God is, man may become." And then a thought from Feuerbach had been drawn to his remembrance: "God did not create man; man created God."

Fruma smiled brightly when he said that. She looked so proud of him, of how Mormon he was becoming.

That week, the Sunday School lesson happened to be about Ruth. The story wasn't new to Hirsh, except in the sense that against the background of Mormonism, all things seemed to be. Listening to class members discuss the first chapter, Hirsh suddenly found himself weeping without understanding why. As soon as church was over, he made his way to Bishop Levy's office and asked if he could sit down. The bishop immediately welcomed him in.

Speaking spontaneously, Hirsh expressed his wish to become a member of the Church. "I want this people to be my people," he said. His heart was pounding. "And your God is the God I want to not believe in."

But Bishop Levy shook his head. "I hope you always feel welcome here," he said. His face was all sympathy, but his next words were a knife. "But if you don't even *want* to believe in God, I can't let you be baptized into the Church."

Well? Hirsh was crushed. Almost he had felt at home here. The beliefs played tricks on you like that. The place for Zion's tent was to be enlarged, spread among the nations, they said. But the stakes in the tent wall were strengthened against him. He could come, yes, but the faith belonged to the Church. No matter how much he read the Book of Mormon, no matter how much he learned about the history, no matter how well he learned to speak their strange language or let himself dream their strange dreams, he would never truly be a Latter-day Saint outside the Church's fixed borders.

He could feel a heaviness settle across his chest. This, he realized bitterly, was the secret he'd been hunting for. Mormonism was more than a set of beliefs. It was an attitude. A reckless commitment to human potential, a certain irrational optimism about the value of a broken world. A wild initial embrace of the stranger who happened to stop in. But everything has its opposite: a faith that could *include* could also *exclude*. And in that, he discovered his driving reason for rejecting the Mormon god.

The umbrella made a beautiful bowl at first. But things can only be wrested so far from their design, and it was made to keep water out, not in. At the center of what was normally the umbrella's top was a plastic cover that kept any water from seeping down along the umbrella's stem. But from the inside, there was no cover and the seal was not quite watertight. As the umbrella filled, water began to weep slowly out of the center.

"It's useless," Hirsh muttered. "I should have known it would be useless. There's nothing quite so stupid as wanting a thing to work." He kicked over the cup, which was still sitting half-full on the floor. "If our useless landlord were called as bishop, would you still believe then?" he asked Fruma.

"I wouldn't be excited," she said. "But I don't see what that has to do with belief. And I don't see what my beliefs have to do with this rain."

Beliefs had everything to do with the rain. The rain, Hirsh figured, was probably the world's oldest theological question. Older than Elijah, and old as Noah. Why was the rain never there when you needed it—and why did it never stop when you'd had enough? "What if Oskar were called as the prophet?" he asked. "He's old enough. Male enough. Opinionated enough. What if God said: that's three for three on qualifications! I'd like to make him my mouthpiece. Would you still trust your God then?"

"You're not very good at being kind when you're frustrated," Fruma said. "You'll feel better when we fix this and your house gets warm and dry."

"My house?" Hirsh said. "Not really. He owns the building, and I don't think he cares that we live here."

There was cold, wet water spilled across the floor and a slow leak still dripping from the ceiling. It could drive a man insane. Hirsh knew he had to get out, get away from it all. And so, before Fruma could say something reassuring, Hirsh stormed out, slamming the door behind him. He stormed down the stairs, and out through the building's aging, Communist-era front doors into the dark of the night.

For a long time, he stood outside in the rain.

Well? God lets it fall on the just and the unjust.

Slowly, Hirsh felt his shirt soaking and his nerves softening. He turned around. Went back into the building, up the stairs. Into his apartment.

Fruma had borrowed the hose from his washing machine. She'd gone up into the crawlspace above the ceiling and left the umbrella there, upside down, with one end of the hose attached to the center. She'd threaded the other end down and strung it across the ceiling, until it came to a stop above a space on the counter where she'd put the pitcher. The pitcher had filled, and now dripped out into the cup. Fruma had placed a folded napkin under one side of the cup so that it leaned just a little forward and dripped into the sink. The water pooled in the bottom of the sink, then slid drop by drop down the drain. From there, it would pass through the pipes, from the pipes to the sewers, from the sewers to the river, and from the river to the sea. From the sea, it would evaporate into the clouds until it fell somewhere as rain. She'd also wiped up the floor, so for now at least, it was dry.

"I'll call Oskar tomorrow," Fruma said. "He might finally call someone to fix it. You never know."

Hirsh was pretty sure he did know. But for her sake, just this one night, he could let the tiniest part of himself hope.

Before Shayna, he used to feel like the more you worried about things, the smarter your decisions would be. If there wasn't a little anguish, you weren't working hard enough to deserve the best outcome.

Yoked

For a few months after Stefan Krause was sealed for time and all eternity to Shayna Selig in the Freiberg temple, he felt like he was on a free-fall through bliss. It lasted after the temple sealing and the evening of dancing, after their first night together (and together, and then together once more), lasted after they went on their celebratory trip to the Baltic coast and returned to an apartment in Leipzig where they would make their first home, after they settled into a routine of warm morning kisses followed by remarkably mundane days at work. Lasted until sometime around the day when Stefan's boss's boss's boss called him in for a one-on-one meeting.

"I hear you got married this year. Congratulations," the crisply dressed executive said. Stefan wondered if having a wedding was truly so unusual as to merit this level of attention. But he just said, "Thank you."

The executive poured him a glass of carbonated water. "I also heard she's from Chelm."

"That's right," Stefan said. He was mildly surprised that particular fact had been noticed, let alone circulated.

"She was born there?" the executive asked. "I mean, she has local roots?"

Stefan nodded.

"Does she miss it?" the executive asked.

Stefan searched his recent memories with her and smiled. "We're quite happy here."

The executive leaned back in his chair. "We own a small mining operation in Chelm—one that's important to our larger supply lines—and a position has opened up. We could use someone with your talents there."

Stefan took a slow drink of his water to give his mind a moment to catch up. In a setting like this, he didn't want to give the impression of being unwilling to do what the firm needed. But he also had a feeling there was probably a catch. They were hoping to move him to a lower, Polish salary, maybe? Or had he upset someone here? "My talents?" he asked.

The executive sat forward again. "I'll be frank. We've struggled with Chelm. There's a . . . different culture . . . in that office. We've had a string of bad luck retaining transferred talent. But there's no easy way around the need." Even though Stefan wasn't far into his water, the executive leaned over to refill his cup. "I don't expect you to stay forever, of course. You could choose to transfer back here after two years, if you'd like." He gave Stefan a long, appraising look. "I can offer you a raise. And I should mention that we view the Chelm post as a prime growth opportunity for future management candidates. Someone who can succeed there shows us they can succeed any-where." He paused. "Give it some thought?"

In words, it all seemed fine. But something about the executive's eager tone left Stefan feeling unsettled. And he had to consider the opinion of his mother-in-law, Fru-ma Selig; if he and Shayna moved to Chelm, she would be more delighted than he felt entirely comfortable with. "Obviously, I'll need to talk it over with my wife," Stefan said. "But I'll let you know soon."

"Please do," the executive said. He stood and offered his hand. "It's been a pleasure visiting with you."

On his way home that evening, Stefan picked up a chick-en döner for Shayna and a halloumi döner for himself. If he and Shayna decided the offer was good news, this could be a sort of celebration. If not? There were worse ways to smother troubles and sorrows. Between bites, he told Shayna the whole strange story of how his work had turned promising and fraught over the course of a single meeting. "What do you think?" he asked her. "Do we take it, or do I find a polite way to turn the offer down?"

"How do you feel about it?" she asked.

"I don't know." He frowned. "I guess it makes sense."

Her eyes seemed to focus for a moment on his forehead before she made eye contact again. "Sense? Who said any-thing about sense?" She waved a hand, which happened to have the remainder of her döner in it. The smell of fresh Turkish bread, roasted chicken, and spicy sauce hit his nostrils and calmed his nerves. "I asked how you feel."

She was right, of course. There was the Holy Ghost to think about; they didn't have to do what made sense. Stefan took a deep breath and tried to listen to his gut. But it was no use: his gut was thoroughly occupied with dinner. "I don't know that, either." He tapped his head. "Too much clutter in the way."

Shayna set her food down. "Then let's get your head cleaned up and organized. We'll talk a little more, and I'll make a list of the pros and a list of the cons. Then we'll talk through the lists like sensible people. After that, we'll throw the lists in the garbage and I'll count to three. When I get to three, we each say what we feel: yes or no. If what we say matches, that's what we should do."

"And if it doesn't match?"

She smiled. Her eyes flicked toward his forehead again; it was a strange habit of hers. Then she took his hand. "If it doesn't match, you're probably wrong. But I love you anyway."

Her eyes sparkled. Everything seemed simpler when she talked about it. He wasn't used to living like that. Before Shayna, he used to feel like the more you worried about things, the smarter your decisions would be. If there wasn't a little anguish, you weren't working hard enough to deserve the best outcome. And then, at a young adult conference, he'd met her. She showed him that sometimes life could be easy—even if it was still completely confusing.

So they talked. He started with the straightforward, almost mathematical parts: better pay, lower cost of living, the carrot of career advancement. She chimed in with how she loved their apartment, while also mentioning that any place in Chelm would put her a full twelve hours closer to her family. He thought about the old Chelm travel brochures Fruma had given him, but decided not to bring up his irrational fear about giving his mother-in-law what she wanted. Instead, Stefan talked about how his boss's boss's boss sounded almost desperate. And about how he didn't trust his own desire to please the office if there was something wrong with the Chelm assignment.

Through it all, Shayna would periodically jot down a line here or there. But when Stefan glanced across the table at the paper to review what they'd covered so far, her lists seemed a little mixed up.

"Hold on," he said. "Why is 'we just moved here' listed under the pros column?"

"I already told you," Shayna said. "This is our first place together. It has beautiful memories for me."

"I don't understand . . . why is that a reason to leave Leipzig and go to Chelm?"

Shayna answered slowly, as if breaking down a basic concept for a small child. "If we leave now, our first place together will have only happy memories. Then, if things get bad later, we'll always be able to think about how happy we were in our first apartment."

Stefan wouldn't have thought of it like that, but he understood how it could be nice to have a sentimental place. "That makes sense," he said. "But why is 'Stefan just wants to make his boss happy' on the pro list?"

She gave him a dreamy smile. "It's cute how you're always thinking about other people. I like that about you."

"But I only brought it up because it might be getting in the way of my judgment."

She shrugged. "Service is good. If you're taking a work assignment no one else wants, that makes life easier for your coworkers. And you'll be happier knowing that you're doing them a favor."

Stefan wasn't sure he always thought about work that way, but it was something to aspire to. "So you think we should go to Chelm because none of my coworkers want to and because we just moved into our apartment here?" Once the words came out of his mouth, the reasoning seemed broken, even though he knew he had just accepted each of those points on its own.

"I don't know yet if I feel like we should go," Shayna said. "Right now, it's just a pro list and a con list, because you wanted to clear your head."

"If that's the pro list," he asked, "what's on the list of cons?"

Stefan pulled the paper in front of him and puzzled over her notes.

"Why did you put being close to your family down as a disadvantage?" he asked.

"Because I love them," Shayna said. "The only people more important to me than my mother and sister are you—and our heavenly parents, of course."

He scratched his head. He knew this about her. He admired these strong bonds of love. But he felt deeply disoriented now about exactly how those bonds worked. "What does that have to do with living here?" he asked.

Shayna gave him that elementary-school-teacher look again. "Absence makes the heart grow fonder." She picked up the last of her döner, then seemed to notice that he wasn't understanding yet. "That's why we came to earth, isn't it? To be away from our heavenly home? If that's reason enough to take on mortality—well, Germany isn't half as bad."

She took a bite of her food. Stefan felt a strange guilt as he thought about how he'd brought her, for all intents and purposes, to start their marriage out in the lone and dreary world, when to him it was just the same old Saxony.

He tucked that thought in his heart and looked back down at the paper. "All right," he said. "But why is cost of living on your cons list?"

Shayna put a hand over her mouth to be polite, but spoke before she finished chewing. "Because sacrifice brings blessings. If lower prices make us more rich, we'll be less blessed. That's just mathematics."

Stefan didn't even try to process, because he'd noticed the next item. He wanted to be reasonable, but this one made him feel attacked. "What about my opportunities for advancement?" he asked. "Surely, that should be good. Can I move it at least to the pro list?"

Shayna shook her head. "It's very dangerous. Do you want to be married to me or to your job?" She took a napkin and wiped the corners of her mouth. "I am ready to support you, whatever we do. But the scriptures say to count the cost. And little promises, bits of praise ... that's how they get you. The most dangerous part of any trap is the bait."

The defensiveness Stefan had felt melted away beneath his wife's words. She had left her world to be with him, and he was all she expected in return. He crumpled up the paper and tossed it toward the paper recycling bin. It bounced on the edge, flew up, and fell in.

"My head is clear," he said. "Let's count."

One, they said. Two. Three.

"Let's take it," Shayna said. At the exact same time Stefan said "Chelm."

And so it was that Stefan found himself, a few weeks later, standing in the back of a small moving truck beside President Gronam, Yossel the Fisherman, Lazar the Blind Beggar, and a deacon named Gimpel. He and Shayna didn't yet have very much to move, so the humble turnout should have been plenty. Before long, though, he felt like it was at least three people too many.

When he and Yossel picked up the dresser, President Gronam shouted for them to put it back down. "Never lift with your knees," he told them. To spare their backs, he had them try again and again until all the movement was in their legs. Even empty-handed, squats are real exercise. Though the dresser was not too heavy, Stefan was beginning to feel winded by the time they got out of the truck.

He came back down to find piles of his books removed from their boxes and set on the shelves. "What are you doing?" he asked President Gronam.

"Those boxes were too heavy: even the strongest knees can pop," President Gronam said. "Since you'll only have to unpack up there anyway, I thought I'd give you a head start." He crouched down to use his leg muscles as he lifted an empty box. "You see? Now, it's no strain at all."

While President Gronam carried the box, Lazar grabbed a few books and took them. Stefan supposed it was just as well for him to clean up after the president. It would be best if the blind elder were not carrying the heaviest furniture anyway.

While Yossel stopped for a drink of water, Stefan looked around for Gimpel. If the two of them could carry the empty bookcase up together, it was possible that the books might end up on it rather than scattered across the floor. But the deacon was nowhere to be found. Stefan looked left and he looked right. He started to wonder if Gimpel had gotten bored and gone home.

Then Stefan happened to glance up. Hanging off the

front of their new building was Shayna's nightstand. And above it, looking down from the window as he tugged at an improvised pulley system, was Gimpel.

Stefan ran helplessly toward the nightstand as it swayed unsteadily upward. "What are you doing?" Stefan shouted.

"Avoiding the stairs," Gimpel called back.

"Are you crazy?" Stefan shouted. "Let it down!"

"Are you crazy?" Gimpel shot back. "Do you want it to fall and break?"

There wasn't anything Stefan could say to that. He stepped back a safe distance and watched it rise and held his breath while Gimpel tugged it awkwardly through the window.

"You see?" Gimpel said. "That worked fine. What's next?"

"Taking the stairs," Stefan said firmly.

By then, Yossel was ready to help. After their experience with the dresser, Stefan and Yossel made sure to lift in the safest way—which was to do so only when President Gronam wasn't looking. While they worked, Yossel shared an old business idea. During a move, the idea had come to him to develop a single piece of furniture which could fill all a family's needs without requiring a thing of the elders quorum.

Imagine a bed, Yossel said, which could be adjusted to different heights. Raised up and stripped of its mattress in the morning, it could be a table. But the table would be made of six separate sections fastened together, so that after breakfast, two could be removed to use as chairs while the other four were raised still higher to use as a desk. For extra comfort, of course, the mattress would also be made of six separate pieces, which could be used as chair cushions during the day. At meals, the chairs could become a table again, and at night, a bed.

"If the chairs are part of the table," Stefan asked, "where would you sit while eating?"

Yossel considered the problem. "I hadn't thought of that," he confessed. "Maybe you could sit first and eat later, or eat first and then sit."

"It might be hard to convince people to do that," Stefan pointed out. "So many like to sit and eat at the same time."

Yossel thought some more. "I've got it!" he said. "We'll make the table legs removable. That way, you can set the table low enough to sit quite comfortably on the floor!"

Stefan admitted he still had his doubts about the product, but Yossel assured him there would be no hard feelings between them. It was best to keep church and business separate. Because Stefan was a ward member now, he wouldn't make a proper customer anyway.

To be fair, Stefan and Shayna's table and chairs and desk and bed took more than one trip. But before long, almost everything was in the apartment. The end table was there, and the bookshelf was there, and the empty boxes that had once stored the books were there.

Only a few of the books themselves were. Apparently, Lazar the Blind Beggar had lost count of floors and doors, so many of the books were in other apartments in the building. Stefan was a little taken aback, but Shayna tapped her forehead and said it was all right. Lazar had done them a service; his deliveries meant that she and Stefan could meet the new neighbors without having to come up with an excuse to introduce themselves.

Within a few weeks, Stefan found himself wishing the rest of his life could go as smoothly as that move. Grocery shopping was overwhelming, public transit perplexing, and work a total nightmare. The budgeting process between the teams somehow involved barter? So Stefan, being unprepared, ended up without the funding his first project would need. It took hours to make sense of his email. He would read a message again and again, trying to follow a coworker's line of reasoning until he found himself walking over to the sender and talking in circles until he could spiral in on what was actually going on. And the lead engineer for the mine—oh, save the innocent from that man!—the lead engineer for the mine was an elderly madman named Reuben Goldberg, who had found the most circuitous possible solutions to adopt in every one of his designs and refused to consider alternatives. No matter what Stefan tried, no one was willing to consider a change to the wildly idiosyncratic ways they did business.

By each weekend, Stefan was desperate for a break. Unfortunately, the weekends started with a Friday night family dinner with his mother-in-law, Fruma, his sister-in-law, Leeba, and Leeba's husband, Noam. It was nice to see Shayna happy there, but the dinner traditions only added to Stefan's sense of disorientation.

For example, at the beginning of the evening, Leeba would light the candles—then immediately cover her eyes. Now that this was to be a regular part of his life, Stefan made the mistake of asking why you'd go to the trouble of making light only to put yourself into artificial darkness. Shayna tried to explain why this made sense—something about how you should only benefit from the light after saying the blessing, but you shouldn't say the blessing until after the work of lighting the candles was done. It was such strange Chelm logic, Stefan decided not to try too hard to follow it. Or, for that matter, anything else he heard that night. If anyone noticed his mind was drifting and asked what was wrong, he had a simple defense: following Chelm reasoning was a kind of work that really ought to be forbidden on the Jewish Sabbath!

The first test of his resolve came almost immediately. Leeba asked how he was doing, and he admitted that the week at work had left him feeling less than sane. She smiled sympathetically and began to tell him an old story she thought would be helpful. The story was about a prince who believed he was really a rooster. This prince stripped off his royal robes, abandoned his room to settle under the table, and would only eat by pecking at scraps set for him on the floor. Naturally, this was a great distress to his mother the queen and his father the king. From every corner of the land, they called healers to explain the problem and offer a cure. But the doctors left—some pecked, some scratched, and some just exasperated.

Finally, a rabbi arrived who understood what needed to be done. He stripped off his clothes, squatted under the table, and bent his neck to eat scraps off the floor.

"Ah," said the prince, "how good to meet a fellow rooster!"

"Agreed," said the rabbi. "Since I left my coop, I've missed the companionship of my fellow birds."

For days, they pecked at food together. They strutted together. And they talked together. One day it was cold; the rabbi took the end of a servant's scarf in his teeth, pulled it down, and wrapped it around himself.

"What are you doing?" the prince said. "I thought you were a rooster like me!"

"Of course I am a rooster," the rabbi said, affronted. "Should it make me any less a rooster if I happen to steal a scarf?"

"Of course not," the prince said. "I'm very sorry."

Well, the next day the rabbi stole another scarf and offered it to the prince. "Would it make you any less a rooster to accept this gift?" the rabbi asked.

"What are you suggesting?" the prince replied. "How could it? I'm certainly no less a rooster if I happen to wear a piece of human clothing."

The day after that, the rabbi began to wear a shirt, and the next day pants, and so on until the both of them were living under the table fully clothed—and no less roosters for doing so.

Another morning, the rabbi slept in. The prince felt bored all by himself. Because he was a more devoted than thoughtful friend, he let himself eat his feelings and finished all the scraps before the rabbi got up.

"Forgive me," the prince said when the rabbi saw that the tray under the table was empty. "You must be hungry. That's my fault. But I'll make it up to you."

"Don't worry," the rabbi said. "I wouldn't be any less of a rooster if I looked a little more widely for food." He stretched his neck, and his arms, and his legs, then he walked out to the kitchen and returned with a warm meal—on a human plate—and sat at the table.

"What are you doing?" the prince asked. "Eating at the table is for human beings!"

"Am I any less a rooster if I take their place?"

The prince considered. "No," he said. "I suppose you're not." And so the prince joined the rabbi for dessert.

Over the next week, the rabbi asked the prince if a rooster would be any less himself if he slept in a bed, or rode a horse, or wrote a letter, or managed affairs of state. And each time, the rooster prince assured his friend that a rooster was a rooster, no matter what.

Before long, Leeba said, the rooster prince was pre-pared to act just like any king. So the rabbi wished him farewell and went off to tend, once more, to the coop he had come from.

Stefan considered the story a long time. "Are you say-ing that work will be easier if I find a way to get on my coworkers' level?"

Leeba looked back at him, confused. "You told me you're feeling crazy. I'm saying that a little insanity never kept anyone from being king."

On the walk home, Shayna asked if he remembered the old Chelm story about the king and the tainted harvest. Stefan didn't, but he also felt that one tale had given him enough to think about already. "Is that the one where they went to the fields and pecked them clean?" he asked. Shayna looked at his forehead, shook her head, and laughed. Then she kissed him and he lost all interest in old Jewish stories.

That Sunday, though, Stefan tried to follow the fic-tional rabbi's example as well as he could. In sacrament meeting, he sang from the wrong hymn. He kept his eyes open during the closing prayer—and discovered that half the ward did, too. In elders quorum, the lesson involved the faith of the pioneers, and devolved into a discussion of their oxen. Stefan not only took it in stride, but spoke of his gratitude for being yoked with Shayna. "Together," he said, "we will make it across these dreary prairies to the promised land."

"Are you moving to Israel?" Aaron Cohen asked.

"Or do you mean Utah?" Menachem Menashe added.

"I mean here," Stefan said. "I think Chelm is where God is leading me. But it's been such a hard week at work. Even though I'm here, I'm not sure I've arrived yet."

The whole quorum nodded sagely, as if he'd made perfect sense. "I know exactly how you feel," Heshel said. He put a gentle hand on Stefan's shoulder—and for a moment, Stefan felt almost as though he was being blessed.

The gesture gave him courage. The next day in the office, he went into the budget meeting and traded his stapler for extra project funds. He skimmed his email and then followed the conventions of a stream-of-consciousness novel in his reply. When he met with Reuben, he pointed out a way they could make the design just a few steps more complicated. Reuben actually thanked him for the advice!

One whole week went by that way, and then another. Stefan made friends. He wasn't sure if he was making any progress—it was hard to tell, given that he was moving more or less at random—but the rhythms of his day had a feeling that reminded him of productivity. Sometimes, the absurdity of it all would start to creep back into the edges of his consciousness, but he'd take a deep breath and that feeling would usually go away. He got a little worried when Reuben began calling his ideas brilliant, but he reminded himself it was all part of a plan.

Finally, he was ready to make his move. Reuben shared a suggestion to add yet another piece to a device, and Stefan told him that he was a genius. Then he pointed to another place on the blueprint. "But would the design be any less brilliant," he asked, "if we took that part out?"

Reuben scratched his head. "Why would we do that?" he said. "It doesn't make any sense."

"We're always adding steps," Stefan explained. "Wouldn't it be more novel and daring to take one out for a change?"

Reuben shook his head. "Lacks elegance," he said. "Just because something has to be useful doesn't mean it has to be ugly. I hate it."

Stefan sighed. He had a sudden urge to take off his clothes and hide under his desk. But he left the office early instead, closed all the curtains, turned off all the lights, and collapsed into his bed, exhausted.

When Shayna came home, it was unnaturally dark. She found Stefan still lying face-down. He was moaning softly.

"I'm not a rooster," he said. "I can't spend the next two years as a rooster."

"Of course you're not a rooster," Shayna said. "Why would you be?"

"Ever since we got here, nothing has made sense," Stefan said. "And that's fine when you're just visiting. It's almost amusing, even. But now, this is my life." He moaned again. "I thought I had it figured out when Leeba told that rooster story, but I can't do this alone."

Shayna climbed into the bed beside him. "Can I tell you another story?" she asked.

"Depends," Stefan said. "Does it involve people going crazy?"

"Oh yes," said Shayna. "I told it to you the weekend we met, but I think you've forgotten."

Stefan could remember the feeling of that weekend so well, but it was no surprise if the details escaped him. "Go ahead."

And so, in the dark of their apartment, Shayna once again told her husband the story about a royal adviser who went to meet with the king. "There's a problem with the wheat harvest," the advisor said. "It's been tainted by a certain kind of rot. It's edible—no one will have to starve—but whoever eats loses their grip on reality. Most of the kingdom will go mad."

"Most?" asked the king.

"There's a little good grain left in storage," the adviser explained. "Enough to feed you and me. That way we'll be able to keep our wits about us through the crisis."

"Are you already crazy?" the king said. "Why should we want to be the only sane people in the kingdom of the mad?"

The adviser admitted that the king had a point. If they stayed sane in a world of insanity, they would be the ones who seemed unreasonable.

"We'll eat the tainted grain with everyone else," the king declared. "But I'm glad you brought this news to me. Because there's something we can do to prepare. Something to offer ourselves some relief, and some measure of wisdom."

The adviser found himself taking the king's hand, Shayna said, as she laced her own fingers through Stefan's.

Stefan turned on his side, facing her in the dark. He remembered her hand in his, but he'd forgotten the ending. "What happened next?" he asked. "What did the king recommend to his adviser?"

"The king said, 'Before we eat, we'll mark each other's foreheads with the seal of madness. That way, when we begin to lose hope, we might see each other. Then we'll understand what's happened to the world around us. Of all the people in the world, we, at least, will know that we're insane.'"

"What does the symbol look like?" Stefan whispered.

"Don't you know yet?" Shayna said. Her eyes went to his forehead. "That's why I married you. I see it every time I look at your face."

*Tzipa made a mental note never to
ask happy people for advice.*

Tzipa and the
Family Proclamation

It was a beautiful spring day when the Silbers blessed their new baby. It was an extra special occasion for the whole ward: the tiny girl with such perfect tiny toes was Israel Lewensztajn's first great-great grandchild. What a joy to bring together more relatives than fit on a four generation chart! Both Israel and his bright-eyed descendant slept like babies through the service, allowing their souls to soak in the blessing without any interference from the conscious mind. After blessing the baby, Brother Silber lifted her up for everyone to see the sweet, sleeping face.

In the pew just behind the chapel entrance, Tzipa felt tears running down her cheeks as the blessing came to a close. She was happy for Hannah Silber, who would be such a wonderful mother. Happy for all the Silbers and the other branches on the Lewensztajn tree. Yes, she was almost exhausted with joy. She knew she must be, because she loved the puff in their baby's doughy legs so much it ached. The emptiness inside her was surely because she was so unreasonably happy for them, had somehow transmitted her own happiness to them in such abundance that she seemed to have none left inside for herself.

When she and Lemel had married, they had planned to wait a year or two before having children. He loved children, yes, but she'd been so busy building up her business and she hadn't felt ready to have tiny feet running through their apartment yet. Had it been selfish of her to want to wait? The question was absurd, but Tzipa clung to absurd questions more and more as she searched for an explanation as to why, when she and Lemel had started trying, no child came. She needed an explanation for how all their love-making and cycle-tracking and doctor-discussing had left her womb empty as two years became three and three became four and four, as it will, stretched on to five.

Tzipa had always thought that *not* having children was what would take work. The women around her had always talked like getting pregnant was dangerously simple. You couldn't let a boy touch you, because that led to pregnancy. You had to be careful with kissing, because that led to touching, and that led to pregnancy. Travel could lead to pregnancy: whether by parking together in a car, or going too far, or somehow managing both at once. Being out past midnight for any reason instead of at home and in bed often led to pregnancy (which was confusing, since bed was where most pregnancies began). And there seemed to be no limits to which drugs could lead to sex and pregnancy: even birth control pills were not beyond suspicion!

Train up a child in the way she should go and she'll remain paranoid forever. After she was married, Tzipa worried obsessively about accidentally getting pregnant. She and Lemel, taking church counsel on emergency preparedness to heart, had purchased a year's supply of contraceptives. They packed others in a 72-hour kit in the closet: during the stress a natural disaster would surely produce, that was the last thing she wanted to be without. In keeping with church counsel, they had made sure to rotate their storage often. They had been creative in the ways they used it. They had followed every piece of advice about preparation with vigor and zeal.

And? On Tzipa, all such caution had been wasted. The only contraceptive she and Lemel needed was their own physiology. Her mother and aunts might have saved their breath; she and Lemel might have saved their money. Why is it that so much of the advice in this world is taken most fervently to heart by exactly the wrong people?

Not that she'd ignored advice about fertility once she realized she might need it. She studied textbooks and collected old wives' tales alike to determine how she and Lemel might try to persuade their bodies to produce a child. Tzipa had never needed a calendar to tell her that her womb might be ready to conceive, but she used one anyway to scientifically confirm what crescendos of desire suggested. On those same days, she made sure Lemel did not take showers that were too hot or wear pants that were too tight. His body, too, needed to be taken care of! She tried making love more frequently, rushing up the stairs from her bakery to their apartment whenever things slowed down. She tried making love less frequently, waiting longer than she liked in the hopes of giving his body more time to produce sperm.

Nothing worked. The doctor prescribed pills, but no babies came. The doctor gave injections, and still no babies came. Desperate, Tzipa and Lemel even drove to Warsaw to have her eggs fertilized and placed, but they failed to attach. It was almost as if they didn't trust her enough to hold on.

Lemel insisted that wasn't true, that it didn't make sense—but nothing made sense. Tzipa couldn't bear to try again. She couldn't stand the thought of her own eggs continuing to reject her.

Tzipa knew it was probably for the best if she could forget about the whole thing and be content with her bakery and her Lemel and her God. Ah, but watching the Silbers bless their baby, she knew she still wanted to carry a child of her own. If only she could discover why God hadn't sent her one!

Tzipa asked discreetly, indirectly, around the ward, to figure out how to trick God into granting a blessing. Not necessarily a child, but just any blessing a person happened to desire with a consuming, tidal force magnified over millennia of evolutionary history.

It was quite simple to get Gretele Gottstein-Kleiner started on the subject. She said that God showers blessings down on his children: on the just and the unjust, the miser and the glutton. Hard times come, she admitted, but eventually they get worn out. With a little luck and patience, everyone would find abundance sooner or later.

Tzipa made a mental note never to ask happy people for advice. Gretele seemed to sincerely believe this to be true, and perhaps it was. She seemed to sincerely expect it to be helpful, which it certainly was not. That was only natural; contentment rarely leads to genuine reflection. God must have realized that for the happy to think deeply would be a waste. Even if a satisfied person obtained some great wisdom, who would be able to hear it through the din of envy?

Recognizing the value of perennial dissatisfaction, Tzipa turned next to the ward's leading overthinker. Menachem Menasche, surely, had spent enough time in his head to have some answer. Tzipa trusted, furthermore, that it would come tempered by his own disappointments and jealousies. (You could trust an intellectual to have a rich supply of those.)

Menachem, of course, couldn't resist a question. He licked his fingers and opened up his scriptures. Flipping from verse to verse, he demonstrated that miracles come by the spirit of revelation. A hypothetical person must study the issue out in her mind, he insisted, employing ancient and modern methods to uncover nuances, apparent contradictions, and hidden layers of meaning. Next, she needed to ask of God, nothing wavering, and believing that she would receive, but at the same time guarding against false spirits and the lust for signs. Above all, she must keep in mind that God cannot lie—but will often equivocate for dramatic effect. Then, if her hands were clean and heart pure and she asked not amiss and God was willing, she could receive the answer or miracle she wanted or the one she needed or perhaps again some mix of the two, God condescending to meet her after the manner of her understanding.

Tzipa concluded that general happiness was not the only disqualifying characteristic in a good advisor. If a person wanted actionable advice, it was also best to steer clear of people who enjoyed ideas.

That standard also ruled out people who fixated on a single short motto, such as Brother Cohen, who said at least once a week that sacrifice brings forth the blessings of heaven, and Lazar the blind beggar, who was forever telling people to stop and smell the lilies of the field.

Who, then, to turn for blessing-getting advice? Oskar the miser was better at clinging to the blessings he had than at opening his hands to receive new ones. Dobra Peretz's only advice was to wait until about 11 am, when things start to feel less cursed all on their own. And if you asked Bishop Levy how to get a blessing, he'd recommend reaching out to your ministering brothers or his executive secretary.

With all these options exhausted, Tzipa turned at last to Mirele Schwartz. Truth be told, there were reasons to believe that the woman was a good choice. Mirele was not temperamentally capable of being satisfied. She was far more a woman of action than ideas. And she intimately understood the nagging sense of wrongness and irrational guilt that Tzipa felt whenever she thought about her struggle to have a baby. Above all else, she had a child. Not an upsetting number of children, like the Levys. Just a single, quiet, precious child. Surely, she'd done something to convince God to trust her with Perla. All Tzipa had to do was swallow her pride and ask.

Mirele did not preach patience or load up counsel with endless qualifications. There is a law, she said, irrevocably decreed in heaven before the foundation of the world, which dictates the relationship between each act of obedience and its corresponding blessing. It may be, Mirele admitted, that this divine law was damaged and bent when it was dropped off on the earth. But sooner or later, God is bound to bless us—literally bound—if we discover the specific law upon which a blessing is predicated and cling to it with exacting obedience.

As Tzipa probed, Mirele was happy to offer examples. People who followed the Word of Wisdom would never get tired of running. Honoring father and mother was the best way to find a job in Poland. Just look at Dobra's cousin Ronia. She quarreled with her mother and ended up in France. And if you wanted to feel closer to the dead, all you had to do was pay a precise and proper tithe and the windows of heaven had to open. Simple as the laws of physics.

And what law, Tzipa dared to ask, might open up the womb?

Ah yes, Mirele said. As far as fertility was concerned, she knew of no surer charm than absolute adherence to the roles laid out for women and men in a revelation known as The Family: A Proclamation to the World.

Tzipa was no Mirele Schwartz. But she felt as if, after years of treading water, she had finally been thrown a rope. How to be a mother need not remain a vague mystery. It was written. In words as solid and seizable as any iron rod. Tzipa went home from Mirele's overjoyed with the hope that comes from fresh guilt. She had been lax, she had been careless, she deserved her suffering. It was so freeing to see it as more than ill fortune, so freeing to feel she deserved it—because then she could change, and stop deserving it, and regain control over her tiny corner of a vast and bewildering universe.

Tzipa's enthusiasm cooled slightly when she got out the Family Proclamation and actually read it. There was an important problem: she wanted to be the perfect prospective mother, needed commandments to which she could be strictly obedient, but there was simply not a lot of strict there. Most of the Proclamation described a theology of longing for family and talked of children's rights. Parents typically appeared as a unit, in gender-neutral terms. As far as defining the unique, God-given roles of women and men which Mirele Schwartz had alluded to, Tzipa could find only two sentences: "By divine design, fathers are to preside over their families in love and righteousness and are responsible to provide the necessities of life and protection for their families. Mothers are primarily responsible for the nurture of their children."

Ah, well. Bare bones still make soup if you boil them long enough.

Lemel seemed well on his way to meeting God's standards for a father. He was certainly loving and undeniably righteous. She was not sure what might count as presiding, but he was probably not so good at that. She was also not sure what it meant to provide the necessities of life. That seemed to be what the placenta did—which was, non-negotiably, a mother's contribution. If it meant rent and groceries instead, her bakery paid for far more of those than his work repairing the town's few pianos. But he had always been willing to provide the necessities of protection, rather than leaving her with the burden of contraception, as many men reputedly did for the women in their sexual lives.

The Proclamation's list for mothers was much shorter. If she was to wrestle with God through these words, he'd played a dirty trick by making her whole sentence about children. However acutely she felt the absence at the core of her divine role, though, she refused to turn away. If you left the children out, what remained? Only "responsible" and "nurture." She could work with that. She would wrestle a blessing out of those two words.

Tzipa was reasonably responsible. In her relationship with Lemel, she was not sure she would go as far as to say that she was primarily responsible for much. Money, yes. But he did more cleaning and most of the reading out loud. Though she was quite capable in a kitchen, all the baking she did in her shop meant she typically left it to him to cook at night in their home. But she kept track of where things were in the apartment and on the calendar, and she always paid their bills on time.

And nurture? She managed. She planned. She calculated. For her, though, taking care of things meant crossing them off a list. Not tending them. Tzipa did not think of herself as very tender.

She and Lemel had real work to do.

Tzipa tried to broach the subject casually the next Sunday after church at lunch.

"Have you ever wanted to preside more?" she asked Lemel.

His face puckered as if she'd snuck a lemon into his borscht. "Not really," he said. "I know you don't see it, but President Gronam already does that in elders quorum more than enough."

"I meant at home," she said.

"Oh, you know I wouldn't do that to you," he said. "Besides, I wouldn't know how to be so gruff."

Tzipa looked at him until he met her eyes. "Well, I'm not asking you to be like President Gronam. Only to call on someone to say the prayers or make some assignments or whatever a president in the home ought to do."

"I suppose I could do better at helping us to remember our prayers," Lemel said. "Are we so bad at that?" For a moment, he studied her face. "Is something bothering you? Am I bothering you?"

Tzipa thought of the baby they did not have. "It's not that I have complaints about our relationship," she said. "I'm just trying to impress God. And apparently he has strong opinions."

"We could try buying him flowers," Lemel suggested. "Lazar says God is very fond of flowers."

"Or," Tzipa countered, "we could change things around in our home so you preside and provide, while I find something to nurture."

Lemel set his spoon down. "You want me to provide? For a place like this?"

Tzipa nodded slowly. "Is that too much to ask?"

He shrugged. "I thought we were happy."

"We were!" Tzipa said. "I mean, we are. But of course, there is more to life than happiness."

"Of course," Lemel said, though he had no idea what she meant. "I will call on you or myself to pray before each meal and I will have us sign a roll each day to make sure we are here and I will try to complain about how we are neglecting our duties."

"I would appreciate that very much," Tzipa said. When he put it that way, she realized that if she did become a mother, she should very much like not to be the only one complaining when their child neglected his or her duties. Perhaps Lemel's practice presiding would be useful after all.

"If you will show me how our finances work," Lemel added, "I will find a way to provide."

Tzipa promised to take him through her accounts. She knew Lemel disliked change, but he loved her, and she was glad to see him so willing to try something new.

Lemel stayed up late that night wrestling with some uncomfortable numbers. Math was never his strongest subject, but he could still see that his income fell far below the sum of expenses Tzipa tracked so carefully across her accounts. That only made sense: it wasn't so hard for Tzipa to pay for a bakery when you took into account what she earned from the bakery. But if he tried to pay for the bakery just from the jobs he did, they would be selling a lot less rugalach and a lot more matzah.

He could try expanding from pianos into the repair of other instruments. An accordion was basically a piano with a bellows. What was a violin but a piano without any hammers or keys? And a harmonica was a kind of mouth organ, which made it something like a piano's second cousin. Lemel typed up some estimates and sighed. It's hard to earn much from harmonica repair. He supposed it could have been worse—at least he wasn't a writer—but it could have been a great deal better. He could have been a baker like Tzipa.

Then again, why shouldn't he be? Lemel had never cared much for early mornings or the stifling heat of Tzipa's ovens, but the Family Proclamation praised Adam and Eve and the Bible said Adam had earned his bread by the sweat of his brow. Why not follow in the footsteps of humanity's ancestor?

There was the small matter of starting a bakery. He briefly considered buying Tzipa's, but he needed to save up for a down payment first. He decided to begin more humbly, doing his own baking in their apartment kitchen until he could afford to buy the big ovens downstairs, and selling his food door-to-door to save the rent he'd otherwise have to spend on a shop.

He wondered absently if customers would mind that he was terrible at baking.

Lemel's first customer was Oskar the Miser, who bought a badly burned roll for a little less than the ingredients cost. His second customer was also Oskar the Miser, who bought a day-old, badly burned roll for quite a bit less than the ingredients cost. His third customer remained Oskar the Miser, who bought most of a batch of two-day-old, badly burned rolls at a temporary discount so steep that there was no price at all.

After that, though, business started to pick up. Lemel got just enough better at baking that he could use sticky glazes and sweet sauces to cover his mistakes. Since he sold mostly to his instrument repair clients, he also found himself with more and more work as a piano cleaner.

Slowly, he crept his way closer to being able to provide. It would not be too many years before he would be able to pay for himself and Tzipa. It would be longer of course, before he would be able to provide for Tzipa's bakery, or the child she wished to have, let alone whatever their child wished to have: perhaps its own butcher shop? He tried not to think about it.

Meanwhile, Tzipa began her first experiment with nurturing. After reading that to nurture was to help a thing grow, she had made a long list of things that might need her help growing. A baby, of course, was what she hadn't been able to have, and pets were a burden she did not want. She had already killed a long line of house plants over the course of her life and did not care to help others limp along to a slow death of thirst.

It finally occurred to her that a sourdough starter needed plenty of nurturing. She hadn't had any sourdough breads on her menu, but that could change. Over the course of several days, she was able to capture some stray cells of bacteria from the air to produce a bubbling concoction with the potential to completely take over her life. What more could God want?

After a little experimenting, she got the bread right. Her customers, who heard her talk of little else, would buy up each loaf almost as soon as she made it and often ask for more. At first, Tzipa flushed at their praise, but then she realized she was neglecting her duties. Nurturing was not to be a secondary responsibility, something to do in the service of bread or customers, but her primary responsibility. She needed to act with exactness.

Tzipa was determined. Late at night, she would research the science of her tender bacteria until she understood exactly the conditions it needed. From one jar of starter she soon had two, and from two, four, and from four, eight, and so on—until her sourdough starter took up all the shop's available storage space.

There was more to nurturing, though, than helping the starter grow. The starter deserved to thrive. If she left it too long, it grew crowded and could choke on its own waste. To stay healthy, a growing starter needed to be divided again or else baked into bread.

Once she ran out of room to divide it, baking was the only option. Her sourdough now took over more and more of the menu. In addition to the rye, she baked sourdough loaves of barley and wheat. She made sourdough bagels and sourdough blintzes and sourdough rugalach. She even tried to come up with a way to make the world's first sourdough matzah.

Her customers struggled to keep up. The more sourdough took over the menu, the faster their early enthusiasm declined. Tzipa made sure to tell them what they were missing. She insisted they buy sourdough slices to go with anything else they wanted to purchase. But no amount of praising and persuading, haggling and threatening was enough.

People simply didn't want enough of her sourdough, and when she forced it on them, more and more customers stopped coming altogether.

Lemel was miserable. For some reason, his business was booming, but the kitchen had only the one small oven. He was spending more and more of each night baking to keep up.

His efforts to preside were suffering. He was often out making deliveries already when it was time for morning prayers, and simply sent a text message to Tzipa reminding her to pray for the both of them. Lost in her obsession with her sourdough starter, she was neglecting scripture study. Though it was hypocritical of him to tell her so (as his own had been all but abandoned for baking) he did his best to speak up. If he happened to say something while she was busy with her starter, though, she often snapped at him.

Not that she was the only guilty one. At Mirele Schwartz's suggestion, Tzipa had also insisted on taking over most of the cleaning. When he saw the simple things she was forgetting, things he never would have thought to neglect, he often snapped at her himself.

What was worse, Tzipa had also taken over the cooking at home. Normally, Lemel wouldn't have minded her help. Now, though, Tzipa's cooking mostly involved increasingly bizarre uses of sourdough. He'd eat sourdough granola bars for breakfast. For dinner, sourdough dumplings in sourdough-thickened soup. Week after week, the sour filled his belly until it soaked into his heart. And still, Tzipa piled more and more onto his plate.

One evening, facing a mound of unsold sourdough rolls on his dinner plate, Lemel couldn't bring himself to eat. He couldn't even bring himself to speak. He only sat, staring at the unyielding mountain of bread while Tzipa sat staring at him, no doubt waiting for him to call on someone to say the prayer. He tried to find the strength to do so, but it was she who finally broke the silence.

"My business is falling apart," she said. Tears welled up in her eyes. "No one in the shop wants my bread anymore either."

"It's all right," he said. "I can almost provide."

But her tears didn't stop. In fact, she began sobbing. "I didn't mean for all this to happen," she told him. "I just wanted us to be more obedient. I just wanted to prove we could live according to the Family Proclamation."

Lemel looked at his plate again. "I know it's an honor to live by the word of God," he said. "But even scripture admits that a man cannot live by bread alone."

Tzipa wiped her eyes. "I am so tired of sourdough," she said, "that I would sleep better if I never saw a container of starter again."

"Are you sure?" Lemel asked.

She nodded fiercely. "With all my heart."

Lemel smiled. "Then let me preside just one more time," he said. And he led her down the stairs, so they could smash jar after jar of the musty stuff together. Like Sampson bringing a building down.

After they had swept up all the broken glass, after Lemel had cleaned the apartment to his liking and Tzipa had replaced her sourdough menu with the names of all the things she'd sold before, after they had collapsed into bed together, their fingers intertwined, after they'd slept in and called Lemel's customers to apologize for deliveries that would be delayed, and Tzipa had helped him bake all the orders in the large bakery ovens—after all that, Lemel dared to get out the Family Proclamation for the two of them to study together.

And Tzipa promised not to nurture any more sourdough. And Lemel asked her if it would be all right if he didn't try quite so hard to preside. As to providing: since Lemel's customers were mostly people who had left Tzipa when she forced them into sourdough, he promised to send them all back. And Tzipa said that from that day on, she and Lemel would be equal partners—just like the very next sentence of the Family Proclamation said that husbands and wives ought to be.

Tzipa did not miraculously find herself pregnant the next month, or the next, or the next, but she did feel at peace: with her home and her bakery and her Lemel and the happy family the two of them could, so often, be.

*The beauty of the gospel was that you could teach
people correct principles and, whether they listened
or not, in the end they would rule themselves.*

Beynish Pays Tithing

Heshel was with Bishop Levy in his office one week, going over the afternoon's appointments, when Beynish walked in, carrying a shopping bag, from which he unloaded seven large jars of schmaltz.

Bishop Levy was surprised to see Beynish there. The man rarely came to the foyer, let alone to the bishop's office. "What can I help you with?" the bishop asked.

"I've been so stressed, bishop," Beynish said, "ever since I lost my job. And now, things have started to spin out of control."

Bishop Levy was surprised. He prided himself on keeping up with the ward's needs. "I'm so sorry to hear that," he said. He motioned for Heshel to go. There was no guarantee the famously distractible secretary would come back, but what was the calling of a bishop other than a juggle between today's lost sheep and the next ones to wander? "Let's talk about how the ward can help."

But Beynish put a hand on Heshel's shoulder before he could get up. "That won't be necessary, bishop. I've only come to pay my tithing, and then God will bless me. If it's the same to you, I'd rather leave the ward out of it."

Bishop Levy was surprised once again. Beynish hadn't paid tithing in years. "It's true that God will bless you," the bishop began cautiously, "though perhaps through an employment specialist—"

"Why would I need an employment specialist?" Beynish interjected.

"—or, when times are hard, some fast offering funds," Bishop Levy continued. Best to get all the options on the table first, then let Beynish think them over. One way or another, the Lord helped those who helped themselves. And at every ward party he had bothered to attend, Beynish had certainly helped himself. It wouldn't do if he walked away now, too proud to accept any assistance. How long, Bishop Levy wondered, had the man gone without a job before coming?

Then his brow furrowed. Bishop Levy was neither the wisest nor the quickest man in Chelm, but something about this situation didn't add up. "Beynish," he thought to ask. "If you don't have a job, what tithing would you need to pay?"

"I told you," said Beynish. "I've been so stressed! I can't stop eating. And then I got on a scale. I won't tell you how many kilos I've gained," he added, then waved a hand sadly toward the jars of schmaltz, "but you can do the math.

That's the same as one-tenth of my increase. Just like it says in the scriptures." Then Beynish looked at Bishop Levy. "Now be honest: is it true that if I pay tithing, the God of Israel can help me lose weight?"

If the Lord of Hosts *was* in that business, Bishop Levy thought, there would hardly be any need for a ward mission plan. Caring for the soul was quite a hard sell when you contrasted it with how easily people fretted over the size of their bodies. He tried to think of a scripture that had something to do with what Beynish was suggesting, but most of the verses that came to mind weren't helpful. Nothing about diets. He wasn't sure the word *thin* even appeared in the scriptures. And there were so many verses about the opposite: feasting on the word, feeding sheep; about free milk and honey, or enjoying the fat of the land. God was like a Jewish mother. Eat, eat, eat, and still: "you have been weighed in the scales and found wanting." Wasn't there any allowance for people who looked in the mirror and didn't like what they happened to see?

Bishop Levy nodded slowly. "I think there's something on the subject," he said, "in Ecclesiastes."

"Wonderful!" said Beynish. "I knew we were blessed to have the Book of Mormon!" And then, whistling to himself, he walked out of the door.

Bishop Levy sighed. If the blessing didn't appear, he hoped Beynish would at least come back to complain. It was nice to see him in this humble house of God, even if he did treat the door as if it were built for revolving.

While the bishop was lost in thought, Heshel glanced down the hallway and noticed that Feiga Cohen had come early for her scheduled meeting. That was not likely to be a quick visit; she would have a thing or two to say! And so Heshel would get a little free time to look around after all. First, though, something had to be done about the bishop's desk. Heshel managed to gather up four of the schmaltz jars in his arms; Bishop Levy grabbed the other three and they walked down to the financial clerk's office to drop them off.

It's interesting, Heshel mused, how different people paid their tithing. Yossel's always came from his net. And Beynish's was definitely gross. The beauty of the gospel was that you could teach people correct principles and, whether they listened or not, in the end they would rule themselves.

*It only made sense that religion was just
as broken as the next thing and needed
at least a few centuries of fixing up.*

Zalman and the
Official Declaration

Zalman the Learned had long struggled to follow the stories in the Doctrine and Covenants. The Torah had never been a problem for him. To be sure, there were some false starts. In the first chapter, for example, the world was created, and then in the second chapter the world was created again, and then by chapter 6, God was getting ready to start the whole thing over a third time. Still, there was some definite forward motion, complete with periodic chapters of begats to show the passage of time. And then from Abraham through Moses the story moved along rather nicely before the plot wandered off in the wilderness.

The Book of Mormon was trickier. Having been born long before there were medications to help with such things, Nephi was temperamentally incapable of sticking to a subject. He was always interrupting his own story (and the supporting streams of complaints about his brothers) with long visions of the future and longer quotes from the prophets of the past. For the first two books, it was often difficult to remember what century you were in. But if you somehow made it to Mosiah, the Book of Mormon's story was not only discernible but actually exciting. You got to see the chosen people be brave and foolish and thoughtful and naive and proud and stupid, just like covenant peoples always are. It didn't always make sense, but at least it had shape. What more could you ask from a book, even if it was God's?

Try as he might, though, Zalman didn't know what to do with the Doctrine and Covenants. He could never find the thread to hold onto. The first section took place in the chronological middle, then the second jumped back in time. If you made it past the first few to section 8, you got some really good stuff about Moses and Aaron, but pretty soon after that, the book started repeating itself worse than Genesis. If he didn't always nod off while studying them, Zalman would swear that sections 15 and 16 said the exact same thing!

What's more, the Doctrine and Covenants never really seemed to pick up its pace. The Saints didn't make it to Kirtland until section 41. Then it took them all the way until section 124 to get to Nauvoo, before rushing off toward Salt Lake at the book's very end—if any readers made it that far. Zalman knew he was supposed to seek knowledge by faith as well as study, but on each attempt, he didn't have quite enough to carry him to the final page of the Doctrine and Covenants.

One year, it occurred to Zalman that if reading left to right wasn't working, it might be better to try right to left, like with the Torah when he was young. And so it was that, on a January morning when Zalman was taking his turn teaching Sunday School class, the members of the Chelm Ward found themselves discussing the 1978 document known as Official Declaration #2.

Things went well enough in their discussion of the declaration's first paragraph, where the prophets said they were grateful that the people of many nations had responded to the restored gospel. Members of the Chelm ward, like so many unfortunate people around the world, lived in a nation. And they had certainly responded to the restoration. Many still remembered Heshel talking about a great repair after he met the missionaries while buying blintzes in Ukraine. As moderately attentive Jews, they already knew about *tikkun olam*, or repairing the world. It only made sense that religion was just as broken as the next thing and needed at least a few centuries of fixing up.

It was when Zalman moved on to the restoration of the priesthood, and what the prophets had done in 1978 to repair the Church, that class turned contentious.

"I have a concern," Brother Cohen said.

Well, of course he did. Everyone knew that before he raised his hand. It was the sort of thing so reliable that you could bear testimony of it before the ward on Fast Sunday: you knew, with every fiber of your being, that Brother Cohen was going to have a concern. But if predictability was a sin, the whole Church was guilty, so Zalman went ahead and called on Brother Cohen.

"This section reminds me of a serious question," Brother Cohen mused. "I have never understood what is so heavy about the priesthood that this Church expects everyone to carry it." He moved a hand to his chest as if the thought itself caused him pain. "Things worked just fine in the priestly lines when there were only a few of us. I have proposed to the bishop, and will propose it now again, that—should our dear Chelm Ward see fit—my sons and I would be more than happy to hold all the priesthood on our own."

Menachem Menasche's hand shot up before Cohen had even finished. Menasche! It was well known he thought of himself as more learned, even, than Zalman. Zalman looked desperately for an excuse to ignore that hand, lifted up as it surely was in pride, and call on someone else. But no one would even make eye contact. It would be out of the frying pan of Cohen's favorite complaint, then, and into the fire of Menasche. Zalman only hoped, against all precedent, that this comment would be quick.

"We are, of course, aware of Brother Cohen's views on the priesthood," Menachem said. "But this passage is not about the priests or the Levites at all, but about a very specific problem in the history of the Saints in America, where people were afraid of Africans and refused to ordain them."

"Afraid?" asked Leah Kantor. "For what reason?"

Before Zalman could answer, Brother Menasche pointed to the open book before him. "As we read in the introduction to this section," he observed, "the position of the Church, which is repeated in the magazines I have studied and the talks I have read, is that we don't know anything."

"Yes, yes," Zalman said, eager to regain control of the class. "And as anyone can observe, it's very easy to go from knowing nothing to holding firmly to a prejudice. The whole thing makes a certain sort of sense."

"I still think it was a bad idea for Americans to hold the priesthood," Brother Cohen interjected.

But the class was ready to move on. "Why the prejudice against Africans?" Tzipa asked. "Don't people usually blame their problems on Jews?"

Zalman the Learned spoke up before Menasche could bore the class further with minutiae from the history of the United States. "There must not have been many Jews in America yet," he said. "If there were Jews, of course, they would have hated Jews," he assured her, "but there is so much hate in the world and there are simply not enough Jews to go around. As we read in the Torah itself, it happened once that Moses married an Ethiopian woman. At that time, Miryam and Aaron objected, believing it unfair of Moses to make her people, too, hateful in the eyes of the Egyptians. But the voice of God came and rebuked them, telling them they would not be the only people hated for his name's sake."

The last details of that story were not exactly written on any scroll, but Zalman was still quite proud of his quick little midrash. His role as a teacher was to bring each tangent back to the scriptures, or at least close enough that the wandering sheep of the Chelm ward could drink from the well. (Unless they were quite attached to wandering, which at least one of them usually was.) "It's not that I object to any particular deacon or elders quorum president," Brother Cohen insisted. "But without the appropriate lineage, I wonder why we hand our fast offerings to young Gimpel or take assignments from our dear President Gronam."

"I object!" shouted President Gronam. "I object to the testimony of Brother Cohen! He is degrading my quorum's dignity."

"This is not a courtroom," Zalman the Learned reminded president Gronam. "Though I am sure that, speaking in general, we do sustain you in this ward." He turned to Brother Cohen. "Certainly in the Church, we believe in ordaining worthy men to the priesthood, whether their name is Levy or Cohen or Johnson or Smith. Once a field is ready to harvest, it's always one hailstorm away from being flat, one soggy week away from rotting. To get the job done in time, we're all called to the work."

"And what a disaster!" Brother Cohen protested. "Consider a mohel as a comparison. If there happened to be a large number of baby boys born in a year, would you hand everyone a pocketknife? No, you would stick to the families with experience. The ones who have been in the business for generations." He sighed theatrically. "You know I love this Church," he added, "but I think that when Joseph Smith ordained anyone at all to the priesthood, he was making a terrible mistake."

"And as we know," Zalman countered, "we came to this earth to make mistakes. Mistakes help us grow. It's written in the hymns. Or the lessons. Or perhaps even somewhere in the long middle of this great and disorienting book of Doctrine and Covenants."

But Brother Cohen only shook his head in disbelief. "Why do the young people today love so much to make mistakes?" he asked. "In the old days, mistakes could kill you. Touch the ark without permission: stricken dead. Come into the priests' court in the temple without precautions: instantly dead. God is dangerous business." He wagged one finger toward Zalman in an emphasis of rebuke. "With God, it's a safety issue to keep most people at a respectful distance. In the old days, priests handled fatal power! We had a whole code for how to safely handle the divine." He snorted. "Now how many of our dear priesthood holders make a careful study of Leviticus?"

Zalman suspected the number was slightly greater than zero, but did not think that saying so would make a strong defense.

Menachem Menasche raised his hand again and did not wait to be called on before beginning to speak. God willing, somewhere in the Book of Leviticus there might be a curse on such behavior. "I am sure that many people in this day and age, not to mention this room, would love to keep far away from God and from priests of every kind," Menachem said. "But God calls us now to enter his presence. And by your own example of the temple's inner court," he told Brother Cohen, "we do so by first becoming a kingdom of priests and priestesses. We may be clumsy. And God doesn't want to be taken lightly. But I don't see another way."

"It makes sense to cast the net wider and wider." Yossel added from the back row, "If God's fishermen stopped with the first load, the sun would beat down on their catch and pretty soon it would start to stink."

Zalman nodded at this. He may not know American history like Brother Menashe or priesthood history like Brother Cohen, but rotten fish was rotten fish. "You see? There is a time and a purpose for everything."

"It still doesn't seem fair," Tzipa blurted out. "I mean . . . what does the example of the Levites have to do with this declaration?" She looked to Zalman for help. "It is one thing to have just one tribe bear the priesthood or step into the inner courts of the temple," she explained. "It would be quite another to give it to every tribe and leave just one out."

The question stopped Zalman. Since he first heard about it, he had assumed this business with the priesthood was part of the great scriptural pattern of God prodding his prophets to get over themselves. God had to drag Jonah to Nineveh. Peter got knots in his stomach at the thought of eating with Gentiles. A long string of modern-day prophets, it reasoned, might need some pushing to take the gospel to all peoples. But in the case of this very first revelation in the Doctrine and Covenants (or the last, if you read the book left to right), the trouble was not with the world, but with a group of those who numbered themselves among God's people. Zalman turned to the class. "Is there a better comparison in the scriptures?" he asked. "Can anyone think of a story when just one tribe was separated from the rest and treated badly?"

There was a pause as the collected great minds of Chelm pondered the problem. Zalman flipped through the pages of scripture in his mind, considering the many times God's covenant people acted less like sheep than asses. The Book of Mormon spoke of a time when the pride of those in the Church exceeded the pride of those outside it, so there was precedent for the Saints' arrogance. And even Moses was making a mess of his health and the people's safety before his father-in-law, Jethro, intervened. Perhaps the failing of the modern prophets was that, being so old, they lacked the counsel of a good father-in-law. But try as he might, Zalman could not think of a direct parallel for the story his class was studying.

Then Shayna's eyes lit up and her hand rose victoriously into the air. "Right at the beginning, in Israel's family, there's the story of how Joseph's own brothers sold him into slavery," she said. "Perhaps this thing in America was more like that."

Zalman sighed with relief. There was a saying about the Talmud: *turn it and turn it, for everything is in it.* The four sets of Latter-day Saint scripture were not nearly so long as the Talmud, but there was still quite a bit there if you looked at it long enough. "Yes," Zalman said. "This is an excellent point. Nothing stirred Judah to greater works than his guilt over betraying his brother. And so may it be with us!"

To begin on the right side of the Doctrine & Covenants, Zalman realized, was indeed the best way to approach the book. The class was beginning with a story like Joseph and his brothers. Next, there would be stories of oppression and captivity, then a crossing of the wilderness. Traveling backwards through time, the Saints could enter their promised land in Missouri and raise up a temple there, before being scattered out into the world, like exiles in Babylon, with only the thought of Zion to warm them. What stranger proof could there be that God was in the long history of this faith than the way the scriptures themselves formed one great chiasmus.

"We're in a young Church," Yossel
said, "even if it wears an old faith."

Are Mormons Christian?

Little Breyndl Fischer came home crying one Friday after school, though there was not a scrape or bruise on her. When Belka asked what the trouble was, Breyndl sniffed back her sobs. "Minah Malkin said it's not good to be a Mormon, since Mormons are really just a kind of Christian."

Belka knew children could be cruel, but felt this was going too far. "Minah Malkin doesn't know what she's talking about," she said.

Little Breyndl shook her head. "But she does! Rachel Weismann said her mother told her so, too. Mormons are just a kind of Christian. We're the same as them all."

The Fischers' older daughter, Golda, was sprawled across the couch in the apartment's main room. Though she was busy giving the barest possible impression of working on her homework, she abandoned that effort to join the conversation. "Did she say that in front of a Christian kid?" Golda asked. "Was there a fight?"

"Golda!" Belka said. How many times did a mother need to repeat that there was more to an education than betting on hallway scuffles? But Little Breyndl had already turned toward her sister, eyes wide.

"Would there be? Really?" she stammered.

"I've never seen one over the issue before," Golda admitted. "But Bluma and Bina said they heard that Saul Gottlieb was picking on poor Zusa Cohen once about her grandparents being Mormon and a Christian kid heard and he laughed at Saul and told him he was full of—"

"Golda!" Belka repeated, more sharply this time.

Golda rolled her eyes at her mother, then searched for words. "He said, um, that Saul was wrong about Mormons being Christian. Anyway, the Levy twins said they got in a fight but the Christian kid had a bunch of friends close and they told Saul to shut the, um, to not talk about that stuff anymore and that Mormons were just a cu—"

"*Golda!*" Starting with the third warning, Belka expected some respect. *Cult* was not a four-letter word she wanted a young child learning.

"Anyway, the kid said that we're definitely not Christian. Bluma and Bina were standing way down the hall when it happened, but they said if you look close you can see a bump on Saul's head from when the Christian kids shoved him against the locker." Golda shrugged. She turned to her mother. "Honestly, though, I don't think Saul was wrong. We are kind of Christian."

Belka could see this needed to be a serious conversation. She stopped kneading the dough for the evening's challah and washed off her hands. "Just because someone might be a little right about something doesn't mean they know what they're talking about," she said. Take baking: everyone with a tongue has an opinion, but hand them an apron and some people will just about burn your kitchen down. And religion? Hand a man a flag and in five minutes he'll think he knows the right way for all civilized people to worship. Putting a label or two in hands like that is a serious fire hazard. At least that's what Belka's grandmother said.

Belka walked over to the couch and nudged Golda over so she could sit between the girls. "Mina Malkin and Saul Gottleib say we're Christian and that's bad. The Christian boy says we're not Christian and that's bad. Golda says we're not *not* Christian, and maybe that's not good—although it's also possible that's *not* not good." She looked at each of them. "Am I getting this right so far?"

"You're not getting it wrong," Golda said.

"Well, let me ask you this," Belka said. "If I put raisins in the bread tonight, would it still be bread?"

Breyndl nodded. She liked raisins in her challah.

"You see? What does it matter if I make it a little different? It's the taste that counts."

"You could add apple," Breyndl said.

"Or pear," said Belka. "Or pineapple. Or melon."

Golda made a face. "That's weird, Mom."

"If Mina Malkin doesn't want to, she doesn't have to try it. But God help anyone who should tell me what to bake in my kitchen!" Belka pulled Little Breyndl close. "Don't ever let someone else's lack of adventure tell you who you ought to be."

Little Breyndl leaned into her, but Golda shifted uncomfortably. "But it is weird. We're weird." Golda asked. "What if we're the ones hiding from obvious facts?"

Belka sighed. "Enough," she said. "Let me bake. We can talk about it at Family Home Evening tonight."

That evening, after they'd lit the candles and blessed the bread and sat down to eat, the Fischers started their regular Friday Family Home Evening. Since they were home and it was evening, Belka figured it was the perfect opportunity to bring difficult questions up.

She looked over at Yossel. "Today," Belka began, "Minah Malkin at Breyndl's school said it's not good to be a Mormon, since Mormons are really just a kind of Christian. I said the important thing about bread is how it tastes, and if it happened to have some apples in it, that doesn't make it a cake." She picked up a piece of bread for emphasis. "But what do you think?"

Yossel finished chewing. "When I have apples in me, that certainly doesn't make me a cake," he reasoned.

"So what would you say to Minah Malkin?" Belka prompted. "Are Mormons Christian? Or not?"

"I'm not sure," he said. "I think I would tell Minah to ask her mother. She's a young girl and I'm a grown man. It wouldn't do for us to fight."

"I'm a girl still," Breyndl said. "I could fight her."

"Hmmm," said Yossel. "Best to do it with your brains. After all, you're a Fischer." He scratched his head. "And I think if we want to understand what a thing *is*, we should ask ourselves first what that thing *does*." He looked back to his wife. "What do Christians *do*?" he asked.

"Run the Parliament, for one thing," Belka said.

"Set all the school holidays," Golda noted with a hint of bitterness, echoing an old Chelm complaint.

"Complain about how much better things used to be," Yossel noted, "while drinking a lot of vodka."

"Tell us it's their country," Little Breyndl said.

"That's not all Christians do," Belka said. "They eat dinner with their families, just like us. They worry when their daughters are crying after school. If a few obnoxious Christians are loudest, the rest can't help that." She sighed. "But it's no wonder Mina Malkin thinks being Christian sounds like such a bad thing."

Yossel looked at his daughters. "Now . . . what do Jews do?"

"Make challah?" Breyndl said.

Yossel nodded. "And eat some together on a Sabbath afternoon."

"Argue about how to keep the commandments," Belka noted. "Talk about the fate of Israel. Remember the temple."

"Get in trouble for not being able to pass as Christian," Golda added wryly.

Belka silently thanked the Master of the Universe. Her daughters understood. "So," Belka concluded. "If your father is right, and if knowing what a thing *does* teaches us what a thing *is* . . . let me ask once more, is Mina Malkin right? Are Mormons Christian?"

Golda put her fork down loudly. "I understand what you're trying to say," she said. "But Minah and Rachel and Saul have a point. We pray now in the name of Christ. The Book of Mormon is 'another testament of Christ.' You have to admit the other Jewish kids are at least a little right for thinking we've betrayed our history. We belong to the Church of Jesus Christ of Latter-day Saints."

"That's it," said Yossel. "Right there in the name of the Church. We are not *Christians*. Just Saints."

"Or at least we are," Belka added cautiously, "when we act like Saints." She looked Golda right in the eye next. "And history is something we still have time to make."

"We're in a young Church," Yossel said, "even if it wears an old faith."

Golda didn't answer. Just chewed the inside of her cheek. Belka didn't know if they'd gotten through.

Meanwhile, Little Breyndl was looking unsettled again. "I don't understand," she said. "*Are* Mormons Christian?"

Belka sighed. "Not in Chelm. Not yet, at least. But in the whole world? I don't always know." She looked once more at Golda. "We will see how we did when the story is done."

"I know exactly what to do," Sara Levy
said. "I'm going to talk to my husband about
calling a matchmaker for our ward."

Matchmaker, Matchmaker

Sara Levy was dreading the next Relief Society lesson she had to teach. The subject was marriage: that sacred covenant, so frequently profaned. She had no idea what to say that would be appropriate for everyone. There was a time, of course, when she wouldn't have concerned herself with such things, but the trouble with being the bishop's wife was that a woman started to worry by proxy about everyone. Being so close to the calling gave her most of the stress and none of the keys.

Well? What was a mere teacher to do? She decided to counsel with her president, Fruma Selig. She'd look for advice, and maybe recognize a little revelation in it. On the Tuesday evening before her lesson, she took a bus to the Selig apartment to see what wisdom she could glean.

"My worry is that everyone's lives are so different," Sara said, as Fruma began to fill a kettle to fix them some herbal tea. "Not everyone has the ideal situation, like Tzipa and Lemel do. How many Feiges do we have in our ward who can't stand their Aarons? And sisters like you—it must be difficult to talk about marriage when you're divorced."

Fruma shrugged. "Don't make it too complicated," she said. "My marriage, for all its faults, taught me a great deal about the worth of souls. Especially my own." She set the tea kettle on the stove. "I don't mind hearing people talk about what a healthy marriage looks like: it reminds me I made the right decision."

"But what if the lesson veers into the importance of shared faith and being married in the Church?" Sara asked. "I don't want to make Shayna feel bad for having married in Germany. And it's hard for Mirele Schwartz to feel like her marriage is good enough when her husband is retired from all religion."

Fruma laughed. "Stefan is in the ward now. We don't worry about what happened before, because each day has trouble enough of its own. And no matter what the lesson is, Mirele will feel like she doesn't measure up. You can't blame the topic for that!"

Sara had hoped for more sympathy, but she held out for some guidance. "What about Leah Kantor? She's never married. And she's no longer young. But also not old enough to write off the whole business for good. It's such an awkward, in-between age."

Fruma was staring at the teapot, but it wouldn't boil. "She may not be married," she acknowledged, "but she's hardly alone. Remember the chickens? The goats?" She looked over at Sara. "Lots of people spend their lives single these days."

"But most people aren't in the Church!" Sara said. "It's one thing to be single if you live with both feet in the twenty-first century. When your faith prefers to mix this and that millennium, the situation's different." At this, Fruma gave up on hovering over the teapot and finally sat down to listen. "We're going to teach that marriage is important," Sara said. "That's practically a fourteenth article of faith—the question is how to tell people what their marriage should look like without making them feel judged."

Fruma sighed. "I understand the problem," she said. "But what's the use of telling people when and how and who to marry when the whole market is broken? If finding anyone decent feels like a fluke?"

Now they were getting somewhere. "Exactly," Sara said. "I don't want to blame any given person. None of this is their fault." That's when inspiration hit her. She sat back in her chair "The trouble is that the community isn't doing enough. We've abdicated too much responsibility."

Fruma leaned forward. "What do you mean?" she asked. "Responsibility for what?"

"There was a time when people didn't have to work so hard to get married. Because the community helped make it happen for them."

Fruma frowned. "We have activities. And there are stake dances, regional gatherings for the single adults. What more do you think we should do?"

"I know exactly what to do," Sara Levy said. "I'm going to talk to my husband about calling a matchmaker for our ward."

Across the room, the teapot began to whistle. The sound was the perfect accompaniment for the expression on Fruma's face.

"No," Bishop Levy said. It was late. He'd just gotten back from a meeting. But Sara wanted to strike while the iron was hot.

"What do you mean, no?" she insisted. "You haven't even considered it yet, Mattheusz!"

"If I could invent callings, do you think Oskar the Miser would be our librarian?" He shook his head. "I'm not the prophet. I'm just a bishop."

Sara sighed. "All right, then maybe Matchmaker is not a new calling. But you could add it as an assignment to a calling that already exists." He ran a hand through his hair. That meant she had him thinking. "Senior missionaries do it all the time! Why not give the same responsibility to the activities committee—or the Relief Society's compassionate service coordinator?"

"I don't know," he said. "These days, people like to find their spouses for themselves."

"No, they don't," she snapped. "You know better than that. No one likes having to date. All the figuring out who to ask and what to say and how to pretend to be: it's exhausting. People are so desperate for help, they invented the internet just to make connections." She crossed her arms. "If religion can't compete with technology, what place will it have in the future?"

He lifted his hands in surrender. "All right. All right. That's enough." He looked at her, weighing some thought.

"But before I give anyone this kind of assignment, I want you to try it. Make one match, one good match, and we'll see."

"And this is for a Church assignment?" Leah Kantor asked. She cradled her cell phone between her shoulder and her ear. "An experimental Church assignment?"

Where had she put her earbuds? They must be somewhere close.

"No, I'm happy to help. I like to do my part for our ward . . . It's nice you're excited; someone might as well be . . . all right . . . yes, I can come to your house . . . I'll talk to you later . . . Yes, later . . . Goodbye."

Had she left them on the kitchen counter after her cousin called? Yes, that was it.

Leah found her earbuds and put on some music—Bedřich Smetana's "The Moldau"—to keep her company on her evening walk.

As she thought over her conversation with Sara Levy, she realized she wasn't entirely sure what she had agreed to. If a matchmaker set up a meeting, that wasn't exactly a date, was it? That is, she didn't have to pretend to be interested in impersonating the kind of attitudes or behaviors you saw in films. For heaven's sake, she was in her early forties. By now, she hoped she had grown out of needing to impress anybody. If it happened indirectly, through her art, that was one thing. But with her charm? Or her wit? Or her body? Please no. She was quite content with all those things, but she had no intention of parading them.

Then again, she'd never been to a matchmaker's meeting. If she could be direct and frank, that could be refreshing. Was she even still open to the possibility of a partner? That was a difficult question. But if you stripped away all the frills of courting and got straight to the negotiations, at least the conversation might be interesting. Menachem Menashe was a mildly interesting man. Not young enough to be annoying or old enough to have grown set and dull; if she said so herself, the forties were a happy medium. And in this unexpected setting, she might get to see a side of him that she'd never met before.

Or maybe the whole thing would be a disaster. That would also be all right. If it was, Sara Levy would probably never ask her to come to a meeting again. And because the request had come through Church, God would owe her a favor.

After Sara Levy reached him, Menachem Menashe was one part intrigued and three parts uneasy. The appealing part was that he had never imagined himself with Leah Kantor. It was something only a matchmaker could have come up with—and maybe that would help. He suspected that he would have married in the old days, and wondered absently how it would have gone. After all, it's one thing to resign yourself to a relationship. It's quite another when you're expected to choose.

The long process of wanting and pursuing and selecting and agreeing, which a person had to go through today to get married, was beyond him. But with someone else starting the process? It was probably still beyond him. He would nevertheless do his best to keep an open mind.

What did he know so far? As far as he could tell, he and Leah had a lot in common. They were both Saints. They were both single. They both read books. If nothing else, those three things were more than most couples in history shared before the spread of women's education. And it's not like modern people who chose their own partners necessarily wound up with much more!

He began to think about what he would even want to ask in their interview at the Levy house. He had never been to a matchmaker's meeting before.

At last, the night arrived. Sara Levy had warned them each to eat dinner on their own—there was no need to test etiquette on a first meeting by having them navigate a whole meal—but she had laid out some rugalach, because a little sweet for the nerves never hurt. And to go with it, she'd made them cups of barley coffee. Was it good? Not particularly. But it honored the Word of Wisdom and it went well enough with a dessert.

Menachem arrived first. He was dressed well, if the tiniest bit rumpled from his studies. Ah, well: people married professors once in a while, didn't they? He was certainly no worse.

When Leah arrived she was dressed neatly, if plainly. She had brought along a notebook. Whether it was to keep track of Menachem's responses or to write in if she got tired of listening to him, Sara couldn't tell. Honestly, Leah already looked a little bored. But maybe that would change.

"I'd like to thank you both for agreeing to participate," Sara said. "Seeing as you are both adults, I left your parents out of this meeting, but I thought I would start with the questions they might ask. You can both answer, and then I'll be out of your way so you can talk amongst yourselves. Because this is an experiment, I hope you'll keep me updated. And I'll call tomorrow to see if you can give me any feedback you might have on the process." She cleared her throat. "Any questions before we begin?"

Leah raised her hand. "Is there a certain time you'd like us to stay until?"

"I'm just glad you came in the first place," Sara said. She looked down at her notes. "First question: do you come from a good family?"

"Yes," Leah said.

"Not exactly," Menachem admitted.

"Second question: how are your prospects? Economically, I mean."

"I live simply, but comfortably," Leah said.

"I live simply," Menachem said.

"Third: do you keep the Sabbath?"

"Yes," said Leah.

"Religiously," said Menachem.

"What are your expectations about marriage?" Sarah asked them.

"I don't," Leah said.

Menachem looked over at her as if surprised at the point of connection. "Neither do I."

That was all the questions Sara had written in her book. She briefly considered following up about Menachem's family but decided it was not her place to pry. Besides, if a person defined family broad enough, everyone's relatives were a mess. "Well," she said instead, "Since you are both religiously observant, with economic differences that are unintimidating and expectations that are compatible, I can in good conscience recommend that you consider this possibility. I'll leave you to discuss whatever is on your minds. Please be as open and honest as possible: eternity is at stake." And with that, she left the room.

Leah began before Sara made it to the end of the hall. "What is the worst thing about you?" she asked.

Menachem thought. "It's difficult to pick," he said. "I am deeply obsessive. Also haunted by my own insecurities. Probably one of those."

Leah appreciated the rapid candor. "What insecurities specifically?" she asked.

"Oh, the usual," Menachem said. At least, he assumed that they were usual. He wasn't in the habit of comparing notes. "Am I good enough? Am I worth people's time? Does my existence justify the burden it places on the fabric of the earth?" Of course, it went deeper than that. It was hard to put into words, but he supposed he owed it to her to try. "Would my life be better if I were invisible and intangible, a silent witness to creation but without any capacity to interfere?" he said.

Leah picked up a rugalach and took a bite. "And are you the sort of person who seeks out constant affirmation in a fruitless effort to calm these insecurities?"

The thought of asking directly for such a thing almost made him want to gag. "Not really," Menachem said. "I'm more the internal, spiraling type. I obsess until I sweat and my mind locks up until, gradually, it becomes exhausted by the strain. After that, things usually don't seem so bad."

"Oh," Leah said. "That doesn't sound like too much, then. A person could live with that."

"I mean . . . I do," Menachem told her.

"I meant another person. You wouldn't actually be the kind of burden you'll always be worried about is what I'm saying."

The sentiment was unexpectedly kind. He wasn't sure he could completely believe it, but he was glad to have the words there to try. "Thank you," he said.

She picked up her barley coffee and took a sip. It was pleasurably hot. "Now you ask me something."

Menachem still felt blank, but it would be rude not to at least try to probe at their hypothetical compatibility. "After you shower, do you remember to pull the curtain back shut? Or do you often leave it open and have to clean it later?"

"I pull it back shut," she said. The question spoke well of him. "Prevention is better than cure."

"If you had a free weekend, would you rather spend it in a city or outdoors?"

"City. One that's old and overgrown."

"I know you conduct the choir. But do you like music?"

"Desperately," Leah said.

"If you had to choose between a randomly selected Slavic composer and a randomly selected German—"

She smiled. "Slavic."

"Do you prefer the library or a bookstore?"

"It depends on the book. To pass an hour? Library. But if I know I'm going to love it, I want it to be mine."

Menachem paused. He picked up a rugalach. It was flaky and just the right amount of soft.

"Why aren't you married?" Leah asked.

Menachem swallowed. "The thought ties my stomach in knots."

Leah laughed. "Marriage is quite a tradition, isn't it?"

Menachem nodded. "I'm glad it exists in the world. Somewhere. And in the next world, likewise."

"The idea of another person in my life exhausts me," Leah said. "I'm happy as I am. I like my space, both physical and psychological. But who knows? Maybe the compromises would be worth it." She bit her lip. "For example, I'd love to know what it's like to have sex with a man."

That was another thing they had in common, Menachem Menashe thought. He'd often wondered about the exact same thing.

"The troubling thing about marriage," he said, "is that it's supposed to work on so many levels at once. You're expected to be practical, but also passionate. To have things in common, while also complementing each other. Marriage is supposed to be the basis for intergenerational relationships—and also the most intensive sort of friendship. It's supposed to be egalitarian and personalized, but with roles that hold up well under pressure and on autopilot." He looked at her sadly. "I think, once upon a time, when some of those things were separate, that maybe it could've worked for more people. But now? It's too much. For me, it feels like much too much."

She took another long, slow sip of the Levys' fake coffee. "I think I agree," she said.

So as not to disappoint Sara Levy, they talked for a long while before they left. But not about the prospect of marriage anymore. They talked about Smetana. And the way rivers wind, gaining force as they flow out toward an unseen river or lake or sea. No one can predict the course in advance. Only appreciate the music of the river's movement.

He offered to walk her home. She laughed at the offer first: since when did she need someone to walk with? But then, realizing she didn't know the best way to end a Mormon matchmaker's meeting, she agreed.

"Do you think we'll feel different after we're dead?" Menachem asked as they approached her building.

"I hope so," Leah said. "I'm looking forward to being able to fly and walk through walls and all those kinds of things when I'm resurrected." She made a face. "I'm also hoping my taste buds change, just in case Jesus offers me fish."

"I meant about relationships," Menachem said. "Do you think God will change what I want? And if he does, will he also change what I want to want? And if he does—if he can—what's the point of working with the me I am in the meantime?"

Leah laughed. "I thought you said you were the kind of person who spirals *internally*," she said.

"I'm not asking you for reassurance," Menachem said.

"What then?"

He frowned. "A sounding board? For my thoughts to be refined? Understanding?"

Leah nodded. "All I know is that whatever relationships we start here have echoes there," she told him. "So I'm glad to be your friend."

The next day, Sarah Levy called Leah, then Menachem. Each gave their reports by phone, rating their experience on various scales, explaining what had happened, and informing her that from them she should not expect any courtship.

"How did it go?" Matteusz asked when he got back from his bishopric meeting. "Did you make one good match yet?"

"A great match," she told him.

He raised his eyebrows. "Really?"

"Some of the best matches are never going to be marriages," she said. "But they're made in heaven all the same."

*Her body was slowly giving way to time's
tides, but her spirit was sharp.*

Henya
the Prophetess

Members of the Chelm ward were always going to visit Henya. She was in her eighties—almost old enough to be a prophet—and so a person might think the ward very charitable for taking such consistent care of her. It was true that Gimpel and Dudel went every week with Yossel the Fisherman as a matter of duty, to take her the sacrament. And Zelda Gottstein made a fine ministering sister; it was lucky that her regular seat in the foyer happened to be closest to Henya's apartment. But mostly, ward members went by the old woman's apartment not out of any altruism, but for themselves. After all, in addition to being the ward's most avid quilter, Henya was a known receiver of revelations and worker of minor miracles.

Her body was slowly giving way to time's tides, but her spirit was sharp. As she stitched or pinned, you could tell her your troubles and she'd listen with a minimum of judgment, topped with a helping of warm curiosity that softened the heart and loosened the tongue. Sometimes, as your story rolled out, she might make a simple observation that put things in a new light. Other times, she'd reach toward you and take your hand and say she would pray for you.

Ah, and that was a treasure! No one knew what gave Henya's prayers such influence in the court of God—maybe being a few steps nearer to death let her glimpse through the veil? or maybe the Master of the Universe just liked people who were a little closer to his own age?—but whatever the cause, there was a power when Henya said she would pray.

Within a few days, ward members swore, something would happen. Persistent pains would ease. Thorny problems would somehow find themselves resolved to everyone's grudging satisfaction. A job offer would come. Menachem Menashe understood the scriptures better after a visit to Henya. The missionaries said that when Henya was praying for them, they always had something to teach. Even fish seemed to be influenced: they'd crowd their way into Yossel's net when his welfare was on Henya's mind.

If the Church called stake matriarchs, Bishop Levy would have rushed to recommend Henya, even though her health would have prevented her from coming to meetings. But apparently, no one at the Church's headquarters had read about Deborah or Huldah, so it was a conversation the bishop never got to have. Instead, he consoled himself over the apparent shortcoming in the Handbook of Instructions by telling himself that maybe the Church couldn't call such matriarchs. Maybe they just appeared.

In any case, members of the Chelm ward did not need any special spirit of charity to visit Henya. Day by day and week by week, a steady trickle of them found themselves driven to her door by need. She was always home, of course, though sometimes she wouldn't call out to a visitor to let themselves in. Around 2 in the afternoon was not good, though ward members disagreed about whether she was seeing a vision while napping or carried up to heaven in an ecstatic trance. And late in the evening, if you happened to come up to her door, you were likely to hear her talking: on and off, in the rhythm of a conversation, but without another voice in the room. If you felt almost selfish enough to interrupt, the sound would stop you—her voice filled with such pleading or conviction that your hand would falter before knocking and you'd turn away. As word of such encounters spread, most ward members agreed that late in the evening—what else?—Henya must be talking with God.

Of course, the world is full of skeptics—and a ward is no exception. Golda Fischer tried to allow ward members the privilege of worshiping according to the dictates of their own disoriented consciences, but she couldn't bring herself to believe that Henya talked with God face-to-face in her apartment's front room.

Did that mean Golda lacked faith? She doubted it. The book of Alma says that faith is a hope in things which are not seen which are true. What Henya did at 2 pm in the afternoon? Who she talked to at night? These things felt observable, even if no one in the ward was willing to look. And truth mattered, didn't it? Even a skeptic like Golda—especially a skeptic like Golda—has a deep desire for truth. She just needs to know where to find it.

In regards to the facts about Henya's activities, of course, the truth's physical location was no mystery. Henya almost never left her house. If she was talking with God, he was coming to her. The only barrier to making an investigation was that it felt like a violation of Henya's privacy. (And, if one was to keep an open mind, potentially also God's.)

But was that really such a crime? If God cared about privacy, then maybe he should stop reading everyone's thoughts. And Henya knew so many people's little secrets that she shouldn't mind giving up one or two of her own. Also, the amount of conversation about Henya's activities made them into a public issue. Someone really ought to see what Henya was actually doing in the afternoon and in that whispered-over evening time.

So Golda told her parents she was going to spend the day with her friend Chava, then went to visit Henya instead.

For the first hour, Golda tried her best not to relax into the conversation. Henya worked on her patch of quilt. Golda shared general sorts of news about the ward and the most mundane details about her own life. She studiously avoided assigning spiritual meaning to Henya's warmth and interest, reminding herself that conversation is simple physics, nothing but waves of sound. After they'd talked for some time, she was able to help Henya up so the old woman could go to the bathroom. She suppressed a laugh when she noticed a quilting book there. A minute after stepping away, Golda pretended to get an important text and asked if she could excuse herself. Henya said she would be fine. Golda walked to the front door, opened it, then closed it and tiptoed to a back room instead.

It was like a jungle of fabric there. Golda hid behind a row of transparent plastic bins so stuffed with bright scraps that she felt quite hidden. After a while, she heard Henya getting back up, washing her hands, and making her way back to the recliner in the front room where she spent her days. Golda's heart began to race. She felt a sudden fear of being caught, a sneaking suspicion that no amount of quilting material could shield her from Henya's penetrating eyes. But that must be superstition and only superstition. She held still. In her mind, she counted heartbeats until they slowed.

There had to be years' worth of cloth in the room, and in the midst of it, time lost all meaning. The minutes seemed to inch by, take wrong turns, get lost in the rows. Still, Golda waited. Henya had an old-style clock that chimed the hour and the sound finally told Golda it was two.

She shifted her position carefully, quietly, until she could peek out from between two bins for a sliver of a look into the front room. But she needn't have worried about making a sound. Henya had replaced her hearing aids with earphones. They were plugged into a tablet. She wasn't opening the heavens or seeing a vision. She was probably watching TV. Or maybe playing a game? Her finger was moving from time to time, scrolling or typing.

Golda decided to creep around the bins for a better look. There was a risk Henya would turn and see her, but she wanted the whole truth. Finally, from over Henya's shoulder, Golda caught sight of the screen.

Golda watched while the Chelm ward's unofficial matriarch spent the afternoon scrolling through social media. She browsed through quilting communities on Pinterest with posts in different alphabets. She watched a YouTube channel that seemed to be a trucker sharing her thoughts while she drove. She spent time on Facebook, frequently leaving the news feed to check on the pages of individual neighbors and ward members. Golda even caught sight of the Instagram pages of friends from school. When Henya pulled up her long message history with Ada Anders, a girl from Golda's classes, Golda looked away. Even from her current position snooping in an old woman's home, peeking at the messages of someone her own age felt like crossing a line.

Golda made her way back into her place in the fabric storage room between the bins. While Henya was still wearing her headphones, Golda took a moment to examine the back window she planned to use later that evening to escape. It occurred to her she could leave early; she had already seen that nothing special was happening. For a woman who spent most of her time at home, Henya certainly got out more than Golda would have expected. But the internet was hardly heaven. Compared with the rumors about how Henya spent her time, the internet seemed downright small. Still, the gift of a skeptic is to be thorough. The longer she hesitated to leave, the more Golda became convinced that she ought to see her investigation through.

In the late afternoon, visitors came and went, but no one noticed anything amiss. They were all so wrapped up in their own concerns—and what sort of person would stop to wonder if there might be a seventeen-year-old girl crouched in a back room? Golda knew some very paranoid people, and none of them had such a thing on their inventories of concerns. Most secrets, Golda realized, were probably equally ordinary. Just personal preoccupations no one ever thought to ask about, because they were too busy making their own assumptions.

The visitors left. The time ticked by. Golda got lost in thought, wondering how she could tell anybody about the truth without revealing how she discovered it. The light in the room slowly faded, leaving the fabric scraps around her more and more muted.

Because there had been no knock at the door, no sound of anything strange, Henya's voice took Golda by surprise. "Hello?" the old woman said all at once, and for a hair's breadth of a second, Golda thought she had been discovered. But Henya was not talking to her. "How are you?" she asked next. There was a firmness and intensity in her voice, as if in warning that she would not accept a partial or dishonest answer. For no good reason, goose pimples spread across Golda's skin. She felt the hairs on her neck tingle.

She took a slow, careful breath and began to inch forward for a clear look at what was happening. A tiny, childlike part of Golda wondered if she was making a terrible mistake. No unclean thing, the scriptures warned, could stand the brilliance of God's presence. But that was silly. This was just an apartment. When Golda got a clear line of sight, there was nothing to be worried about. All she could see was an old woman wearing headphones and the blueish light from her tablet illuminating her face.

"I know," Henya was saying. "I know . . . I never went through the things you're going through, but people—have mercy on us!—are always people." She sighed, and Golda understood how a sigh like that might leave an impression on a more superstitious eavesdropper. "But I'm glad to know you," Henya said. "I see you."

See who? Golda craned her neck just a little higher to peek over the back of Henya's recliner and caught sight of Ada's face on the screen. Her makeup was streaked from crying. Her mouth was moving. Golda, of course, couldn't make out the words—but she recognized the sorrow. The ache of loneliness. The weight of the world's expectations. Golda wouldn't have expected such raw need from a quiet girl like Ada. And Henya said this or Henya said that, but all Golda heard was love.

What more could there be to see than that? Ada would tell Henya what was on her mind. Henya would probably pick up her quilting and work while she listened. It was nothing; it was everything. Golda turned away and she let herself out the back window.

In the Chelm ward, they still talk sometimes about Henya's powers. How she understands things no ordinary person would know. How she works minor miracles. And her prayers! They swear that there's no better cure for life's troubles than to know Henya is praying for you. If all she leaves is a comment online, it's as good as hands on the head in blessing. Sometimes, a person will mention how they stood outside her door one night and would swear they overheard her talking straight with God!

When Golda hears these stories now, she bows her head. "And if you listen closely," she whispers, "God answers."

It was important that choir members have a good
experience, because—in a Church run on unpaid labor—
choir was one of the few truly volunteer positions.

The Chelm Ward Choir

Sister Leah Kantor had one of the most challenging callings, perhaps, in all the Church. Many choir directors had to put up with people singing in different keys, but in the Chelm ward choir, singers were frequently on a completely different hymn. No amount of cues or reminders to sing the same song seemed to make a difference: it was just their way. In matters of argumentation and debate, there was a saying: "two Jews, three views." In Chelm ward choir practices, where people sang whatever combination of words and melodies they could call up from their uneven memories, it was "two Saints, three songs."

Still, Sister Kantor had tried to unify the group. They needed some sort of harmony. Half the joy of being in choir was different voices meeting. So if a choir member did not want to sing "Now Let Us Rejoice," she might try to nudge them into bringing the words of another song, like "The Spirit of God," onto the same melody. It was important that choir members have a good experience, because—in a Church run on unpaid labor—choir was one of the few truly volunteer positions. Sister Kantor might be called of God whether she was interested or not, but her singers needed to feel drawn in.

For purposes of recruiting and retention, then, she simply had to make the numbers memorable for choir members and the congregation. To set apart choir numbers as *performances*, a special offering distinct from ordinary congregational singing. Obviously, volunteer singers were an unwieldy tool for pursuing that goal. When she tried to divide them into sopranos, altos, tenors, and basses, for example, a certain member of the Cohen family derailed practice with complaints about how four was too many genders. So Sister Kantor worked other angles as well. For example, she met early with Belka Fischer, who played the piano and was called of God to pretend to play the organ. "When you practice a song for the choir," Sister Kantor suggested, "don't start from the beginning. Start by practicing the last few lines. Once you've really mastered them, you can work your way forward." The effect was striking. While most hymns slowed down between the beginning and the end, choir numbers began to speed up!

Sister Kantor, however, did not rest on her laurels after accelerating the organ accompaniment. There was so much more a choir director could do. In her pursuit of a complete artistic experience, Sister Kantor thought of ways to accompany choir numbers visually, through lighting or props. These efforts did not always go smoothly. Like the time she prepared them to sing "Lead Kindly, Light": it was only after she lit a candle and darkened the chapel that she discovered no one had memorized the words, let alone the tune!

Next, she'd tried "All Creatures of Our God and King," but at the final rehearsal the hens she brought in had roosted in the piano, the goats took a bite out of her sheet music, and one of the sheep got lost. They'd all had to leave practice then to search for it, until Lemel carried it back on his shoulders. For the actual performance, she scaled down to a few strategically placed fishbowls. Nothing went wrong with them—it occurred to her that they were a nice alternative to putting flowers on the stand, and might add visual interest to a funeral—but they failed to capture the scale of grandeur in the hymn and left her unsatisfied.

After that, she made a strategic pivot in her pursuit of excellence. In essence, the pivot was to aim for good enough instead. She still rehearsed the choir for months, of course, but she accepted that their rendition of "Israel, Israel, God is Calling" would likely include a few strains of "Welcome, Welcome Sabbath Morning." She resolved to be the live prop she wanted to see in the choir, conducting with the poise and visual flourish of a master, and leaving any extra chickens out of it. Given the theme of the song, a part of her hoped that the audible voice of God would make a guest appearance, "but if not," as the scriptures said, she would still keep the people singing.

At last, the great and terrible day of their performance came. Little Breyndl Fisher, the choir's youngest member, froze halfway up the aisle with stage fright, but after checking to see if she still wanted to perform, Lemel scooped her up just like a lamb to carry her to the stand. Breyndl stood there, stiff, ready to mumble-whisper the words. Fair enough, Leah Kantor thought. When many are called it's all right if a few get frozen. Though she couldn't help but feel a little of that same petrifying nervousness as she glanced from Belka at the organ to the unfocused faces of her singers, the feeling fled as she lifted her arms to conduct.

The men's voices rang deep and resonant through the chapel as they sang, "Israel, Israel, Sabbath morning" and "Welcome, Welcome, God is calling." On the second line (or third, as they saw fit) the sisters came in with "now we rest from lands of woe" and "calling thee from every care."

And then, three miracles happened.

For just one glorious moment, everyone in the choir sang in the exact same key.

And old Israel Lewensztajn, who *always* slept through sacrament meeting, suddenly stirred, blinked, rose up and looked around . . .

. . . as, for the first time anyone could remember, the phone in the bishop's office began to ring.

Sister Kantor smiled. She had always wondered what God's audible voice would sound like.

*The time had come to organize the
ward's first-ever group temple trip.*

His Brother's Keeper

On the Sunday when 97-year-old Israel Lewensztajn woke up during sacrament meeting just before the meetinghouse telephone began ringing, no one was sure at first what to do. Was this a part of the choir's performance? A vision from God that came to their ears? Or was someone actually trying to reach them on the telephone? It was several seconds before Gretele's mother, Zelda Gottstein, walked over from her usual place in the foyer to confirm that a real telephone was ringing and answer it. She soon appeared in the chapel doorway—the closest she'd come for many years to entering—to summon Bishop Levy. Apparently, the stake president had been trying to reach Chelm's humble shepherd for some time and was beginning to suspect that caller ID was standing between them. The president had concluded that a call during meetings, with the whole ward as witnesses, might help the bishop overcome his hesitations and return to their unfinished business.

Feige Cohen, Mirele Schwartz, and a few other sharp-eared Saints sitting near the chapel exit could make out bits and pieces of the meetinghouse half of the conversation. Bishop Levy was discussing an event to take place in the spring. He mentioned the city of Kyiv, the chartering of a bus, and potential arrangements for some sort of overnight stay. He did not sound enthusiastic (except when raising objections).

But all Bishop Levy's efforts were fruitless. No excuse or evasion was enough. The stake president was insistent. After each interruption, he showed such a clear increase in love that Bishop Levy slowly realized he was being rebuked. When the bishop returned to the chapel, it was to announce that the Saints of Chelm were about to put their faith in God and the modern nation of Ukraine: the time had come to organize the ward's first-ever group temple trip.

Talk immediately turned to who planned to attend. Old Israel Lewensztajn surprised everyone twice: first, by still being awake, and second, by saying that he would not miss the trip for anything short of an urgent call from the other side of the veil. (In his capacity as ward executive secretary, Heshel put down Brother Lewensztajn as a "maybe.")

Oskar the Miser's reaction to the sudden proposal, in contrast, was unsurprising enough to restore ward members' sense of normalcy. "Why should I budget for a trip all the way to Kyiv now," he asked, "when soon enough, someone else will be able to do my work by proxy for me?" (Beside Oscar's name, Heshel wrote "next time.")

There were other nos. Zelda Gottstein said the trip to the phone had been quite enough. Lazar worried about carsickness. There were also other yeses. Mirele Schwartz, predictably, was willing to make any sacrifice to attend. The Cohens, shockingly, decided to go together. Menachem Menasche was excited both for the temple and for time together on the road with other ward members. The Fischers suggested games they could play along the way. From there, vigorous discussion about bus-friendly entertainment picked up among the likely goers while the stayers fell quiet.

Before long, Bishop Levy cut through all the chatter. Whoever decided to stay or go, he insisted, the trip would be for the whole ward. Over the next few months, they could all prepare family names to send. He challenged everyone to find five names for sealings, or else for the prayer roll. Heaven knew every family had need enough for both.

And so it was that the members of the Chelm ward went to work on their family histories.

No one would plant a tree by tossing a leaf into the sky and waiting for it to grow a branch, and the branch a trunk. To Brother Cohen, it seemed equally absurd to start one's genealogy in the fickle present. When talk turned to family history, he preferred to begin at that roots. During many a talk and many a lesson, he had opened up the good book to trace his way from Abraham to Levi, from Levi to Aaron, and then on down the generations through the many lines described in Leviticus and Chronicles and Ezra.

But those ancestors had already served in one temple or another in Jerusalem and hardly needed an invitation to drop in on the one in Kyiv. And sometime before the temple was destroyed on a long-ago 9th of Av, the genealogies stopped. It simply wasn't possible for the fathers to make it down in an orderly, linear fashion to the children.

So Brother Cohen sighed and opened up a blank page in the back of his book. Perhaps it would have to be backward after all, with the children driving across the centuries in reverse for as long as the engine could hold out. "Aaron was the son of Eleazar," he began, "who was the son of Amram, who was the son of Ezra, who was the son of Gotlib, who was the son of Chaim." Writing scripture of one's own, he realized, was remarkably simple if one stuck to the classic plot.

Meanwhile, in the quiet that descended on her apartment in the evening, Clever Gretele was using a very different method to figure out which ancestors to begin with. It did not even occur to Gretele to move forwards or backward, since she had always thought of families as being more round. Relatives sort of circled around each other in her experience, waiting to pounce on the less alert. The person Gretele most desperately wanted to see in heaven was her mother, but Zelda might never die and, if she did, was probably too stubborn to leave the foyer even for the courts of God. Gretele decided that the best way to help herd the woman toward celestial glory would be by setting up some peer pressure in advance. To fulfill the bishop's challenge, she set out researching her mother's aunts, who had been pushy in this life and had hopefully retained that same virtue in the next.

Oskar the Miser felt little need to search out his fore-bears in the Wiener family. Considering family legacy to be a kind of wealth, he counted his regularly. There was his uncle Nachum the cheapskate, who refused to pay for ice even in the hottest of summers because in a few months, everyone would get it free. He thought of his grandfather, Kopel the penny-pincher, who lived off a special soup made by filling old tea-bags with dried vegetables and letting the broth steep. There was a maternal cousin once removed, Libkind the extortioner, who narrowed the local wage gap by refusing to pay anybody for anything. And then there was the greatest of his great-aunts, Gryna the gold-digger, who had married seven brothers in succession and made it through a combined total of fourteen weddings and funerals in the same hand-me-down gown.

It occurred to Oskar that Gryna had left him one last gift. He could send her first five marriages on this temple trip and still have two left for the next! That just went to show that it paid to plan ahead.

In other homes, too, there was a great turning of the hearts. Leah Kantor started it with an old record player and a turning of the albums her relatives had loved. She thought it might coax their spirits closer and give them a head start preparing for the temple trip. Menachem Menasche faithfully chronicled the siblings and cousins in each generation leading up to his own, appreciating the crystalline shapes of stops and starts in his wide family tree. In the Levy house, Bluma and Bina put together a four-generation chart in which almost no one was dead and almost everyone needed blessings. Especially their father, whose worn nerves surely deserved a mention on the temple's altar.

If there were truly blessings coming, Bishop Levy wanted a divine advance. He had accepted that the trip would happen, but as he planned the particulars anxiety still twisted his stomach like a wrung-out rag. It was not that the bishop had anything against the temple. (It was true that his ancestors' luck with such buildings had run out more than once, but so had his grandfather's cow—and they'd chased her down each time to keep the milk up just the same.) No, the problem was Ukraine.

Bishop Levy's ancestors were not all from Chelm, and he knew a thing or two from old family stories. Growing up, he had heard wild tales about gangsters in Odesa. As for Kyiv, Bishop Levy's mother's cousin's great-grandfather was a humble milkman from the nearby village of Boyberik and he had experienced nothing but scams and misfortune in the big city. The people of Chelm knew an offer too good to be true when they saw one—but they didn't know how to turn it down. Naturally, he worried for them.

Nor was Bishop Levy's own family safe. As the father of daughters, he was hardly eager to pass through Anatevka, where they might fall in love and break his heart. These days, a girl might choose a man who had a double life online as a Nigerian prince, or a live-in boyfriend who only wanted to make it as an influencer, or a perfectly likable wife. Yes, a father could never really know what would happen in Ukraine.

The stake president had assured him it would be all right. After all, Ukrainians had recently elected a Jew as their head of state. What could go wrong, the stake president asked, in this day and age? Ah, but Bishop Levy had inherited an active imagination. He assured the stake president he could think of a few things.

The only person who felt more conflicted about the trip than the bishop was Yossel the Fisherman. Ukraine didn't worry him. The temple building looked perfectly nice, and he knew from a song his children sang that he was going there someday. But it would be with a little twinge of uncertainty, the nagging doubt that he was missing something. When the topic of family came up in the Church, as it so often did, Yossel always felt an extra burst of gratitude for the family that had taken him in as an infant after losing their own baby. But sometimes, he also felt curious about the anonymous parents who had given him birth.

Thoughts of his birth parents could lead Yossel down a dangerous spiral. In church once, he had heard a story about an illiterate peasant who learned, after his death, that he was celebrated in heaven as his world's greatest poet. For the angels, the speaker said, what truly mattered was not the man's poverty, but what he could have written given the opportunity. That story was meant to be comforting, but it gave Yossel a sudden vertigo. He was a fisherman. He could hardly imagine himself as Yossel the Poet. Then again, his adopted father was a fisherman. If his birth father had raised him, would he be something else entirely? Perhaps, in a different life, he would have been Yossel the Trash Collector or Yossel the Car Salesman. Truth be told, he probably would not have been a Yossel at all.

So what had happened to Not-Yossel the Not-Fisherman? Was he only in hiding, waiting to reveal himself in the eternities as the self who might have been? Or had an inheritance of fishing, through accident of the time just after his birth, sunk itself for the eons into the very shape of Yossel's soul?

At the same time he pondered his own post-mortal identity, Yossel found himself wondering about the brother he had never known. In his parents' house, there was a thick silence about that lost son, the one who could have had Yossel's life. Someday, perhaps, Yossel's parents would develop an interest in the Church. Perhaps then he would bring up his missing brother—and his mother's eyes would not grow misty and his father would not change the subject, because they would see that there was a way to be together with their son again. Their son, who could've been the fisherman. Their son, who might have filled the house with laughter. Who might've fallen in love with the girl next door, maybe even married Belka. All while, in the orphanage, not-Yossel the not-Fisherman might've been left without knowing any parents at all.

In the next elders quorum meeting, President Gronam talked about family history. Family history, he said, was not simply a walk down memory lane, but a duty with a firm basis in doctrine. President Gronam liked duties because he hated indecision. Much better to go through life with the days resolving into neat sets of accomplishment and guilt than to wander through a sucking morass of possibilities.

A man should know what to do. Projects, lists, even busywork, were some of the most gracious gifts God gave mankind. Even if it had nothing to do with family, genealogy would be useful because it was concrete, measurable, and all-but-inexhaustible. Until the Millennium, the dead were a renewable resource. The work for them was good as any wheel to put your shoulder to. And for all its challenges, it was hardly the most complicated part of belonging to a family.

And so President Gronam reminded his quorum members what they were under obligation to do. He expected them to do this work, to do it right, and to do it right now. Like many kinds of paperwork, the urgency was no less than apocalyptic. According to Malachi's prophecy, Elijah the prophet would come before the great and dreadful day of the Lord—to turn the hearts of the fathers to the children and the hearts of the children to their fathers. A Saint should do something about that.

Brother Yossel Fischer raised his hand. He asked what it meant for the hearts to turn. He wondered, further, exactly which fathers were meant in the verse.

President Gronam sighed. He liked the idea of family history as something to do better than he liked dwelling on the turn of phrase about Elijah turning hearts. Privately, President Gronam suspected that no other prophet had been given a more harrowing task. So many fathers' hearts ran hard or hot—and who knew what would happen if you tried to wrench them aside from their accustomed courses? And children: their hearts were so hungry. It took years for most to accept the limits of what their fathers could offer and turn their expectations elsewhere. It was madness to turn those hearts back again. A kind of divine madness to expect that a collision of the hearts would go well.

It was no wonder that Elijah slipped by so many houses each year for a sip of Passover wine.

"Think of the temple like a factory," President Gronam told Brother Fischer. "This factory packages relationships for transport—to a faraway country, or another world. And our duty is to feed in the raw materials. I don't know what Elijah does with them."

As Yossel considered the raw materials of his own life, he thought of both families who had played roles in his creation. He was so much a product of the family he knew: good and loving parents who had always been there for him with noble ancestors who had lived pious and faithful lives. But, in some ways, he was also a product of the family he didn't know: parents who, for whatever reason, had not wanted to raise a child. Had they loved him once? Had they loved each other? He didn't know. He hadn't ever looked for them because a part of him didn't really want to know.

But maybe President Gronam was right. A person's duty was to find the names of his ancestors and offer them to God. Absent as they were, Yossel's birth family were a kind of ancestors. Maybe not in the same sense as the parents who had given him a home and an identity, but he could claim them nonetheless. If he could find them, who knew what he might learn?

On Wednesday, he decided to walk down toward the orphanage to see if they had any records about his origins. He wondered briefly if his birth parents still lived in Chelm. He considered the possibility that he had passed his birth father on a street or helped his birth mother reach a bottle off a high shelf while shopping. He wondered if they would want to meet him now, if they would be proud of the fisherman he had become.

It was possible, of course, that his birth parents were dead and he would have to wait for the next life to find out. What if his birth father had died in an accident before he was born and his birth mother had died in childbirth? Maybe they'd been watching him all his life from the other side of the gauzy veil between the living and the dead. Or maybe they had been alive when he was young, but each died in the many years he wasn't looking for them. He had growing children of his own: plenty of people old enough to be his parents were no longer among the living.

But if they were alive. If they were alive, and he could find them, and he went to talk to them, what then? It was quite possible his absence had never troubled them. Maybe his birth mother had thought of him only in passing and with shame. Maybe his birth father had never known about him at all. What then if he found them and knocked on the door?

Yossel walked past the orphanage. He walked past it without giving the building a second glance, but thoughts of his birth parents followed him down the block. He stopped in front of a small grocery store. If his birth parents were dead and in God's hands, he didn't need to understand in advance what God would do with their names. And if he didn't need to understand what God would do if his parents were dead, maybe he didn't need to know in advance what he would do if he discovered that his birth parents were alive. After all, hadn't the prophets taught that Yossel was a god in embryo? If that was true, he was entitled to some mysterious ways.

Yossel turned back toward the orphanage, not knowing beforehand what he was getting into. He walked past the corner store where Isaac Peretz used to buy his cigarettes. He picked up speed as he passed the front door of Fruma Selig and Hirsh the Atheist's aging building. He ran past a cafe, where Leah Kantor and Menachem Menasche were having a heated discussion about the relative merits of Shostakovich's fifth and tenth symphonies. Finally, he composed himself and walked up to the orphanage door, sure that the Lord would provide a way.

Apparently, though, the Lord was not in a hurry. On Wednesdays, the front office told him, the place was short staffed and the records office was closed.

Late that same evening, so late that she supposed it was night, Feige Cohen was thinking about her marriage. Aaron was not an easy man to know. She suited him well enough: she was not an easy woman. They were both so brittle; that was the trouble. Once either of their minds got set, it was stuck. After the barest hint of decision, both found it all but impossible to change course. And in any collision that followed, neither knew how to give, so the obvious alternative was to break. He could be so thoughtless and bull-headed, he would hurt her feelings without realizing it. Being more perceptive, she hurt his feelings on purpose. In a great leveling across their difference in emotional intelligence, the results were essentially the same.

As the years passed and her heart calloused over, she found it easier and easier to forgive him in theory. But by then, her reflexes were too strong to forgive him in observable practice. Whether she thought he deserved her hard feelings was beyond the point; they were simply a matter of habit. She clung to each offense. She savored the bitter taste that came with licking her wounds. Yes: when she joined the Church, she'd found it surprisingly easy to give up coffee because she held on to her firm rituals of resentment. Having a chip on her shoulder energized her. A little spite gave her reason enough to get out of bed.

She still loved her husband, and she wanted to be with him in time and eternity. Just not too close. Was there anything so wrong with that?

Her children certainly thought so. They were of the opinion that there were better ways to grow up than on freezing glares and icy silences. Their parents' way of relating left the children inside them feeling insecure and the adults they had become feeling embarrassed. A few years ago, the children had briefly hoped that Feige and Aaron's conversion to Mormonism proved—against all previous evidence—that they were capable of change. There had been a brief window when her children had even been interested in the strange religion and its potential to transform. But after immersion failed to wash Feige's personality away, their interest dried up. Except for the occasional visit from her granddaughter Zusa, Feige was left in the Church without branch.

She would go to the temple on behalf of her ancestors. But she had no illusions. It was clear to her that she and Aaron were a weak link in their family's long chain.

Bishop Levy couldn't sleep that night, either. As he lay in the bed, tossing, his thoughts turned to Benya Krik, the famous gangster they called the King. He imagined the King's men stopping the bus and looking the Chelm ward members over. He felt so weak as he thought about how he must look to those tough old Odesa Jews and their modern successors. What an unflattering mirror the past could be.

In the bed beside him, Sara Levy was also awake. She was tired, but every time she started to fall asleep, her husband would turn again. She wished for a moment he had a less sensitive heart. "I understand that you're worried," she finally told him, "but I still don't understand what you're so worried about."

Her voice pulled him from his thoughts. Once he left the churn of them, the figures of the gangsters thinned but his embarrassment remained. He felt small. Silly. But since his wife was still up, he felt that he owed her the truth. "I was thinking about the ghetto where my great-grandmother grew up," he said. "And wondering about this temple trip."

"That was a long time ago," Sara said. "Why should those things keep you from sleep? The old ghettos and shtetls don't even exist anymore."

She was right, he told himself. There were no more czars, no pale of settlement. No dance on the rooftops of an empire's fringe. No Russian Empire. That world didn't exist. Benya Krik was only a ghost. The village of Boyberik didn't appear on any map.

But maybe that was the problem. The most frightening thing about the past was the way it had of disappearing. He was afraid to go back and meet it, yes, but he was also afraid to go back and find it gone.

The next day, the attendant at the orphanage records office received Yossel warmly. As soon as he had explained, to the best of his limited ability, who he was—and provided official documents to support his story—she was happy to retrieve his file.

It was thin. The report did not list any names, descriptions, or contact information for his birth parents. Instead of mother and father, it offered the identity of the police officer who had retrieved an abandoned baby from beneath the sauerkraut in a nearby grocery store and the orphanage nurse who had recorded that lost baby's length and weight. So far as the official paperwork was concerned, then, he was the descendant of two different departments of the state. Otherwise? His name: unknown. His birth date: unknown. The place: likewise unknown. And then, staring up at him from the midst of the vast unknown, Yossel noticed a strange thing. Even as an anonymous baby, his religion was listed as Jewish.

After a moment's puzzlement, he realized what this must mean. He had not been abandoned at birth. For at least eight days, someone outside the orphanage had cared for him.

That thought pierced his heart. And made the dead ends on the rest of the page feel so heavy. He was accustomed to thinking of his past as a nothing, but the fields on this form showed that his early life must have been made of missing somethings. For the first time, he wondered if he'd had a middle name. If he'd been named after someone. What the first blanket his mother had wrapped him in looked like. Now that he had one tiny glimmer of his past, he was more attuned than ever to the darkness. There were such specific things he did not know.

Israel Lewensztajn was looking forward to the temple trip. He liked falling asleep in the chapel well enough, but he had never fallen asleep in an official house of the Lord! He only hoped he would not snore.

He was especially looking forward to seeing family and friends there. Maybe, while sleeping in the temple, he would dream of his parents, his aunts and uncles, or his own great-grandfather. He could still remember the man's forked white beard, and snatches of the melodies he used to sing around the table with his fellow Hasids. Maybe those friends of his great-grandfather would all come, too, still singing, and Israel would hear that old music again with the same wonder he had experienced as a small boy. It would be nice to be the young one at a party for a change.

Over dinner, Israel thought to wonder about the food in heaven. He had spent long enough on earth to see tastes change, ingredients change, kitchens change, even dietary laws change. Speaking for himself, he wouldn't mind having a little wine again in heaven. Then again, even if an angel brought it out on a platter, he'd feel suspicious of shrimp. He wondered whether most of the dead would prefer to eat and drink what they were used to. If you sat at a heavenly banquet with a medieval rabbi, for example, would he want a bite of potato latke? Or turn up his nose at the strange root? This struck Israel as an important question the prophets ought to spend more time praying over. What sort of feast would it take to coax the generations to the same table? For God's work to progress, his people surely needed to know.

It occurred to Israel that the scriptures suggested even angels enjoyed a little novelty. Hadn't the three messengers who came to Sarah and Abraham rejoiced over her food? They could have packed their own to bring, in tiny heavenly boxes. But they didn't. Mouths watered. Hearts turned. He resolved not to get out of touch after he died: he would come take a look at his descendants from time to time and see what was on their plates. Yes, he'd smell the sweet savor of whatever meats they decided to cook, in whatever strange future gravy or sauce. Earth surely had a surprise or two for eternity. Maybe that was part of the whole purpose of their partnership.

Zelda Gottstein thought about eternity far less as she prepared not to go to the temple. As the ward planned for the trip, she thought instead, with a mix of longing and revulsion, about the bus ride. Everyone stuffed together for all those hours, with no more free air than from a window cracked a centimeter open. Yossel smelling, as he did, of fish. She wouldn't miss that.

But she would miss them. Fools that they were, bigger fool that she was, she would miss them while they were gone. She would miss the warmth of having them in a very next room.

Zelda had never been one to fixate on sin, but separation? That was a problem she hoped this faith of hers really would solve. In time, and maybe after the darkness she expected when life reached its end.

As Belka Fischer comforted her husband Yossel, it occurred to her that the way might not be so blocked as it seemed. So the orphanage didn't know his birth date? The hospital must have records of any babies born there. He ought to check on the eight days or so before the policeman brought him to the orphanage. For that matter, a mohel might keep notes on the babies he had circumcised. So far as she knew, there was only the one who had been active in Chelm four decades ago: the old dentist, Moritz Froim. It seemed likely enough that her husband would have been abandoned in the same general geographic area as he was born. After all, a mother looking to be free had no reason to flee very far. A newborn baby couldn't even crawl. With a little more looking, Yossel could surely find a few candidates, at least, for the person he might have once been.

And so it was that Yossel the Fisherman went out on another expedition.

The hospital was less accommodating than the orphanage. Polish privacy laws simply weren't designed for people with only a general approximation of their identity. They were happy to show a person a record regarding his or her own birth, but they expected you to know already with a great deal of precision who you were. There was no provision for possible selves, let alone the proximate selves Yossel wanted to fish through. The records staff were sorry, of course, that he had lost both parents—in whatever senses of the word—but they needed him to understand that even as a baby, he had a right to privacy, which would last for his whole natural life. They couldn't just let a stranger like him look at his birth records. If he could prove that he was dead, of course, that would change the story. Intruding on the living was a crime, but on the dead, it was research.

Yossel thought and he thought. He was not in any hurry to die, but an opportunity was an opportunity and he felt he ought to take advantage of it somehow. After a few moments of consideration, he asked to see the records of any deceased babies from the time period in question, in the weeks before his arrival at the orphanage. That would at least give him a place to start, he pointed out, by showing which of Chelm's children he was definitely not. The staff agreed to look, but the search led to another dead end. No babies matched that description, and Yossel had to leave without so much as a scrap of new knowledge about who he wasn't.

Given that disappointment, Yossel was low on hope by the time he reached the old mohel's door. He had been assured that Dr. Froim was very likely still alive, though his hand was no longer steady enough to continue in his former lines of work. Sure enough, those hands rattled against the locks for several minutes before the retired mohel welcomed Yossel into his apartment. But when Yossel shared his story and asked his question, Dr. Froim readily agreed to take a look. He had not kept, he admitted, a direct list of the baby boys who had been brought to him. But families usually brought along a little money or a gift, which he had always listed in an account book alongside the parents' names. It wasn't much, he warned, but he could check and see about Yossel's theoretical parents' generosity.

Yossel's heart fluttered as the mohel's hands flicked shakily through the pages in the year and then month of his mysterious birth. Sure enough, Dr. Froim announced at length, a couple had brought him a child at that time. Their names were Jakob and Rochla Fischer.

The hope Yossel had felt rising in his chest was instantly deflated. Of all the possible names the mohel could have read, those two were the least helpful. The one documented baby was his brother. Truth be told, a part of Yossel felt jealous. It hardly seemed fair: why should Yossel's brother, who needed no answers, have inherited this clue? He could hardly blame the child, but it was still frustrating. Why was it so often that those who had, received, while those who had not were left empty?

But Yossel refused to give in to resentment. He would be his brother's keeper. If he could look past his disappointment, Yossel realized, his trip had not left him entirely without insight. Given his parents' silence on the subject, he had never known that his brother lived to be circumcised.

On the night when Yossel found a clue, Menachem Mena-sche was reading in his scriptures about covenants. He'd made it past the promises of descendants like stars in the sky or sand in the sea, like fruitful branches growing over a wall, and was trudging through the stories of those descendants getting stuck like sand in uncomfortable places, when he happened upon a familiar story in an unfamiliar way. In the book of Samuel, David and Jonathan made a covenant. Jonathan loved David as his own soul. He gave him his robe and his garments.

Menachem stopped and looked up. He didn't know just what sort of covenant those two had made. But he wondered what they would mean to each other in the time beyond all time. Yes, David had broken a whole tablet's worth of commandments. According to the Doctrine and Covenants, he had forever broken relationships with his wives. But Nathan the prophet said God forgave David. The scriptures showed that God could sometimes equivocate, but they were quite clear that he could not lie. The Psalms said God would not leave David's soul in Sheol. What kind of heaven would heaven be without some kind of relationship with people he had known and loved?

Menachem loved his parents. Their very memory was a blessing to him, so he wanted more: to see them again, to be theirs and for them to be his. When that reunion came, he also wanted them to see how he had loved the world, to feel themselves extended through his relationships. He wanted them to feel what a good talk with Lazar or Leah meant to him, to see him studying with his students in Sunday School. To understand all the tiny ways he expressed life's many loves. Of course, those were hardly the kinds of relationships a person took to the temple for transport across the veil. The truth was, and might well always be, that he had no new relationships to mark on a chart. Only the connections he carried in his heart. He supposed that he could, at least, bring that into God's house. Lay it on the altar. Who knew what Elijah would do with it?

President Gronam had never been particularly fond of thinking about his father, but that same night he decided it would be best if they were sealed. It was possible the shock of death and the vast expanse of the spirit world had opened his father to change. If that was the case, he might as well throw the man a rope, with the sealing's weight acting as an anchor against the storms he was likely working through as he reflected on his life.

Though he balked a little at the thought, President Gronam reassured himself that there was little enough danger in such an act of conditional charity. After all, if his father was still the same man he had once been (or at least seemed to be), then the sealing could work to his condemnation. The anchoring weight of family obligations would be no balm to a spirit still kicking against the pricks. And if it dragged him down instead, President Gronam felt no need to be sorry. Once mercy had claimed her own, justice and vengeance would be the same. Vengeance was not President Gronam's, but it was quite emphatically the Lord's. In life, kindness could easily slide into carelessness. There had to be boundaries. But when it came to questions of judgment and redemption, you didn't have to be a fool to trust love. President Gronam was confident that God's love would sound in the proper key.

And on that same night, Feige Cohen dreamed of her mother. They had quarreled, sometimes, when Feige was young, but they often seemed to find their way back out of an argument without any lingering damage. After all these years, it finally occurred to Feige to wonder how. But she hesitated to ask. If her mother had a secret to resolving conflict that she had never shared, Feige would feel bitter. She'd say something curt, and her mother would say something back. Feige wouldn't be able to stop herself, then, even though she wasn't in the mood to fight over how their fights had ended. Not when her mother was sitting quietly, bent over some needlework.

Since it wouldn't do to disturb her, Feige leaned closer instead to see what her mother was working on. Her first impression was that it was beautiful. Delicate lacework in the shape of a tree. But the pattern was irregular, asymmetrical, and Feige felt a sudden itch to fix it. She found a needle and bent beside her mother to count the stitches on each row until she could see what had gone wrong.

Looking closely, there were problems with more than the symmetry. As she scrutinized the stitching, it was clear the piece was filled with little mistakes. Sloppy. Slapdash. She was surprised her mother hadn't given up. And yet: when Feige looked from any given stitch to the larger pattern, those quirks stopped looking so much like flaws. The longer she looked, the more they each seemed to be part of the design. There were odd twists worked into the leaves and fruit, almost-snarls made to conjure knots in the wood. The piece's genius transcended planning: it was the product of inspired improvisation.

Feige clutched her useless needle. She wanted to make things right, but she couldn't tell what right was. It was so frustrating. A woman should know what to do. She wished, looking at the lacework, that she had her mother's eyes, her mother's gift. But that was hard to imagine. Feige had trouble letting anything go. Ah, she couldn't stand it.

And then her mother's fingers were in her hair, stroking gently like she was a child again, drifting off to sleep. Those careful fingers. They were love, they were love, they were love.

The next time Bishop Levy saw the stake president's number appear on the screen of his cell phone, he answered. But before he could report on his progress since their conversation on the meetinghouse phone, the stake president asked for his forgiveness.

"It was wrong of me to push you," the stake president said. "Sometimes I forget that eternity is a long time." He cleared his voice. "The temple can wait for the people of Chelm. After all, waiting for us is most of what heaven does. If anyone has names they would like to send now, they can send them with another group. You should follow your judgment when it comes to your ward."

But Bishop Levy no longer felt quite such a strong desire to escape the journey. "Even if you were wrong, I think you were also right," he admitted. "I don't think that our ancestors would want some anonymous Christians poking across the veil and asking them to be baptized." It would be better for them if their own family members came, inviting them to be sealed. Reaching across history was no small thing, but what better place to do it than in Ukraine? "We should be the ones to carry those names to the temple," he said. "We'll be ready in the spring, God willing, for a trip to Kyiv and a wonderful time." Sara was right. There was nothing to worry about.

After reassuring the stake president one more time that this really was his choice, Bishop Levy brought the conversation to a close and turned his attention to searching for old family names.

At that very moment, Yossel was making his way to his parents' apartment. They would be happy to see him—they always were—but he wondered how they would react when they found out he'd been looking not only for himself, but also for the son they never talked about. Would they feel as though their children were conspiring against them? Since one of them was dead, the two Fischer boys had never done anything like this before.

Yossel didn't want them to feel bullied, but he wanted a question or two answered for a change. He wanted his brother to be remembered. For someone, finally, to say his name.

Jakob Fischer threw his arms around Yossel right after he opened the door, and for a moment Yossel almost decided to let the sorrows of the past stay silent between them. But he had not visited an orphanage, a hospital, and the office of a retired dentist for nothing. He needed the truth. "I went to visit the old mohel," Yossel began, "and he didn't know anything about me."

"Well, why would he?" Yossel's father said. "Both your children are daughters."

"I mean about me before I was me, or when I was a different me. When I was a baby. But your names were written in his account book, because of my brother."

Yossel glanced over at the couch where his mother was sitting. Sure enough, a faraway look came over her and her eyes turned misty.

For an instant, he could see a cloud pass over his father's face, too, but then it was bright again. "How is Dr. Froim, then?" Jakob Fischer asked with a forced lightness. "I saw his nephew the other day, and he was telling me—"

But Yossel refused to let him change the subject. "I wish I knew more about my brother," he said.

His father met his gaze. "That was a long time ago," he replied. "And there's not much to tell. Why don't you tell me about my granddaughters? I can make you some tea."

But Yossel pressed forward. "I want to know more about my brother. I believe he's still there, in heaven. I believe I'll see him again someday. But I don't even know his name."

"It was Beniamin," Yossel's mother said suddenly. "Our little Beniaminek."

Yossel's father moved to sit beside her. He put an arm around her in a way that struck Yossel as half-comforting and half-protective.

Yossel's mother began to cry. "And he may not be in heaven—" she said, before her tears gave way to sobs.

Yossel's father stroked her hair. "Hush now, hush," he said. He gave Yossel a reproving look. "You don't have to talk about it."

Her shoulders continued to shake for a moment, but then they stilled. "He's a grown man," Rochel Fischer told her husband. "He deserves to know my shame."

Yossel did not know what to think. Shame? He could never have imagined his mother being unfaithful to his father, but then again—he knew her as a parent more than as a person. And that would've been long ago, years before his memories began. Like so many things.

Yossel's mother turned toward him. "Your father wasn't even there," she told him. "It was my fault we lost your brother," she told him. "I lost him."

"Even if you made a mistake, I don't see how you would be to blame for his death," Yossel said. That was old, magical thinking. God didn't punish by taking away children.

"His death?" his mother said. "God forbid."

"She lost your brother," Yossel's father said. "We never could find him, but it's possible that he's still alive somewhere."

Then the words began to pour out of his mother in a torrent. "I was so tired. I could barely think. One day, I was coming back from some errands. It wasn't until I stepped through our front door that I realized I had my bags, but his carrier was missing. I ran back to the stop, but it wasn't there. I rode every bus I could find, but there was nothing. We contacted the transit authority, questioned the drivers, but none of it was any use. No one could remember anything. And how could I blame them—when I had forgotten my own suckling child?"

"For a week, she was inconsolable," Yossel's father said. "She wouldn't go to work, would barely leave her bed. We had wanted a child so badly, and to lose him so soon . . . you've never seen a heart so broken. When a friend of mine, who worked at the orphanage, told me there was a baby there, I thought we should raise him. At first, she resisted—"

"I couldn't bear to lose another child—" his mother said.

"But I promised her I would keep you close to me, always. That's why you never went to the yeshiva. Why I trained you to become a fisherman. I know it might not be the life you would have wanted, but you have to understand how frightened we were."

"Even after we adopted you, we spent the next two years looking for your brother," his mother said. "But there was no sign of him. It was as if he had vanished into thin air."

"We didn't want you to grow up thinking that your brother was all that mattered to us, so eventually we gave up the search," Yossel's father said. "I only pray he's happy somewhere."

Yossel turned to his mother. "What else do you remember about that day?" he asked her.

"Besides the blind panic? The despair? The tearing my hair out searching?"

"I need to know," said Yossel, "exactly what was in the bags you were holding when you came home."

"Nothing of value!" Yossel's mother cried. "Nothing worth losing a child! Some bread, some cheese, some potatoes. A jar of sauerkraut."

Yossel's heart felt ready to burst. He had just lost a brother, but he had found himself. He was the product both of the parents he had known, and the parents he was just meeting, with their tragic secret and their hidden motives and their terrible self-doubt. "Oh mother," he said. "How could I be angry at you for losing me in the sauerkraut aisle? I am only thankful for the policeman who left the note in his report at the orphanage that helped me find you again."

His mother looked at him in confusion. Then something dawned in her eyes. "Could it be?" his mother asked. "All this time?"

"Our Beniaminek?" asked his father.

"No," Yossel said. "I am Yossel the Fisherman. The man I am is because of the child you raised. But yes," he said. "You did give birth to me. And today, your lost son is found."

Communication went so much more smoothly,
Stefan realized, when you didn't have a goal. And
wasting time? That was a universal language.

Like a Foyer is Burning

Within a few months of moving to the city, Stefan Krause was getting used to many things about Chelm. Work was still hard, but he could go home and look at Shayna and laugh about it. He'd given up on correcting his mother-in-law, Fruma Selig, when she said that he and Shayna might not have been married in the Church, but they'd brought their marriage to the ward. He let himself be flattered by her happiness instead—and quickly found it to be contagious. That joy reached all the way back to Leipzig, where his employer was still celebrating how long he'd lasted in the Chelm office.

Once in a while, though, he still struggled. Church could be especially hard because back home, the ward had always been his safe place, the little village that watched out for him against the backdrop of a big and bustling city. There, the rhythms of worship were part of his muscle memory. He knew by rote what to do and what it meant. Thanks to callings, he always had a way to give back. He might not agree with every crackpot comment people shared—but serving and being served, there was no question he belonged.

In the Chelm ward, they practiced the same religion. But the culture was just different enough that he fell easily out of step. The hymns were familiar but the singing was strange. The testimonies never seemed to fit into the familiar grooves in his mind, even though he recognized the conviction. He'd sometimes finish sacrament meeting feeling like someone who'd had a stroke and was once again learning to make sense of language.

And then came the second hour. In elders quorum, President Gronam's tone always managed to make him feel guilty. But for the life of him, Stefan couldn't figure out what he was feeling guilty for. And Sunday School? He came to class and by reflex, he started the scriptures from what was apparently now the wrong side of the book. It made him think of Jonah and all those poor, lost Gentiles in Nineveh. The way everyone else so easily turned pages, he wondered briefly if he could still tell his left hand from his right. Stefan was part of the covenant people, yes, but he also felt so foreign here.

Some weeks, he just needed a breath. Shayna had a calling in primary, so she would head off to class, and he would find himself hesitating in the hall, then sitting in the foyer. Zelda Gottstein was always there, but she didn't feel a need to speak. The first time he skipped class, they both just sat in the quiet. Without words, there was no sense. Without sense, there was no nonsense. It was nice.

Sometimes, Zelda brought sweets to share after the meetings were over and she'd let Stefan get a little head start. Over food, they'd chat about nothing in particular. Communication went so much more smoothly, Stefan realized, when you didn't have a goal. And wasting time? That was a universal language.

Soon Stefan got quite used to skipping the second hour. He didn't really miss elders quorum; this foyer quorum was better. Different people would drift through each week, and he'd get to see a different side of them. But he and Zelda were the regulars. One week, he finally thought to ask her how she ended up as the space's anchor. Why did she sit in the foyer all the time?

Zelda looked off into the distance for a moment, then began. "It started when Chava—that's my granddaughter, Heshel and Gretele's girl—learned how to say amen. When you're that young, every word has a use. She'd say *more* to ask for food, *mama* to ask for comfort, and *amen* when she thought a person should be done talking and go sit down. Whenever a talk felt long—and it doesn't take long for most talks to feel long—she would say it loud and clear, like a command. If the speaker kept going, she would say it again, louder and louder. Amen . . . amen . . . AMEN!"

"And you brought her out here to keep her quiet?" Stefan asked.

"Only if the speaker didn't get the message," Zelda said. "I didn't want her to get frustrated and give up—it's good for a child like that to keep her faith in language." Her eyes settled on the crumbs left behind the Silber baby's first rice cakes. "It turned out all right. Most of what trained her immune system came from this floor."

Stefan nodded. His own body's library of antibodies had been stocked in much the same way.

"Eventually, Chava learned to raid her mother's bags, distract herself, and stay quiet through sacrament meeting. So if a speaker ran long, I was the one who would cry and needed to be taken out." She smiled. "Although it's good I brought myself here, because when Chava hit running age, she started sneaking off the bench and making a break for it."

"The children run in Germany, too," Stefan said. "I suppose that children are the same everywhere."

"Watch closely," Zelda told him, "and you'll notice that there are actually two kinds of children, who turn into two kinds of people: those who run for the stand, and those who run for the door." She shrugged. "Chava ran for the door, but she was cleverer than most children. At the most chaotic moment in nursery, she would seize the opportunity to run again. That's why I started to stay and guard the foyer through the second hour as well."

"And afterward, you just stayed?" Stefan asked.

"Who said anything about afterward?" Zelda said. "Now that she's a young woman, the only thing that's changed is that she tries to bring friends. And it's only a matter of time before she'll be running off with some boy instead." Zelda shook her head.

"You said she's a clever girl," Stefan pointed out. "She'll be all right."

Zelda leaned toward him. "Gretele is clever too, and she married Heshel anyway."

Stefan frowned. He liked Zelda's story, but he still wasn't sure if he knew why she stayed. There had to be more keeping her here, orbiting the meetinghouse at the edge of its gravity, than her granddaughter. "In a few years, she'll be grown up," he said. "Do you think you'll stay in the foyer then?" He paused. "And if you don't, is it back to sacrament meeting and classes, or off to other Sunday adventures?"

Zelda gave him a long, searching look. "No, I won't leave. I wouldn't know what else to do with myself."

They were quiet for a moment.

"And I like it here," Zelda said. She pointed to a specific spot on the wall. "You see that? That dent, right there? Gimpel and Dudel were wrestling with each other one day. I think Yossel had just taught them about Jacob and the angel. In any case, you can still see where Gimpel's shoulder left a mark!" She pointed to the carpet. "Right there; you see that dark spot? My son-in-law the clerk tripped over his feet and dropped some lard, which turned out to be Beynish Finder's tithing. The stain will linger for years. So many things do."

And then Zelda stood up off her usual couch to show him a small tear in the fabric behind the very chair he was sitting on. She told him it had been made by a goat Leah Kantor brought in for a choral number. On the wall inside the window sill, she showed him faded crayon marks, which never quite washed all the way off. This faded blue one from Chava, the trace of yellow from Bina, this big, dark swirl from Dinah Peretz just last week. Every stain, tear, or dent had a story, down to the drop of juice spilled by Elijah the prophet on his way out of the blind beggar's ward Passover feast.

As she spoke, Stefan felt an overpowering sensation: one that was familiar, one that would nevertheless always

be strange. It radiated out into the room, the spirit rushing through the years like a mighty wind. Translating
this world for him, translating him into it.

Zelda looked over at him quizzically.

Stefan leaned down and fished under the couch until
he found an orange crayon. Then he pulled back the curtain on the windowsill and made his mark on the wall.

People need chances to run into each other by accident,
especially when they would never do it on purpose.

The Scattering of Israel

In the months before the ward's planned trip to the temple in Kyiv, Menachem Menasche started to follow a story online. He was always doing things like that—to be honest, it drove Zalman the Learned a little crazy. *Vanity, vanity,* the preacher says, *all is vanity.* And why did he say that? Because he saw our day, Zalman argued, and all the tiny things that would slip out of cell phone screens to trouble our minds.

Never mind that, Menachem countered. This story was important, because it involved a disease that people had contracted by eating bats. According to the Torah, bats are trayf, so the story was—in a way—religious. It could remind the members of the Chelm ward that there was value to keeping the Word of Wisdom and otherwise eating kosher. Even if God wasn't so strict about certain points in this last dispensation—every parent gives up on enforcing the rules by the time the youngest children are coming of age—it would still never be a good idea to eat bats or pangolins or pigs. This obvious moral was the proof that one could still find little nuggets of wisdom on the internet.

But when have the children of this world ever listened to sense? They ate bats, and they got sick. Fortunately, most of them survived. Ever since God put the breath of life into Adam, people have been quite stubborn about holding onto that original gift. Unfortunately, they also tend to leave it lying out in public. Breath quickly became one of several key suspects (along with restroom doors and polluted handshakes) for how the disease spread.

Menachem kept the ward updated as the virus came closer. It hit South Korea. Japan. It hit the United States, and he got worried: that country was not capable of keeping anything to itself. When the first cases were confirmed in France, he knew there wasn't much time left. France had taken Frederic Chopin and Marie Curie from Poland—not to mention Dobra Peretz's cousin Ronia—and it would be just like them to send a virus back in return. He told his fellow ward members that any day now, they should expect the disease to come knocking.

Sara Levy laughed the warning off. The virus wasn't Jesus. It had better ring the bell as well as stand at the door knocking if it wanted to be let in. Zalman also remained skeptical about this whole viral story. He agreed that eating bats was unwise but thought a backwater like Chelm might be safe from whatever disease happened to be fashionable in Paris.

At the beginning of March, however, doctors in Poland confirmed medically that the country was, in fact, part of the larger world. By then, who knew how many people in Chelm had secretly become agents of infection? Ward members who had spent the first part of the year studiously ignoring Menachem suddenly wanted to know what they should stock up on in case society collapsed. Would they need an emergency supply of board games? Or to quadruple their collections of pajama bottoms?

Not necessarily, Menachem reported. After some quick research, he was able to inform them that the market had settled on toilet paper as the preferred pandemic craze. He predicted that skyrocketing demand for toilet seat covers, toilet plungers, and toiletries in general would soon follow. Isaac Peretz responded to this news by rushing to install a bidet. Several other ward members made a feverish run on various bathroom-related companies' stock.

In the midst of this panic, Oskar the Miser was calm as a summer's day. *If ye are prepared, ye shall not fear,* the scripture says—and for once, a verse was worth the thin paper it was printed on! He had already stockpiled bathroom supplies eight years earlier, when a small drugstore went out of business. At his current rate of use (which involved a pair of scissors for precise portioning), he'd have toilet paper enough to last for decades. And toothpaste? If you watered it down enough, a single tube could outlast a measly pandemic. He didn't need any external vindication or praise, of course, for his exceptional foresight. He was, in fact, rather looking forward to not having to listen to other people at all. But still, it didn't hurt to know he was far ahead of the curve. If more people took advantage of life's little opportunities, he thought, no misfortune would be a crisis. Just another opportunity to eliminate waste.

Because not everyone was so prepared (temporally or temperamentally) for an intermission in the world as they'd known it, Fruma Selig and President Gronam set to work measuring the ward's needs. Surely, everyone would have some. Lazar the Blind Beggar would probably have to break his tradition of meeting the bishop to collect the first fast offering. Henya would need to be protected from visits. Even Oskar might require some help if he got sick, Fruma thought. Hard as it may be for him to grasp, there was more to life than keeping a closet full of floss.

Yossel the Fisherman and Mirele Schwartz also had their organizations move into action. Gimpel and Dudel went from door to door to collect offerings from a special fast. Golda and Chava took responsibility for health communication, making a video message for ward members about the importance of not touching your face. Theirs, Mirele though, was truly a chosen generation.

Still, some people somewhere must have kept touching their faces, because a few days later, everything shut down.

It wasn't so bad at first. For example, doing school from home allowed Golda an opportunity for some career exploration. While helping her younger sister, Breyndl, manage her online homework, she was able to rule out careers in technical support, elementary education, and prison administration. By keeping an eye on the news, Golda was also able to rule out nursing, retail, and basically anything that involved interaction with the general public. She was learning a great deal about the world and herself.

At the Peretz home, Dinah took advantage of the close quarters to drive her brothers crazy. After all, God expected people to be nice once they were old enough to get baptized and she only had another two years.

But as the mandated lockdown dragged on, such silver linings lost their luster. Tzipa watched video after video of mimes, desperately studying their craft, as she tried to keep up with the demands of running a bakery mostly via gestures through her shop's front window. Mirele Schwartz wiped down groceries—jars, cans, loaves of fresh bread—to keep her family safe. As usual, she was sure that she wasn't doing enough. This time, however, trustworthy experts seemed to agree. The news felt like a long list of ways you could accidentally make somebody die. Having her fears taken so seriously was far less pleasant in practice than she'd always expected.

Sundays were especially bad for some people. Israel Lewensztajn missed the meetinghouse; he never slept as well at home. Zelda Gottstein disliked the stale quiet of her living room. It might've been more bearable, she thought, if there were a few cranky babies passing through. No such luck: people could bless the sacrament at home, give little talks at home, study the scriptures at home, but nothing at home could replace a meetinghouse foyer.

Everyone felt the loss in their own way. The truth is that all kinds of people need a little time in a foyer. Even when it's not under mandated lock and key, the modern world is sorely lacking in shared but barely-governed spaces. People need chances to run into each other by accident, especially when they would never do it on purpose. Take that one small inconvenience away and they go a little crazy. Even by the high standards set in Chelm.

The longer Aaron Cohen stayed at home, the more paranoid he got. Not about the virus. He didn't really believe all that propaganda about how sickness comes from germs. No. As anyone who reads the scriptures knows, the leading cause of disease is wickedness. (Direct trials from

God take a distant second, unless the disease in question is a skin condition like boils or leprosy.) The best medicine, therefore, is repentance. And maybe a nice offering to God to go with it. Preferably something shiny. Returning the ark of the covenant with an offering of little golden mice, for instance, or setting up a bronze serpent. Maybe this time a bronze bat? Aaron wasn't an expert on the details, but the big ideas were all laid out somewhere between Numbers and Judges if a person only had eyes to see.

But did the doctors today read the scriptures? No. They were too busy stuffing their heads with all the body parts and smut in their anatomy textbooks. In their arrogance, they genuinely believed they could stop a plague by sending people home. But idle hands do the devil's work. So the consequence—the totally predictable consequence—of all the lockdown measures was that people grew sicker. You could see it in the case counts as they rose and rose and rose. Aaron Cohen could see the daily proof and had to bear the constant agony of having a solution the experts weren't smart enough to look for. If only he could make them understand! "Of course, no one ever listens to me," he complained bitterly to Feige. "Not even my wife!"

Feige was in fact hearing her husband's rants. But because she had grown as a person, she decided not to respond in any verbal sort of way. They were happier like that. It was better for everyone if they didn't argue over the fine and potentially hurtful distinctions between hearing and listening. Years ago, she'd learned that no one really wants to be told which one you're willing to do. In her own way, though, she did think about the words that kept dribbling out of Aaron's mouth. That was something. For instance, his comment about idle hands and the devil helped motivate her to get out her lace work. While

Aaron railed against the entire medical profession, Feige fended off Satan by knitting face masks.

She wasn't the only one thriving amidst the adversity. Heshel was having an excellent pandemic. He'd often found himself remote from work in one way or another, and now he had plenty of company. Meanwhile, Clever Gretele was enjoying the administration of their temporary home branch. She kept the talk assignments short and sweet. In an echo of her favorite calling, she assigned herself to focus on the Young Women. And, since there was no one around to stop them, she asked Heshel to serve as her assistant. During midweek activities with Chava, the three of them were able to build up a thriving business inventing things like digital receipts for physical cookies, which they were able to sell quite profitably online to speculators and bored futurists.

Across the ward, life's ordinary trials also continued. Hirsh's roof still leaked. Out on the lake for Yossel, fish refused to bite. Bananas that were green in the evening still became perfectly ripe at 3 am yet mushy by morning. People committed sins in most of the same old ways plus some mildly inventive new ones. Beynish's weight continued to fluctuate.

During the pandemic, however, many routine problems got worse in a subtle, soul-sapping sort of way. With a glut of toilet paper came a corresponding rise in toilet clogs. Routers groaned under the weight of people's need for connection. Before long, they seemed to have unionized and would randomly go on strike. Pet dogs got indigestion from licking too many scraps off the floor; pet cats got depression from being cooped up with the humans always at home and dropping those crumbs. People said stupid things by text message, then never got a chance to be less offensive in person. Selfishness and despair prowled for victims and had quite a feast.

Even outside of Chelm, of course, the human mind has a limited capacity. Add a few extra troubles and the nerves strain like an overstuffed plastic grocery bag preparing to rip open at the least convenient time. Bishop Levy tried and failed to keep up with the few ups and many downs in people's lives. He could feel them scattering not only to their own homes, but into neglected corners of their own hearts. He wanted to reach out to his people, to do something to keep the Lord's little flock together, but in the early days of the pandemic, most of his energy went to canceling old plans instead of coming up with new ones.

He closed down the meetinghouse. He let everyone know that he didn't know when they'd next have any meetings. One grey morning, he called the charter bus company to postpone their trip to Kyiv and its temple until such a time as the world got better. "Don't worry," he told himself and the other ward members. "The moment this pandemic lets up, we'll reschedule. Right now, the spirits of the dead are probably busy ministering to people anyway. Soon enough, they'll have more time on their hands for ordinances and we'll make it to Ukraine."

In the meantime, to keep up ordinances for the living, Bishop Levy contacted each priesthood holder in the ward to tell them they could bless the sacrament at home. After checking the Doctrine and Covenants, he said it didn't matter who passed it—so long as it was done with an eye single to God's glory. In a pinch, he admitted, an eye flitting between God's glory and the carpet would also do.

Houses without a priest or an elder presented a problem. On a call, Bishop Levy asked the stake president if some members could lay out bread to be blessed through a window, but apparently Church leaders were opposed to performing ordinances through screens. Maybe it struck them as too Catholic. Instead, Bishop Levy suggested that members who couldn't get the sacrament break a little bread and take a moment for the memory of how, in the Bible, Jesus and his friends really liked to eat. Over the centuries, there would surely be times when memory was all anyone had. It wasn't so bad to get a little practice now quietly keeping God's stories alive.

Still, one theological problem troubled him. The scriptures say that wherever two or three gather in his name, Jesus is there with them. Suddenly, of course, that had become a higher bar. It seemed like such a tragedy to leave ward members who lived on their own without the Master—for who knew how long—just because of immune conditions.

Bishop Levy thought and thought, until at last, a solution came to him. To those who were alone, he recommended setting out a cup for Elijah. If his spirit came, that would turn one into two, and then Jesus would turn two into three—and three . . . well, three was company! It was pure inspiration. His clearest revelation. And proof, above all, that even in the darkest, the most isolating of times, if you'd only look for it with a little prayer and a desperate degree of faith . . . there is always some way of gaming the system.

Chelm Glossary:
A Perplexing Guide

Chelmish

Gefilte Fish—literally "stuffed fish." Since stuffing a fish is more work than it's worth, however, that step got left out several centuries ago, and now the ground fish stuffing is plopped into greyish-white patties and served on its own. As part of the restoration of all things, Yossel has apparently been searching for some food to once again fill with gefilte. See also: hamentashen.

Geniza—you wouldn't want to just throw something with God's name on it into the garbage, would you? A geniza is a place to stash things that might be holy but are also past their prime (sort of like a meetinghouse library). Some genizas have remained in continuous use for hundreds of years (not unlike the average junk drawer).

Halakha—religious law, determined by commandment, precedent, and argument. So much argument. See also: Talmud.

Hamentashen—a pastry made of dough folded into a triangle, with jam or other sweet filling in the middle. The name means "Haman's pockets." Maybe if the original Haman's pockets had been full of jam, he'd have been a happier man and would never have tried to commit mass genocide.

Latke—a potato pancake that is perhaps the greatest gift the Inca ever gave to the Jewish people. Tastes a little like cheeseless, crispy funeral potatoes.

Matzah—a flat and, in the modern industrial age, brittle bread known variously as bread made in haste or the bread of affliction. Eaten, if not enjoyed, by observant Jews during Passover.

Mezuzah—a thin box with a small scroll of scripture which can be placed on a doorpost as a reminder. One famous rabbi said to hang them vertically; another said they should be placed horizontally. You don't have to be from Chelm to conclude that it's best to put them up on a slant.

Mohel—a mohel is a person who performs circumcisions. What's a circumcision, you ask? Well, it's a kind of symbolic operation performed in Judaism, Islam, and many American hospitals. It's sort of like sharpening a pencil, if that pencil were attached to a baby boy's groin.

Passover Seder—the world's oldest form of dinner theater, an elaborate escape-room type experience that involves getting out of slavery in Egypt.

Purim—a holiday celebrating the actions of Queen Esther, who saved Jews across the Persian Empire by revealing her heritage to her husband. Which is not the easiest thing to do when your husband also happens to be a casually violent totalitarian ruler with genocidal friends.

Rosa Luxemburg—a famous early twentieth-century Polish-German, secular Jewish, anti-Leninist Marxist revolutionary who had a lot of enemies across the political spectrum while she was alive and a lot of streets in East Germany named after her a few decades after she was safely dead.

Schmaltz—rendered fat, usually of chickens or geese, that can be used for cooking or spread on hearty rye bread as a non-dairy substitute for butter. Only acceptable as tithes if you're paying on gross.

Talmud—have you ever wondered what it would look like if the Bible and the proceedings of the Supreme Court had a baby? The Talmud is a collection of questions, majority rulings, minority opinions, and other commentary from several centuries of sages and scholars. Just barely longer than the original Encyclopedia Britannica and at least twice as fun.

Vashti—maybe the bravest royal in the Hebrew Bible, she had the courage to tell her husband "no thank you" when he ordered her to come to a party to show off for all his guests. This is a big deal when your husband happens to be a casually violent totalitarian ruler. She was banished; the Bible doesn't record whether she considered this a punishment or a relief.

Yahrzeit—literally "year-time," the anniversary (on the Hebrew calendar) of a loved one's death. Traditionally, a yahrzeit is marked with special prayers and the lighting of a slow-burning candle. Some people fast on their father's or mother's yahrzeit, either out of affection or because no one is there to say, "Eat! Eat!"

Mormish

Chiasmus—an ancient poetic device where concepts are repeated in reverse order. In 1967, John W. Welch discovered the presence of chiasmus in the Book of Mormon, because that's how Mormons were spending their time in the late 1960s.

Elders quorum—in the English language, an "elder" is a person who is considered old and possibly even wise. A "quorum" is the minimum attendance in a voting group before it's time to give up and go home instead of conducting business. Neither of these definitions has anything to do with an elders quorum, which is a group of men age 18 and above who are specifically taught not to give up and go home when most of the group fails to show up.

Fast offerings—once a month, Latter-day Saints go without eating and donate extra money to the poor. Fasting every month may seem like a lot, but it's really not. During the early years of the Great Depression, some Saints fasted twice a month. During the Utah famine of 1855–1856, some Saints barely ate at all!

General Murmurer—Heber C. Kimball once suggested that each pioneer company call a general murmurer. His reasoning was that as things stood, the pioneers were duplicating an awful lot of work.

Mission—a rite of passage in which young adult Latter-day Saints prepare for the little, unavoidable awkwardnesses of modern life by doing something extremely awkward for eighteen to twenty-four months in a row.

Relief Society—when sacrament meeting runs long, Latter-day Saint women are quite relieved to finally get out to enjoy each other's society.

Prayer roll—in the Bible, one of the items placed before God in the temple is the *lehem hapanim*, a baked offering often translated as "shewbread" or "bread of the presence." It would make sense, then, to have a baked roll on the altar in Latter-day Saint temples today. Through some accident of language, however, the modern temple "roll" is not made of food at all. It's only a list of names of people who are sick or need help for serious problems. See also: ward.

Primary—literally, "first." In a ward or branch, the Primary is the first line of defense against invasion by the next generation.

Ward—an old term for a voting district in a town, now used mostly to describe different wings of a hospital, such as the "maternity ward" or "psych ward," or else to describe local groups of Latter-day Saints in need of comparable spiritual support.

Word of Wisdom—what substances are prohibited and permitted by the Latter-day Saint standard known as the Word of Wisdom? Well, imagine everyone bet their favorite vices in a game of poker and lost.

A Note on Pronunciations

Learning how to correctly pronounce the name of a living person is a valuable gift of attention and respect. In some stories, speaking a true name is even associated with magical powers. Never be afraid to ask a person for help, pretend to know in advance by rehearsing with the help of web searches and audio files, or otherwise prepare to say a name right. Most people appreciate the effort.

Fictional characters, in contrast, seldom care. You can pronounce the names of people in Chelm however you want. If you mess them up, Gretele Gottstein-Kleiner and old Israel Lewensztajn are not going to like you any less.

That said, here are a few tips if you happen to be reading out loud in front of your Yiddish-speaking friends:

1. Lots of female names end with *a* or *e*. These are pronounced the same way, as an *uh*. For example, Gretele is pronounced as if the color grey is trying to say something but lost its train of thought (*grey-tell-uh*) rather than as two colors (*grey-teal*). See also the Selig (*say-lig*) family, whose names are pronounced *froom-uh*, *shay-nuh*, and *leeb-uh*.

2. An *ei* is pronounced like the body part *eye*. That makes *grey-tell-uh's* last name *got-shteyen kl-eye-nur*. Leicht, which is the last name of Lemel (*lehm-uhl*) and Tzipa (*tsee-pah*), sounds a lot like "liked."

3. Speaking of the Leichts, the *ch* in Yiddish names is never pronounced like the *ch* in *chocolate*. It is, somewhat ironically, much more like the *ch* in *Christmas*. The Loch Ness Monster, in addition to being Scotland's favorite cryptid, is a great example of how to say the Yiddish throaty *h* or *kh* sound. In the Chelm ward, Chava's name is pronounced *hah-vuh* with a hard *h* that flirts with, but is too young to marry, *kha-vuh*. In English, you can go all the way to *khelm* when you're pronouncing Chelm. (Since this is fiction, there's no need to be embarrassed if you already pronounced it like a portmanteau for "chocolate elm." Hopefully you weren't too disappointed when the town turned out to be mostly pickles and onions instead.)

4. Most Yiddish names come from German, but a few ward members have spellings from Polish—a language that has no fear of its consonants. Israel Lewensztajn doesn't usually say his own last name, since he's been around so long that everyone knows it already, but if he did, he would say it *leaven-shtayn*. Bishop Levy (whose last name rhymes with Chevy) has a Polish first name. It doesn't come up much, what with him being the bishop and all, but his wife Sara (*ser-uh*) calls him Matteusz (*matt-ay-oozh*).

5. Many members of the ward share names with famous people you could look up. Menachem, for example, happens to have the same first name as an Israeli prime minister with a markedly different temperament. Isaac Peretz has the same name as a famous Yiddish writer. And Oscar "the Miser" Wiener, of course, has almost the exact same name as a hot dog.

Acknowledgments

Writing a novel is sort of like running a marathon, in the sense that a sane person probably shouldn't do it. Having survived this book, I would like to take some time to thank people who helped along the way.

First: my co-authors. Back before the pandemic, when my brother Mattathias was still living with us, he, Nicole, and I would stay up evenings brainstorming various idiocies and laughing ourselves short of breath. Thanks for indulging me when I thought they would be a 20,000-word collection we'd knock out in a few months. Several years and 90,000 polished words later, those early conversations are a distant memory . . . but the laughter still echoes.

Next: thanks to everyone who passed through my writing group, Consensual Lobotomy, during this process. It's been a relay race. Megan Walker, Chris Husberg, Ruth Owen, Heather Clark, Heidi Summers Creer, Mike Barbeau, Teira Wilson, Mary Denton Taylor, and Lee Ann Setzer were there for the beginning. Dantzel Cherry, Chanel Earl, Jeanine Bee, and Holly Venable swapped in along the way and crossed the finish line with me. Two dear friends and comrades, Janci Patterson and Lesley Hart-Gunn, got the whole book—some stories several times. Special thanks to the group for helping me turn my single, wandering girls camp epic into the far more readable standalone pieces they became. Special thanks also to Lee Ann for reading the whole draft manuscript at the end in one go to make sure it worked as a novel and not just a series of punchlines. From their favorite café near Chelm's orphanage, Leah and Menachem salute your work. To everyone: in addition to the craft advice, your encouragement and company sustained me. And thanks for reading some of the funniest bits aloud to your spouses—there's no better fuel forward than hearing about a passage that demanded to be shared.

As if it weren't enough to write a book, we decided to publish it! As a Mormon author, I sometimes think Moroni had the right idea burying his manuscript in the ground once he was finished. I am indebted to the phenomenal teams at Wayfare magazine and BCC Press for getting this away from the dirt and into people's hands. Huge thanks to Lori Forsyth, who serves on both staffs: for selling me and Wayfare on the serialization concept, for providing editorial support, and for all the behind-the-scenes work you do in Mormon intellectual spaces.

Among the Wayfare staff, special thanks to general editor Zachary Davis for being so supportive of literary writing as a part of the magazine's larger vision, to Jeanine Bee for juggling the entire town of Chelm along with her regular fiction editor duties, and to Katie Lewis for trying to teach me the difference between "that" and "which" and helping me make sense of when to use commas.

At BCC Press: Michael Austin is a gentleman and a scholar, Steve Evans is a problem-solver extraordinaire, and Conor Hilton is a welcome digital shepherd for this wandering sheep. Andrew Heiss makes pages so pretty, Jeremy Ames brought an artistic eye to the cover design. My hat is off to all of you.

A special thank you to David Habben for bringing heart as well as hands to your illustration work. It's a dream come true to have the lightness of your style gracing these pages.

To name my Patreon people I've included a whole separate list. But I also want to say here that you guys are so great. I was between jobs for part of this project, and the money also meant hope for the future and belief that this work matters. I've loved your comments and emails over the course of the book. Cris: sorry for spying on your ward council. Bryan: thanks for putting music in my head.

Cece Proffit, who accepted a position helping me manage the logistics of my many Mormon literature projects, helped save my sanity down the stretch. Thanks for the help, tracking, planning, communicating, and following up—and it's a good thing you already had a finger in so many pies! Thanks also to Madison Beckstrand for help making a manageable revision plan.

For the Jewish elements in this book, I am indebted to a long list of dead Yiddish writers and the readers and critics who kept their work alive long after their world was wiped away. On a more personal level, I owe a debt to my grandfather and middle-namesake, Art Goldberg, for sending us Jewish books all through my growing up years and for long talks on the phone. To my father, David Paul Goldberg Westwood, for lighting candles and telling stories. To Jason Olson, for all the swapped stories and shared sensibilities at BYU and again when we worked on *The Burning Book.* Collective thanks to Congregation Beth Tikvah in Columbus, Ohio, for always treating me with warmth, and to Congregation Kol Ami in Salt Lake City, for hosting leaders of what is arguably the world's last remaining Jewish shtetl, Krasnaya Sloboda in northern Azerbaijan, right at the time when I was finishing up the book. Thanks to Miryam Farrar Chandler, who I fell for in eighth grade but wouldn't admit I was dating because I was a good Mormon and we weren't yet sixteen, and to my aunt, Juli Moscovitz, for memorable seders, songs, and conversations in my adolescent years.

Finally, I want to thank my children—Kira, Elijah, Leif, and Laila—for their patience with all the times I was off hunched over a computer. Thanks for laughing so hard that time I told you about Yossel finding out he was his own brother. And thanks for your own gentle attitudes toward the real world's many, many fools.

—James Goldberg

Special Thanks to James's Patreon Supporters

We'd also like to express thanks to the people who provide regular support to James Goldberg's writing through his Patreon account. Figuring out how to tell our people's stories well takes time and resources. This book and many others are possible because of people who invest in the dream of a richer Mormon literature:

Bryan Catanzaro
Jena Catanzaro
Jared and Selina Forsyth
Devin and Marites Galloway
Greta Hobbs

Rosalie Stone
Cris and Janae Baird
Jessica and Zac Wiest
Mark Olson
Andrea and Andrew Hurst

Anna Erickson
Merrijane Rice
Dan Call
James and Taylor Egan
Kjerste Christensen
Miranda Wilcox
Tony Gunn
Travis Austin
Hillary Stirling
David and Anne Healey
Jason McDonald
Robert Bennett
Sheila Gill Hadden
Gene Jones
Arlene Ball
Margot Bradford
Ardis E. Parshall
Chris Burnham
Jeanna Stay
Vaughn Johnson
Walker Frahm
Nick Senzee
Melissa Leilani Larson
Camilla Stark
Rebecca McCulloch
The Kevin Klein family
Adam and Laurie Stradling
Rebecca Bateman
Ashley Gephart
Peter Olson
Kayela Seegmiller
Craig Yugawa
Joah Fussell
Jennifer Eichelberger
Kristine Haglund
Kami Bratten
Heidi Creer
Christopher Bradford

Eric D. Snider
James Jones
Katherine Cowley
Edward M. Goldberg
Michael Haycock
Vilo Westwood
Rachel Helps
Stephen Whitaker
Jonathan Stone
Andrea Landaker
Benjamin Christensen
KyneWynn le Kind
David and Sunitha Gill
Karl O.
Scott and Pam Frost
The Jankovich Family
Elizabeth Mott
Michael Ellis
Colleen Baker
William Morris
Annalisa Waite
Carl Rossi
Ian McKnight
Kate Shipman
Ryan Saltzgiver
Austin Smith
Brian Ebie
Conrad Dietrick
Taylor Petrey
Kellie Nuss
Rosalynde Welch
Tara Hawks
Curtis Cahoon
Vilo Elisabeth Westwood
Jennifer and Ryan Rauzon
Robison Wells
Diantha Hopkins
Zachary Davis

Jason and Sarah Olson
Christopher Angulo
Dallin Earl
Steve Otteson
Steve Peck
Tanner Sperry
Natalie Brown
Emily Falke
Janae Stubbs
Kristine Anderson

Danielle Badger
David Habben
Emily Hess-Flinders
Emma Franks
David Fletcher
Troy Salmon
Andrea Landaker
Austin Smith

Also by James Goldberg

The Burning Book
(with Jason Olson)

Jason Olson felt God's presence in the Jewish tradition he was raised in. So what was he supposed to do when he also heard God's voice in the Book of Mormon?

The Burning Book traces Jason's spiritual journey from aspiring rabbi to Latter-day Saint missionary, from Brigham Young University student to Israeli immigrant, and from Jewish Studies scholar to military chaplain. It's a memoir about one man's experience finding God: in two faiths, in two countries, and in the lives of other people.

Co-written with novelist and poet James Goldberg, *The Burning Book* offers readers a glimpse into Jewish and Mormon cultures and asks what it means to seek the voice of prophets in a modern, multicultural world.

The Bollywood Lovers' Club
(with Janci Patterson)

Amrita Sidhu belongs: in her Indian extended family, in her Sikh faith, in her California home. But when a family fight makes up her father's mind to take a job in Ohio, she's torn from the fabric of her community and left to find her footing in a new high school and a new life.

In Ohio, Amrita meets Dave Gill, who's funny, part-Indian, and Mormon. At a series of Bollywood movie nights with friends, they begin to connect—despite the pressure they both feel not to date outside their own faith.

As Amrita stares down diverging paths for her future, she knows only one thing for certain: she can't hold on to everything.

The Five Books of Jesus

It starts in the desert. John the prophet lowers Jesus under the Jordan's muddy waters and pulls him up, just as a bird swoops down to skim the river's surface. It spreads next to Galilee, where some welcome Jesus as a disciple of John and others grow wary of his rising influence—fishermen are leaving their nets, tax collectors their offices, and students their masters to listen to this new saint. After abandoning his nets, Andrew ties knots in the threads of his shirt to remember Jesus' teachings. After escaping his slum, Judas waits for Jesus to call down the legions of angels who can end a broken world. But just as Jesus' movement in the north is gaining strength, he turns south toward the Temple and a fate his followers will struggle to understand. *The Five Books of Jesus*, James Goldberg's lyrical novelization of Jesus' ministry, tells the story of the gospels as Jesus' followers might have experienced it: without knowing what would happen next or how to make sense of events as they unfold.

Let Me Drown with Moses

The forty-nine poems in *Let Me Drown With Moses* are not for those who think of religion as another name for self-help. They are for those who still believe in a God who wrestles. For those who think faith should challenge as much as it comforts. For those who would follow a prophet chest-deep into the Red Sea, even before the waters part.

Drawing on imagery from scripture and Mormon history, *Let Me Drown With Moses* gives voice to the spiritual longing of a people and does its own small part to keep religion a living language in the 21st century.

Phoenix Song

In this follow-up to his 2015 collection, *Let Me Drown With Moses*, James Goldberg explores themes of suffering, community, faith, and discipleship with both an unflinching commitment to God and a clear-eyed perspective on the difficulties of mortality. Whether telling stories from Goldberg's ward, chronicling his experience in chemotherapy, imagining alternate histories, or commenting on the scriptures and society, the poems in *Phoenix Song* describe what it means both to feel burned to the ground and to rise from the ashes.

Song of Names
(with Ardis Parshall)

In 2015, Beirut's district president takes the dangerous road to Damascus once a month to bring the sacrament to Syrian Saints. In 1904, a ward rallies around a mentally ill member in Salt Lake City after he's institutionalized. In 1844, a sister gathers new members on the South Pacific atoll of Anaa and teaches them the gospel by singing hymns from dusk until midnight. The twenty-two poems in *Song of Names* draw images from the lives of ordinary Latter-day Saints from many times and places to make a mosaic of discipleship. Accompanied by historical introductions, reflective essays, and original fine art sketches, this collaboration between James Goldberg, Ardis E. Parshall, and Carla Jimison is a monument to two centuries of struggle and faith.

A Book of Lamentations

In his fourth volume of poetry, James Goldberg writes in a register of religious lament as he wrestles with a changing climate, a pandemic, and fissures in the fabric of society. The collection's fifty-three poems, accompanied by original artworks by Camilla Stark, map anxieties the world faced in the years leading up to and including 2020 and raise a warning voice about the destructive choices we collectively continue to make.

The First Five-Dozen Tales of Razia Shah

Razia Shah—a promising, bright, suicidally-depressed seventeen-year-old living in New Delhi—has to tell herself a new story each day to convince herself to keep living until the next. Amir Mousa, a Palestinian shopkeeper in North Carolina, finds his thoughts jolting back to his lost village after he wins the lottery. Soon Punjabi, Congolese, and Mexican immigrants' stories are told following the structure of the Jewish liturgical calendar, the folk hero of a forgotten people embarks on a quest to gather stories like grain against a famine, the leader of a merchant household in an alternate Indian Ocean trading culture is forced to confront his failure to keep a covenant with his slaves, and a hospital patient begins hallucinating the life history of his Indian-American anesthesiologist's father. The novella and five short stories that make up *The First Five-Dozen Tales of Razia Shah and Other Stories* combine fantastical imagery and lyrical language to meditate on the pressures human beings face in an era of migration and rapid social change—and the power of storytelling in the face of those pressures.

Remember the Revolution

In 2006, 22-year-old James Goldberg moved to Utah, dreaming of possibilities for Mormon artistic community. Though the ride was often rough, he spent the next five years feeling his way forward, finding a voice to speak the language of the tradition in his own distinct register. The twelve essays and short stories in Remember the Revolution chronicle those experiments, giving voice to the idealism, anxiety, and insight of a young Mormon writer.

Whether imagining the experience of a Mormon Bollywood playback singer, giving the German Jewish philosopher Walter Benjamin a seat in Primary, telling the story of the early Restoration through an imagined sequence of Joseph Smith's anxious dreams, or writing an inverted theology in the form of spam emails, Goldberg grapples with ways Mormon thought can engage with the cultures around it and speak to the pressing questions simmering beneath the surface of the modern world. At turns sincere, satirical, surreal, and somber, *Remember the Revolution* is vital reading for anyone interested in the potential of a distinctly Mormon literature.

James Goldberg's family is Sikh on one side, Jewish on the other, and Mormon in the middle. He won the Association for Mormon Letters awards in Drama (2008, for *Prodigal Son*) and Novel (2012, for *The Five Books of Jesus*) and has been a finalist in Poetry, Creative Nonfiction, and Criticism. He is also the recipient of an Orson F. Whitney Outstanding Achievement Award, which honors his body of work and contribution to the Latter-day Saint writing community. His recent collaborations include *The Bollywood Lovers' Club* (with Janci Patterson), *The Burning Book: A Jewish Mormon Memoir* (with Jason Olsen) and the online multimedia project *A Dance of Light* (with Lisa DeLong and Nicole Pinnell).

Nicole Wilkes Goldberg teaches persuasive writing and LDS literature at BYU. Since its inception in 2012, she has been co-editor of the Mormon Lit Blitz. By day she is grading and raising children. By night she is a witch of the woods, stuck in the suburbs.

Mattathias Singh is a child of the lands of Punjab and Ashkenaz at their deeply unexpected border in Deseret. Like his brother James, he grew up on tales of the unique wisdom of Chelm and is proud to have helped add to their number within these pages

Illustrations by David Habben • davidhabben.com